Praise for *Category 7*

"Take a healthy dose of the paranoid scenarios from *24* and governmental intrigues from *The West Wing*, then spike them liberally with the atmospheric minutiae that armchair meteorologists know and love. Fast-paced storytelling . . . Satisfying."   —*Kirkus Reviews*

"Kate Sherman, a plucky meteorologist, and Jake Baxter, a CIA weatherman, are the last line of defense between New York City and a Category 7 hurricane, which was created by a top-secret weather-control weapon. A fast-paced action-adventure that promises a rousing finale and delivers it."   —*Booklist*

"What would happen if a massive superstorm hit New York City? And what if the storm's ferocity were enhanced by human activity? In the authors' apocalyptic scenario, much of New York would be destroyed. Buildings would topple, tunnels would flood, and the death toll would be enormous."   —*Library Journal*

"A hurricane is not only possible in New York City, it's happened before. But because no one alive today has been through that experience, people are not aware of the devastating potential. But Bill Evans knows New York, New York weather, and New York weather history."
—Bryan Norcross, CBS News hurricane analyst

"A well-researched thriller whose building devastation will keep the reader 'churning' through the pages."
—Steve Alten, *New York Times* bestselling author

"A most creative piece of fiction. Author Bill Evans certainly knows what he is talking about. *Category 7* will have you thinking the next time you hear the pounding rains and the whipping of the wind. You might be more in awe of nature after reading this book."   —*Shelf Life*

Category 7

Kate Sherman is a brilliant young meteorologist who can't understand how she recently missed predicting three major storms—storms that cut into the profits of her employer, Coriolis Industries. Afraid of being fired, Kate throws herself into an analysis of the strange storms—and headlong into the path of a secret plot that may cost her her life!

Hurricane Simone is a Category 7—the biggest, strongest storm in recorded history—and she's clawing her way up the East Coast. When she hits New York City, skyscrapers will fall. Subways and tunnels will flood. Lower Manhattan and much of Queens and Brooklyn will disappear under more than thirty feet of water. Thousands, if not millions, will die.

Created by secret, cutting-edge weather science, Simone is not just an unnatural disaster—she's a weapon. Kate and CIA weatherman Jake Baxter must figure out how to stop the storm before she flattens New York City . . . and identify Simone's master before he has them both killed.

CATEGORY 7

BILL EVANS AND
MARIANNA JAMESON

A TOM DOHERTY ASSOCIATES BOOK
NEW YORK

This is a work of fiction. All of the characters, organizations, and events portrayed in this novel are either products of the authors' imagination or are used fictitiously.

CATEGORY 7

Copyright © 2007 by William H. Evans and Marianna Jameson

A Tor Book
Published by Tom Doherty Associates, LLC
175 Fifth Avenue
New York, NY 10010

www.tor-forge.com

Tor® is a registered trademark of Tom Doherty Associates, LLC.

ISBN-13: 978-0-7653-5671-0
ISBN-10: 0-7653-5671-6

First Edition: July 2007
First Mass Market Edition: September 2008

Printed in the United States of America

0 9 8 7 6 5 4 3 2 1

ACKNOWLEDGMENTS

I always felt that I had a great story to tell because those from whom I sought advice told me so! Not one person told me to give it up. But would you believe that a meteorologist like me, who tells the story of how the weather is going to be every day, had no clue as to how to go about getting this story told? It has taken me ten years to get this project completed, and I never could have done that without some great advice from some really wonderful people like Bob Miller at Hyperion, Rich Malloch and Renée Simkowitz at Hearst, and William Pecover (Sir William), the British publishing magnate. They were so kind and generous with their time, especially Sir William (over multiple bottles of red wine), and each was willing to introduce me to others who might further my project. I am so grateful to each of them for their support in sending me down this path despite my never having published a single word.

I also want to thank all the people with whom I have spent so many years talking about this book for their great advice—Bryan Norcross, Dr. Max Mayfield, Dr. Bob Sheets, and Dr. Nicolas Koch. Thanks to the office of Mayor Michael Bloomberg and the New York City Office of Emergency Management, especially Press Secretary Jarrod Bernstein and Deputy Press Secretary Andrew Troisi. Their input was immeasurable, especially when it came to figuring out how much flooding would occur in the event of a hurricane in New York City, who would need to be evacuated, and where they might go. It was reassuring to learn how well prepared these offices are for the hell on earth that the city might become in the event of a major hurricane. Thanks also to Ellen Schubert and the energy staff of UBS for giving us the run of that massive trading floor in Stamford, Connecticut, so we could learn how commodities are traded.

I really want to thank Tom Doherty Associates for having the chutzpah to take on a first-time wanna-be novel writer. Melissa Ann Singer has been fabulous, and the staff and sales department have been very encouraging, which is wonderful for someone in my position.

I offer great heartfelt thanks to my coauthor, Marianna Jameson. If not for her, this work would never have been set down on paper. When I first met with her, we talked about weather for days and days. We shared the same excitement for meteorology and the same sense of humor as well. When I saw what we talked about turned into words, I could not believe what I was reading. When you are a meteorologist like me, you look at weather data day and night and dream of putting those beautiful phenomena into compelling words. Marianna captured my vision, complete with raging hurricanes, devastating tornadoes, torrential rain, massive thunderstorms, whipping wind, blazing sun, and clear blue skies. She has written such powerful lines that I can feel the wind-whipped rain on my face. It is the weather in words—she does all that and tells a fantastic tale as well.

In addition, I want to thank James Howard and Verna Evans, my grandparents, who raised me to grow up to be whatever I wanted to be. They also taught me to always remember to thank God each day for getting to live this life he planned for me and for the weather he created. And, I want to thank the most important people in my life, my family. I have a smart and beautiful wife and four wonderful children. My wife, Dana, has not only been such a great source of support, but she reads about 175 books a week, so she is a great resource!

Bill Evans
Stamford, Connecticut
Summer 2007

AUTHOR'S NOTE

People who become meteorologists often say that a single weather event that impacted their lives is the reason they came to the science, and I was no different. Growing up in Mississippi, my life was changed forever in 1969 by Hurricane Camille, which caused a tremendous loss of life and property to my homeland and changed the way I saw the world.

When I moved to New York City in 1989, I looked at all the development along the coastline and morbidly thought, *What a place for a hurricane to strike*. And thus this project began.

In 1997, while I was hosting The Bahamas Weather Conference, I saw a presentation by the great professor Dr. Nicholas Koch, a geology professor at the City University of New York. Dr. Koch gave a riveting presentation on the great hurricanes of the Northeast and what would happen if such a hurricane were to hit New York City today. Every seventy years a major hurricane has struck New York City with devastating results. Hog Island, which was situated south of Roosevelt Beach, southeast of Manhattan, was totally wiped off the face of the earth in the middle of the night during a hurricane. The last big hurricane to hit New York City was what was later called "The Long Island Express." This storm destroyed a great portion of Long Island, Connecticut, and New England. That was in 1938—nearly seventy years ago—and now we find ourselves fast approaching that anniversary.

Entire generations in the Northeast have come and gone without experiencing the devastation of a hurricane of any category. As I walked the streets of New York City, I realized that the people here had no clue as to what would happen if a hurricane were to make a direct hit on the city.

When asked, the overwhelming majority of city residents responded that they would take shelter in the NYC subway in the event of a hurricane. The subway? Obviously people have trouble understanding what a hurricane could do to the city, let alone what they should do if one strikes, even after seeing the devastation caused by major hurricanes in the last few years.

Plus, the New York City area is a much different animal than the U.S. Gulf Coast. The city lies at the point of a right angle formed by the New Jersey coast, running north-south, and Long Island, running east-west. Since a hurricane spirals counterclockwise, water would pile right into the five boroughs of New York City at an amazing rate, faster than in any other part of the country. Also, the land underneath the Atlantic Ocean in this area is bedrock, not sand as along the Gulf Coast—and it slopes upward toward New York. So in the Northeast, a Category 2 storm easily becomes a 3, a 3 becomes a 4, and so on. . . .

To me, this information was so overwhelming that I wanted to write a book on the subject. I wanted to take this data and write what I expected would be a science book about a hurricane hitting New York City: what the losses might be, estimates of the damage and destruction. After all, it's happened before and in weather, history repeats itself.

I first took my research to my employer, WABC-TV, and I convinced them to do a half hour special on what it would be like if a hurricane of category 3 magnitude struck New York City. We now run that hurricane special and a series of other weather specials throughout the year.

But I believed that the great story of a New York City hurricane needed to be told, so I kept pitching my idea of a science book to anyone who would listen. Fortunately, for me, the ears were there. As I sought advice from friends and acquaintances in the science, television, and publishing industries, my science book began to take on a different look. One day I was having lunch with Jeffrey Lyons, the great movie reviewer and a personal friend with whom I have played softball in Central Park for twenty years, when he asked me, "Why in the world would you want to write a science book when the story of a hurricane hitting New York City would make a great movie? Write the screenplay!" he said. So I compromised. I changed my idea from a science book to a novel—not a screenplay. Thanks for the advice, Jeff!

Then, September 11th happened. That moment changed the world. I immediately shelved the book idea. Another disaster hitting New York City—no way! The story took a little nap until the spring of 2003 when I went back on the offensive, looking for someone to help write and publish this book. The hurricane seasons had been relatively quiet up until that point, but the sea surface temperatures were rising, and it looked more and more as if we were going to see an increase in storms—as the Hurricane Center termed it, "a multidecade period of higher than normal storm activity." From this point on, every year the "big one" doesn't hit New York City, is one more year that we are closer to it.

In early 2004 while I was playing in a charity celebrity golf outing at Innes Arden Country Club in Old Greenwich, Connecticut, I had the pleasure of meeting Jeff McGovern. Jeff, a great guy and a great golfer with a great "past," took an interest in my book idea and in a roundabout way introduced me to Marianna Jameson, my coauthor.

Now I know how the Wright brothers must have felt. After working tirelessly for so long and hard, my project has finally taken wing and is off and flying.

AUTHOR'S NOTE AND ACKNOWLEDGMENTS

The chronology of my involvement with this project differs from Bill's in part because it began with a conversation that took place without me. And without Bill, in fact. My good friend Brian Mitchell happened to run into an acquaintance of his named Jeff McGovern one evening as their train pulled out of Grand Central Station, and their conversation took a turn I can only call serendipitous. Jeff mentioned that he had an acquaintance who wanted to write a novel; Brian mentioned that he has a friend who is a novelist. Thus, my first thanks must be to these men, whose casual conversation begat the working partnership between Bill and myself.

Our introduction took place over the phone. I'll admit now that I was leery of working with a celebrity, but Bill's warmth, down-to-earth personality, and easygoing approach to life were more than I had hoped to encounter. We hit it off at once, realizing that we had the same offbeat sense of humor. We also shared a fascination for the mechanics and mystery of weather, an interest in high technology, and a love of thriller novels. I offer my deepest thanks to Bill for bringing me onto this project, which has brought to fruition something that had been a dream of his for so long and which has been, quite frankly, a lot of fun for me.

Determined that this project would work out, we forged on. Thanks to the creativity, support, encouragement, and steady, savvy business sense of our literary agent, Coleen O'Shea of the Allen O'Shea Literary Agency, we shaped and refined our story until it was ready to see daylight. It lay, wrapped and stamped, on Coleen's desk the first week of August 2005 as we and the rest of the world watched Hurricane Katrina bring to life the worst fears of so many. We agreed without discussion to withhold the manuscript until the waters receded and some of the initial horror began to settle into the nation's consciousness.

A few months later, our manuscript landed on the desk of Linda Quinton, vice president and associate publisher at Tor, who loved it and passed it on to senior editor Melissa Singer. We could not have been luckier than to have our manuscript land in their hands. Linda's enthusiasm gave our book life, and Melissa, a dream of an editor, helped us smooth out the story's rough edges and provided spot-on editorial insight. This book would not be what it is without her help. The production, art, marketing, sales, and publicity departments at Tor found Linda and Melissa's enthusiasm for our book to be contagious, and both Bill and I deeply appreciate that. Especial thanks must go to Jamie Stafford-Hill, the art director, for designing our fabulous cover.

In the process of researching and writing this book with Bill, I called on many experts in many fields, all of whom were unfailingly patient and most generous with their time and information. First, I must again thank Bill, who gave me a crash course in heavy weather. Lori Bast, who handles public relations and outreach for NOAA's Aircraft Operations Center at MacDill Air Force Base, was tremendously helpful and put me in touch with hurricane-hunter pilot LCDR Carl Newman and Flight Director/Flight Meteorologist Paul Flaherty. Both men answered all of my questions and provided wonderful information about what it's like to fly into hurricanes when most other aviators try like the dickens to avoid them. Paul, in particular, proved to be a candid, engaging, and extremely patient correspondent whose enthusiasm for what he does came through in every answer to my many, many questions.

Thanks, too, to three people at UBS in Stamford, Connecticut, who took time out of a very busy afternoon to tell us what we needed to know about working in a trading environment: Ellen Schubert, who brought Bill and me onto the trading floor at UBS and gave us a quick but comprehensive overview of what happens there; Elizabeth Maxwell, who was extremely generous with her time and provided candid information regarding what traders do and how and why they do it; and Gary Gray, who explained thoroughly, candidly, and with charming good humor the rather significant role meteorologists play on a trading floor. Thanks, too, to Bernd Pfrommer for helping me to understand weather derivatives. Jarrod Bernstein and Andrew Troisi provided tremendous information about New York City's Emergency Management operations. The technical information imparted by all was received gratefully and used with the best of intentions; however, a few things had to be nudged to fit our story. All mistakes are my own.

I owe many thanks personally, too, not the least to the BSC posse: Joanna Novins, Deirdre Martin, Karen Kendall, Alisa Kwitney, and Liz Maverick—wonderful writers, good friends, and deeply, darkly funny women. Dane McSpedon and Kathy G., the most avid, critically thinking thriller readers I know, who gave me great suggestions, which I duly co-opted. Joanna Novins deserves additional thanks for sharing the insights and experiences gained during a decade and a half spent serving the United States as an analyst for the Central Intelligence Agency. You may throw a grenade like a girl, but you wield words like a master.

Very special thanks are due my father, who served this country as an officer on several U.S. Navy supply ships in the Pacific. I grew up hearing stories of his often hilarious, always thrilling adventures at sea, and I especially loved the ones about how ships sailed around and occasionally through typhoons. One story resurfaced full force as I worked on this book, one in which the ship he was on was heading into a typhoon. The high winds and heavy seas caused part of the deck and support structure to crack. As damage-control officer, the situation was his problem. He wasted no time in stripping the ship of every iron handrail, ladder, and bunk, and anything else he could find to use to patch the fault, and drafting every available person on the ship to begin welding it back together around the clock. Those who didn't know an acetylene torch from an anchor chain (I'm paraphrasing—he was a sailor after all) became accomplished welders in a hurry. The ship was saved with no loss of life or cargo and limped into port, astonishing those who later saw the full extent of the damage.

In my early twenties, I thought that story was likely a minor incident he'd embroidered to get unruly children to settle down; I rolled my eyes at its next retelling. A few days later, I was quietly handed a copy of the commendation from the Department of the Navy that detailed in language less colorful but no less stirring than his own the precise story he had told. I was humbled and awed and, not for the first time, immensely proud to be his daughter. It's a pity he's not here to read this book. I think he would have enjoyed it.

Thanks, too, to my friends and family, who not only still love me but are still speaking to me after I went into occasional electronic exile while I worked on this book. Particular thanks to Deb Dufel, Amy Hymans, Nancy Mitchell, and Melanie Cochran for their understanding and support.

Special thanks is due Kevin Przypek ("Super K"), who was the high bidder for the opportunity to have a character named after him in this book. Kevin's generous donation to the Newfield School Playground Fund was a great boost for a great cause. Mike O'Connor gets an honorable mention, too, because he kept upping the ante by strategically bidding against Kevin. Thanks, too, to their wives, Angela and Tara, respectively, for encouraging their husbands' spending habits.

Finally, endless gratitude to my husband and children. You're my oxygen.

Marianna Jameson
Summer 2007

Friends who set forth at our side,
Falter. are lost in the storm.
We, we only, are left.

—Matthew Arnold, "Rugby Chapel"

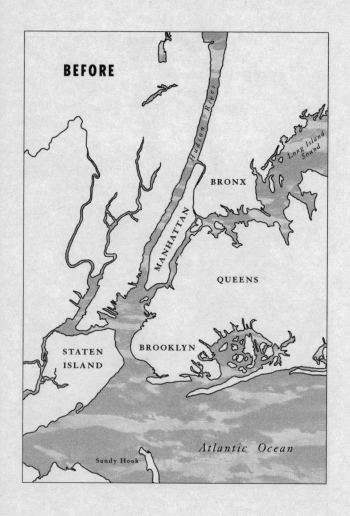

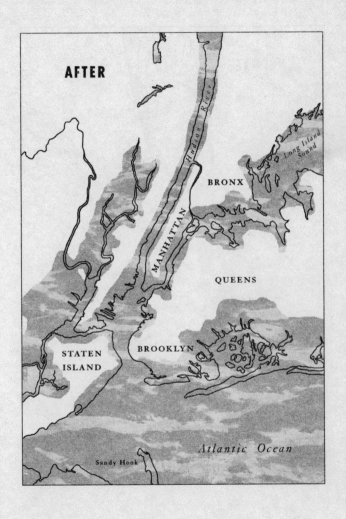

CATEGORY 7

Rain lashed through the hellishly hot Saharan sky, hurling itself groundward with chaotic fury only to evaporate before it made contact with the dying earth. The newly dry air was sucked up again into the wet layer to repeat its journey until the storm subsided.

An hour later the edge of the desert was as it had been days, months, and years before, revealing no signs of having been changed by the storm. Heat shimmered over still-parched, endlessly shifting sands, sending eddies of fine dust into a sky brilliant with unrelenting light. The very air seemed to glitter as sunlight sparked away from the myriad minute planes of mica and silica particles the earth sacrificed to the sky in convective obedience.

Some of the grains of sand and minerals, the spores and bacteria, had already traveled untold distances. Abandoned by winds long since vanquished, they had lain here for days or decades ready to be lifted once again to the sky. Some particles came from the beds of ancient seas and primeval jungles; others were more recent, formed only a few millennia ago when the earth writhed, heaving rock and ash into chaotic skies as it gave birth to the African lands, the implacable massifs and the dusty plains encircling them.

Smaller than dust and immeasurably light, the particles were swept upward and overland, floating westward on the hot winds, taking with them the harsh and timeless lessons of the desert. Without will, without desire, they hovered over dunes as the airstream steadied. Silent travelers, they dipped to the earth and rose above it, blinding eddies in a river of wind, and swept over scoured plains that kept untold secrets, that hid the treasures and the miseries of civilizations long dead.

As they entered the dense, sticky air above the city, the microscopic particles of dirt and minerals, of pollen, fungi, and bacteria, of long-dead plants and creatures, began to cluster. Unavoidably, they collided with the irresistible, heavy carbonaceous particulates that humankind hurled into the sky. Since humans had discovered fire, they'd mimicked the actions of the earth itself, sending ash and smoke heavenward with abandon, dulling the atmosphere, dirtying it.

The wind kept the particles aloft, leading them on an endless, nomadic flight, its mission inexorable, its duration eternal. They'd blown through refugee camps and over embattled lands, embracing the death and desperation that rose in the unholy heat on the fetid air. They swept across wasted fields and villages, depositing remnants of times both better and worse and lifting into their midst both the hope and the destruction that lay beneath them.

Mountains rose before the particulates, precipitating many to the earth, sending others ever higher. Lakes and rivers beckoned, swelling the air with moisture unknown to many of the particles for countless ages.

Some fell. Some remained aloft, continuing their traversal of savanna and desert, plantation and city.

Eventually, the particle plume reached the sea. In a startled tumult it dispersed, broadening its sweep, extending its reach, no longer limited by the boundaries of a landmass beneath it. Like a heat-dazed serpent uncoiling under sudden shade, the pale gold shimmer of dust unfurled a lacy haze above the deep blue waters of Africa's western coastline. Its elegant leading edge undulating toward the lush distant lands of the Caribbean and the Americas, the golden filigree of ancient dust was visible from space. Thousands of unseen eyes began to watch it, waiting and wondering what effect it might have on distant shores and distant lives.

CHAPTER 2

May 31, 4:57 P.M., eastern coast of Barbados

"Did you cut *every one* of my classes?" Richard Carlisle—senior meteorologist for a major TV network, professor emeritus of the meteorology department at Cornell, and generally mild-mannered Southerner on the receding edge of middle age—stared at his former student with undisguised disbelief. He might have laughed if his safety weren't at stake.

Barely sparing it a glance, Richard pointed, straight armed, to the breadth of paned glass behind him. The window framed the limitless expanse of the Atlantic Ocean from the steep, rugged cliffs dropping below him to a horizon nearly obscured by an encroaching, churning late-afternoon sky. Thick layers of cumulonimbus mamma clouds resembled sinister, undulating bubble wrap as they stretched across the water.

"In case you were asleep at the wheel that semester, Denny, what's brewing out there is called a tropical storm. The sustained wind speed is fifty-five miles an hour and gusts are hitting seventy-five. Does that mean anything to you, son?" He paused. "Let me refresh your memory. A person can't remain vertical against anything stronger than that. And you want me to go out there—on a rooftop terrace—and do my stand-up? Are you plumb crazy?"

He would have preferred to say something stronger, but there were too many between-shift waitstaffers bustling through the rooftop dining room of one of Barbados's most luxurious oceanfront hotels on the eve of hurricane season. The island, the easternmost in the Caribbean and arguably the first that would feel the effects of the season's weather, was facing the upcoming storm season in typical Caribbean style, with a languid shrug.

Twenty-four-year-old Denny Buxton, Richard's former student and current assistant producer, grinned with the unique idiocy of someone who has seen just enough of life not to realize he hasn't seen nearly enough. "Dude, c'mon. The Weather Channel guys do it. Hell, Jim Cantore is somewhere on a beach right now getting his ass sandblasted six ways 'til Sunday." Denny paused. "Okay, how's this? We'll tie you down. I saw some of those loop things in the floor that they use to tie down tents."

Richard continued to stare at him, dumbfounded. The kid was a fool. Unfortunately, he was also right. Viewership spiked during bad weather, but doing something crazy never hurt.

Denny's idiot grin never faded. In fact, it grew broader. "You want to do it. Holy shit, man, I can't believe it. You're gonna do it." Laughing, Denny exchanged an exuberant high five with the cameraman, who was not much older and no more sensible.

Richard looked over his shoulder at the wall of windows and the dark, glowering bank of cumulonimbus clouds beyond it. The smooth, caplike pileus cloud had stabilized, as the last radar report had indicated it would, and the storm hovered over the ocean, threatening to come ashore at any moment in a rush of wind and hot rain.

The storm would be fast and furious, probably gone within an hour. Not overly dangerous, it would wallop the coastline, annoy the residents, and scare the hell out of the tourists, dousing the hardiest, or foolhardiest, among them who remained outdoors. After the rain ended, the island would return to being steamy and still, the weather a suitably sultry backdrop for its summer season.

"C'mon. Let's mosey. We're on in thirty." Denny and the cameraman pushed through the door, and into the wind.

Richard took a deep, resigned breath and followed them onto the roof.

"We'll just do the teaser out here. If it gets too bad, we'll go back inside," Denny yelled over the howling wind.

"A decision only a moron could make," Richard drawled under his breath.

Denny squinted at him and mouthed, *What?*

Richard smiled tightly. "I said, 'Good idea.' "

Denny nodded. "You stand there," he shouted, pointing to an open area that afforded no protection from the elements. "That way if you get knocked over, you won't fall over the edge."

Shaking his head, Richard moved to his marks and grimaced against the wind as Denny gave him the countdown with his fingers. As the producer's last finger folded into his palm, Richard flashed his on-camera smile.

"Hello, America, from the not-so-sunny Caribbean. On the day before the official start of the hurricane season, we're already bracing for a close encounter with the second named storm of this year. In what is already shaping up to be a remarkable hurricane season, I'll be providing you with a bird's-eye view of Tropical Storm Barney from the coast of beautiful—" He stopped speaking as he saw Denny's eyes widen and his jaw sag.

Microphone in hand, Richard glanced over his shoulder. His gut clenched as he watched the bloated, menacing clouds exploding over the open ocean with the unholy force of a mid-air detonation. Furious plumes burst in all directions and the sea's dark, choppy swells erupted into a frenzied expanse of boiling, churning whitecaps thundering a crazed ambush on the suddenly puny cliffs and the beach at their base, fifty feet below.

Faster than his mind could register what was happening, the wall of wind hammered at Richard, knocking him to the floor and sending him skidding headfirst into the stone skirting wall that surrounded the roof. As unconsciousness rushed over him, Richard remembered the last time, the only time, he'd witnessed anything like those clouds.

The South China Sea in 1971.

Those storms hadn't been pretty.

They hadn't been natural, either.

CHAPTER **3**

Tuesday, July 10, 5:00 A.M., Campbelltown, Iowa

Carter Thompson stood in front of the picture window in his cozy home office, staring through it without seeing the dawn break over Iowa's broad, green horizon. His mind was two thousand miles away in the still-dark skies above the seared, arid wasteland skirting the edges of Death Valley in the Mojave Desert.

The final test of his skill, his ingenuity, his intellect, was about to begin. He'd spent millions of dollars and thirty years waiting for this moment to arrive, and nothing was going to stop him from bringing his life's work to its fruition. He was about to create rain. Not just bring it forth from clouds produced by Nature and seeded with man-made chemicals. That had been done for decades. No, he was about to *create* rain from clouds he'd brought into being where none should exist.

Success would bring the means of salvation within reach for so many creatures, so many species and environments.

Closer than that.

It would make salvation imminent.

Feeling his heart do a small, excited somersault in his chest, Carter frowned and closed his eyes, bracing himself for the slight, dizzying head rush that always followed the errant heartbeat. The sensation annoyed him, always seeming to strike when he felt the most powerful. It diminished his sense of being in control, as if Nature was reminding him that he was but one cog in a vast, complex mechanism. He kept his breathing evenly paced and waited for the return to normality. Fighting it was useless; he'd learned to keep his excitement in check to reduce the occurrences. But now—he opened his eyes and let go of the windowsill, straightening up as the sensation of free-falling was replaced once again by stalwart equilibrium—now there was no need to restrain his elation. He'd made his commitment to the earth, to humanity, decades ago, and now fulfillment rested in his hands. The knowledge that there could be no greater good to bestow upon mankind than what he was about to do resonated in his soul.

Deeply satisfied with himself, Carter smiled. Over the years, he'd accepted every risk, every cost, with a scientist's pragmatism and patience. He prided himself on it. Even the latest inexplicable atmospheric quirk, which had kept the jet stream unusually far to the south, bringing remarkably mild weather to much of the U.S. for the last month, had been accepted with equanimity, even though it had put his final field trials in jeopardy and his program at risk of discovery. It was difficult enough to build or modify a storm when large swaths of the country showed up green on Doppler radar screens, but he'd overcome that challenge several years ago by using those storms as camouflage for his own. Building storms when the skies and the radar screens were clear and showed virtually no signs of precipitation, leaving him with nothing to mask his tests, was the last obstacle to success. And he would overcome it.

Today he would build a rainstorm in the clear skies over the desert. He would prove himself to be more than a mere cog in the universe. Today he would receive Nature's benediction.

He would become Nature's equal.

The speakers attached to one of the computer monitors on his desk emitted the soft click he was waiting for. Carter walked with a measured stride back to his chair and seated himself within the white-blue halo of light from the screen. A light tap on the mouse brought up the windows displaying live satellite radar and infrared feeds, as well as live streaming video. The data came from a leased transponder on one of the many satellites in geosynchronous orbit twenty-two thousand miles above the equator.

He'd had no trouble getting the transponder through his quiet, well-funded research program, blandly titled the Environmental Replenishment Foundation. Getting the right encryption software had proven a little more difficult, given the laws barring the import or export of encryption algorithms that the U.S. government can't break. Moving the operations offshore had taken care of that problem and a host of others. Paying big salaries to talented physicists, atmospheric scientists, engineers, and software developers in a cross section of poor countries went a long way toward ensuring the foundation's work progressed as quickly and as inconspicuously as it needed to. Generous consulting fees paid to local politicians had neutralized the messy issue of regulatory oversight, which only served to slow down the advancement of science.

The images on the screens before him brought a smile to Carter's face. The sky at the edge of the desert was perfectly clear except for a small cluster of cumulus fractus clouds centered on each screen. His clouds.

He tapped the on-screen control for the microphone. "Go ahead."

The clipped, smoke-roughened voice of the foundation's chief pilot, Raoul Patterson, Maj., RAF (Ret.), came through the speakers as clearly as if he were in the room. "Earth-Four. We're on approach."

"Copy Earth-Four," Carter replied quietly as he zoomed in on the small cluster of clouds that had been painstakingly created less than half an hour ago. Pulling back slightly to gain a broader view of the area from the streaming video, Carter saw the speck that was his plane. But the modified, stealth-enhanced Lockheed P-3 was absent from the radar screen. Nor would it show up on any military or aviation radar that might be doing routine sweeps of the area. His smile widened as he acknowledged, not for the first time, that sometimes his inventiveness and his resourcefulness surprised even him.

The pilot's voice broke into his thoughts. "All systems are go and on standby. Awaiting orders. Over."

"Drop on approach to the target as planned."

"Copy. We're on approach. Over."

The plane wasn't traveling particularly fast and, holding his breath, Carter watched the timer run down to twenty seconds.

"Drop the sensor on eight and initiate on one, Earth-Four, then depart the area. Over." Carter said the words softly and a sudden, harsh tightness in his chest made him suck in a hard breath. The sensation—hovering on pain, short of ecstasy—was so different from the free-falling sensation of a moment ago that he wondered if he were having a heart attack.

Surely not. God would not take from me this moment.

"The sensor is in the chute and ready for release." As ever, Raoul's voice was bland and expressionless. Carter didn't care. Gasping against the chest-crushing vise holding him in rigid stillness, he fought against normal, irrational fear and struggled to remain focused on the test that was about to commence.

An argon-filled, weighted racquet-ball-sized canister would drop from the chute in the bottom of the plane and burst open five seconds later, releasing dozens of delicate microsensors that would activate on contact with the desert air. Smaller than a dime, with a working life of no more than twenty minutes, the sensors would gather data and transmit it to the plane's transceiver at a furious pace before burning up from the heat generated by their splinter-sized silicon processors. If they made it as far as the ground, they would disintegrate into metallic confetti that would scatter onto the desert floor and be hidden under shifting sand.

"Ten, nine, eight. Sensor released. Seven, six, five, four, three, two, one. Initiating the laser."

Carter felt his heart rate spike again as he imagined the invisible beam of infrared energy, releasing more heat than one hundred thousand 100-watt lightbulbs, blasting through the atmosphere and into the heart of his clouds, heating them and releasing the energy they stored. Releasing the life-giving rain they held.

The pause from the cockpit lasted less than twenty seconds. "It's a go. Two pulses of one-point-five seconds discharged at a point-five-zero-second interval. Mission complete. Earth-Four out."

Carter had zoomed out slightly as the cumulus congestus clouds on the screen began to billow in all directions, frothing against the black sky, evolving from pristine silvery paleness to dark, dirty gray, obscuring the small, empty square of desert as the counters on the bottom left of the screen flashed new readings. Altitude, temperature, air pressure, relative humidity, wind strength—each variable was moving steadily in the correct direction until the data came to an abrupt stop as the sensors were incinerated or simply shattered against the ground.

The constriction in his chest began to ease, and sitting back in his chair, Carter let a satisfied grin steal across his face as the intensity of his breathing lessened. His lungs ached as they expanded. Dreamers and scientists alike had long strived to create rainfall on demand. The world needed it, and now, thanks to his tenacity and talent, the world had it. *He* had it. Nothing, not even death, could take that from him.

He closed his eyes. Earlier successes had been sweet, but never as sweet as this. This was vindication, and after a lifetime of waiting, it tasted like nectar. Like cold, pure water. It tasted like rain. It tasted like power.

Man had been attempting to control the weather for centuries. From the days of sacrifices offered to ancient gods to chemical cloud seeding experiments still underway, people had clung to the belief that it could be done. For decades, the world's most advanced intelligence services and military organizations had spent countless millions trying to control the weather. Carter knew that firsthand.

As the American military was being ground down in Vietnam in the sixties, the Central Intelligence Agency had plucked him and a small group of other scientists out of their doctoral programs in the atmospheric sciences and made them part of a highly classified, highly special-ized, fast-track research team devoted to weather control. Intelligence had confirmed that the Soviet Union had sur-passed American efforts to dominate and control the weather. The U.S. was determined to win—the weather war, the Vietnam War, every war.

With an enormous budget, virtually no oversight, the best technology in the world at their disposal, and an unassail-able cover as government staff scientists, Carter's group quickly outstripped the fledgling Soviet attempts to break the chaotic "code" of weather patterns. The key to Carter's team's many successes was that, unlike the Soviets, Carter's team hadn't focused on manipulating the weather or con-trolling it. They'd focused on creating it.

As the geopolitical situation grew worse, other issues took precedence in the minds of Soviet leaders. The Soviet weather program devolved and practically disappeared, leaving the American program the victor by default. Not long after the Agency learned of the demise of the Soviet program, hints about the American program appeared in major newspapers across the country, leaked by anony-mous sources.

Carter had always assumed—known in his heart—that the leak came from the offices of Winslow Benson, a young, ambitious junior senator from New York who had a healthy respect for power but no respect for science or na-ture. Having the power to create and control the weather was an awesome responsibility and a staggering opportu-nity, but Benson, who was heavily if quietly backed by the emerging nuclear power industry, had also seen its potential damage to his backers. Skillfully playing upon the fears of a distrustful, Cold War–hardened public, Benson had openly decried Carter's program, the very program that Benson's committee had secretly funded for nearly ten years, as being part of a Strangelovian scheme that would prove more destructive than beneficial. It didn't take long for the CIA to eliminate the program.

Unwilling to accept the decision, Carter had fought back in Agency offices and Senate hearing rooms, to no effect other than to watch his scientific career and his credibility go up in flames. Livid, humiliated, but with stubbornness that bumped up against the edges of rationality at times, Carter had abandoned the conjoined worlds of government and academia and had gone into business, continuing to do independent weather research whenever and however he could. Initially, the realities of having a family to support and a business to run had slowed his progress and reshaped his objectives, but the passage of time had also hardened his resolve into something a little less flexible than steel. And now, thirty years and many millions of dollars later, he'd achieved his goal.

In every cell, to the very depths of his soul, Carter knew this morning's accomplishment was more than just a technological breakthrough, more than arbitrary luck or the result of hard work. It was deeply, magnificently symbolic. Managing the weather on a global scale was the ultimate authority man could assume over the earth. Exacerbating a storm here, diminishing one there, literally keeping the rain outside of the city so it didn't rain on the government's parade—the Russians and the Chinese had been doing that openly and unapologetically, almost whimsically, for years, without any concern for the interruptions they caused to the flow of Nature.

But what Carter had done today was different.

He took in an easy, reverent breath. He'd created clouds where Nature's tortured climate denied their presence. And from those clouds, from that bone-dry desert air, he'd created rain.

He'd created the means of Life.

The thought resonated in his head as strong and pure as the last note of a hymn in a towering cathedral.

The means of Life.

His talent, his intellect, had wrested from Nature this privilege, this gift beyond comprehension. Over time, regulating rainfall locally, regionally, even globally, could return denuded rain forests to their natural state and reverse desertification, counteracting the effects of global warming. It could reduce Third World poverty and hunger while diminishing poor nations' dependence on the First World's extortionate largesse.

He gripped the arms of his chair, the well-worn leather meeting his palm, giving way beneath hard fingertips as the second realization of the day struck him.

Rain.

Reign.

His hands relaxed as the duality of peace and purpose surged through him. There couldn't be a mandate more clear: With this privilege came the equal and opposite responsibilities to punish the destroyers and to protect the innocents.

It was the ultimate philanthropy.

An electronic crackle from the speaker jolted him from his euphoria.

"Sir. We may have a problem." The pilot's voice still conveyed cool British disinterest.

The challenge wasn't finished. Carter leaned forward and smiled. "Go ahead."

"The flight director thought he might have seen some campers in the path of the storm. Reconnaissance confirmed the presence of a small camp in a canyon not far from ground zero."

Carter went still. "How far?"

"Less than half a kilometer."

This wasn't good news. While it was occasionally unavoidable, collateral damage—human deaths—occurring on his test beds tended to distract the crew and increase the risk of discovery.

"Why didn't you see them earlier?" he asked, his voice calm and matter-of-fact.

"The night-vision video camera and infrared scanner had already been shut down. Standard ops. We would have had to be directly over them to pick up a picture anyway. It's a tight canyon."

Alone in his office, Carter nodded, knowing every step of the test procedures. As a routine precaution, non-essential electronic instrumentation in the specially equipped plane was powered down before the big, power-sucking laser was brought to life.

He took a decisive breath. Initiating a rescue would not only reveal too much, it would likely be useless. Unable to absorb any appreciable amount of water quickly, the hard-baked desert floor would speed the copious rainfall along the path of least resistance. The canyon walls would act as a funnel, pushing the water, making it deeper and more deadly. Even if they were awakened by the roar, the campers would likely be dead before they could identify the sound.

So be it. "Proceed per orders, Earth-Four. Contact me when you close your flight plan."

The pause was minuscule, but Carter picked up on it and frowned as the pilot's voice came back online. "Roger that. Earth-Four out."

Carter sat back in his chair, deeply annoyed and unable to enjoy the green undulations on the screen before him. He didn't like mistakes. Nor did he like anything to impinge on his moments of glory. They were private moments, a time of communion between himself and his destiny. He sat in the darkness trying to recapture that fleeting sense of wonder until a light tap at his door broke his concentration.

"Daddy?"

His eyes opened at the softly spoken word, and he saw the face of his youngest daughter, Meg, framed in the doorway.

"Are you okay?"

He smiled and stood up, tightening the belt of the light flannel robe he wore over his pajamas. "Meggy, I don't think I've ever felt better. Where are you off to?" he asked, clicking the mouse to lock the computer screens before crossing the hardwood floor.

"Jane and I are going out for a run before the hullabaloo starts. The kids are all still asleep, or at least we think they are." She stopped talking long enough to give him a kiss on the cheek, then turned to walk with him to the kitchen. "There's no noise up there anyway. Mom's still asleep, too."

His next youngest, Jane, sat at the breakfast bar tying her shoes. "Hi, Dad. Why are you up? Too excited to sleep?" she asked with a grin. "It's going to be a long day."

"I haven't been up long," he said, brushing away her question with a smile. "It's just great having everyone together. It doesn't happen too often anymore, so why should I waste my time sleeping?"

Both women laughed.

"When the population of the house goes from two senior citizens to two senior citizens plus fourteen twenty- and thirtysomethings plus ten children under the age of seven, you should be flat-out exhausted," Meg pointed out.

"Never. I've always said you girls and your mother were the sources of my energy. That hasn't changed. Except that there are seven husbands and the grandchildren in the mix now. Everyone being healthy, happy, and here is more important to me than the reason you've come."

Jane stood up and kissed him lightly on the cheek. "We wouldn't miss it, Dad. This company has been part of our lives forever. We've watched you build it from scratch. You deserve the party. You deserve more than a party."

"We're so proud of you," Meg added in a whisper. "You've shown them all that no one can keep Carter Thompson down."

The looks on their pretty faces brought back a faint, fleeting version of the squeezing sensation in his chest and he forced a smile against it. They were good girls. Smart girls. All of his girls were. And they were sincere, honest, and worthy of his trust. That's why they had all wanted to work for him when they'd finished their studies, and that's why he'd hired them to work for his companies, the companies that had made everything else possible. He was blessed, so truly blessed in so many ways.

"Go have your run before you start getting soppy," he said gruffly, waving them to the door. "Stay near the pond. I think the airstrip has been secured for the president and I don't want you getting shot by those Secret Service hooligans."

Rolling their eyes with gentle, amused exasperation, they left the house. He watched them launch into an easy, steady pace as they headed along the grassy path to the small lake half a mile away, then made his way through the silent kitchen of the old farmhouse and upstairs. His wife, their other five daughters, and their families, all asleep, had no idea that he, Carter Thompson, had just secured the health and prosperity of the world and its people.

Of course, an inevitably steep cost would be borne by a few, but it would be far outweighed by the inarguable benefits to so many.

It was a matter of simply restoring the world's equilibrium. The thought made him smile.

CHAPTER **4**

Tuesday, July 10, 6:35 A.M., Washington, D.C.
Freelance work had its perks, but meetings like this wasn't one of them.

Tom Taylor, eco-terrorism expert and special advisor to the Director of National Intelligence, shifted in his chair. He'd been sitting too long and wanted more than anything to get up and get some circulation back into his lower extremities. But first he had to subdue this beast that would not die and *would not fucking listen to him*.

Being dismissed on sight as too young to be in the position he was in was an ordinary enough occurrence. His gene pool had conspired to give him the face of Dorian Gray. The older he got and the more brutal, brain-fogging shit he saw, the younger people thought he was. It worked to his benefit in its own weird way, but he had to put up with condescending crap for the first few minutes of every God-damned meeting he'd ever had. He handled it, though. It was better than the alternative. If his face revealed half of what he knew or half of what he'd seen, he'd scare the hell out of the Angel of Death. But right now, he wouldn't mind doing exactly that to the prick with the chest full of ribbons sitting across from him.

He looked up from his papers to meet the eyes of the general seated at the end of the table in the comfortable, secure conference room several stories below the ground floor of the Pentagon. "With all due respect, General Moore, you're not going to change a thing. The jet stream stays parked where it is."

"You don't mess with Mother Nature, Mr. Taylor," the general replied, his jaw barely moving as he spoke. "This isn't what HAARP was intended for. It's called the High Frequency Active Auroral Research Program for a reason. It's a communications and surveillance *research program,* not a weapon. We've never applied consistent, continuous, wide-scale atmospheric interference for this length of time before, even when a situation clearly warranted it. What we're doing right now is what whack-job assholes have been accusing us of doing for years."

Stand down, you fucking prima donna. "I understand your concerns, General," Tom said in a calm tone calculated to infuriate people who thought they were the AIC, which was his shorthand for the role he normally occupied: Asshole In Charge. "The CIA's Director of Operations and the Director of National Intelligence understand that HAARP is strictly an atmospheric research tool and that to use it otherwise is to give credence to the rants of conspiracy theorists. But the Pentagon's public relations machine is not our highest priority at the moment. We're looking at a bigger mission right now, sir. One with incalculably high stakes and a potentially catastrophic outcome. We're changing the rules, and you have to play along."

The general's skin was as coarse as granite and nearly the same color, or had been until a moment ago. Now it was turning a deep shade of red. His eyes were blue and burning with anger at being overruled. Given that he'd been on the Joint Chiefs of Staff during the former administration, powerlessness probably wasn't a sensation the man was used to experiencing, but that was too damned bad. He wasn't calling the shots this time. The CIA's DO was, at the direct request of the DNI.

Nevertheless, Tom wished again that he'd brought along some technical backup for the meeting, especially since the general had brought reinforcements. But his best researcher had died unexpectedly and his replacement wasn't up to speed enough to warrant bringing him in now.

"General, I have a meeting at Langley in a little while, so I propose that we cut to the chase. We're confident that a terrorist cell operating within U.S. borders has devised a means of controlling the weather. We've asked you to cover our backs while we hunt for the members of this cell and to keep the weather over the continental U.S. stable until we're able to flush them into the open by making them blink first. Thanks in part to your cooperation, we're close to identifying the terrorists, General Moore. Now, I'd like to understand your objections to continuing this operation."

He could practically see the man's blood pressure spike. "My objection is that we're disrupting necessary, critical cycles that fuel global weather, including thermohaline convection. My objection is that we don't know what the consequences will be if we continue interfering with weather systems at this level, Mr. Taylor. And at this point neither do we know what will happen when we stop the

interference." He paused, apparently waiting for some response.

Tom provided none and instead leaned back in his
chair, masking with nonchalance his alarm at the general's
admission. This was not the way things were supposed to
play out. He knew that, the general knew that, and the DNI
knew that. Smoking out terrorists was not supposed to
take this long. It had taken eight months to find Saddam
Hussein, Osama bin Laden had been more fucking elusive
than anyone had anticipated, and now these bastards—

When he'd been tapped to head the task force, the DNI's
staff had briefed him with everything they knew at the
time, which was basically the *what:* The weapon of mass
destruction under discussion was the weather. The sinking
feeling in his gut had been offset by an adrenaline burst.

*It was a damned big weapon to hide. And yet someone
was hiding it all too effectively.*

For the last two years, the attacks had been scattered,
small-scale, and on foreign soil. They had been test runs
most likely, but too damned effective and too damned
subtle to prevent or even discover ahead of their execu-
tion. Whoever was behind them knew how to lay low and
how to get people to keep their mouths shut.

The pace of the investigation had picked up when fresh
intelligence gave the task force a reason to believe that
over the last few months operations had moved inside the
U.S., indicating the increased probability of an attack. Despite being armed with that knowledge, the task force had
quickly run into an impressive set of dead ends. To a small
degree they'd narrowed down the *where* to the western
U.S., but after three months they still had no strong leads
on the *who,* the *when*—as in when the next strike would
be—or the *why,* although on the surface, the latter was
pretty simple to figure out.

If you controlled the weather, you controlled the world.

The U.S. had been trying to achieve that for decades. So
had its enemies. And one of them was succeeding where
the rest had failed.

Tom realized the general was glowering at him.

"Mr. Taylor, I'm sure you're familiar with the laws of thermodynamics, but let me refresh your memory anyway. The first law of thermodynamics states that energy can neither be created nor destroyed; it can only be transformed from one state to another, from potential to kinetic and back again. The second law states that the potential energy in a system will always be less than the initial state. What you've caused us to do, to put it bluntly, is to shortchange the system. Over the last five weeks, we've prevented an immeasurable quantity of potential energy from being converted, or released into the atmosphere as storms and other weather events. But we can't keep doing that."

Tom glanced down at his notes. "There have been small storms scattered around the country in the last five weeks. And the Atlantic has been active earlier than usual. There have been twenty-two named storms so far, including two that happened before the official start of hurricane season, but none of them have done much more than generate headlines and a little heavy surf. That hardly sounds like you're holding back anything, General. Who's responsible for those storms?"

Colonel Patricia Brannigan, the general's aide, had been quiet until now. She broke into the conversation. "We are. We had to bleed off energy where we could, when we could. Holding that much energy more or less stationary put us at increasing risk."

"Of what?"

"A disaster, Mr. Taylor. With a cool upper-level high parked over the center of the country, the Gulf air has nowhere to go, so it just stays there and gets hotter. And the water beneath it gets hotter. Right now, the Gulf is averaging eighty degrees Fahrenheit, which is significantly warmer than it should be at this time of year. Hot water heats the air and the hot air rises. If a hot spot of sufficient intensity develops, with all that latent energy behind it, a column of air could burst through the system's cap like a volcano."

"Without the ash and fumes," Tom pointed out dryly.

She didn't even blink. "No ash. No fumes. Instead, you'd have violent weather at altitudes not naturally available to storm systems. Convection cells would be moving at unnatural speeds backed by unnatural pressure, creating hurricanes that could spread for thousands of miles in all directions and throw off tornadoes, waterspouts, and severe thunderstorms. Airplanes would be blown out of the sky, ships caught in transit would be sunk, and communications would be disrupted all over the northern hemisphere. There would be massive flooding, heavy hail, strong winds—Would you like me to continue?"

"No, I get the picture." He reached for the coffee cup at his elbow and glanced into it. Empty. He met her eyes. "As dreadful as it sounds, Colonel, that outcome relies on a fair bit of speculation, doesn't it?"

The general leaned forward across the table with something close to bloodlust in his eyes. "Listen, you fucking spook," he said, his voice dropping to a steel-edged rasp. "We're talking about the weather. There are too God-damned many variables to predict exactly what *will* happen, but any one of the probable or improbable scenarios we've come up with would be enough to give the DNI a laundry bill. Read my lips. *The energy is building.* We're treating the upper atmosphere as if it's some big battery, but even the atmosphere has its limits and at some point, a point we may reach very soon, we are not going to be able to keep Nature from taking its own course."

"What does that mean, General?"

"It means that unless we begin to dissipate that energy on a larger scale now, while we can still control the rate of dissipation, we could have a hemisphere-wide disaster on our hands."

Tom held the general's eyes. "No."

The general leaned forward again. "Mr. Taylor, perhaps I'm not making myself clear. *We have to stop this operation now.*"

"I understand what you're saying, General Moore, but we can't stop the operation," he replied calmly. "We're going to continue Operation DOWNPLAY as planned until an anomaly occurs that isn't of our making. And when that happens, we can have this conversation again."

Colonel Brannigan leveled a grave stare at him. "Mr. Taylor, please try to understand that we've already moved beyond any models we've designed. The bottom line is, as the general said, that we don't know how much longer we can continue to deconstruct and diffuse the natural weather patterns, nor do we know how much longer we can contain the energy those disruptions are producing, nor do we have a plan for dissipating the energy currently stored."

The military admitting defeat. There's something you don't hear every day. Tom watched the aide's face, keeping his own expressionless despite the furious churn in his gut. "Did I hear you correctly, Colonel? You don't *know how* to release the energy?"

"Yes, Mr. Taylor, you heard me correctly."

"Here's a suggestion. Continue bleeding off the energy as you said you've been doing. Brew up some bigger storms if you need to. Just don't do it over the continental United States. Cuba and Venezuela come to mind as convenient targets." He spoke softly and glanced at the general's face, which had deepened toward a more purplish-red hue.

"You can't move massive cells of energy like they are pieces on a chessboard, Mr. Taylor," Colonel Brannigan replied before the general could open his mouth. "As the general said, we've taken a dynamic system and rendered it static for the last five weeks. We've essentially cranked a powerful engine far beyond its capabilities. There *is* no place to release the energy other than right where it's stored."

"Surely there's some natural mechanism—"

"For releasing an artificially created, supersized energy field? No, there isn't. This situation has never existed before." She folded her hands in front of her on the table and stared him down with a cold smile. "Naturally, Mr. Taylor,

the Russians, NATO, and most of our allies already suspect we're up to something, and they're not happy. Neither
are the Chinese. We're scaring the heart out of them because their physicists can't explain what's happening by
any natural means. Neither can ours, other than those per-
petrating it. Nor can any climatologists. No one has ever
seen anything like it, or read any theoretical work suggesting something like it. But, without knowing anything
about this operation, people are hypothesizing about energy gradients being radically out of alignment, which is
not a situation that has ever been produced except in computer models. Conspiracy theorists are having a field day,
particularly those with HAARP in their crosshairs."

Tom raised an eyebrow. "Thank you for sharing that with
us, Colonel Brannigan." He shifted his attention to her left.
"General, please keep me apprised on the situation."

The general leaned back in his chair and fixed his eyes
directly into Tom's. "I don't know if you're a religious
man, Mr. Taylor, but you may want to become one. Asking
God to have mercy on us all for what we've done may be
the only option open to any of us now."

Tom stood and gathered his papers into a neat stack,
slipped them into his briefcase, and met the general's
eyes. "I'm not, General Moore, but I'll take it under ad-
visement. Good day."

He nodded at Colonel Brannigan and left the room. The
nearest men's room was fifty feet down the hall. He managed to make it into a stall before losing his breakfast.

Depleted and shaking, he leaned against the cool metal
wall of the stall and closed his eyes.

*Those assholes had better make a move soon. Damned
soon.*

A couple of splashes of punishingly cold water snapped
his spine back into place before he left the washroom. He
didn't make it ten feet down the hall before he heard the
colonel's cool voice call his name.

Swearing under his breath, he stopped and turned
around to watch her walk toward him with a stride more

appropriate for a body encased in desert camo and combat boots than a tight Army green skirt and low-heeled pumps. She came to an abrupt halt a foot away from him.

"What can I do for you, Colonel?"

"Issue the order to release the jet stream," she replied bluntly. "There was an inexplicable cloudburst near Death Valley less than an hour ago. I think it's the anomaly you've been waiting for."

He let a few seconds tick over as he stared into the icy blue of her eyes, not quite ready to believe her, not quite trusting the triumphant burst of adrenaline flooding his veins. "Let's go back to the conference room and you can tell me about it."

And you had damned well better be right.

CHAPTER 5

Tuesday, July 10, 11:00 A.M., Campbelltown, Iowa
Meteorologist Kate Sherman stood at the edge of the large, crowded tent watching the warm early-summer rain fall steadily in front of her. Her mind, for once, was not on the weather. She was wondering if making the mad ten-foot dash to the next tent and getting soaked to the skin was a reasonable trade-off for remaining within earshot of the endless drone coming out of the face of Ted Burse, a network security guy and indisputably the most boring human being ever to come out of a mad scientist's petri dish. She was convinced Ted had. There was no way the man could have been produced by a force of nature. He was that bad.

Glancing to her right, she gave Ted a polite smile, the same one she'd been giving him every ninety seconds or so for the last ten minutes, which was when he'd cornered her. Enduring situations like this was just one reason she despised company parties, especially the ones held outdoors in the rain in Iowa. Campbelltown, Iowa, population 416, where there was nothing but the weather on people's minds and nothing but farm fields in every direction. The only bump on the horizon in any direction was the low-slung, unassuming headquarters of Coriolis Management, the company she worked for, the company that had paid her to sit on a train for two days to come out here for one day and would pay her to begin the return trip to her office in Lower Manhattan and real civilization the following morning.

Imminent salvation appeared fifty yards away in the business-casual-clad body of Davis Lee Longstreet, global director of strategy for Coriolis and her boss. Envious, Kate watched him do the executive weave in and out of the crowded, colorful tents, his progress through the drizzle-soaked landscape as smooth and easy as that of a shark through calm, dark water. Kate knew from experience that Davis Lee never got stuck talking with one person for too long.

That was about to change. He was going to be stuck with her for as long as it took her to get the hell away from Ted.

Kate stuck out her arm and grabbed Davis Lee as politely as she could without attracting the attention of the many Secret Service agents and private security personnel milling around on the corporate campus. He stopped and, with a single look, absorbed the situation.

His Princeton–Yale Law–Kennedy School brains well hidden—as usual—behind a charming, Southern façade, Davis Lee slung a casual arm around her shoulders and gave her a crooked grin that made his attractive face even more handsome.

"Well, if it isn't my favorite weather bunny," he drawled in his best *Green Acres* voice. Kate forced a smile and refrained from stepping on his foot. Hard. "How you doin', Miz Kate? Never can bring myself to say your last name. It would set too many of my relations spinnin' in their graves." He sent Ted a smile that stopped just short of vacuous. "Hey, Ted. I didn't know y'all knew each other."

Ted smiled back and was on the verge of replying when

Kate pre-empted him. Once the man got started, he was impossible to stop.

"Hi, Davis Lee. I'm so glad we bumped into each other. We need to talk. About that report," she added meaningfully.

"What report would that be? This is a social occasion, Kate, or didn't you get the memo?" He sent Ted a conspiratorial wink that, as Kate could have predicted, was lost in translation. Ted was that dense.

"I'm here, aren't I? And you know what report I'm talking about. *The* report." She paused, waiting for him to quit playing dumb, to jump in and back up her lie.

He didn't, and she knew it was deliberate.

Great. "The report on episodic fluctuations of rainfall patterns in the Gobi Desert. I believe you needed help with some of the vocabulary." There was just enough New York saccharine in her smile to make his eyes narrow although his smile never dimmed. That was permanent, just like a shark's.

"Oh, *that* report. I just plumb forgot, what with the excitement of gettin' to meet the president again and all." Davis Lee extended his hand toward Ted. "Kate and I have to have a chat, Ted. I'm sure you'll excuse us."

They weren't ten steps away when Kate glanced up at him. "How do you do that?"

"Do what, darlin'?"

"Seem sincere and sappy at the same time."

Davis Lee steered her out of the tent and through the wet grass to the asphalt, sheltering her under his golf umbrella. They were heading across the main parking lot to the building where their boss, Carter Thompson, would be meeting with the President of the United States in a few minutes. Kate wondered how close to the building she would be allowed to get before the swarm of beefy men in dark windbreakers detached her from Davis Lee.

"Well?" she prodded.

He paused for a heartbeat, then looked down at her. "You ever been accused of being subtle?"

"Never," she replied. "I'm from Brooklyn. We don't do subtle."

"Now that's just too damn bad, honey. My mama might like you if it weren't for that."

Kate rolled her eyes. "Quit channeling Jethro Bodine. I need to talk to you, Davis Lee."

He grinned. "See now, Kate, I just follow J. R. Ewing's basic rule of life. 'Once you can fake sincerity, you can achieve anything.' It's a Southerner's eleventh commandment, at least when dealing with y'all."

Kate shot him an exasperated look.

Davis Lee just laughed and snugged her against him for a second, then dropped his arm. "So, how's things, darlin'? Looks like you're having some trouble these days."

"Uncharacteristically, yes, I am. And I can't figure out why."

"Maybe your voodoo dolls have too many pins stuck in them." He lifted a hand in greeting to someone Kate didn't recognize.

"Voodoo is for people, not weather," she snapped. "I'm serious, Davis Lee. And seriously pissed off. I missed a hailstorm in Montana, a flood in Minnesota, and a straight-line windstorm in Oklahoma. Three events in three states in three months." She shook her head. "It makes no sense. I've reviewed the data from the land stations and satellites. Cross-checked everything. I don't know how I missed them. And don't try to make me feel better by saying everyone else missed them, too. It won't work. I'm better than everyone else and we both know it."

"I can't disagree with you there. You're damned good." He took a sip from the bottle of beer he held. His hand completely covered the label, but she knew it was non-alcoholic. Davis Lee didn't like mistakes—his own or anybody else's.

"Don't stop there," she said dryly. "What about the storms?"

His eyes were still on the crowd when he said, "It's not an exact science, is it?"

The offhand comment took her by surprise, and she swallowed a tart reply. "No, it isn't."

He glanced down at her. "You rollin' over and playin' dead so soon?"

"What's the likelihood of that?" she replied, forcing a grin. "I intend to find out what went wrong."

"Let me know when you do."

Here goes. "It might be sooner than you think. I wrote a paper about those storms and submitted it to a conference. It was chosen for presentation. You don't mind, do you?"

He studied her for a moment and then said, "I don't know. Do I? What conference is it?"

"An annual conference on severe local weather."

"Local where?"

She gave a silent laugh. "Anywhere. Everywhere. Look, you send me to it every year—"

"I do?"

"Yes, you do. Do you remember what it is I do for you, Davis Lee? I study local weather and make forecasts."

"And y'all have conferences about it?"

Great. Jethro's back. "We do," she replied patiently.

"So with this paper you'll be contributing to the body of knowledge?"

"Yes. But you don't have to say it with such skepticism."

Smiling, he bobbed his head. "My apologies." He paused. "You've done some pretty good things for us, Kate, with that streaming data going straight from those feeds into those woo-woo databases you made. You're not going to give away the farm, are you? Or tell all your secrets?"

"Hardly. The presentation doesn't have anything to do with me or the company, as such. It's limited to those storms."

"What are you going to say about them?"

"That they exhibited atypical behaviors due to criteria that remain unidentified and for reasons that remain unexplained."

He stared at her. "That's it?"

She nodded.

"You're just telling everybody that you found a problem and you're not offering any solution?"

She nodded again.

He ran a hand through his amber waves of plugs and let out a long breath as he stopped and faced her. He didn't look happy. He didn't look pissed off, either, which was good, but "annoyed" might fit the bill. "You have to answer me some questions, Kate. First of all, what's the point of doing that? It doesn't exactly make you sound like the hotshot you are. And, second, why in the name of all that's holy would you admit that to your peers?"

And people call you an intellectual. She put her sarcasm in a closet and met his eyes. "Well, someone else might have an answer or be studying the same thing from a different perspective. Like you said, it's a contribution to the body of knowledge. A colleague and I were talking about it and he said he thought it had some potential."

"Someone in-house?"

"No. I spoke about it with Richard Carlisle. He's a former professor of mine and—"

"The weather guy from TV? The one that nearly got blown off that building a while back?"

"Yes, that would be him."

"How do you know him?"

"We're friends."

"Isn't he a little old for you?" He raised an eyebrow.

She resisted the temptation to fold her arms across her chest and glare at him. "Yes, Davis Lee, he would be if we were dating, not that that's any of your business, but we're *friends.* Can we get back to the conference?"

"No offense intended. When's the conference?"

"The end of next week."

"Where?"

"D.C."

"You taking the shuttle?"

"The train." She glanced at her hands for a split second, fighting the mingled residue of shame and anger that shot through her whenever the issue of travel arose. Her rational side knew she shouldn't have to explain her decision every time, especially after six years had gone by, but the other side trumped that thought process because her decision was less a choice than a traumatic imperative. She'd been hard at work just before nine on September 11, 2001, in her thirtieth-floor office that faced the World Trade Center a few blocks away. The memories could still leave her paralyzed if she let them.

Kate cleared her throat and returned her eyes to Davis Lee's face. "I'm taking the train," she repeated in a voice that had lost its fire.

Davis Lee nodded. "That sounds fine. By the way, good call in Nebraska last week. Saved some wheat futures."

"Thanks. Make sure you tell my boss," she replied dryly.

They resumed walking, and before she realized it, he was steering her toward another crowded tent, this one full of tables laden with food. "I'll be back in New York early next week. We can talk more then. In the meantime, I have to go see a man about a policy." He turned to a heavyset woman behind him and flashed that charming smile at her. "Well, I'll be damned. Tammy Jo. Isn't this just lucky? Do you know Kate? She's from the New York office. Kate, this is Tammy Jo, one of my assistants here in Campbelltown. My right hand, as a matter of fact. Kate is one of our meteorologists, Tammy Jo. Maybe you can get her to tell you why it's rainin' on our parade." With a wink and a smile, Davis Lee drifted into the official-looking group of armed and headset-wearing men milling in front of the headquarters's main door.

Damn it. Kate forced herself to smile back at the blushing, beaming woman, who put a bottle of Bud Light into her hand and was urging her to get in line for the food coming off the grills.

Kate put the chilled bottle to her lips and swallowed. Although she'd never admit as much to Davis Lee, learning that her paper had been accepted for presentation at the conference had left her with mixed feelings. It was an honor, of course. She'd be speaking to a pretty potent audience of weather research professionals, a growing number of whom were her fellow forecasters in the ever more cutthroat investment and financial markets.

For the other half of the audience—the wonks, academics, and TV talking heads—standing up and saying that you didn't know something was a perfectly acceptable thing to do. But if you called Wall Street your home away from home, it was less acceptable. Much less. Fund analysts and managers, stockbrokers, bond and commodity traders, and the rest of them would not only never do it, they also had a limitless supply of jargon and weasel words to get around acknowledging the fact that they weren't actually God. If they heard that a person whose expertise they relied on had publicly admitted she didn't know something that she should—well, it wouldn't go down well. That's why Davis Lee's fairly calm acceptance of her plan had come as more than a surprise. She had plenty of doubts about what degree of career suicide she might be engaging in. She'd been prepared to drop it if he'd made a big enough fuss, and part of her had sort of hoped he would so the decision would be taken out of her hands.

On the other hand, those storms were just so damned weird that maybe she wouldn't have let it drop. She took another sip from the bottle.

Despite what she'd implied to Davis Lee a few minutes ago, the truth was that Richard—friend, mentor, weather junkie, and the nation's most-watched morning weatherman—had most definitely *not* been supportive of her research into the storms or of her decision to turn that research into a conference paper. He'd tried to talk her out of pursuing the research entirely by pointing out one possibility that she hadn't considered, one that she hadn't been able to forget.

In his easygoing way, Richard had reminded her that weather fanatics and conspiracy theorists continually combed scholarly and scientific literature for unanswered questions. They turned these into "proof" of improbable threats, dire scenarios, and evil government plots.

While Kate was hoping her thoughtful questions would capture the attention of someone with answers, according to Richard those very questions could lead the loo-lah brigade to hijack her hard-won credentials and excellent reputation by identifying her as yet another expert who had come over to their side. She'd be an unwitting poster girl for the legions of lunatics who put up homemade Web sites with black backgrounds and white type, and in badly written, slightly hysterical prose declaimed paranoid theories, anti-government rants, and junk science.

Not quite what she had in mind for her fifteen minutes of fame.

On the other hand, she was a trained scientist and unexplained phenomena chewed at her brain.

"Excuse me, ma'am. Rare or medium?"

Kate blinked, realizing she'd been shuffling along the buffet line in a daze. She focused on the shiny, soot-streaked, entirely too earnest face of the young man smiling back at her. He was stationed between the hot, smoking grills and the tables sagging under the weight of brimming, steaming stainless-steel chafing pans. His paper chef's hat had wilted in the humidity and sat in a flattened pouf on his sweaty head, perfectly complementing his char- and blood-streaked white coat. His right hand reached for her plate while his left held aloft a long-pronged meat fork with charred bits of many a steer clinging to its tines.

"Sorry. Wrong line." She smiled her thanks at the young man and headed for the salad bar.

Unexplained phenomena were welcome to chew at her brain. Mad cow disease was not.

CHAPTER 6

Tuesday, July 10, 11:30 A.M., Campbelltown, Iowa

If it was true that power was the greatest aphrodisiac, then surely proximity to power had a similarly potent effect. Being waved into the tightly secured inner sanctum of a presidential enclave had given Davis Lee a serious hard-on. The fact that he was headed to his own office only enhanced the experience: His office was inside the ring of fire.

He didn't have to fake a smile as he walked past the phalanxes of Secret Service agents and presidential aides milling around the entrance to Coriolis's headquarters and the various security checkpoints. As he pushed open the door to his office, his smile grew wider.

There she was, the quiet, earnest, painlessly plain Elle Baker, whom he'd lured away from a low-level position in the White House chief of staff's office to be his senior assistant for special projects.

She was the perfect choice. He'd known it the first time he'd seen her during an interminably long and utterly boring party hosted by one of the wildlife conservation lobbies. Elle had been working her way along the walls of the room, following the sophisticates like a shadow and laughing without catching the jokes. Knowing big breaks inspire big loyalty, he'd made a point of finding out who she was and chatting her up, and then he'd had HR check her out and make her a Manhattan-based offer she couldn't refuse. It had all taken less than ten days.

She had come on board a few weeks later fully armed with undergraduate degrees in statistics and history, a master's degree in library science, and an unexpected tenacious streak. Despite having lived and worked in D.C. for two years, Elle still bore all the hallmarks of an ambitious but clueless small-town girl from a flyover state. According to what HR had been able to find out, she'd gotten her position in the White House the old-fashioned way—she'd earned it.

No connections to any significant Washington power structures had surfaced during a routine background check. Her name had never appeared on any blogs, scandalous or otherwise, and her Internet presence was limited to a tame page on Facebook that hadn't been updated since she'd graduated from college. A deeper background check had revealed that although her mother had gone to the same college as the First Lady and they had belonged to the same sorority, Elle's father was a staunch and vocal supporter of the wrong party.

The director of personnel for Coriolis had laughed that it was more of a miracle than a mystery that Elle had been hired by the White House, and Davis Lee hadn't argued. After her research internships at the national party headquarters and a private think tank, the White House had been an unusual next step, but two years in Washington had obviously garnered her some kind of connections. Elle wasn't the most politically astute twenty-six-year-old Davis Lee had ever hired, but if she'd been able to pull off something like that, she was clever enough to do what he needed her to do.

She had quickly shown herself to be gifted when it came to research, which made her more than tolerable until his current special project—he'd told her it was a behind-the-scenes biography to be privately published for Carter's upcoming sixty-fifth birthday—was complete. In truth, there was no biography planned. Davis Lee simply considered comprehensive, clandestine digging around in someone's personal history due diligence in the realm of corporate politics. Carter Thompson was a canny gamesman who held his cards close to his chest, but that didn't preclude him from having a few up his sleeve.

"Hey, Elle, I was wondering when you were going to get here," he said as he walked toward his desk.

"I flew in this morning. Tammy Jo picked me up at the airport and brought me out here a little while ago."

"Good girl. They didn't give you any trouble out there, did they?" he asked, tipping his head toward the front of the building.

"The security people?" She shook her head as she began to blush. "No. A few of the agents recognized me from the West Wing, so they checked me in pretty fast."

"Good. Now tell me what you're doing in here when you should be out there having fun."

She smiled up at him, too widely and, frankly, too adoringly. If she'd been good-looking, it wouldn't have annoyed him, but she was as plain as a picket fence. No makeup, no fashion sense, no efforts made to improve her looks. . . . He winked at her anyway and watched her quickly turn away. "Are you about to make me a happy man, Miz Baker?"

Settling into the chair behind his imposing walnut desk, Davis Lee tapped a key on the keyboard to bring his computer's monitor to life, then leaned back and slid his feet out of his thoroughly soaked hand-sewn Italian leather loafers. *Damned Iowa mud.*

"I think you'll be pleased, Davis Lee. I thought you'd want to see these right away and I didn't want to leave them lying around. That's why I waited for you here," she replied softly as she stood up and carried a file folder to him. It was stamped with the word *"CONFIDENTIAL"* across the front in large, dark blue letters, followed by *"DAVIS LEE LONGSTREET ONLY"* handwritten with a red felt-tip marker.

Subtle.

With a deep breath, he accepted the folder from her, flicked it open, and gave it a two-second glance before setting it on his desk. He met her eyes. "More articles he wrote? I thought you found them all a while back."

She dropped gracelessly into the wing chair in front of his desk. "I thought so, too. But these weren't archived in the same way. They're not from what would be considered academic or scientific journals. They're from . . ." She paused.

"Well, they were cited in some old off-the-wall books I came across. About weather conspiracies. Like weather control and things like that."

He realized that he hadn't breathed out and forced an easy laugh to cover it, then reached forward and keyed in his password. "Elle, you have to come clean with me. What do you mean you 'came across' old books about weather conspiracy theories? I find the fact that you were reading them almost more alarming than the citations you found in them. Don't tell me that's what you do for fun at night because I just won't believe it."

"No," she replied, with a smile that looked a little strained. "But in one of those dry papers Mr. Thompson wrote while he was at the Weather Service in the mid-sixties, he made an allusion to a topic I hadn't come across before, so I decided to see where it led me."

His gaze moved from his screen to her face and he sent her a look intended to let her know this wasn't a conversation he'd entertain for much longer. "And it led you to the whack-job world of weather conspiracy theorists?"

She nodded and started to laugh. "Well, you told me to find whatever I could. I thought that there might be a little bit of color behind all the drab information I'd found so far. You know, something to spice up the biography a little. So far, I can't imagine whoever writes it is going to have much to work with. I mean, most of his papers were about jet stream fluctuations and cloud physics."

"So what did you find?" he asked, his eyes drifting to his computer screen. One tap to the keyboard brought up his e-mail application. There were sixty-three new messages.

"College term papers."

Davis Lee looked up. "Say what?"

"He was interested in the role of meteorologists during times of war." She leaned forward, eyes bright with geeky excitement. "He wrote about theories of weather manipulation throughout history. Like in the time of Shakespeare and Napoleon. And he was a big fan of what was going on weather-wise during the world wars. You know, like forecasting strategies and weather research. Cloud seeding and—"

"Slow down there, Elle. You're losing me."

She smiled, delighted with herself, and looked almost pretty.

"I think it might have been an early hobby or passion or something, Davis Lee. Have you ever heard him talk about it?"

He shook his head, a growing uneasiness whispering against the hairs at the back of his neck.

"Then I guess we've stumbled across something, haven't we? I mean, it shouldn't come as too much of a surprise. His senior thesis was on the British Meteorology Service and the D-day invasion, and his graduate work focused on the evolution of large-scale weather patterns. He must have dropped it as a hobby or whatever by the time he was getting his doctorate, because his dissertation is real scientific and pretty dry, but—"

She read his dissertation? "Elle, stay on point. The term papers?"

"Right. Sorry. So, this cluster of papers struck me as a little weird because, basically, he wrote ten undergrad term papers that were all variations on a theme. And they were all written in different years for different classes— even an English lit class. It's kind of a stretch to be able to do that, and I think you'd have to really love the topic to be able to approach it so many ways."

"How did they end up in these books?"

She shrugged, her hands tightly folded in her lap. "I guess he must have thought they were good, or important, or something, because he probably sent them to the people who cited them. I mean, I'm conjecturing here, but they didn't have computers or the Internet or anything then— well, DARPA Net, but he wouldn't have had access to that—but he had to have been in touch with these people somehow. How would they know about his work otherwise? He was just a college student. So if he contacted them, that means he had to have been pretty into the subject and must have thought his papers merited some attention. Don't you think?" She paused for a quick breath. "I mean, why else would he have even corresponded with these people?"

Her words were coming faster and her voice was getting breathy. If he didn't stop her, she'd talk herself into a fit of hyperventilation.

"Okay, just give me a second." He held up one hand as he glanced at the title page on the top of the stack. *"Playing God: Man's Search for the Means to Control the Weather."*

Davis Lee kept his face expressionless. *Carter, what the fuck were you up to?*

He flipped through the rest of the papers. "The Role of Weather Prediction in the Outcome of the One-Hundred-Year War." "'Typhoon' Halsey and Weather-Induced Losses in the Pacific Theater." "The Role of Electromagnetism in Mythology and Superstition." "The Effect of Climatic Changes on Commerce and Social Structure in the Nineteenth Century." "Weather Imagery in Shakespeare's Tragedies."

His heart skipped a beat. Damned if Carter's name wasn't on each cover sheet, along with the name of the course, the professor, and the date. No matter what the course was, Carter had found a way to work weather into it.

This won't play well on talk radio.

Revelations of college fuckups hadn't been kind to Bill Clinton, Joe Biden, or anyone else in the public eye. But theirs had been more typical transgressions—smoking dope and committing plagiarism. Contributing to conspiracy theories that challenged the U.S. government's morality or policies was in a different category. Howard, Al, Rush, and G. Gordon would have a field day with it no matter which angle they chose to discuss. Then the teletaters— Davis Lee's private term for TV commentators—would get hold of it. When that happened, the shit would not only hit the fan, it would stick.

Not gonna happen.

Davis Lee looked at Elle, who was glowing. "How did you get your hands on these?"

"I contacted the authors of the books and told them what I was doing. They were happy to help and sent me what they had. Then I requested Mr. Thompson's undergraduate transcripts from the University of Iowa." She shrugged. "I tracked down the professors. Some of them are still around and had hung on to this stuff. Some said they knew he was destined for greatness, but others admitted that they just hung on to everything. But now that he's such a household name, I think they were delighted to be recognized as part of his history. They were sort of honored to be asked. You might want to think about mentioning them in the acknowledgments."

Feeling a little winded, Davis Lee nodded absently and stared at his computer screen to buy time to collect his thoughts. He knew Carter well enough to know that he wasn't a guy to drop a subject if it meant something to him, yet ten years at the man's right hand had never provided Davis Lee with an inkling of this—what was it? "Hobby" seemed a bit tame. Knowing Carter as well as he did, "obsession" might be the right word.

When Davis Lee had met Carter, Coriolis Engineering had been twenty years old and nothing special, just a big construction firm that cleaned up after natural disasters and made a healthy profit doing so. He'd been the one to persuade Carter to use his weather forecasting skills to get into the financial markets, primarily futures markets, and that's why Carter had brought him on board. Making money off both ends of weather events had never occurred to Carter before Davis Lee brought it up, but it had occurred to Davis Lee right away. Hell, if you could figure out which storms were going to kill a few thousand acres of soybeans or take out a drilling platform or pipeline before the other guys did, you could make serious money. And if you had a company that could go in and clean up the mess afterward, which Carter already had, you could win twice. Pointing that out was all it took. They'd been cleaning up, literally and figuratively, ever since.

But if you knew how to make things happen the way you wanted them to—

"Davis Lee?"

He blinked and brought his attention back to Elle, who was slowly crawling back into her shell. "I'm sorry, darlin'. I'm just a little blown away by all that you've accomplished. What did you ask me?"

"I said you might want to thank them in the book's acknowledgments."

He had no idea who she was talking about, but he smiled anyway. "That's a great idea. You keep all the information together so we get it right. And why don't you keep on working this angle? Find whatever you can. It's great stuff, Elle, great stuff. Try to get originals when you can, so we can keep them in the archives."

She stood up, slowly, understanding that she'd been dismissed but not quite ready to go.

"Something else on your mind?"

"Well, I know this probably has nothing to do with the biography, but I'm curious. What do you suppose made someone so interested in this sort of, I don't know, topic or research area or whatever, who studied it all the way through the Ph.D. level, take a job with the Weather Service studying jet stream fluctuations? I mean, doesn't that seem out of character? It seems so, I don't know, dull."

Damned if that's not the question of the day. "Real life, I assume. He had a wife and two babies by that time, Elle. And in the 1960s, I'd say there was more money in being a public servant than in being a weather historian or conspiracy theorist." He tilted his head toward the door, forcing a grin. "You better get gone before I think up more things for you to do."

Thirty minutes later, Davis Lee shifted his posture minutely. His feet were still damp from walking through the muddy grass, his ass was numb from sitting on the couch for too damned long, and part of his brain was still absorbing the strange news that Elle had given him. But the rest of his mind was fully attuned to the conversation taking place a few feet away from him.

If the two most powerful men in the room had been dogs, they'd be snarling and lunging at each other's necks about now, and a big bucket of cold water dumped from a height of four feet would end it. The mean old curs in question were his boss, Carter Thompson, and Winslow Benson III, the President of the United States, and they were smiling instead of snapping, but the undercurrent was just as vicious. Throwing a bucket of water on them would only land Davis Lee face down on the carpet with a couple of kneecaps in his back and a gun or two at his head.

The trim, taut, silver-tipped President Benson was looking at Carter with that sincere, wide-eyed, feel-your-pain look that he did so well. It was the look that worked on soccer moms when he was explaining why cuts in education were necessary and retirees when he was carving up what was left of Medicare. It had won him the election two and a half years ago.

Damn, but the man had it down to an art.

Davis Lee swallowed his smile of admiration before it made a public appearance. He knew that the fourth man in the room, the president's son, Win IV, was watching him while pretending very convincingly not to be doing so. Win Lite, as Davis Lee liked to call him, was as much a snake in the grass as his father, but he was more obvious about it and, because of that, would never go as far.

President Benson was leaning forward, nodding at the right moments, offering a concerned frown as needed. Not that he was fooling anyone. Davis Lee knew that the president wasn't listening because the topic interested him; he was looking for ammunition to use against Carter when Carter ran for political office. It was an open secret that Carter was contemplating a candidacy. Neither the president

nor anyone on his junkyard-dog team of advisors was sure
which office that would be, but Davis Lee could guarantee
they were all hoping it wouldn't be oval.

"You've heard the arguments before, Mr. President."
Carter Thompson, down-home man of the people and, per-
versely, a multi-billionaire, gave the president a casual
shrug and spoke in a voice that was calm almost to the
point of being eerie. "It's not just a theoretical problem and
it's not just a political flash point. There are facts that must
be taken into account. There have been hundreds of serious
safety incidents since the advent of nuclear power." He
smiled his trademark, avuncular smile. "You've got some
aging and vulnerable plants out there. They're in areas that
are critical to markets and population centers and they're
ripe for trouble, whether accidental, natural, or deliberate.
We don't need another Three Mile Island, we don't need
another September 11th, and we don't need another New
Orleans. It's time to shut the plants down and replace them
with other, diversified means of energy generation. Safer,
renewable means. What I want from you now is a promise
that you'll have your people actually look at the data. It's
that simple."

"Simple," the president repeated with a predictably grave
nod. "You know, Carter, there are some people who might
think you want the federal government to bail out small
farmers *again*—this time by paying them to dig up their
corn and soybeans and replant the fields with windmills and
solar panels." His smile was anything but benign. "Is that
what you're asking for? Another federal subsidy? Most voters think farmers already get too much free money."

Next to the president, who was every inch the high-
gloss East Coast elitist, Carter looked like a pudgy farmer
straight out of a B movie, complete with a comfortable
slouch and an unruly thatch of grizzled gray hair. All that
was missing was a stalk of something clenched between
his teeth.

He rocked back on his heels. "Not a subsidy, Mr. President. Congressional support in the form of research and

start-up money for small businesses whose owners are willing to turn their backs on generations of family farming and proud tradition to help wean this nation from its dangerous dependence on foreign oil and provide a safer alternative than nuclear energy," Carter replied in that voice better suited to the confessional than the negotiating table.

The president stared at Carter for a full minute. "That's touching, Carter. Almost profound. Make sure you use it when you're campaigning." His disdain for Carter and the conversation had finally leaked into his speech.

Davis Lee wanted to applaud. Everyone knew the president had been in bed with the nuclear power industry since his first election to the New York State Legislature. Why Carter still bothered him with the subject was a mystery to most people—other than Davis Lee. He stood up, shoved his hands into the pockets of his pressed Dockers, and leaned a shoulder against a window that framed lush, rain-soaked cornfields. The movement caught Win Lite's attention and Davis Lee grinned at him. Win smiled back. They both knew that in a few years they'd be facing each other without the old men in the room.

Davis Lee had done some research of his own; he knew that the first documented meeting between Winslow Walters Benson III, a promising young U.S. senator from New York, and Carter Thompson, a self-righteous prig with a Ph.D. in meteorology from the University of Chicago, was during heated budget hearings for the fledgling National Oceanic and Atmospheric Administration, to which Carter had moved briefly after a long and uneventful stint at the Weather Service.

Even prior to Elle's arrival, Davis Lee hadn't been able to discover anything indicating that the men had met before the hearings, but the tone and content of their sparring during the hearings was all wrong, and indicated to Davis Lee that it was not their first face-off. Nobody talked to a senator the way Carter did, on the record no less, unless he'd done it before.

By the time he'd risen to a level high enough to warrant

appearing before the subcommittee, Carter had spent ten years producing a slow but steady stream of white papers on topics of little social or scientific importance and, as far as Davis Lee had been able to discern, marginal utility. To date, Davis Lee had found nothing that gave the slightest hint as to why Carter had been worthy of notice by Benson. Or why he'd been worthy of Benson's derision. Nevertheless, the transcript of that first set of hearings was full of sharp exchanges that gave credence to rumors of an early and intense dislike between the two men.

In the ten years Davis Lee had spent at Carter's side, all discussions with Senator and, later, President Benson had always been like this one: controlled and contrived, but imbued with mordant undercurrents Davis Lee wasn't supposed to notice and a dark history he wasn't supposed to understand.

Today's revelations about Carter's early interests might be important, or might not. His interest in that bat-shit crazy stuff had apparently faded with the beginning of his serious employment and, as far as Davis Lee knew, had never been revisited. If Carter had been that into it, dropping the subject would have been uncharacteristic, but knowing how the man worked, Davis Lee figured it was likely that Carter had simply never had time for it again.

He shifted his concentration from Carter's ordinary face, which had aged and gone jowly in the last two years, to the well-maintained, patrician glossiness of the president's. On the surface, they were as different as two men could be. Winslow Benson was elegant and overbred, like some high-priced bird dog, as opposed to Carter's backwoods coon-hound sensibilities. But underneath those manufactured appearances, they both possessed minds, morals, and ambitions that made Machiavelli look like a limp-wristed, dickless amateur.

"But getting back to the point, which is money, I'm glad you understand the terminology, Carter." The president smiled. "It really won't matter how you describe it, because the word 'subsidy' is the one our people on the Hill will be using to describe this plan if you push it, and it's what we'll be saying to the press. Believe me, 'amber waves of windmills' just doesn't cut it as a sound bite."

The president shrugged casually, as if the conversation were about nothing more important than the chance of rain tomorrow. His loose denim work shirt, handmade but designed to look rugged and off the rack, moved with him. "You'll come off as a crackpot. Frankly, Carter, I can't believe you're wasting my time with this. After the last blackout on the East Coast, the whole subject of energy cutbacks fell off the table and nobody's brought it up since—except you. Nobody wants to talk about shutting down anything. They just want to be sure that they can get to work in an air-conditioned train or SUV with a fully charged Nano in one hand and a fresh cappuccino in the other. Even the hurricanes in the Gulf didn't make people want to change things. It just made them hug their plasma TVs a little harder before they went to bed at night." He shook his head, wearing a cold smile. "Americans are energy gluttons, Carter, and we're not about to apologize for it. I personally can't wait for the day some storm flattens one of your God-damned windmill farms, and when it happens, believe me, the whole world will be watching to see how fast you come back online." He paused. "But if you still just don't get it, Carter, I'll have someone from my staff spell it out for you."

Not a thing about either man changed, not their expressions or their postures or the rhythm of their breathing, but the tension in the room surged.

There was one place you didn't hit Carter, and that was in his ego.

Unless, apparently, you were the President of the United States.

Davis Lee felt sweat trace a cold path along his hairline. He spared a glance at Win, who seemed to be biting back a smirk.

More proof that he's an idiot.

"Mr. President," Carter began slowly as he rocked back on his heels again. "I *have* talked to your staff and that of the last administration. On several occasions. And believe you me, those conversations have always resulted in some action." He smiled. "Not the right kind of action, unfortunately. You see, when they're not actively stonewalling us, your staff members inevitably direct the Nuclear Energy Commission or some conservative think tank to launch a long-term study on the effects of something minor on something irrelevant. The results of those expensive studies, after a few years of data analysis, are always unclear, and the public war of words that follows always overshadows the pointlessness of the study." Mimicking the president's shrug, Carter shoved his hands into the pockets of his worn and rumpled khakis to jingle the change he'd deliberately put there.

His pulse rate back to normal, Davis Lee found himself fighting a smile as he watched a muscle flick in the president's cheek. The man hated fidgeters. Hated them.

"The subject needs to be taken to the next level, Mr. President," Carter continued slowly, "and that would be you. It's that critical. You need to give this some serious attention. I think it will be an important issue in the upcoming election cycle." He inhaled, sucking his lips against his teeth, then let the breath out as a sigh. "In fact, I can pretty much guarantee it."

The president's eyes lit up with manufactured delight. "That sounds like a threat, Carter."

"Come on, Winslow. You know me better than that. I don't make threats. Nor do I make empty promises." Carter paused, but his smile didn't change. "As a scientist, a businessman, and a concerned citizen, I promised the environmental and anti-nuclear lobbies that I would bring this matter to your personal attention. I've done so because I'm a man of my word. Now, as a voter, a party member, and a major contributor to the party coffers, I expect to be listened to and taken seriously. I don't think that's unreasonable. In fact, I think it's the least you can do."

The president's smile widened, taking on all the sincerity and subtlety of a high-end hustler in a low-end pool hall. "I just don't understand your logic, Carter. What makes you think it will make a difference? Shutting down a nuclear power plant hardly improves the playing field. It's a long administrative process and then the plant has to be decommissioned. That can take years. Then the fuel rods have to be transported, maybe even through your precious grain belt, and then stored somewhere. Your little band of organic, Birkenstock-wearing fruits and nuts wouldn't like that, now would they? And think about the farmers. I mean the serious farmers, Carter, the agribusiness conglomerates. They like cheap, reliable power. Lots of it."

"Your loyalty to the nuclear industry is touching, Mr. President, but it's wearing thin. Grassroots organizations are—"

"Grassroots organizations are a waste of my time, Carter," the president snapped. "You may be the big man out in front, but the people behind you aren't even on the radar screen. They only think they are. Airheaded fuckers. They're like a swarm of gnats, Carter. Annoying as hell but too small to be significant. Your crunchy-granola friends may not realize the days of starting social change over a dinner of organic homemade tofu are gone, but as you just pointed out, you're a businessman. You know better. You know the number of people chaining themselves to fences or marching on the Mall or whining on limp-dick liberal blogs will never come close to equaling the number of dollars the energy industry spends to reassure the rest of the country that they'll always have lights that don't flicker." He stopped then, and laughed. "Hell, Carter, I'm waiting for you to ask me about the state of my conscience, or how well I sleep at night, and then I'll know for sure how far you've slipped." The president reached down to unbutton a cuff and began to roll up his sleeve. "If you're going to continue to be a player, Carter, cut the bleeding-heart crap and get on board. If not, get the hell out of the way." President Benson turned away, dismissing Carter and the conversation.

Carter didn't move. Davis Lee couldn't even see a gleam

in his eye, although his desire for blood had to be running high. Carter wasn't a man to accept being dismissed by anyone.

"Get out of whose way, Winslow?" he asked quietly.

"Mine."

Carter didn't have time to answer before an aide tapped on the door and then stuck her head into the room.

"Mr. President, it's time to go. Mr. Thompson, Mr. Longstreet, the agents would like you to go downstairs first. The president will join you onstage in a few moments." The aide's smiling courtesy stopped just short of being obsequious.

"Thank you for taking the time to speak with me, Mr. President," Carter said with a brief nod, then walked out of the room with his face arranged in its familiar jovial smile.

"Thank you, Mr. President," Davis Lee repeated, shaking the man's hand and then following his boss out of the room. He smiled at the pretty young woman as he passed her. She was blond and either smart or well connected, maybe both.

It was too damned bad the White House had gotten so tidy.

CHAPTER 7

Tuesday, July 10, 12:00 P.M., Campbelltown, Iowa

Win Benson watched in silence as his father rolled up his other sleeve. After a moment, Win brought his iPod out of his pocket and set it to his most frequently used recording, then turned it on. As the low hum of white noise filled the room, the president looked up and met his eyes.

"If he declares, he's not going to be an easy man to beat. It will be a three-way race," Win said.

"It's been tried before. He'll pull votes from the other side and make it easier for me just like Perot did for Clinton and Nader did for Bush," his father said dismissively.

Careful not to show any sign of concern, Win smiled easily and slid his hands into his trouser pockets with a casual shrug. "He's as wealthy as Perot but more popular, and he's got the same core constituency as Nader with more businessmen in the mix. I think it would be a mistake to underestimate him."

"Don't spend too much time thinking about it, Win. He's not going to run. For everything else he's got going for him, Carter is a loose cannon who wouldn't last a week on the campaign trail. His ego is out of control, as you just saw, and he can't stand being questioned or second-guessed. And he can't let go of things." He paused as if he was going to continue, then shrugged. "We go way back, and things like that don't change."

Win froze, staring at his father's profile. "How far back?"

"Far enough."

Asshole. Before his annoyance at his father's condescension could show on his face, Win turned and walked to the window. There was a hell of a crowd out there in the rain. It was a tribute that so many people would come out in this kind of weather. His father naturally thought they were here to see him up close and personal. Win, however, had spent some time walking through the crowd. The group was upbeat and energetic despite the shitty weather, and many of the conversations he'd overheard had to do with Carter or his company. He'd come away with the uncomfortable feeling that the crowd was actually here primarily for the company's thirtieth anniversary party and only secondarily to see the president. Now, watching the stage being set up a few hundred yards from the building he was in, Win realized too late that his father might be even less of a draw in this dog-and-pony show. After all, it was a relatively young crowd, and there had a been a surprise announcement a little while ago that Bon Jovi and Hootie and the Blowfish were scheduled to play later in the day. The anti-Benson contingent was well represented among the faces swarming in the press tent; they would doubtless label his father the warm-up act.

It had to be deliberate. Even if it weren't, the fallout would be ugly and responsibility for retribution would fall to him. He needed a weapon. Now.

Win turned to face his father. "How do you know Carter? Why do you go so far back? You were in the Senate and he was a nobody. Just some low-level bureaucrat in an agency that had no power."

His father glanced away for a moment before answering. "He was with NOAA when it started up, and he wasn't that low. He had some budget responsibilities. He testified before my committee back in the seventies."

"Lots of people have testified before you. Not all of them hate you."

The president acknowledged the statement with a wry smile. "Long story short, we canceled his program and he made such an ass of himself that no other program wanted to take him on. He was basically driven out of government work. That's why he started his own company. He was too much of an upstart—no one would hire him."

"What sort of budget did he have? What program was he running?"

"Climate research," his father said after another slight pause.

The caginess was completely in keeping with the president's personality, but the underlying discomfort with the subject was not. There was more to the story. "What did he do?"

His father's expression now held unmistakable irritation, letting Win know he wasn't going to get many more answers on the subject.

"It was the early seventies. Lots of people were into lots of crazy things, and Carter's was the environment. He was angry when he heard that his program was being canceled, but he went ballistic when he heard that there were plans to build more nuclear power plants. He saw connections that weren't there. Nuclear power was completely outside his research area, but the topic made him crazy. Still does, as you just saw. So he took it upon himself to sit there in the hearing room lecturing us on 'deep earth' ecology and how the Earth was an organism and not just a green and blue rock floating in space. He said that working against Nature was working against the Divine." He gave a silent, awkward laugh. "Can you believe that? Anyway, he said that on the record, and proceeded to get so worked up that he—" The president shook his head. "He made a complete ass of himself. Sounded like some tree-hugging hippie. And he blames me for it, apparently."

"That's not in any hearing transcript that I've read."

His father's smile faded. "That was during a closed hearing. He didn't do much better in the public ones, though. The point is that he might get to be governor of Iowa, but he's no contender for the presidency."

"Then why are you here?"

His father frowned at him. "Because he's got money and he spreads it around. If he didn't, believe me, he'd have been marginalized long ago."

Another light tap at the door captured their attention. The flavor of the week stuck her head in and smiled. "Whenever you're ready, Mr. President."

He was going to crush Winslow Benson.

The realization took Carter by surprise. It wasn't so much a decision as a promise to himself; it felt different from the decisions that had driven him for the last thirty years and the decisions that had driven him for all the years before that. This was cold and pure and solid, immutable, irreversible. He would make sure the president became a blot on the political landscape due to his own shortsightedness and greed. It needed to happen.

"Well, that went well, didn't it?"

Carter continued down the carpeted corridor for several

steps before glancing at his senior advisor. The fury churning in his gut was carefully contained, but he knew Davis Lee wasn't fooled. He was one of the few people Carter could trust with the truth. Not the whole truth, but versions of it, and only because Davis Lee was so good at manipulating it.

Davis Lee Longstreet looked like a beach bum, spoke like a hillbilly, and strategized like Genghis Khan. It was a profitable but irritating combination of traits and served to automatically deflect reproach. Even the press was fooled; Davis Lee was too easygoing and quick to laugh to be considered ruthless, and yet, in ten years, he had never flinched from making the hard call and implementing the necessary plan, all the while making sure his fingerprints weren't on the results.

"There's no need for sarcasm," Carter replied. "It went as well as expected."

"There's always a need for sarcasm when dealing with authority," Davis Lee replied, flashing the grin that disarmed so many. "It keeps things in perspective. What next?"

"Lunch," Carter said, pausing to look through the wall of glass that fronted the building. Dozens of large, colorful tents covered his corporate campus, and hundreds of people swarmed beneath them. The turmoil in his gut began to ease, and for the first time in several hours the smile on his face felt nearly genuine. This was his land, in his town, in his state. Those were his employees out there, and his family and guests. The president was his guest.

Carter took a deep, satisfied breath. Even the president had known better than to turn down his invitation. Today's party, celebrating thirty years in business, wasn't quite a command performance for the commander in chief, but it was close enough and, despite the conversation that had just taken place, the president knew it. Winslow Benson might hold the office—for the moment—but Carter had the money, he lived in the right state, and he had accumulated enough power that the president felt some faint obligation to keep him happy. It was another sure sign that Life was unfolding as it was meant to.

On cue, Carter's vice president of human resources introduced him. His wife, Iris, and their daughters, clustered on the stage, began to clap. The crowd followed suit, cheering wildly. Carter stepped past the Secret Service agents and pushed open the building's heavy doors just as a few weak rays of sun broke through the clouds. A roar erupted from the audience. He jogged up the steps to the stage, shooing away with convincing humility the implication that he might have had something to do with the break in the weather.

It was quite masterful really, because he'd had everything to do with it.

CHAPTER 8

Tuesday, July 10, 3:00 P.M., McLean, Virginia

Jake Baxter clenched his right hand into a loose fist and let the phone ring a second time before picking it up. In ten years of working as a forensic meteorologist in the Directorate of Science and Technology at the Central Intelligence Agency, he'd never been on a project that fired his imagination—or his brain cells—as much as this one did. He'd been on the new task force for less than a week and it still kicked his blood pressure up a notch when he thought about it, but he was trying hard to make it seem like it was just another line item on his to do list: *No. 5. Get up to speed on the God Squad Task Force.*

That was how Operation DOWNPLAY had been introduced to him by Candy Freeman, the most atypical candidate the Agency had ever promoted to the level of Branch Chief. Small, loud, inappropriately named, and sarcastic as hell, Candy was also incredibly smart and had the unique talent of being able to think outside the much-touted box. Way outside. And that, he figured, was part of the reason he'd been tapped to fill the job within hours of Wayne Chellner's death: he was an unlikely candidate for it. Wayne's specialty had been predictive weather analysis, not forensic analysis as Jake's was.

Wayne—poor son of a bitch—had been assigned to the interdisciplinary task force for only a month before he'd failed to completely swallow that last, fatal bite of a pulled-pork sandwich with extra Tabasco during his habitual Friday lunch at Jimmy Joe's BBQ Shack. When Candy had not-so-casually mentioned the task force in the same conversation in which she'd announced the news about Wayne, Jake knew he wanted to be the one to pick up the ball and keep running with it.

And here he was, in over his head and working too damned hard to think about it.

He picked up the handset on the third ring. "Baxter."

"Hi, Jake. We're ready for you." The West Texas twang in Candy's voice was barely discernible. That in itself spoke volumes. She didn't tamp that down for just any-body, so whoever was running this task force had to be way up the food chain.

"I'll be right there."

As he stood up and reached for his laptop, Jake admitted to himself that he hadn't had this much adrenaline pumping through him in entirely too long. Not knowing who was in the conference room he was about to enter was only part of it. He knew little about the task force and its mission other than to know his role was to provide in-depth weather research about highly classified pinpointed locations. Some of the locations made sense to him, like Chicago and Kabul, and others, like the town of Prayer, Oklahoma, and a geographical coordinate marking an uninhabited part of Sudan, made no sense at all. It didn't matter, though. The operation was functioning under a strict need-to-know policy, and

Jake knew his role at the moment was to provide answers, not ask questions.

Except that the information he had been told to compile wasn't just standard weather data. It had included enormous amounts of geographical and hydrological information as well as historical weather data, and in a lot of cases it went back twenty or even thirty years. It had been a surprise to Jake to realize such detailed information was available. Comprehensive weather data gathering had been in its adolescence thirty years ago, or so he'd thought. The files that had been delivered to him had borne classifications he'd never seen before.

He knocked on the door, which opened almost immediately. As he stepped inside, the first thing he noticed was that there were only two people in the room, Candy and the guy who had opened the door. He looked young enough to be an intern.

Great. I report to Junior. Jake's adrenaline shut off as he moved into the room and set his laptop on the wood-grain Formica surface of the table.

"Hi, Jake. Come on in. This is Tom Taylor. He's leading the task force for the DNI."

Candy's voice was subdued and Jake hid his surprise as he extended his hand to his new boss. If he was working for the DNI, that meant he wasn't Agency.

That has to be thorn in a lot of executive asses. "Nice to meet you. Jake Baxter."

"Dr. Baxter." Tom Taylor's grip was exactly calibrated to convey overt confidence and subtle superiority in direct defiance of a chin that looked like it might never have met a razor. After releasing Jake's hand, he gestured for Jake to have a seat. "I'm glad you were available to step up to the plate on such short notice."

"It's an interesting project."

"That's one word for it," Tom said after one second of deliberate hesitation, and Jake wondered if the kid expected him to look uncomfortable.

Not in this lifetime and not for this asshole. Ten seconds in the guy's presence was enough to establish arrogance as the kid's most memorable credential.

"I trust you've been given access to all of Dr. Chellner's materials?" the asshole continued, walking to the end of the table where a short pile of manila folders was neatly stacked. Each folder was hashed with thick diagonal lines of dark blue that went from the upper right to the lower left corners. The words "TOP SECRET/SPECIAL COMPARTMENTED INFORMATION" rested in a rectangle of open space in the center of the lines.

"Yes."

The other man nodded and motioned for Candy to be seated. Then he sat down and picked up a pen, leaning back in his chair.

They must have taught him that in business school.

Jake tried not to stare as Tom frowned slightly and stuck the pen in his mouth as if he were taking a moment to collect his thoughts.

Make that nursery school.

Jake sat down and crossed his arms, leaning on his forearms as he met Tom's eyes. *I learned this in the Marines, pretty boy; now start talking.*

The flatness of his eyes told Jake bluntly that Tom was unimpressed. At least the playing field was even, which was more than it had been a minute ago.

"How much do you know about weather manipulation and control? Specifically processes that could be considered undetectable weaponry."

"I know there's a UN treaty forbidding it and there are a lot of crazies out there who think we're doing it anyway," Jake responded without a second's hesitation.

"Not just crazies."

Jake shrugged. "Okay, educated crazies as well as the less-educated kind. History and a lot of junk science have given them reason to suspect it. America hasn't always played nice in the sandbox."

"We didn't have to. Ever since it started to matter, it's

been our sandbox." The shadow of a smile crossed Tom's face, sending a chill down Jake's back.

Jake didn't like chills. He blinked and didn't smile back.

Tom continued, "I realize that speaking so cavalierly about the weather can be offensive to those who have made it their life's work. Unfortunately, the reality is that it remains the last frontier and, as such, it begs to be conquered."

Spare me the flowery shit. Jake kept his face bland.

Tom set his pen down on the tabletop, the flat of his hand coming to rest on top of the files. "The subject of weather manipulation had its heyday in the fifties and sixties with a few successes, like when Operation POP-EYE rained out the Ho Chi Minh Trail and helped to cut off the North Vietnamese supply lines, and a few disasters, like when Project STORMFURY steered a weak hurricane away from the east coast of Florida only to have it strengthen, turn on its own, and tear up southeastern Georgia." He paused. "All of that happened in the good old days, when the Agency's involvement was never acknowledged, but it nonetheless called the shots. Then security started to get a little too porous in Washington, what with the Pentagon Papers being leaked and Deep Throat doing his thing—you get the picture. There were obvious but false indications that the Soviets had stopped plowing money and their brightest minds into the effort and that the field was ours for the taking. All of Congress saw an agitated constituency and a lot of TV cameras. Around the same time, the Pentagon got tired of taking all the heat. So the U.S. officially dropped out of the weather game. Overt funding fell off the budget as a line item in the mid-eighties. Like you said, though, there have always been crazies spouting wild-ass theories and producing so-called 'proof' that the research never stopped."

"A lot of fairly credible scientists think the same thing."

Tom glanced up. His brown eyes were dark and devoid of expression. "And they're right. There were too many projects under way to stop everything. Some things had to be abandoned, but others simply went—I suppose I can't really say they went underground, can I?"

It was an effort not to cringe. But the bad joke served one purpose. With a flash of belated insight, Jake realized that the man across the table was no kid but what he'd always called a vampire: an ops guy who had stayed on the dark side so long he couldn't function in the light anymore. At least not without scaring the hell out of people.

"Money was allocated from special project funds."

As Tom stopped to let his words sink in, Jake felt a menacing twist in his gut. Special project funding meant money from the "black budget," the billion-dollar slush fund that Congress handed the Agency every year without an expectation of progress reports or accountability.

"The Soviets had already dropped out of the race. Their deep research stopped in the seventies," Jake pointed out, "other than agricultural research and efforts to keep Moscow skies clear for parades."

The vampire smiled. "And you believe that? How disappointing. On the contrary, there have been incredible strides made in benign climate management in the last several decades and these files"—he patted the stack in front of him—"will detail that for you in case you want the background. What we're more interested in at the moment are the less benign activities."

Benign climate management. Coming out of that mouth, the words made the hair on Jake's neck stand at attention.

Anyone who had studied weather for more than five minutes knew that nothing about it was benign. Meteorologists knew it wasn't the final frontier and that it wasn't anyone's tool. It was the most powerful engine on earth. It could start up anywhere at any time and do just about anything. Very few things could interfere with a developing weather system, and there wasn't a force on earth that could stop a storm once it got going. Anyone who thought otherwise was either a fool or a madman.

Jake unclenched his jaw. "Who's doing what?"

"A lot of people are trying lots of things, Jake—may I

call you Jake?—but the important thing is we think some-one is succeeding. We need to find out who, why, and how, and then take their toys away."

Jake shifted his weight to lean back in his chair, his re-laxed attitude belying the adrenaline bubble that had just burst near his heart. As Fang Boy had stated, manipulating the weather for economic or political gain had been tried for centuries to very small success. Developing the technologi-cal means to make the weather an offensive weapon had been tried for only a few decades, resulting in no significant advances. That, in Jake's opinion, was a good thing. Achiev-ing success would render all other weapons pointless, which would be a bad thing no matter who got there first. He cleared his throat. "Could you be a little less vague?"

"No." His pause reinforced Jake's opinion that he was an asshole. "You don't need to know more than that. Not now anyway. What we want from you is an analysis of the data you've been given. We need the history of the weather pat-terns and trends within those patterns, and the scientific ex-planations as to why they are what they are. We need you to identify points at which predictions failed. Identify the anomalies and explain them."

"Identify the point at which *whose* predictions failed?" When Tom only raised an eyebrow, Jake let a few seconds tick by before he added, "Are we looking at a credible threat?"

"We've got a task force mobilized, don't we?" Tom replied. "But, while credible, the threat is not considered imminent. We need to know more about it before we take things to the next level. But we need intelligence and cer-tain circumstances are constraining us."

In other words, experiments were being run inside U.S. borders, where the Agency wasn't allowed to operate. Openly.

Holy shit. Jake shifted his posture again and made a point of staying calm. "Eco-terrorism isn't exactly break-ing news."

Tom smiled that creepy, bland smile again, as if he was

actually enjoying the discussion. "Actually, it depends on what sort of eco-terrorism we're talking about, and the information you come up with is going to help us identify and define those talking points. If something's happening, and we're pretty sure it is, it's going to become public sooner rather than later."

"Are you talking about the jet stream—"

"No. We did that," he said bluntly. "We parked it over the Plains to force the bad guys into the open, and they complied, but barely. Weather isn't easy to hide, and neither are the fuckups that inevitably follow it. And I'm not talking about e-mails discussing who's going to be drinking what on Trent Lott's new front porch after the waters recede." He began winding the pen through his fingers with tight, controlled movements.

"Any bad storm gives the lunatics a fresh platform and Katrina was Christmas come early for them," he continued. "Between them seeing faces in the clouds, accusing FEMA of staying away because of government-activated plasma fields and particle beams, accusing the Army Corps of Engineers of dynamiting the levees, accusing the Agency of using steering mechanisms to decimate a Democratic stronghold—" He stopped and looked Jake in the eye. "I'm sure there are more theories, but you get the idea. By the time the hearings on Katrina rolled around, the lunatics might as well have been tap-dancing naked down Pennsylvania Avenue, because they were getting as much press coverage as if they were. We don't want that to happen again."

"How do I fit into this?"

"You're going to give us what we need to stop what is already happening and to own the discussion when it happens. Public discussion of anything related to weather manipulation or control inevitably turns into a PR nightmare. You so much as mention cloud seeding and you've got the environmentalists coming at you from one side, the water use, land use, and agricultural lobbies from at least six other directions, the real estate developers, and then there's the tourism industry. Politicians start doing vocal warm-up exercises and the intelligence community gets to bend over one more time. The only happy people are the scientists, because somebody's finally going to ask their opinions."

Tom straightened abruptly and leaned toward Jake, his face grim and angry. "But I really don't give a rat's ass about any of them. Katrina, Rita, and Wilma stirred up enough shit in the public pot that even people who know better started looking nervous. And not just on the Weather Channel. They were out there sweating and looking nervous on CNN, and FOX, and God-damned MTV. So keep this in mind as you're crunching your numbers, Jake. Next to finding out who's doing what, why, and how, my highest priority is to make sure that we own this discussion." He paused and leaned back in his chair again, his stilled fingers a good inch away from the pen. "Any questions?"

"Yes."

Tom pushed a hand through his hair, reasserting his control. "Now would be a good time to ask them."

Jake knew better than to expect a promise of any answers. "What am I supposed to be looking for? Specifically."

"Local weather patterns and the reasons they exist."

"With all due respect, most weather patterns in the world have been documented for decades, if not—"

"Which makes your job that much easier," Tom snapped. "Obviously, we're not interested in El Niño or the Siberian Express. We want local patterns. Very local, in some instances, and we need to know what differentiates one from the norm or one from another. For example, what are the parameters that influence the way the Santa Ana winds affect one locality as opposed to another one nearby or across the state? And, of course, we need to know what the anomalies are and what causes them, and if they repeat elsewhere under similar conditions."

Of course. "In other words, you identify the microclimates and I fingerprint them?"

Fang Boy allowed a hint of a real smile to flick at one corner of his face. "Yes, that's what we want you to do." He paused. "Other questions?"

It was less an invitation than a change of subject.

"Not at the moment."

"Excellent." He slid the stack of manila folders across the table. "Here are a few more coordinates and the background material. You can send your reports to Candy when they're complete. Thanks very much for your time."

Jake glanced at Candy, whose face was uncharacteristically expressionless, and felt a coldness settle in his gut.

"Thanks, Jake," she murmured.

"My pleasure," he replied easily, then stood up, nodded to both of them, and left the room.

Back at his desk three minutes later, he glanced at the new data points he'd been handed. Two were map coordinates somewhere off the west-central coast of Africa, one was in Death Valley, and the fourth was off the coast of Barbados. He shook his head as he plugged his network cables back into his laptop, then sat down to add the information into the multi-level database he'd created.

It was well after eight o'clock when he felt someone's eyes on his back. Secure workspace or not, it was still an uncomfortable sensation. Without so much as a telltale stiffening of his back, he swiveled in his chair to face the opening of his cubicle.

"It only took you five seconds. Not bad. Of course, if I were a bad guy, you'd be dead."

He frowned at her small fairy face surrounded by a cloud of bottle-blond curls. "You have the weirdest sense of humor of anyone I know."

"I save it all for you, Jake." Candy's twang was back in full force, its easiness betrayed by the dark circles that were emerging from underneath her ubiquitous girly eye makeup. "I was hoping you'd still be here. You got a minute?"

He nodded. She straightened and bobbed her head in the direction of the bank of conference rooms across the Cube Highway, the wide central aisle that bisected the myriad featureless cubicles that the DS and T called home.

A minute later they were in one of the nicer conference rooms, one that had chairs that didn't squeak when you sat in them and an under-counter refrigerator in the corner. She opened it and took out a Diet Coke for each of them.

"Tom isn't always that much of a prick," she said, handing Jake his soda across the table.

"Seemed like he knew what he was doing," Jake replied easily, which made Candy laugh.

"Well, I did say 'isn't always,' didn't I?" She sat down at one end of the table, popped the flip top of her can, and poured the contents into a glass tumbler. "I'm not allowed to give you a complete brief yet, Jake, but I will be soon. I did, however, squeeze him enough that he's allowing me to fill you in on a few things he neglected to mention."

"I'll be sure to write him a thank-you note."

She met his eyes. "Got it. Now can we move on?"

Drinking straight from the can, Jake nodded with a grin. "As long as we're clear."

"You were going to be brought on in about a month anyway, when the project entered the next phase. When Wayne died, though, I fought to bring you on now. That's why you're doing all of Wayne's work. I know it's outside your usual tasking, but I'm going for continuity here." She fought off a yawn. "Sorry about that. Late night. This project is interdisciplinary, as you know. Everyone is involved at some level, but its home is Counter-Terrorism and we're on a fast track. We're shifting gears shortly."

"Shifting into what?"

"Ops. You'll be front and center."

He blinked at her.

"You okay?" she asked over the rim of her glass.

"I'm a meteorologist."

"I meant your health. You look a little funny."

"I'm fine, just surprised you're putting me in the field."

"I could have phrased it better, couldn't I? Still want it? You're ex-military, aren't you?"

"Semper Fi. And hell, yes, I still want it."

"Thought so." She took another sip. "You won't be covert, if that's what gave you that funny look. Just involved in things in the field. Techie things."

"Hey, it hasn't been that long. I can still—"

"You won't be covert," she repeated softly.

The very lack of emphasis on any particular word made it clear that her statement was non-negotiable, and the part of him that had already begun to smell cordite wafting through humid jungle air returned to acknowledge the filtered air of Langley.

Candy sat forward, hands folded primly on the table in front of her. "Like I said, I can't tell you everything, Jake, but I can tell you that we're scoping wide right now. Intelligence and Operations are involved, naturally, and DS and T is bringing up the rear. We've had to go outside for some of the talent, but it's a crack team so far. Homeland Security and the military are represented, obviously, but we also have vulcanologists and seismic guys, avalanche gurus, a whole slew of atmospheric physicists with specialties ranging from cloud structure to solar flares— we're even tapping into those conspiracy whack-jobs who keep mawing over plasma fields and electromagnetic mind control. What's that Tommy Lee Jones movie where he's bitchin' about looking for someone in every henhouse, doghouse, and outhouse?"

"The Fugitive."

"That's it. Love that man." She kicked off her pink highheeled shoes and shifted in her chair, bringing her feet up underneath her. "We're looking for subtle, non-specific weather anomalies, which makes finding the old needle in a haystack sound like a much easier task. You're on first string, Jake. We need everything you can pull together as soon as you can pull it together. For all Tom seems like a jerk—and he is one—he has an open mind. No theory will be rejected flat out. My daddy used to say that you should never wrestle with a pig in the mud because you'll both get dirty, but the pig will enjoy it, and sometimes that's the only way you can win."

Jake kept his eyes on her. "What the hell is that supposed to mean?" he asked after a minute, and she laughed in response.

"My daddy was a hog farmer, so he liked his pig references. He was also a barnyard philosopher, and was fond of saying that it doesn't matter a damn if hindsight is twenty-twenty if you don't learn from it. Well, to my way of thinking, part of the reason the September 11th attacks were possible was the incredulity factor. The idea of using an airplane as a weapon had been raised a couple of years before the attacks, but not enough people took the idea seriously because it was just so wild-ass crazy. People said the logistics, training, and what-all needed to carry off an attack like that were too complex, too numerous, et cetera, but then someone did it. And not just one attack, but four coordinated attacks. That's when people realized we're fighting a deranged army who are willing to take all the time in the world to kill us." She shrugged. "Well, devising the means to use weather as a weapon would be even more time-consuming and expensive, and is even more ludicrous to imagine being successful, but guess what? It's happening." She paused and gave him a tight smile. "The kind of people who think up this stuff measure time against the backdrop of eternity, Jake, while too many of us measure it against traffic on the GW Parkway or the closing bell of the New York Stock Exchange. We gotta fight crazy with crazy, Jake. Like I said, no idea, crazy or otherwise, will be dismissed without discussion."

He nodded grimly. "And the locations?"

"Some are places of interest and some are potential targets that we want to assess."

"Who are we looking at?"

She let a minute pass before letting out a slow breath. "I'm supposed to tell you that I can't tell you, but the truth is that we don't know. This whole topic is one that has been kicked around for decades, like you were discussing earlier. I'm not even sure why somebody finally started taking it seriously, but the threat level on this one recently passed 'Oh shit' and is now firmly at the 'Holy shit' stage. I'm not sure what the next level is, but I wouldn't be surprised if it's 'Duck and cover.' " She smothered another yawn and sent him an apologetic look. "Sorry to make you stay up past your bedtime, honey, but you need to get over to the archives. Bring a dust mask and a miner's lamp. You're cleared for things that probably haven't been looked at in decades. I don't know if any of it is going to help you, but it might give you some context. Let me know if you need anything."

"Like what? More information?" Sarcasm wasn't the best route to take with Candy, but she understood it.

She stood and slipped into her shoes. "I've told you as much as I can. As soon as I can tell you more, I will. In the meantime, go get dusty. It'll do you good."

She left the conference room with a forced smile, leaving Jake to rehash once again everything he'd learned in the last few hours.

The bottom line was that someone was manipulating the weather, and if the CIA didn't already know who it was or how they were doing it, then it wasn't any of the usual suspects. Which meant that no one knew what their motivation was, or their timetable. And that was the most unnerving thing of all.

CHAPTER 9

Tuesday, July 10, 11:30 P.M., Campbelltown, Iowa

Carter was ending the long day exactly where he'd begun it. The moon, edging its way toward full, shone down from a brilliantly clear, starlit sky, illuminating the fields and the pond beyond them and flooding his home office with soft silvery light.

"I thought I'd find you here."

He looked up to see his wife, Iris, standing in the doorway, smiling at him. Her hair was brushed out and loose around her shoulders, the way he liked it when they were alone. It had once been blond, but now it was a mixture of gray and silver. It still looked good against her dark blue bathrobe. He'd told her that on their honeymoon, and every bathrobe she'd owned since then had been dark blue. He smiled back. "My work is never done."

She gave a light laugh and came into the room, seating herself in one of the chairs opposite his desk. "I'm about to turn in. Are you coming up soon?"

"Yes. Soon. How are you doing, honey?"

"I'm tired. It was a good day, though. A lovely day. I can hardly believe it's been forty years," she said softly.

"I wouldn't have made it this far without you."

She smiled. "Yes, you would. You accomplish whatever you set out to do, Carter. You always have."

He accepted her praise with a smile. She was a good woman. He'd known she was the right one from the first time he'd seen her. And he'd been right. She'd moved from rural Iowa, the only home she'd ever known, to Washington, D.C., with a few tears but no complaints. She'd borne every one of his setbacks with stout loyalty and inexhaustible inner strength, and every triumph with quiet dignity.

Shy at heart, Iris didn't like being in the public eye, much preferring to stay home and take care of her family. But as the companies had grown and he'd asked her to make appearances with him and even on her own, she'd handled each situation with genuine grace and the patience of a saint. She was a very, very good woman and, from the start, had proven herself worthy of his trust and affection. "You did a great job, Iris. Thank you."

"Meg said you were already up when she went running this morning."

He nodded, turning his head as he caught, out of the corner of his eye, televised footage of a washed-out campsite in a desert canyon. "Breaking News" flashed across the screen below the FOX News logo. Reaching for a remote, Carter brought up the sound.

"—this morning's tragedy in Death Valley. A Park Service helicopter pilot who was investigating reports of a freak rainstorm discovered the washed-out camp of a group of college students. According to the National Weather Service, the heavy rains occurred before dawn and lasted less than an hour, but dumped two inches on the parched desert floor. The eight nineteen-year-old students, who were trekking across Death Valley as part of an attempt to raise money for a friend who'd been stricken with cancer, were apparently sleeping when a flash flood caused by the storm roared through the canyon where they'd made camp. We go now to Carmella Noyes, who is on the scene in Death Valley. Carmella, just how unusual is it for a rainstorm to—" Carter hit the Mute button.

Two inches in less than an hour. In the desert.

The air temperature in their target zone at two thirty this morning had been 98°F with a relative humidity of 11 percent. And he'd produced from that hostile environment not only clouds but clouds that had produced two inches of rain in less than one hour. He folded his hands on his desk to hide their trembling and took a slow, deep breath to contain his elation before turning back to his wife, who had just emitted a soft sniffle.

She knows better than that. He felt his brows furrow.

"What a tragedy." She met his eyes, tears pooling in her own, and shook her head slowly. "They were so young."

Carter sighed. "They were in the wrong place at the wrong time, Iris. It's an unfortunate coincidence and it's a damned shame. We'll send a donation to their cause."

"Carter," Iris began, her voice close to a whisper, "please tell me you didn't know they were there. That it was—"

"As it happens, I didn't know they were there. But I wouldn't have stopped the test if I had, Iris. It's happened before. It will happen again. We avoid it when we can, but science has always required sacrifices. You know that."

"But—"

She's arguing with me? His frown deepened and anger began to stir inside him. "There are no 'buts,' Iris. The test was a success. A huge success. Raoul is already heading out of the country to refine the procedures, and then we can begin to do what we've always wanted to do. What we've talked about doing for thirty years." He stood and walked around the desk to take her hand. She rose out of the chair and his arms went around her as she nestled against him. Her warm, comforting curves melted into him as they had for more than forty years.

"Carter, you know I'm proud of you. You've achieved so much. And you're so kind to want to use it for good," she whispered. "But, as a mother, I just can't help thinking about—"

"No." Tilting her chin up so she had to look at him, Carter made sure he had a gentle smile on his face even though his voice was firm. "No, Iris, you can't focus on those kids. Focus on the results. As a mother, you should be thinking about all the other children who will be saved. All the children whose parents have never seen rain, who have never known anything but heat and dust. The generations who have never lived anywhere but refugee camps, who have never eaten anything that wasn't thrown to them off the back of a truck. We're going to save them, Iris.

We're going to save so very many of them." He pressed a kiss to her soft forehead and gave her a tight hug, which she returned.

"Where is Raoul going?"

"The Caribbean."

Her body stiffened against him and he knew she was holding her breath. Anger stirred again and, again, he suppressed it.

"But the last time—the tests you ran there before went so terribly wrong. Those storms were so dreadful and then—" He felt her chest rise against his as she took a deep breath. It didn't keep her voice from cracking. "It's not going to be like last time, is it, Carter? It's not going to be like Mitch, is it?" she whispered against his chest. "Or Ivan? Those storms were so big. So many people were hurt."

Carter clenched his teeth. How many times had he told her that mistakes were best forgotten once you learned the lessons they offered? And he had learned plenty from the mistakes he'd made nine years ago. His first field attempt at manipulating a hurricane had had disastrous results. He'd been too eager, too full of pride, to temper his enthusiasm. Instead of proceeding with moderation and restraint, he'd gone for big results. Nature, in the form of Hurricane Mitch, had punched back hard and fast.

One of the most powerful and destructive storms of the twentieth century, Mitch left meteorologists dumbfounded as they watched its power rise and fall and rise again. Its deadly, staccato path was unprecedented and virtually unpredictable, its destructive force almost incalculable. Eleven thousand people had died; thousands more were missing or had been displaced by the time the storm finally dissipated. Mitch had nearly destroyed a country; nine years later, Honduras was still recovering.

All Carter had been able to do in reparation was have Coriolis Engineering personnel on the ground there from the moment it was safe to deploy them.

And he had heeded Nature's lesson. He'd waited, refin-

ing his calculations and his equipment, and three years ago
he'd tried again. His intervention with Hurricane Ivan had
been better. The storm had been clumsy and erratic, but it
had been powerful, and that in itself was success. Reminders
of early failures were completely unnecessary. And Iris
knew that.

"I thought you had faith in me, honey," he said calmly,
but there was a challenge in his voice.

She clutched him tighter. "Oh, Carter, of course I do.
You know I do, but—"

Mollified, he tightened his embrace slightly, then
stepped away, placing her at an arm's length and holding
her there while he looked directly into her eyes. Her fright-
ened, loving blue eyes. "No 'buts,' Iris," he said again,
softly. "People are the inconstant variable. They always
will be. But I can control the other things now. You know I
can, don't you?" He gave her a small shake. "Don't you?"

Still wide-eyed, still silent, she nodded.

Satisfied, he relaxed his grip on her shoulders. "It won't
be like Mitch. I promise you, honey. It will be nothing like
Mitch."

Even as the soothing words were coming out of his
mouth, Carter knew his sweet, gentle wife had inspired
him yet again.

There was truly no better means of focusing people's attention on the fragility of life, on the power of Nature and
the vulnerability of man-made structures, than the simple
means afforded by Nature herself.

The world, and the president, needed to be taught a lesson.

And what Carter needed to teach them that lesson was a
storm.

**Thursday, July 12, 11:00 A.M., 500 miles
east-northeast of Barbados**

Raoul heard Carter's rasp through his headphones and
mostly ignored it, though part of his focus shifted.

He wasn't getting too old for this shit; he was getting too bored with it.

The first few years, when they'd been doing the real research, had been interesting. Doing all the test runs while they were testing laser strengths and sensor life cycles had been a challenge, and plotting courses to find shitty weather and meddle with it had been a change from what pilots usually did, which was plotting courses to avoid it. But that had been more than a decade ago. For the past five years, every test run had been more or less the same as the one that preceded it. The scenery changed and occasionally the crew did, but procedures and results were essentially the same with small variations.

The last real excitement had been in the nineties when Carter had begun playing with hurricanes. *Fucking madman.* At first they'd deliberately stirred things up in East Africa to get some storms going. As far as Raoul was concerned, that was Carter's first mistake. The flooding had gotten out of control too damned fast.

You just don't fuck with the Nile.

Unless you're Carter Thompson, who thought it was his right since his company would be the one called in to repair the damaged infrastructure.

By the time they'd finally manufactured a storm that had done what he wanted it to, which was blow out to the Atlantic, Carter had decided to use that storm to test his newest contraption, a laser that could superheat swaths of the ocean surface. It had been late in the hurricane season in 1998. Carter had been attempting to simply cause more rain by increasing the amount of water vapor in the air. What he got was Hurricane Mitch, which tore the hell out of the Caribbean and Central America. About as unnerved as Raoul had ever known him to be, Carter had immediately canceled the rest of the field tests—*a bloody miracle, that*—and hadn't trotted out the updated version until 2004. That debacle spawned Ivan, which chewed up most of the southeastern U.S.

After that, Carter had gotten more cautious and more

paranoid and had started spacing the tests further apart and in more disparate locations. One result was that during the last few years Raoul had had less to do and more time to think about what he was doing.

And what he was doing was despicable.

He could have dismissed it as a midlife attack of conscience, but the reality was that he could no longer fool himself into believing the foundation's activities were as benign as they had once been. Raoul had become a millionaire at some point in the last few years, which was more than he'd ever thought he'd be, but the hunger for excitement that had once driven him was gone. He had no passion left in him. Carter knew it, and Raoul was certain that was part of the reason he was six thousand feet above the Central Atlantic right now. Carter had made it clear he wouldn't let Raoul retire without a fight, and it seemed to Raoul as if they both knew the time for that fight was drawing near.

He adjusted the volume on his headset and acknowledged the second squawk.

"We're on approach," he said, bringing his full attention back to the bank of clouds ahead and below him. "We'll drop the sensor on eight and initiate the laser on one. Over."

"Proceed, Earth-Four."

His co-pilot began the countdown and his flight director launched the sensor and initiated the laser on cue. The clouds boiled over and the plane bucked in the sudden turbulence. Raoul banked and increased altitude, watching the churn beneath him with dispassionate eyes.

It was another fucking storm, another fucking dollar. Maybe his last.

CHAPTER 10

After floating parched and light for so long over hot lands, the dust-laden wind had reached the sea and spread across the limitless sky. Impregnated with salt and heavy with water vapor, it drifted destinationless over the waves, spiraling lazily as it rose and fell in tropical eddies. Cooling currents aloft kept it from reaching the heavens. Warmth from the sunlit water kept it buoyant as it flowed, unhurried, to the west.

More than two miles beneath those eddies, along the long, jagged seam where the earth nudges the northern continents farther apart and inexorably widens the sea, life simmered around a meandering chain of steep hydrothermal vents.

The vents functioned according to the imperatives of Nature as they had for millennia. Without agenda, with no awareness of consequences or purpose, they had laid the foundations of civilization and trade, of art and greed and war, as their effluvia layered the ancient ocean floor with copper, gold, and other metals Man would eventually find and desire. The freestanding chimneys, many rising nearly two hundred feet above the seafloor and grouped intermittently along a line that roughly paralleled the spreading center, were the pathways for toxic clouds of superheated minerals the earth released from her deepest recesses.

Ceaselessly, the primitive, elemental spew emerged from the vertical chambers at temperatures reaching 750°F and combined with the dense, icy water to birth an impenetrable, poisonous black fog that billowed with hellish fury. Pushed skyward by unimaginable pressure from the chimney, the dark cloud alters in density, in chemical makeup, in salinity, until it has inevitably altered itself beyond dis-

tinction and become part of the sea. Its fearsome heat also dissipated on the journey.

On reaching the surface currents, the column of primeval heated water represents little more than the earth's eternal contribution to the steady, timeless current that sweeps warm African waters to the temperate shores of Caribbean Islands and North America before turning to the east to bring its warmth to Europe.

This day, however, the earth's crust shifted minutely, accelerating infinitesimally the movement of magma through her caverns. Its rhythm altered, a single white-hot wave moved through the sea of molten rock with a different intensity until, encountering the vented chamber and the sudden reduction in the pressure upon it, the wave released its excess energy and so returned to entropy.

Surging forward with greater force than usual, the superheated ejecta rose higher, hotter, and faster through the water column. Even so, when it pushed through the distant surface, its content mostly was dispersed, its fury mostly abated, retaining but a fraction of its birthright heat.

Still, that heat was greater than that of the surrounding water.

The ancient, geothermal vapors held enough discrete warmth to distend the surface wave it fractured on its release, and to extend minutely that wave's errant slap at the wind. The barely warmer air rising from the surface collided with the well-traveled particles resting on a languorous breeze softly sweeping the midday sea.

Excited by the burst of wet warmth that had risen from the waves, the wandering eddy embraced it. As the eddy rose in a slowly accelerating swirl, its speed, heat, and moisture proved an irresistible attraction to other low-lying banks of torpid air. The gathering winds spiraled toward the picturesque scattered cirrostratus clouds overhead, like a novice dervish practicing its art.

Twenty minutes later an arrow of intense, man-made heat shot down from above, searing the heart of the spiraling winds. Photons scattered, evaporating molecules of water vapor and transforming their latent energy into the cell of an embryonic storm. Recovering only slightly from the instantaneous blast of excitation and fury, the superheated air spun upward, climbing hundreds of feet as its appetite for the dense, warm air beneath it became voracious, sucking it in, and devouring it.

Now part of the emerging vortex, the particles would next meet at a distant landfall.

CHAPTER 11

Thursday, July 12, 12:00 P.M., McLean, Virginia

Jake was poised to lock his computer when he heard the soft chime that announced new e-mails. He knew he could safely ignore them. He wasn't expecting anything urgent, and besides, he was already on his feet, more than ready to head to the large cafeteria to have lunch and a brief respite from the electronic glow of his computer screens. But, like everyone else in the place, he was addicted, so he clicked on the icon in his status bar. His e-mail application appeared on the screen displaying eleven new messages at the top, color-coded according to sender. Only one caught his attention.

He sat down again and clicked to open the broadcast message from the U.S. National Weather Service. Nearly an hour ago, a rapid and unanticipated escalation had turned an unnamed tropical depression in the Central Atlantic into Tropical Storm Simone.

Lunch was forgotten.

Thursday, July 12, 12:10 P.M., Financial District, New York City

"Did you not get my e-mail or are you trying to tell me something?"

Kate swiveled to see Lisa Baynes, the newest addition to the meteorology staff, standing in the doorway, hands on her hips. Only two years out of her undergraduate program, Lisa had already been head-hunted by most of the firms on the Street. Kate had made her the offer she couldn't refuse—more money and an office with a door, plus a generous cab-fare allowance—and she'd happily left one of the big brokerage houses down the block to work for Coriolis.

Kate raised an eyebrow and gave her a mock frown. "Something like 'you're fired' because you refused to help me when you saw me stranded in that tent talking to Ted Burse?"

Lisa put up her hands in surrender. "Hey, talk to the hand. I got stuck sitting next to him on the flight out there and I was ready to kill myself before the landing gear was up. Besides, at those kinds of parties, it's every woman for herself."

"Some team attitude."

"Martyrdom is *not* in my job description."

Kate laughed. "When did you send the e-mail?"

"Ten minutes ago."

"Then I didn't get it. I have it set to update every twenty minutes."

The younger woman's eyes widened. "Are you serious? What if something comes up? Like, something important."

"Yes, I'm serious. I'd never get any work done otherwise. Of the three hundred or so e-mails I get every day, most are either pointless or are just exercises in ass covering. If something important goes on, whoever needs me to know it immediately can call me," Kate replied with a one-shoulder shrug. "So what did you want to know?"

"I was wondering if you were doing anything for lunch."

"No plans. Where are you going?"

"We're heading over to that hot-dog cart on Pine and then we're going to sit on the steps of Chase Plaza and get some sun."

"Sounds good to me. Anything to get me away from the blogs. They're going ballistic over the Senate hearings. The markets are getting worked up over them anyway," she said, tapping the keys that would lock her computer.

"Kate, for the record, I have no idea what hearings you're talking about," Lisa replied. "But I think I want to trade jobs. I've spent the morning doing two things: staring at those two lows that are churning over the Plains, trying to figure out what else they're going to destroy, and hanging up on commodities traders who want to know the same thing. I'd rather read blogs."

Kate stood up and grabbed her sunglasses. She pulled the office door shut behind her with a grin. "You've got to work up to that. Besides, I didn't say that was the only thing I've been doing. I've been hanging up on traders, too. I'm trying to figure out if any of those tropical depressions are going to do anything."

"Yeah, what's with that? They're lined up across the Pacific like the Rockettes waiting to go onstage."

Kate shrugged with a laugh as they crossed the trading floor, which was operating at its usual steady hum. "I have no idea. The two in the Atlantic don't have me concerned, but I'm just hoping those Pacific systems fizzle out. If even one of them escalates to a tropical storm, we could be in for some bad news. It's still monsoon season on that side of the big pond. So you said 'we' were going to lunch. Who's 'we'?"

"Elle Baker. She's working for Davis Lee on some special project and hasn't met a lot of people here. Did you know she used to work at the White House?"

"I heard that. I've seen her around, but I haven't met her."

"I sat next to her on the flight home. She's nice. A little quiet but interesting enough to talk to if you get her going. She's from the middle." Lisa shrugged. "Minnesota, Montana. I don't know; I think it begins with an M. Nice kid, though."

"Says you. You're twenty-four."

Lisa shrugged expressively. "Hey, I'm from Trenton. You stop being a kid there when you're ten."

Smothering a grin as they rounded the corner, Kate came to a stop at the elevator bank where Elle was waiting for them. She'd seen Elle in passing a few times and each time had had the same thought: The young woman existed at the intersection where elegance meets dowdiness. Elle was slender and tall but usually wore clothes that seemed to be cut for a teenaged boy in prep school; today she had on angular khaki pants, black leather flats, and a loose oxford-cloth button-down shirt. Her blunt-cut blond hair was scraped into a too-tight ponytail, and tiny earrings made her ears appear larger and more prominent than they were. She had very white teeth and a pretty, orthodontically perfect smile, which somehow made everything else about her appearance seem even more off-kilter.

Lisa made the introductions as the elevator car began its descent.

"So is Davis Lee keeping you busy?" Kate asked for lack of anything more brilliant to say.

Elle nodded with a smile. "It's non-stop."

"That sounds like Davis Lee, all right. What sorts of things are you working on?"

"They have to do with the anniversary."

Kate blinked at the dismissive reply. *You're not getting off the hook that easily, Miss Snippy-pants.* "Like what?"

Elle glanced at her, as if weighing Kate's title and position against her own, and a second later gave a small shrug, which announced her protected status with the subtle precision of a paper cut. "PR-type things, mostly. I'm working on a history of the companies and pulling together some background information on Mr. Thompson for a short biography. Working with Marketing on the invitation lists for some of the events that are being planned for later in the summer." She paused, then smiled. "That sort of thing."

"A biography of the old man? Has he done anything interesting besides make lots of money?"

Kate cringed at Lisa's blunt question but was curious about the answer.

"Well, he started out as a meteorologist," Elle replied.

"You knew that, right? And he worked for the government for a while before starting his own company. I think the jump from doing pure research to starting a construction company is sort of unusual. Pretty much a polar extreme, if you think about it. From all brain to a lot of brawn, at least in the beginning."

"Well, yeah, that's what I mean. What made him do it? Did he get picked up by a tornado and see God before landing in a cornfield or something?"

"It was probably just money, Lisa. Nobody gets rich working for the government," Kate replied.

"See, that's the thing," Lisa argued. "He *did* get rich working for the government. Who do you think pays him to rebuild all those roads and bridges? Our rich Uncle Sam. But in spite of the money, I still think the move from research to reconstruction was a weird one." She glanced at Elle. "So, okay, here's what's really on my mind. How many more company parties are there going to be this summer to celebrate the weirdness of his decision? In the city. I'm not interested in seeing any farms again any time soon—unless the president shows up again."

Elle gave a small laugh at Lisa's question. "The president or the George Clooney–esque Secret Service agent you wouldn't stop talking about on the flight back from Iowa?"

"Funny you should ask," Lisa replied a little sheepishly, and glanced at Kate. "Until I saw one up close, I never knew I was such a sucker for men who talk to their cuff links."

"Instead of just talking *about* them?" Elle retorted under her breath, provoking a burst of unexpected laughter from Kate.

Okay, the kid deserves a second chance. She has a sense of humor, if no sense of fashion. "You've heard the tales of the cuff links of the Confederacy, then?" she asked.

Lisa looked from Kate to Elle. "What are you talking about?"

"Davis Lee has a pair of cuff links made from the buttons of some relative's Confederate Army uniform. Supposedly one of them has a dent on it from when it deflected a bullet and saved the man's life," Kate explained, rolling her eyes. "He brings them up all the time."

"Surely not more than once a week," Elle murmured.

"It's things like that that made me swear never to date anyone from the Street. Their level of self-absorption would interfere too much with my own," Kate said with a wry grin. "There have to be a lot of those guys in Washington, too. Especially in political circles."

"Plenty," Elle agreed. "Although meeting men other than at work is a challenge if you don't have a network."

"Or even if you do," Kate added.

"What, no hometown honey?" Lisa said, blatantly sarcastic.

"We broke up around the time I moved up here," Elle replied tightly.

Kate winced and changed the subject. "So other than enduring conversations that never die, how has it been? I mean the transition from the West Wing to Wall Street?"

Elle tucked a stray hair behind her ear with a graceful hand and cocked her head, thinking about her answer. The movement revived that subtle uneasiness at the back of Kate's mind. Something about Elle seemed so out of place. She wasn't self-assured or well dressed enough to fit the Ivy League/Wall Street stereotype, but she was no wide-eyed small-town girl, either. Maybe the small-town prom queen, given her attitude. And the thin streak of ingrained bitchiness. Elle wasn't stupid, though, and had to realize that if she wore makeup and better clothes, she'd attract a lot more attention. That made Kate rule out the idea that Elle was just here looking for a husband, as she'd overheard one of the admins sniping a few weeks ago. But there was still something about her—bitchiness aside, Elle just didn't seem tough enough for Wall Street. Maybe that was it.

Once through the revolving doors and on the street, Elle

started to speak and Kate brought her mind back to the conversation.

"I think it's been a pretty smooth move. In one sense, I suppose, an office is an office and a job is a job. The details change, like who you work for and what you do, but you still have to get in at seven o'clock, get things done, and then go home and get ready to do it again the next day." She smiled again. "I found the bigger change to be the difference between living in Washington and living here. I lived there for two years and, even though I've only been here a little over a month, I can tell that the cities are so different."

"I thought Washington was pretty cosmopolitan," Lisa said as they waited for the traffic at the corner. "Looks that way on TV, anyway."

"Oh, it is. It's a very sophisticated city, but in a different sort of way than New York. D.C. is smaller, for one thing. And there I think the challenge is more about accumulating power and fitting in, whereas here it seems to be more about accumulating money and standing out. I mean, even the clothes people wear are so different. Down there, the Brooks Brothers look rules. Up here, it's Donna Karan."

"Depends on your neighborhood," Lisa pointed out. "In mine, it's sparkly Lycra a few sizes too small and platform stilettos. Of course, that's mainly for the women."

Elle looked aghast. "Where do you live?"

"Uptown. *Way* uptown. Let's just say that if I haven't been killed by the time my neighborhood goes chic, I'll sell my apartment and make a frigging fortune." She shrugged. "Meanwhile, it's a great way to end a lousy date. I just invite the guy back to my place, and as soon as I give the cabbie the address my date decides he's more fond of life than he is of me."

Elle said nothing for a moment, and Kate just watched the two of them.

"Are you serious?" Elle said finally. "Aren't you afraid?"

Lisa gave her a look that spoke volumes about the difference between Midwesterners and girls from South Jersey.

"Of what? Hookers? I introduced myself the day I bought the place just so they wouldn't think I was interested in a turf war. They're actually pretty interesting once you get to know them."

"You *know* them?"

Lisa frowned. "Well . . . yeah. They're neighbors. Sort of. They know everything going on in the neighborhood. On the flip side, I've gotten to know a few cops, too. Cute ones."

"Secret Service agents and cops? I think you just have an authority fetish. But if you don't quit talking about your neighborhood, Elle here is going to sprain her eyebrows," Kate interjected with a grin. "So, did you have any trouble finding a place to live, Elle? The city can be pretty over-whelming if you don't know your way around. And apart-ment hunting requires you to decide whether you prefer dealing with cockroaches or extortionists."

"No. I found a place right away."

Kate glanced at her in surprise. "That's great. Where?" she asked at the same moment Lisa stated flatly, "Nobody finds a place right away."

"Oh, um." Elle stopped and looked around as if to get her bearings, leaving Kate to wonder what she was up to now. "I always get sort of confused. I think I live that way." She waved a limp hand vaguely uptown.

"Well, I hope you live in that direction, honey; other-wise you're living on a boat," Lisa said as they came to a stop in front of the hot-dog stand. "Hey, Yuri, how you do-ing? A hot Polish with the works today, buddy, with extra mustard and kraut. Two pickles. Oh, and a diet orange car-rot Snapple."

Kate grimaced. "Oh my God, Lisa. That sounds revolt-ing."

"Which proves that you've never tasted paradise," she replied, unfazed. "Well, it is if you finish it off with a root-beer Popsicle."

Elle met Kate's eyes and shuddered, then ordered a plain hot dog and a bottle of water.

When Kate got back to her office, she sat down, kicked off her shoes, clicked to check her e-mail, and watched as the messages populated her in-box. Thirty-five of them. She triaged them, responding to the most urgent first, and it was twenty minutes before she opened the mass-distributed one from the Weather Service.

She immediately launched the application that allowed her to view the data and download the satellite feeds, then sat speechless, staring at her screen.

It happened again.

She ran the short videos again, then focused on the data tracking the atmospheric changes as they happened. At first glance, there was nothing that should have sparked the escalation and, although the numbers seemed off-scale, she knew the data-gathering satellites were just too good these days to doubt their findings.

Swiveling to shut her door, she punched in the number of Richard Carlisle's cell phone with her other hand.

"Simone," was all she said when he answered.

His silence lasted a few seconds longer than she expected and that made her nervous. She stood up and paced a tight circle, coming to a stop in front of the window. Looking out, her eyes were drawn, as always, to the vast pit, now a construction site, that had been home to a pair of majestic towers. And, as always, she looked away before emotion could grab her.

"A research vessel in the area noted some minor seismic activity near some underwater vents," Richard replied calmly. "Temperatures in the water column bear it out. Natural causes."

"That could explain that first small spike, but not the escalation that happened eighteen minutes later."

"What do you want me to say, Kate?"

That I'm right. "That I'm not making it up."

"You're not twisting facts. I'll give you that."

She shoved a hand in her hair and gave a small frustrated tug to the roots. "Richard, you have to admit this is— The forward speed has increased already and its wind speed is nearing the lower boundary of a Category 1 hurricane. This is *not* normal," she hissed into the phone. "It's happening *too fast.*"

He paused again. "Are you still coming over for dinner?"

"Yes."

"Good. I'm on my way home right now and there's an accident up ahead, so I really have to pay attention. Are you driving up or taking the train?"

"The train. The six twenty-four. It gets in a little after seven."

"Great. I'll meet you at the station. We'll talk then."

Damn right we'll talk. "See you later." She clicked off the phone and swore under her breath as a window appeared on her screen to remind her that she had to lead a weekly teleconference in five minutes.

Thursday, July 12, 6:30 P.M., Washington, D.C.

Tom grabbed the handset of the secure phone before it completed its first ring. Only task force personnel had the number and it was rare that anyone used it. "Taylor."

"It's Lieutenant Commander Smithwick, sir."

He didn't bother trying to put a face to the name. "Yes?"

"About two hours ago, one of our ships picked up the crew of a pleasure boat that capsized under the build-up of Tropical Storm Simone. They reported seeing a plane in the area immediately before the escalation."

He sat up straighter. "What kind of plane, Commander?" he demanded.

"It was too far away for them to make out many details. They couldn't see any markings."

"Who had aircraft in the area?"

"There were no U.S. planes in the area at that time, sir. And a preliminary review of radar data does not corroborate their story."

"Thank you, Commander. Send me what you have and keep me apprised."

"Yes, sir."

He hung up the phone and looked at the blank wall ahead

of him. There was only one kind of plane that could evade radar. And it didn't fly into hurricanes.

Without stopping to analyze or check the urge, he picked up a heavy crystal paperweight—awarded to him for the successful completion of a particularly heinous operation—and hurled it at the wall with all the force of his anger. It embedded itself deeply in the drywall and hung there motionless for a few seconds before it fell, hitting the hard floor. The force of its landing broke the crystal into a few large pieces that flashed as they tumbled to a stop. The scatter pattern lay within a patch of late-afternoon sunlight. One shard threw a broad streak of brilliant colors onto the drab walls.

He stared at it for a moment, then leaned back in his chair and closed his eyes.

We just fucking lost.

Again.

CHAPTER 12

Thursday, July 12, 7:00 P.M., Greenwich, Connecticut
As Kate stepped off the train onto the platform in Greenwich, Connecticut, she could see Richard Carlisle's aging mud-spattered Land Rover idling in the pickup area. It was the same car he'd had since she'd met him, when she was a freshman at Cornell, and it hadn't been new then.

Settling her backpack on her shoulder, she descended the steps and crossed the parking lot.

"Just once can't you pick me up in your Sunday-best car instead of the heap you haul your dog around in?" she asked as she climbed into the front seat, gently pushing the huge head of an Irish wolfhound out of the way to drop a kiss on Richard's cheek.

"Finn McCool here likes to go for a spin every second Thursday of the month at seven."

"No offense, Finn," she said, giving the gentle giant a rub on his aristocratic snout, "but I'm not buying it." She turned back to Richard. "One of these days I'm going to check the mileage on that Jag of yours. I'm beginning to think the only time you drive it is when you pull it in and out of the garage to have it detailed."

"One of these days I'll surprise you," he drawled, pulling away from the curb.

"When?"

"When you quit bitching. Could be years from now." He sent her a grin. "How was Iowa? You were there last week, right?"

She nodded. "Hot, flat, and boring as bedamned. I don't know how people live there. There are hardly any buildings and the air doesn't smell like air; it smells like cow manure and dirt." She looked out the window and watched the suburban scenery evolve from business to gentility before continuing. "Got my backside properly situated in a sling while I was there."

"Who did you insult?"

"Thanks for your support." She let out a frustrated sigh. "And I didn't insult. I *disappointed* everyone from the bean counters up to Davis Lee. My famous storms. They're getting me into trouble every time I turn around."

Richard chuckled quietly. "Kate, come on. You missed two storms in how many years?"

"See, that's just it. It's not years. That would be acceptable. I missed three big ones within *three months,* Richard. I still don't know how I did it." Shaking her head, she turned to him again. "I was tracking the systems, made all the right calls, and then—wham. Kate Sherman's credibility takes a thirty-five-mile-an-hour hit. And now, Simone is rearing her ugly head."

"Not so ugly and not so big," he pointed out.

"Yet."

"And not at all unexpected," Richard continued. "With all the strange weather that has been going on over the entire middle of the country for the last few weeks, something big was bound to kick up soon. Anyway, shake it off, Kate. I've got a whole mess of oysters to roast on the grill—"

"Oh God." She slumped against the seat. "You're going to poison me with that down-home cooking again, aren't you? I keep telling you, Chinese takeout is fine, Richard. Pizza, even. The real stuff, I mean, not the Greenwich goat-cheese-and-shredded-weeds kind."

Richard laughed as he turned down the private beachfront road toward his house, one of the few remaining 1920s bungalows in Old Greenwich that hadn't been stripped to its foundations and rebuilt as Versailles Lite.

Still only one story with three small bedrooms and one bath in a neighborhood of three-story palaces with more square footage than the average elementary school, the home's ramshackle coziness seemed to Kate to be tangible evidence of Richard's view of life.

Richard Carlisle was a national fixture in the mornings. All across the country, people tuned in to watch him and find out what to wear and whether a storm was going to hit their city. Such popularity could have made him a real jerk instead of merely wealthy. But he'd remained the same guy Kate had taken classes from a decade and a half ago: simple, unpretentious, and concerned with little more than the basic necessities for himself and the world at large. He cloaked his hippie sensibilities in a buttoned-down demeanor, delivered good science in an easy, accessible way, and didn't have much use for outward shows of wealth. Except for that 1961 E-type Jaguar he'd remodeled his garage for.

He brought the Rover to a stop near the back door, and Kate climbed out with some encouragement in the form of a large wet nose placed against the back of her neck. Moving only slightly ahead of Finn, Kate pushed open the back door that Richard never locked and dropped her backpack on the kitchen floor, then headed straight for the refrigerator and a Red Stripe. The room's comfortable clutter was witness to the ten years he'd spent in the house with his wife. And the last two years he'd lived there without her.

"You need a maid," she muttered.

"You need some manners."

She grinned at him as she pried off the cap. "So what's on the schedule besides dinner?"

"I just got another set of blooper tapes from Joe Toliver if you're interested," he replied. Joe had been a classmate of Kate's at Cornell who had become one of the new breed of meteorologists who hit the beach when the big waves did, microphone in hand and camera in tow. He also collected blooper and audition tapes from God knew where and compiled them for snide, private fun.

"One of these days he's going to get sued." Kate grimaced. "I haven't recovered from the last set. The image of that sweet young thing going ass-up into the air when lightning struck the news van has stayed with me."

"Good thing she wasn't closer to the mast or she would have ended up with more than a broken arm and a bruised ego." Richard took a beer from the refrigerator and leaned against the counter as he opened it. "Anyway, a new set arrived today and Joe assures me they're the best so far. I think he's getting ready to market them, because he's starting to organize them according to weather event. Snowstorms, lightning strikes, and the all-important non-event of good weather."

"Speaking of bloopers, when is your adventure in Barbados going to make it into his collection? It's not every day you see the granddaddy of television weather reporting slide headfirst into a stone wall in a seventy-five-mile-an-hour gust."

He raised an eyebrow. "It's not going to be included by private agreement. Besides, everyone has already seen it on YouTube. Come on, let's go outside. We might as well enjoy the sunset while I get the grill fired up. That low-pressure system is going to move in by ten."

Kate shook her head with a smile. "I don't care what your bones are telling you, Richard. It won't get here till after midnight."

It was close to ten, and Kate was sitting on the small flag-stone patio overlooking Long Island Sound, watching the muted glow of Queens beyond the end of Richard's small, dilapidated dock. She set her drink on the weathered teak table next to her and leaned back against the cushion of the chaise lounge. The sky was still clear, but the humidity was edging toward being oppressive. The stars had gone from being bright over the water to slightly smudged, and the parade of strobing aircraft transiting above Long Island had remained steady as the night air thickened with the impending storm. Night-blooming flowers growing in pots near the house lent an intoxicating sweetness to the darkness but didn't overshadow the lingering pungence of sun-baked seaweed and freshly cut grass. Kate had long ago traded this rich, earthy lure for the sharp, man-made tang of city air, but it would always be the perfume of summer on the water, of childhood, of growing up two blocks from the beach in Brooklyn.

She turned as she heard the footfalls of Richard's bare feet as he crossed the lawn behind her.

"Well?"

"The fact that I made a pig of myself by eating several dozen isn't enough for you?" Kate laughed. "Okay, I hereby state for the record that oysters roasted on—what kind of wood did you say that was?"

"Apple wood."

"Well, they're fabulous. And your potato salad wasn't bad, either."

"That came from Whole Foods," Richard admitted, idly scratching Finn's head.

"Well done, you, for choosing it, then." She watched

him set a long, cylindrical case on the smooth, weathered stones. "It's getting too hazy to see anything. Why bother setting up?"

"It's not too bad yet. And I watch the planes if I can't see anything natural," he replied with a smile as he extended the legs of the tripod and set the telescope gently into its mount. "How's your dad?"

Still dying. Kate lifted the sweating glass of Diet Coke to her lips and replied over its rim, "Slowing down."

"I'm sorry to hear it, Kate." His voice held sincerity but stopped short of sympathy. He knew better than to try that.

She lifted a shoulder with a casualness her heart didn't share. "It was sort of inevitable, wasn't it? You volunteer to work in the smoking pits of Hell because you're patriotic and you're devastated and you don't know what else to do. And while you're there, you breathe in billions of toxic particles every day for months and then your lungs start to fail. It's what happens."

"How's your mom handling it?"

"When she's with him, she's a saint, and I don't know how she keeps herself together. But when I'm around her, I definitely detect the scent of burning martyr."

"Taking care of someone isn't easy." He said it mildly, but Kate cringed at her thoughtlessness. She didn't have to hide much from Richard, but this was a topic she usually sidestepped. He'd spent five months taking care of his wife as a fast and furious cancer overtook her. It had been two years since she'd passed and he still hadn't quite come to terms with her absence. The state of his house gave that much away. Ever since Jill had died, the house had been missing something vital. So had Richard.

"I'm sorry, Richard. That was really crass."

"Yes, it was, but it's understandable."

"Maybe." She took another sip and let her head fall back against the wooden slats. She focused on the reflected lights shimmering in the barely moving water at the end of the dock. Other than some blame-avoiding bureaucratic non-name—Ground Zero Pulmonary Syndrome—no one had identified what was wrong with her father or the hundreds of other early responders who were sick with the same thing. The lack of certainty about what her father had and how it would progress afforded the family some time to adjust. Maybe too much. Either way, it was a small comfort. She was still watching her father die one breath at a time.

"Dad doesn't complain about a thing. Ever. I mean, he's working his way through the reading list for some course in classics at Columbia that he found on the Web. He told me that he never had the nerve to read books like those. He thought he wasn't smart enough, but now he figures it would be a shame to—" She took a deep breath and pushed back against the emotion she felt accumulating in a hard knot at the back of her throat. "Anyway, I do what I can, but the help Mom wants isn't the help I can give. I offered to hire someone to come in a few times a week and give her a break, but she said no. She wants me to move into the building instead." She let out a slow, controlled breath. "I live twenty minutes away by subway and it's not enough. Meanwhile, any discussion of my sister coming home from LA for a visit is sacrosanct."

"She's got her own problems."

So do I. "If it's all the same to you, I think I'm going to change the subject before I get maudlin or just plain angry. It hasn't been a good week on the home front."

"Fair enough. How about those Yankees?"

"Like I care. You know I'm a Mets girl," she replied, forcing into her voice a lightness she didn't feel. "I have a better topic than that one."

"I doubt it, but let's hear it anyway."

"I've added two more storms to my repertoire."

"Why weren't you this obsessive when you were taking my classes?" Richard replied without lifting his head from the eyepiece of his telescope.

She smiled. "Because I was eighteen."

"And now?"

"I'm greedy. Don't you want to know which ones?"

"Do I have a choice?"

"Of course not. Your storm—"

"I have a storm?"

"Yes. Barbados."

He lifted his head. "Oh, for Christ's sake, Kate, don't drag me into this."

You're already in it. She shifted in her chair. "I'm not dragging you into anything. I'm including that storm and the Death Valley storm in my discussion. You have to admit that both of those were pretty damned weird. Too weird to write off as coincidence."

"We're talking about weather, right? The quintessential chaotic system?" he murmured as he adjusted another knob.

"Yes, and our chosen field." She paused. "I'm holding off on adding Simone until I see how she plays out."

"She's comfortably a Cat 1 now. Did you know that?"

She frowned. "No. When did that happen?"

"Not long ago. I checked the status before I went to pick you up just in case you bashed me over the head with it first thing."

She rolled her eyes and took another sip from her soda. "Okay, so we have another one in the mix. And, come on, Richard, you know every one of these was more than weird. They were spooky. Off-the-charts spooky."

"We already hashed this out, Kate—," he began after a barely discernible hesitation.

"We talked about it, but I don't recall coming to any conclusion. Look, I know you think I'm nuts, but that's okay, because I think I'm nuts," she interrupted.

"No comment."

"I still say the escalation in all the storms happened too quickly. You can't change my mind on that. All five of the storms were building within normal ranges for their circumstances, and then with no warning and for no reason I can find, they became way more intense than any reasonable worst-case prediction. It was like they just exploded without anything pulling a trigger. Like, I don't know, spontaneously."

"Kate, storms just don't escalate for no reason. You know that. There *was* a trigger mechanism. In the case of Simone, it was an underwater seismic event. That's been documented. And compounding that is all the upper-air turbulence caused by the storms in the Gulf and blowing from the Plains to the Atlantic. Half the country is in flux right now from the jet stream anomalies. As for the other ones, you just haven't found the triggers. But if you keep looking, you'll find them eventually and realize they provide perfectly natural explanations."

She shook her head. "The jury's still out on that seismic thingie, but *there is nothing there* for the rest of the storms, Richard. I've checked every measurement, every parameter. All the obvious things and even a lot of things that have never been known to play a role—"

"Like pork belly prices? Maybe a butterfly in Tokyo flapped its wings a little harder one day that week—" He raised his head and met her eyes. "What's this really about? Is something going on with your family?"

The question sliced into her like a paper cut, deep, sharp, and unexpected.

"Don't go all pop psychology on me," she said, barely containing her annoyance. "It's about scientific curiosity. Something you have always revered. There was a time when you would have encouraged me to pursue this instead of practically insisting that I forget it. What changed?"

"Don't get so annoyed. Nothing has changed. And I'm not insisting that you drop it. You've already conducted an in-depth review, so now I'm suggesting that you learn something from the experience, move forward, and apply it," he replied mildly, bending his head once again to look through the eyepiece. "Maybe absorb a little humility while you're at it. This is Nature we're talking about, Kate. It can't be neatly compartmentalized. Its very essence is chaotic and it operates in at least four dimensions with an infinite number of variables that change constantly."

"That's just it, Richard," she snapped. "I *haven't* learned anything. I *want* to learn something. I want to learn how five entirely unremarkable storms can blow up to extraordinary proportions when there's no weather system in place to support that level of escalation or intensity, and how one additional storm—the one in Death Valley—*literally* came out of nowhere."

He shook his head. "Why don't you type 'weather anomaly' into Google and see what comes up? Maybe you'll find something interesting."

"I really don't see any cause for getting snide. Besides, I've done that and I definitely *don't* want to go there. I'll stick to real science, thanks."

"Kate, you're a very good forecaster, but everyone makes mistakes. Just move on." Thunder rumbled in the distance, making him straighten up. "What was that you said about midnight?"

"I haven't felt a raindrop yet."

He laughed, but when she didn't respond in kind, he met her eyes and released a sigh of resignation. "What do you think you're going to find, Kate?"

"I don't care what I find, Richard. Anything from a hidden microclimate, to a wind anomaly, to—yes—a conspiracy theory if it can withstand some scrutiny. I just want an answer."

He busied himself with minute adjustments for several minutes, muttering commentary on the night sky, which was beginning to get hazy with water vapor.

Kate glanced at her watch only to find Richard's gaze on her when she looked up. He wore the same smile she'd seen during class so many years ago.

"What time is it?"

She frowned at him, noticing the faint breeze kicking up. "Twenty after ten. Which bone was it this time?"

"Just an achy back. The rain will be here any minute."

"Not likely."

"Come on, help me bring in the cushions; then I'll take you back to the train before the rain really gets going." He helped her to her feet with a smile. "If it's keeping you up at night, Kate, then I hope you find your answer, or at least run into someone who's interested in your questions. You might as well get some mileage out of the time you put into the paper."

Reluctant to leave the comfort of the chaise lounge prematurely, she got to her feet slowly. "So, out of curiosity, have you actually read it yet?"

"It's on the top of the stack," he assured her.

She gave him a look. "How long has it been there?"

"I'll start it tonight. Look at that. Perfect timing." He grinned and, as she lifted the cushion she'd just been sitting on, Kate felt a warm, fat raindrop land on her arm with a splat. It did nothing to bolster her confidence.

CHAPTER 13

The tall channels of wet, salty air rose steadily through the night-dark sky, spinning helixes of water, heat, and wind into a single vast vortex of sound, speed, and fury. Fed by the ocean's trapped heat, the engine spun tirelessly, its convection towers contracting as they passed over cool spots, expanding as they coaxed up from the depths water that should have been colder. Thin outer walls of white at the distant edges of the storm gave way to ever denser walls of gray that spun fast and tight around Nature's most spectacular creation, the eye of a hurricane, arguably the eye of the gods.

Moonlit calm reigned within it. Seabirds coasted along currents in the thinning air, trapped inside until flung out by an errant updraft, or, too tired to continue circling, they drifted to the calm, dark waters below to test their fates. Beneath the storm the sea rose, pushing upward and outward as it sought to offset the falling air pressure, to move away from the vast energy the storm pushed beneath the churning waves. Those low walls of water bullied their way ahead of the storm, announcing to any creatures with the sentience to know danger that the force without which life could not exist was also the force of death.

Hundreds of miles to the west of the storm, along America's luxuriant southeastern coast, the night sky was clear and bright with stars. Wanderers on the moonlit beaches of the many lush, verdant barrier islands reveled in the freshening breeze, a welcome respite from the oppressive heat of the day. By morning, those beachcombers knew, the same stretches of sand would reveal small wonders from the sea, pushed landward by the silvered surf that now pounded the shore perhaps a little harder than it had earlier in the day.

Any thoughts of menace from the growing storm far out to sea were casual; right now the storm had no bearing on their lives and thus garnered little attention other than the idle speculation of vacationers enjoying the subtropical ennui for which they had planned and paid.

CHAPTER **14**

Friday, July 13, 2:00 A.M., Greenwich, Connecticut
Richard turned his head away from the softly glowing numerals on his bedside clock and resumed staring at the ceiling.

Two in the morning.

The rain had begun softly but had gotten heavier as he'd driven Kate back to the train station. The silence between them had been nearly as dense as the air. The ease and good humor that always marked their monthly dinners had been strained by the topic of their conversation. Even now, many hours later, he couldn't shake the shadow that her determination had cast over him.

Tenacity had never been a characteristic he associated

with Kate, which made her stubborn refusal to drop this line of questioning all the more curious. He had a feeling she'd latched onto these storms to avoid a few of the human variety that were bubbling up in her parents' small apartment in the Brooklyn neighborhood of Gerritsen Beach. And that meant she wasn't likely to give up on her pursuit quickly or easily. When one was confronted with an unpleasant reality, speculation was always a comfortable refuge.

He let out a heavy sigh. Kate was smart. It hadn't taken her long to come to some intriguing conclusions, but she couldn't see that those very conclusions could become a flash point because, for all her brains and Brooklyn bluster, Kate was naïve. She wouldn't rest until she had a theory she could both verify and be comfortable with. Unfortunately, there were a lot of people out there who didn't care much about that. The conspiracy nut bars in cyberland would seize upon those perhaps-valid questions and turn them into weapons that could fatally damage Kate's career and credibility. If there was a whiff of scandal that could in any way point to the man who signed her paychecks, Carter Thompson, Kate would lose her job. Carter Thompson was not a man to suffer fools or to suffer being made to look foolish.

Pushing back the covers, Richard got out of bed and walked barefoot through the dark house to the small screened porch off the dining room. Or what used to be the dining room. Now the table served as a cluttered way station for things in transit to other parts of the house.

He didn't bother to close the door behind him. The fresh air would cool off the house.

After he'd dropped Kate at the station, he'd gotten online and looked up the storms she was obsessing over just to verify what she'd told him about all the parameters being normal. He had to admit that, based on what he'd discovered, she was right. The storms were anything but ordinary, and that left him even more unsettled. Not that he'd ever admit it to Kate, but ever since that debacle in Barbados, he'd been wondering about it himself.

It.

He took a deep breath, not wanting to think about it.

On a global scale, the ferocity of storms in general had increased in the last few years, seeding the already-fertile soil of weather watchers' minds with theories old and new. In little more than an hour on the Web tonight, he'd read white papers that flatly stated the increased intensity was due to global warming, others insisting it was due to unusually strong solar flare activity, and even one that ascribed it to geomagnetic disturbances resulting from minute gravitational fluctuations in outer space. And those were just a few of the hypotheses floating around the scientific establishment.

When he took into account theories espoused by the borderline whack-jobs of the science world, the list became exponentially longer and more ludicrous. There were dire warnings about bombardments of electromagnetic pulses from ultrasecret Soviet-era satellites still in orbit and about the U.S. military bouncing high-frequency waves off the ionosphere in an effort to effect wide-scale mind control. And then there were the dubious sources that insisted that shadowy, acronym-heavy military/intelligence/industrial organizations were getting involved. The most widely espoused theories described special radio frequencies used to create artificial stationary pressure ridges in the jet stream to provoke floods, droughts, and general economic devastation or, conversely, excellent weather for fun and profit. The calm weather in the early part of the summer, and its sudden cessation a week or so ago, had helped fuel that discussion beyond all bounds of reason.

He rubbed his eyes. Many—most—of the theories were closely held and passionately defended, and not just by the wing nuts of the world, either. Not long ago, two prominent scientists in the meteorology community had been invited to a major industry conference to debate the cause of the increasing intensities of the Atlantic hurricanes over the last few years. What was supposed to be a frank and candid discussion of the effects of human-influenced global warming versus a natural cyclical trend in the earth's climatology had been preemptively canceled amid an unexpected and heated escalation of opinions. And that was involving cool-headed, real-world scientists.

Richard stared across the small moonlight-streaked patch of wet lawn to the thick cluster of trees at the edge of his property as two disturbing words kept reverberating in his mind like the endless rhythm of a bad dance band. *Carter Thompson.*

When they'd met forty years ago as handpicked recruits for a CIA weather-research program, Richard had known right away that Carter had the skill and the drive to accomplish anything he set out to do. He'd had a tenacity unlike anything Richard had ever encountered before, and he'd been a relentless team leader, taking every success, every failure, personally. A man with a deep, passionate, almost mystical respect for Nature, Carter had embraced the program's goals so completely that the rest of the team had been a little in awe of him.

Eleven of the best meteorological minds the government could buy had worked in that stuffy, cramped, windowless computer lab in Langley to create the ultimate weapon—one that was untraceable, unstoppable, and potentially less lethal but exponentially more effective than conventional or even the newly minted "unconventional" weaponry being developed at the time. They'd been working on harnessing the force and fury of weather.

Their mission was to take the relatively small amount of existing weather research and twist, stretch, and reshape it to create the ultimate Cold War "force multiplier." Other researchers working under the same umbrella program were building on the cloud-seeding and other rainmaking experiments that had been under way for more than a decade, but Carter's team had been told to *create* weather. To build storms and escalate them. To learn not just how to track them, but how to steer them. And how to stop them.

With the specter of Russian success breathing hot against their necks, they'd had the freedom to follow every crackpot theory, every off-the-wall idea, and they'd done so at an exhausting pace, sometimes forgetting to eat or sleep or go home as they worked to turn hypotheses into refined computer models and to push those computer models to the field trial stage.

They'd been so close to achieving their goal.

Operation POPEYE had been dumping rain on the Ho Chi Minh Trail for the better part of a few years when the public, already fed up with the war, had learned of its existence due to a leak. The pressure on the Pentagon to answer questions on weather research was getting intense, as was the pressure on Carter's team to achieve a positive result. They had been doing calculations using every piece of data available to them to perfect a recipe for a typhoon, and Carter had persuaded the military that directing targeted sequential bursts of high-intensity lasers at both an embryonic storm cell and the surface of the ocean surrounding it would produce the heat needed to speed the convection cycle and grow a storm. With almost evangelical zeal, Carter had assured the Agency higher-ups that his team could create a cyclonic storm with a size and intensity that could be modified at will. Finally, in the late summer of 1971, they'd received orders to take their ideas out of the lab and into the Pacific Basin.

They hadn't needed to be told twice. To conduct what they didn't realize would be their only field trial, he and Carter had boarded a military transport in Maryland. Seventy-two hours later, after hopscotching across the country and the ocean, they'd arrived at a U.S. air base, the name of which they never learned. After a harried day or two getting details organized and crews briefed, Richard and the surface-mounted monitoring equipment had been flown in a thundering open Huey to a ship waiting to take them to their target zone in the South China Sea. Ground Zero was nothing more than a specific coordinate chosen for its atmospheric predictability and the likelihood that it would provide the conditions they would need. It was also far enough into the open ocean that nobody would see anything—but if by chance someone did, they wouldn't understand it.

He'd been a young, skinny CIA scientist with no combat training and no sea legs. He hadn't had much more than his Southern ways to keep him going on that ship, surrounded as he was by a mixture of silent Agency observers and an annoyed, twitchy pod of high-ranking, beribboned, battle-hardened military officers representing all the branches. Everyone was waiting on deck impatiently for Carter to appear over the horizon in the specially modified C-130 Hercules cargo plane that carried the enormous machinery that generated the laser, which, in those days, was a technology few people inside or outside the military had worked with or understood.

It had been as near to perfect a day to run the test as they could have wanted. The majority of the clouds were few and high, wispy mackerel cirrus that wouldn't interfere with anything; the rest were the mid-layer cumulus, the puffy cotton-ball clouds that every schoolchild learns to draw. They were the typical, ordinary clouds that formed every day over the ocean as the result of a tropical sun beating onto warm water. They drifted through relatively stable air all day long and dissipated overnight, only to reestablish themselves the next day.

Until he and Carter had gotten hold of them.

When the Herc bearing Carter and the laser finally appeared on the horizon, Richard had suggested that the observers might want to watch from the bridge. Stony, silent macho glares had greeted his words, but he quickly put the uniformed men out of his mind as he readied his equipment. Brief, terse radio exchanges identified the targeted cloud cluster, and he'd watched the plane bank slowly as it rose higher into the painfully blue sky, heading for the strike zone.

A single, searing pulse of heat, measurable in seconds, burst from the pod hanging below the belly of the aircraft, scorching the air and sending the benign, picturesque clouds into a billowing, explosive frenzy that drew gasps from the men behind him. Lightning and thunder shattered the air as churning, chaotic winds pelted them with hot, fat raindrops that stung like hordes of angry bees, wilting the knife-sharp creases of a dozen starched uniforms.

Twenty minutes later, the storm was over, the sky was clear, the plane carrying Carter was a speck on the horizon, and most of the officials around Richard had regained the power of speech.

He and Carter stayed in the region for a month, playing fast and loose with Nature as if they were a pair of playboy gods, in the process creating the most active typhoon season ever recorded in the Pacific—a record that had never been broken. By the time they headed stateside a month later, Southeast Asia had been battered by seven typhoons inside of five weeks, including two that had achieved sustained winds of 140 miles an hour.

By all accounts, their work had been more than a success. It had been masterful, and the buzz had made them nearly drunk with victory.

Then, in what had to be one of the cruelest twists of fate, the day their last storm dissipated over China after having smashed into Taiwan with deadly force, Senator Claiborne Pell, chairman of the Senate Subcommittee on Oceans and International Environment and under relentless pressure from the public, began demanding the Pentagon surrender information about weather manipulation programs.

By the time he and Carter had returned to their desks, they were no longer heroes except to their fellow team members. The entire program had been disbanded.

Enraged beyond the boundaries of prudence or fore-sight, Carter protested at Langley and later during secret hearings on Capitol Hill. He forcefully explained that the Soviets were masters at copying what the U.S. achieved and the successes enjoyed by his team would eventually be reproduced behind the Iron Curtain. If the U.S. didn't con-trol the weather, the Soviets would, he'd argued, and who-ever controlled the weather would truly rule the world.

The more passionate Carter's arguments became the more they met with tight-lipped, dispassionate rejection from the higher-ups at the Agency and with cold, unsympa-thetic smiles from members of Congress, including the man who now held sway in the Oval Office, Winslow Benson.

Richard and the rest of the team had left Carter to his anger, eventually accepting that it would have been im-possible, not to mention dangerous, for the Congress to ig-nore the public outrage. The furor that erupted when the fearless *Washington Post* reporter Jack Anderson broke the news about Operation POPEYE in March of that year had not died down as insiders had hoped it would; how-ever grudgingly, Congress had to be seen to be responsive.

Weather control, Carter's team was told, was too much of a hot-button issue and conjured up too many science-fiction scenarios. Even secret weather research funding was duly cut in favor of research advancing nuclear tech-nologies, which few voters understood but most accepted because of nuclear power's perceived connection to the triumphant horrors of the bombing of Japan.

The team had been unceremoniously dispersed, with most of them asked to spend six months in their "cover" roles at the infant National Oceanic and Atmospheric Ad-ministration before heading back into civilian life. Nearly all had slipped quietly back into their lives as soon as they could. Like Richard, many went into academia. None had become researchers, barred as they were from working on anything related to what they'd done at the Agency.

Carter alone had lingered at NOAA for more than a year, finding and, when necessary, creating battles with the funding subcommittees. Richard knew the impetus behind those debates hadn't been policy or even principle; it had been vanity. The smirking junior senator from New York, Winslow Benson, who had been a member of the body that eliminated their program, was also a member of the committee that funded NOAA. None of their group had liked Senator Benson with his patronizing manner and William F. Buckley–esque intonation; however, most of them had tried to ignore his condescension.

Not Carter.

Carter had taken the senator's blithe dismissal of his arguments as a personal affront. Years later, when the senator's quiet allegiance to the emergent nuclear power industry became known after the Three Mile Island debacle, Carter reached what Richard considered his tipping point.

Enraged, Carter had spoken of the accident as would a man speaking of witnessing the rape of his wife. The fury of Carter's diatribe had been so unsettling that Richard had eased away from further contact with him, but he knew that from that moment forward, Winslow Benson would be to Carter the embodiment of government treachery and environmental perfidy. That the man now sat in the White House had to be gnawing at Carter's already-bloodied sense of justice.

A wet nose nudging him in the small of his back brought Richard out of his reverie. As he opened the screen door to let Finn wander in the yard, a grim truth introduced itself in his mind.

Carter had always had the imagination, skill, and drive to help the team achieve its goals. After the collapse of his scientific career, Carter had put that same imagination and energy into creating not one but two highly profitable companies, and his net worth was now measurable in the billions of dollars.

Which meant for the past decade or more he had had the means and the opportunity to resume their research.

But was there a motive significant enough to spur Carter to pick up where we left off?

The unspoken question sent an icy tremor down Richard's spine. It would be so simple—reassuring actually—to say that mere greed could motivate Carter to engage in something so chilling, but Carter had never been money oriented. Even now, the media continually marveled at how simply he lived considering how wealthy he was. The sickening reality was that Carter's personality allowed for only two possible motives: power or vengeance. With Winslow Benson contemplating reelection and Carter sitting on billions of available dollars in his beloved Iowa cornfields, either motive—or both— could apply.

As he opened the door to let Finn in from his quick predawn sniff, Richard looked up at the dark, cloudless sky. Another beautiful day was in the making.

It sent another cold shiver down his back.

CHAPTER **15**

Friday, July 13, 8:00 A.M., Financial District, New York City

Elle,

I know you're busy with tons of stuff for Davis Lee, but I was wondering if you might have time to take a look at something for me. I've attached a paper that's been accepted for presentation at a meteorology conference, and before I send it to them in final form for inclusion on the CD-ROM they hand out to attendees, I'd like another pair of eyes on it. It's not too long and, given your background, I figure you'll pick up on things like mistakes with grammar and footnotes, etc. When it comes to that, I'm one of those "last year I couldn't spell meteorologist and now I are one" types. ☺

Any suggestions would be appreciated. I owe you one.

Thx,
Kate

Kate sat at her computer and debated whether to send the e-mail she'd just typed. It was against her character to doubt herself, but since her conversation with Richard last night that's about all she'd been doing. She needed another opinion, and Elle seemed like the perfect person to ask for it. She had a background in research, so she'd probably be able to tell if Kate was wandering down the path of bad logic, as Richard had implied. And Elle wasn't a meteorologist, which meant that her perspective as an intelligent outsider could offer some insight.

On the downside, she might end up thinking that I'm just as much of a nut bar as those conspiracy theorists out on the Web.

Exasperated by her own dithering, she clicked on Send and then opened the spreadsheet she had to get to Davis Lee by noon.

Friday, July 13, 9:00 A.M., Campbelltown, Iowa

The chirp of a cell phone brought Carter's gaze to the small bank of them aligned along the left edge of his desk. They were reserved for family members, which meant Iris and the girls. Not even his sons-in-law had the number of the one that now chirped for the second time.

The small screen displayed a Washington, D.C., exchange, which meant it had to be Meggy. He frowned. As his assistant counsel for legislative affairs, she routinely called him on his office line. Something had to be up if she was using a private line.

He flipped open the phone. "Yes, Meg?"

"Daddy, turn on CNN." She sounded breathless.

Without a word, he glanced up at the bank of TV monitors on the forward wall of his office and tapped the remote to bring up the sound on the third one from the left. The White House press secretary was standing in the Rose Garden, his hair blowing artfully in the wind as photographers jockeyed for an angle that would keep the sun from blinding them.

"—the President of the United States," he said, finishing his introduction.

The cameras pulled back and Carter's jaw tightened as he saw who followed the president to the lectern. Ranking members from every energy- and environment-related committee in both the House and the Senate, plus half the cabinet, stood there looking somber as the president flashed his orthodontically perfect smile. Carter flicked on the other four televisions on the wall and glanced at the one to the left of the one showing CNN. FOX News's camera was panning the crowd, and the sight of the faces made Carter's gut clench. His anger was fringed with dread. The seated audience comprised a balanced mix of activists and lobbyists, interspersed with enough sycophants and famously disenfranchised minority icons to ensure that whatever was about to happen would get a lot of play in the press.

The crowd applauded, if not enthusiastically at least with good grace, and the president waited for the greeting to subside.

This can't be good.

"What is this?" Carter demanded.

"Daddy, I swear I don't know. Nobody knows." She sounded almost frantic.

He let out an explosive breath. "For pete's sake, Meggy. Somebody has to. Nobody can keep a secret in that town."

"Daddy, I swear I don't. I've got calls out everywhere. If anyone knows, they're not saying. I—"

"Wait."

The applause had stopped and the president glanced at his notes, then up at the cameras.

Carter glanced quickly at the other screens. Every network had cut to the same scene with their "Breaking News" logos littering the visual real estate.

"My fellow Americans, a little over two hundred years ago, a small group of courageous, forward-thinking patriots—farmers, lawyers, merchants—declared independence from a foreign regime. That regime, while initially serving us well, had slowly begun to limit our freedoms, undermine our self-determination, and strangle our emerging economic strength. The situation the patriots faced was born thousands of miles from our shores and it was born out of greed and out of fear." The president paused and looked from his live audience straight into the camera. "But the patriots were not without blame. To a certain extent, those early citizens allowed and even encouraged the situation to develop. That is, until our Founding Fathers realized that the old way was no longer the best way, and decided it was time for a change."

Carter eased back in his chair, all senses still on high alert, the phone in his hand forgotten.

"One week ago," the president continued, his voice rising, his well-bred New England intonations ringing with righteousness, "this great nation of ours celebrated the anniversary of their courageous and historic decision to throw off the tyranny of a power external to their land and antithetical to the ideals of their fledgling nation. Those strong, brave men of high morals and like minds crafted a declaration of intent to face down their oppressor, to wrest from that foreign power a new way of life, one that nurtured the Divine within and Nature without. With words that continue to stir the hearts and souls and fire the imagination of men and women all over the world, their declaration of independence from a foreign power that fateful day in early July of 1776 changed the world. Their words, their deeds ushered in a new reality, a new philosophy, a new method of seeking to attain a quality of life and of liberty that had never been enjoyed by any civilization in the history of mankind."

The president glanced down at his notes with just the right hint of humility, the right edge of patriotic anger. Carter felt his eyes narrow.

"Their words were backed up by the noble sacrifices of the citizens of our young nation. Our forebears faced a future that would have been uncertain had it not been for their unshakable faith, their steadfast hearts, and their stalwart backs. And they prevailed. Despite myriad hardships and privations, despite the huge cost of shattered families and destroyed property, they triumphed. And we, the citizens gathered here today in the Rose Garden and the millions of Americans in cities and towns around the country and around the world, are the beneficiaries of their prescience, their conscience, their faith, and their call to action." The president waited for a beat that Carter felt echo in his brain, then looked straight into the camera again, straight into Carter's eyes.

"I stand before you today, surrounded on all sides by patriots filled with the same sense of purpose, driven by the same desire for self-determination, inspired by the same call for freedom and liberty. It is with the greatest pleasure and pride that I announce the creation of the Coalition for an Energy-Independent America, which will be led by Frances Morton, whose roots extend to the *Mayflower* on one side and much farther back to the great Quinault Indian Nation on the other, and who has been the Undersecretary of the Interior since the first days of my administration. Under the strong, committed leadership of Ms. Morton, the coalition will work toward achieving its goal of complete American independence from foreign energy supplies by 2030."

Carter didn't move. He barely breathed as he watched the president bask in the most enthusiastic applause he'd received in months.

I should be there. He knows it. I know it. The country knows it. I should be there shaking his hand, smiling at the cameras, taking questions.

But I'm not there.

Carter unclenched his jaw and stood up, proud of his self-control even as rage threatened to consume him. "Why didn't we know about this, Meg?"

She was in tears, sobbing into the phone. "I don't know, Daddy. I swear I don't know. This is—"

He tuned her out as the president resumed speaking.

"This is America's second declaration of independence and it, too, will call upon the strength and fortitude of all Americans as we work together to shift from our dependence on foreign supplies of fossil fuels to new, home-grown methods of heating our homes, powering our cars, and lighting our cities. It won't always be easy or comfortable. As it did for the early patriots, the shift from one way of life to another will involve sacrifice. We must keep in mind, however, that just as the sacrifices made by our forebears helped shape not only our nation but the world, so, too, shall our sacrifices change the world we know for the better." He stopped to allow the applause to swell, then continued as it subsided.

"The creation of this broad, bipartisan, cross-industry, and inter-agency coalition is a turning point in our nation's history. My administration has been working for months behind the scenes to bring together representatives from all sectors of the energy industry: regulators, lobbyists, CEOs, and researchers. We sat them down at tables and fed them lunch and made them talk to each other." He grinned at the crowd. "We didn't tell them what to say any more than we told them what to eat. We just put out some ham, chicken, tofu, and sprouts, and let them make their own sandwiches. After all, you gotta pick your battles."

His man-of-the-people role confirmed, his expression and his voice grew sober again as the polite laughter died away. "It was an inspiring event. It was small-*d* democracy in action. Everyone was on equal footing. Wind farmers had a chance to talk, really talk, with representatives from major utilities. Ethanol producers discussed ideas with the CEOs of petroleum companies. Manufacturers of geothermal and solar energy–collection equipment shared their views with automobile manufacturers and the people who operate the nation's natural gas pipelines. It was a free flow of information among people who, until then, had seen each other as competitors, if not as outright enemies. Now, everybody realizes that we're all on the same side of the fence, that we're aligned to fight the good battle, and that we're going to fight to win." He paused, sending an intensely soulful look to the cameras, one that made Carter's stomach churn as much as Benson's words did.

"I'll say it again. Today is a great day for the nation and for the world. Led by this coalition, America will take the lead in the research and development and production and utilization of clean energy, and we'll do it within our borders and within our means. That is why I am asking Congress to give fast-track approval to a three-billion-dollar appropriation to fund the research and development activities that need to be undertaken by the coalition. To sweeten the pot, I've asked all of the players involved, from the biggest to the smallest, to contribute money, talent, and other resources to the coalition to the best of their ability. Working together, members of this broad coalition will study every method of energy generation that's ever been devised and implement every method that's feasible within the boundaries of safety for our people, our environment, and our economy. And like our nation's forefathers, our determination and our sacrifices will ensure that our grandchildren and *their* grandchildren will live in a safer, cleaner, more prosperous nation. Thank you all for coming today, and God bless America."

Declining to take questions, Winslow Benson crossed the stage with a purposeful stride and self-confident smile and disappeared under the portico, followed by a covey of dark suits.

Every network immediately cut to a talking head, each of whom tried to fill airtime with a repetition of what the president had just said until they could get hold of an "expert" to discuss what had just been said.

"Meg, how many people have you—"

"Everyone. They're all already on their way to the Hill and K Street to find out what's going on. Every phone in the office is busy, Daddy. I'm so sorry I didn't see this coming. I just . . . There wasn't a hint of it. Not a hint." Her voice was breaking again with desperation.

"Enough about that. Keep me apprised of what you find out."

He ended the call with Meg and looked at his assistant, who had been standing in his doorway looking nervous for the last few minutes. "Track down Davis Lee and get him on the phone. And tell Pam I need to see her immediately," he said calmly, referring to another daughter, his vice president of public relations.

"Yes, sir. She's already on her way up."

Feeling the erratic thump of his heart, Carter nodded and watched her shut the door. The dizziness began to encroach on his consciousness, and ignoring the constellation of flashing lights on his phone console, Carter leaned back in his chair, resting his head against the faded doily one of his daughters had crocheted for him years ago. Trying to focus on keeping the rhythm of his breathing slow and easy, he could not block the thoughts crowding his head.

So that is Winslow's answer. The greens get a pat on the head and another empty promise that they'll be listened to, while the nukes and the derricks and the drillers get new leases and more money and less oversight.

The light-headedness wasn't dissipating as quickly as usual, and he slowed his breathing further, trying to parse the information into manageable pieces.

Everyone was going to "contribute." The big boys would send in their hired guns, who excelled at spending time and wasting money, and the little guys would give up their scientists and their credibility to the cause. And it would all be for the greater good. Everyone would get a chance at the table, and everyone would walk away a winner.

As a strategy, it was brilliant. And, unsustainable though it was in the long term, it would likely work in the short term, just as it had for the canny political persuader who had used the same philosophy to great effect in the last century, Karl Marx. For all that Winslow Benson had wrapped his message in Old Glory and the Founding Fathers, the packaging neither softened its effect nor hid its origin.

From each according to his ability, to each according to his needs.

The difference was that in this situation, the shoestring organizations would give everything they had and the big corporations would take everything they could get.

Carter's rage surged again, harder to control, seeping through the hairline cracks that had formed in his composure. The environment was *his* issue, not Winslow Benson's. *He* was the one with the mandate to protect it. *He* was the one who had developed the means to harness the power, to restore life. The president would destroy it—the environment, the planet, all the life on it. It was as much a certainty as the sun rising tomorrow morning. He'd kill it with his pet cause, nuclear energy. It had lined his pockets and sent him to the White House. It owned him, hard heart and black soul. It owned him.

And it would ultimately kill him. Carter would see to it.

The disorienting roar in his head stopped then and, shocked, Carter was able to rein in his fury.

Surely he hadn't just thought about killing the president. That would be wrong. As a man of honor, he wouldn't. He couldn't.

His eyes snapped open. He slammed a clenched fist onto the solid American oak of his desk.

Damn Winslow Benson's soul to Hell for what he is about to do to this nation and this world.

What about what he's already done?

The small voice echoed inside him and Carter's breathing stopped.

Of course. The jet stream.

It had been parked over the middle of the country for weeks in the early summer, constraining the warm, humid, mostly stable Gulf air from moving north, inhibiting the cool Pacific fronts that usually swept down the eastern side of the Rockies. The weather had been wonderful for most of the country, not unbearable, not droughtlike. There had been no catastrophic storms in the Midwest, no tornadoes in the South, not even much notable activity in the Caribbean or the Gulf. A slew of named storms had built up in the Atlantic and broken up without much ado. And then, suddenly, the jet stream had begun to return to its normal position, sparking localized storms of surprising violence across the South and throughout the Midwest.

He'd known in the back of his mind that such uninterrupted good weather followed by such inexplicably bad weather couldn't possibly be natural, but now, acknowledging that the alternative was probably the reality, a chill ran up his spine.

If the jet stream anomalies weren't natural, it meant he wasn't alone out there.

It meant someone else could manipulate the weather. And that someone could only be the U.S. government. And the only means possible was HAARP.

Anger ripped through him. It had to be a test—a hell of a long test—or maybe it was a show of strength. God knows there were enough reasons the White House would want to flex a little muscle. The Benson administration had been a glowing target for so long and even its usual allies had been beating it up from all sides, deriding its trade agreements, environmental accords, foreign policies. No one was happy right now. Not even the electorate.

The electorate.

Near-perfect weather in a summer before an election year would give the president something to crow about all winter long as he built up his campaign war chest. During the long period of unremitting but not extreme warmth, electricity usage had shot up and remained there, making the president the darling of the industry while calling a lot of attention to the role of so-called "clean" nuclear power in the nation's energy mix. Reduced levels of rainfall had pushed reservoirs and water tables below normal volume but not to the drought level, putting environmentalists into the spotlight without actually framing agribusiness as the bad guy. And the lack of severe weather initially had not only helped to fade the nation's collective memory of recent failed responses to critical situations, but had robbed critics of the administration's emergency operations of their anticipated ammunition. Not to mention what the lack of natural disasters had done to his own company's profits, which were not as high as they usually were at this time of year.

Now the pendulum was swinging back, but this time, the president was ready for it.

The son of a bitch.

The adrenaline burst carried Carter to his feet and he stared at the American flag hanging proudly in the corner of his office, undulating in the breeze from his open windows. It had flown over the graves at Arlington National Cemetery and had been presented to him by the governor of Iowa.

With liberty and justice for all.

For all.

Carter felt his head clear as he stared at the red, white, and blue. His inner vision intensified and narrowed.

The president is wrong. Terribly wrong, and history will bear witness to it.

Shaking off the trance, Carter refocused on the flag. As a patriot and believer in democracy as well as destiny, there was only one way he could interpret the president's words.

As a declaration of war.

He has to be stopped. The people have to see what he truly stands for, what has fueled his career.

Carter was reaching for his phone when movement on the screen of his monitor captured his attention. The small, tight swirl of clouds and rain that had recently entered the easternmost Caribbean Sea had continued to gain momentum without any additional help from him and was gradually climbing toward being a Category 2 hurricane. They were calling her Simone, and she was a perfect storm: compact, slow, worthy of attention. Near the top of her spin, a wisp of clouds resembling a spear pointed north-northwest. Carter let his gaze drift along an invisible trajectory from the spear point to a pronounced indent at the "corner" of the eastern seaboard, where New England distinguished itself from the mid-Atlantic states.

Carter's eyes came to rest slightly north of the indent. His anger dissolved and he was filled with a calm, clear-headed resolve.

He would level the playing field.

He had already taken Simone from a minor tropical depression to a Category 1 hurricane. Now he would nurture her to bring the world's attention to the tremendous danger posed by Winslow Benson and his support for nuclear energy. Under his guidance, Simone would become a storm so big, so powerful, that she would dwarf anything yet recorded by man. And he would bring her to the one place that would make the world take notice.

New York City.

And the aging Indian Point Nuclear Power Plant that lay thirty-five miles to the north of it.

CHAPTER **16**

From the tip of Florida to southern Virginia, foaming breakers were bright with the sunburned flesh of rookie boogie boarders and the neon-covered bodies of more serious surfers paddling furiously farther out to catch the next wave, the best wave, the one that could fuel stories for the rest of the season. On the Chesapeake Bay, executives and politicians played hooky on the water, their egos swelling in unison with the sails of their sloops and cata-marans. Along the piers and jetties that spliced the Atlantic from the Delaware peninsula up to the Jersey Shore, children squealed with feigned fear and unfeigned pleasure as they dodged the spray from crashing waves. Fishermen off coastal New England hauled in above-average and occasionally perplexing catches as creatures typically seen in deeper waters followed feeder species into the continental shallows.

Simone, the cause of all the giddy seaside delight, spun tirelessly in the Atlantic, having paused in her path as if contemplating a change of direction or plan. Undisturbed by the aircraft penetrating her walls or the many eyes watching her, she continued her inexorable churn.

CHAPTER 17

Friday, July 13, 1:00 P.M., the outskirts of Port-au-Prince, Haiti

Raoul Patterson walked through the small, dirty shack, his usual confident, military stride made longer by the anger simmering beneath his composed exterior. He was providing an unscheduled wake-up call to Jimmy "Tiger" Strathan, a former USAF pilot who had been headed for his second tour in Iraq when he'd decided he didn't like getting shot at or being underpaid while doing so. Tiger had relieved himself of his duties, walked away from his country, and gone contract, bumming his way through Central America and the Caribbean until eventually landing in Port-au-Prince, Haiti, where Raoul had run into him four days ago.

While Major Patterson, RAF (Ret.), had no respect for

deserters, he had a lot of respect for the U.S. Air Force and the training they gave their pilots. And mercenaries can't always be choosers. He'd hired Tiger right away, knowing there was a good chance it was a mistake.

That's why learning that Tiger's faint pretensions of intelligence had indeed disappeared came as no surprise. That it had only taken a few days of living in this Caribbean shit hole for him to complete the transformation was more of one.

The cause of it wasn't the humidity or the heat, although both were hellish. And, given Tiger's not-so-latent sociopathic tendencies, it wasn't the job. Flying test operations for the foundation, which was nothing more than a front for a secret and completely illegal, immoral, and unethical research and development project, was like flying any wartime mission. You focus on the results and ignore everything else. Drop the bombs and win the war or, in this case, zap a cloud with a laser, change the weather, and get rich.

So it definitely wasn't the job.

What had changed Tiger was the apparent absence of civil structure. Amidst the squalid lawlessness that defined much of this small, desperate nation-state, Tiger had thought to become the master of his own fate. And so he had, Raoul acknowledged with a grim smile, by forgetting Raoul's rules for his crew.

Coming to a halt, Raoul stood in the doorless opening of the bedroom, surveying the scene before him with disgust. He wasn't sure which was worse, the stench or the sight.

A miasma of sweat, booze, farts, and sex hung in the room like an impenetrable fog. Six bare legs—two male, four female—stuck out at odd angles from beneath a tangle of filthy sheets and torn mosquito netting. Two empty bottles of Jim Beam lay on the floor. One appeared to have spilled when a stray limb had knocked it over. Judging by the nearly bestial cacophony of sounds coming from the bed, the other had been consumed.

The bottle blonde draped across Tiger's chest was Annike, a European of blurry provenance and invisible means of support who turned up anywhere there were flyboys. She had bad taste in clothes and worse taste in men, but she had big tits and liked weird sex, which made her slightly more than tolerable in this part of the world. Raoul didn't know the other woman, but given the position in which she'd fallen asleep or passed out, she knew both Tiger and Annike intimately. Her skin was black as coal and streaked and dotted with scars. She couldn't have been more than twenty at a push and was likely far younger.

To each his own.

Raoul crossed the room and drove a knuckle deep into the instep of the cleaner of Tiger's feet, causing the younger, stupider man to jerk his legs up, dislodging both women. They fell to the floor in an obscene sprawl, one on either side of the bed, but didn't wake up. The stereophonic thuds and grunts, and perhaps the pain, brought Tiger up on one elbow.

"What the fuck—," he rasped, then peered through barely slitted eyes. "Oh. Hey, boss."

"Get your ass down to the hangar. We're flying," Raoul ordered, his clipped words belying the calmness of his voice. He couldn't stop the occasional trace of his native Yorkshire seeping into his painstakingly acquired high-street accent when he was annoyed, but he made a point of never raising his voice. He'd discovered early in his career that not shouting scared more people more of the time. It worked for Clint Eastwood and it worked for Raoul Patterson.

"Uh, I don't think I can—"

"I'm not interested in what you think. I said we're flying. Now get your sorry, drunken ass out of that bacterial stew and into your clothes. I'm giving you five minutes and then I'm leaving. Permanently."

Tiger's twenty-six-year-old eyes widened painfully.

Clearly, Raoul's rules hadn't been fully taken to heart by Tiger, who, despite the warnings, had decided last night to show himself to be an arrogant, sloppy drunk and, according to the juju amulet around the younger woman's neck, a defiler of local religious taboos. Either condition could get him killed in this part of the city, where ignorance fed irrationality and local gangs had a penchant for blood and violence.

A lesson in crew discipline was required.

"I need—"

"If you're thinking of a shower, stop. There's no water. You have four minutes and thirty seconds. I'll be in the other room." Raoul turned his back and left the doorway.

A minute or so later, Tiger stumbled into the small central room of the house, shirt hanging open, jeans buttoned at the waist but unzipped, underwear lost or forgotten. He leaned against the wall and blinked, his movements uncoordinated and lethargic as his reflexes struggled to come online.

Raoul studied him dispassionately. "Where's your documentation?"

Keeping his papers safe, if not always immediately available, was another critical point.

"Huh?" Tiger looked at him with unfocused eyes.

"Your passport."

"Oh. Somewhere." He patted his bare chest absently in search of a pocket.

Raoul let the search continue for fifteen seconds before he Frisbeed the small folder across the room, where the corner of it hit Tiger at high speed in the solar plexus. He grunted and pitched forward but caught himself before he fell, then straightened up, clutching the flat missile to his stomach. Raoul began a silent countdown from five. By the time he got to three, Tiger bent over and began to throw up.

Ten minutes later, Raoul had his depleted, dry-heaving co-pilot by the arm and was pulling him to the door. "Better here than in my cockpit," he muttered. "And for God's sake, Strathan, tackle in."

After a bone-cracking twenty-minute drive along the coast on badly paved roads and pocked dirt tracks in an open Jeep, they arrived at what passed for a hangar. Tiger was in much better shape, relatively speaking. He looked like hell and stank like a whorehouse, but he'd achieved relative cognition by sucking on a canister of oxygen for the whole drive. Now he was downing small cups of hot, bitter coffee one of the mechanics had offered him.

Raoul knew Tiger was in no shape to fly anything. However, given the pre-determined flight plan and mission, that was a moot point.

Raoul walked back into what someone had generously termed "the office" and handed Tiger a beat-up black canvas bag. "On your feet. Let's go."

"Look, could you cut the commanding-officer crap? This excursion of yours wasn't planned, okay? I thought I had the day off," Tiger griped.

"Plans change."

"Your plans changed. That doesn't mean mine have to." He stood up gingerly, as if the sudden change of altitude might send him crashing. "Where are we going, anyway?"

"Inland."

Raoul allowed himself a smile as the few people within earshot turned to look at him for confirmation. From their location on the coast, "inland" meant only one thing: drug running.

Of the half-dozen men in the room, only Tiger was openly incredulous. The rest had seen and heard too much in their lives for anything to surprise them, and after a moment they looked away, never having displayed the slightest curiosity. Theirs was a world in which questions were not asked and tales were not told. Doing either could get you killed.

"You gotta be fucking kidding me," Tiger said.

"Actually, I am. We're going sightseeing." Raoul turned and walked out of the small room at the back of the building. Calling it a building was a compliment. It really wasn't much more than a supersized shack.

When he reached the aging chopper, Raoul climbed into the pilot's seat and began the pre-flight checks. Tiger climbed in beside him, more subdued than he had been at the house.

"This thing's older than me," he said derisively, looking at the stripped-down display that had dials that were actually connected to mechanical equipment and real fluids instead of circuit boards and sensors.

Raoul spared him a glance. "It may well be older than your mother." *And held together with spit and rubber bands.*

"Do you know how to fly it?"

"I did thirty years ago. I'm sure it will come back to me," Raoul replied as the rotors groaned into a slow revolution. Even that kicked up dust devils. Getting airborne as soon as possible was a necessity. "Are you in?"

"Yeah. No headset?"

"No need. The radio was stolen a few years ago."

Tiger looked distinctly uncomfortable. "What happened to the doors?"

"Took them off," Raoul replied absently as he monitored the gauges. "The wind coming through all the bullet holes made a hell of a racket."

Ten minutes later they were cruising over the edge of the coastline heading northeast, toward the open ocean.

"So, what are we really doing?" Tiger shouted over the loud and unhealthy whine of the ancient engine.

"A little bit of freelance recon," Raoul replied, and pointed to the canvas bag at Tiger's feet.

Tiger gingerly opened it and stared at the video camera, then looked back at Raoul in confusion. "Uh, how much are we getting paid for this?"

"A once in a lifetime price," Raoul replied after a moment's consideration. It wasn't a lie. "I'll tell you when to start filming."

Tiger nodded and stared straight ahead. The uneasy silence lasted longer than Raoul had anticipated.

"So, I heard you had a wild night," he said eventually.

A slow, debauched grin spanned Tiger's face. "You saw the results," he said. "Those bitches did things I didn't think were possible."

Stupid git. "I meant before that. In the pub."

Calling the place a pub was as much a misnomer as calling the place they parked the planes a hangar, but it was the best description he could come up with. In that part of the city, any place a non-local could get a drink without getting knifed deserved to be called a pub.

"What about it?"

"You made a lot of friends last night."

Tiger clearly wasn't happy with the indirect approach. "What the hell are you getting at?"

Soon enough, mate. "Okay, get into position."

Tiger shook his head in disgust and lifted the camera out of the bag.

Raoul pointed at a patch of shallow water off the starboard side. "Start filming when we get to that reef."

"What are we looking for?"

"Sharks."

"You're kidding."

"Just turn on the bloody camera."

Tiger brought the camera to his eye and aimed it downward. Raoul saw the zoom lens fully extend.

"Hey, there *are* sharks down there."

"Imagine that," Raoul replied drily. "How many?"

"Three. No, wait. Four."

"What are they doing?"

Tiger raised his head and gave Raoul an unsubtle look. "They're swimming, Raoul."

Arse. "I'm going to try to go a little lower on the next pass. Can you get down on the floor? I want to get the cleanest shots that we can so I can wrap this up and get back before anyone notices."

Tiger looked back at him with wary eyes. "Notices what?"

"Just get on the floor and keep shooting."

Raoul watched the young fool unbuckle his harness and wedge himself onto the floor in front of the seat, legs dangling over the side, feet not seeking the security of the skid. He held on to the door frame loosely with one hand as he turned to give Raoul a quick, delighted grin over his shoulder.

"I feel like those guys in 'Nam. You know, the ones in the movies who were always riding shotgun." He turned back to the unsecured opening and lifted the camera to his eye again.

You stupid, ignorant fuck. Raoul shot past the small, reef-rimmed cay and began a slow loop as he dropped to fifty feet. He didn't want to scare the fishies too much. That would ruin the effect.

"You were quite chatty in the pub last night," he said conversationally.

Tiger froze and the hand wrapped around the video camera slowly drifted to his lap. "Say what?"

"You got pissed—sorry, hammered, as you Yanks say— and started talking about what you were doing earlier in the week." Raoul's voice was nearly cheerful over the roar of the rotors. "The storm, the plane, the equipment—you were having quite a lot of fun, weren't you? Regaling the other poor sods with tales of your glory." He paused. "Unfortunately, the trouble is that not only was that bad form, but you really don't have a fucking clue what you were talking about."

The look in Tiger's eyes had gone from caution to fear, which left only two stages before reality sank in. Raoul knew he wouldn't have to wait too long.

"I wasn't talking about—"

"I was there to babysit. I heard you, *Jimmy.*"

"Hey, don't call me—"

"I thought I made it clear that I don't tolerate that sort of behavior on my team, *Jimmy,* even for shit-hot Yank flyboys like you. Do you remember the part where I told you that I don't care what you drink or when or how much as long as you can fly when I need you to? And that I don't care who or what you fuck but that if you talked about the missions to anyone you'd be taken off the team? Do you remember that little chat?"

"Okay. Yeah. Got it. I'll . . . I'll keep my mouth shut."

"No, Jimmy. I'm not giving you a warning. I'm telling you good-bye."

The kid's Adam's apple was working overtime and he looked like he was about to wet himself. He'd shot right past panic into terror. Stage Four.

"Fine. Okay. As soon as we get back—"

"It's too late for that, Jimmy. Cheers." Raoul tilted the chopper abruptly and the stunned, unsecured Jimmy "Tiger" Strathan fell out, too terrified to scream.

Righting the old bird, Raoul gained a little altitude and set a new course, not bothering to notice where Tiger fell or whether he survived splashdown. He didn't have to. Such an outcome would be temporary at best given the only signs of life within twenty miles were four sharks.

Besides, he had other things on his mind now that Tiger had been taken care of. Like getting his crew out of the country before any of what that fucking Yank had been yapping about last night made it back to anyone who might care. Of course, in a conveniently perverse twist of happenstance, most everyone who might care was busy preparing for Hurricane Simone, which was projected to cause heavy rains and strong winds as it skirted north of the island sometime in the next forty-eight hours. If the storm track changed and the island took a direct hit, tens of thousands of people would be in trouble.

But not as much trouble as Raoul and his crew would be in if they didn't make it out of the country. Today.

CHAPTER 18

"Have a minute?"

Kate looked up to see Elle in her office doorway, looking a little more frazzled than usual. "Sure. Come on in." She lifted a stack of file folders from one of the chairs and set it on the floor.

Elle walked in and closed the door, then sat down. "I finished reading your paper a little while ago."

"Thanks for taking a look at it. I didn't mean to make it sound as though timing was critical," Kate said, then grimaced. "So how is it?"

"It's good. Interesting." Elle smiled and leaned back in the chair.

Even slouching, she didn't have any belly fat. It was reason enough to dislike her.

"Is that the research equivalent of saying it has a good personality?" Kate asked drily.

Elle laughed. "No. That means that I thought it was interesting, Kate. It was a nice change to read about something current. Most of what I've been working on is a few decades old."

"So do I end up sounding crazy?"

"Define 'crazy.'"

Kate rolled her eyes. "Great."

Elle brushed away the reply with a languid hand. "I'm joking. You don't sound crazy. But since you brought it up, I take it you won't be surprised if some people think you are after they read the paper?"

"A friend of mine hinted at it," Kate admitted. "More than hinted. I think he said I'd become the poster child of the Weird Weather Weenie Society once the paper gets posted online." She sighed. "So the maybe-crazy factor aside, does the paper make sense?"

"It definitely does make sense," Elle confirmed. "I'm not a weather watcher, so I couldn't completely follow all the equations. I don't know what some of those variables are or what they mean, but your arguments seem pretty sound." She paused. "Is your presentation going to focus on the science or the speculation?"

Good question. "I'm not sure I can separate one from the other," Kate replied with a shrug.

"But you think that the storms were—what would you call it? Enhanced by technology?"

Kate shifted in her chair, uneasy at the direct question. "They seem that way to me, but I think it's too far-fetched a notion to bring up in front of an audience of serious scientists. Now, if I were speaking at a *Star Trek* convention—" She let the sentence drift with a grin.

As tired as Elle seemed, the gaze she fixed on Kate was clear, focused, and intent. "But that's what you're really getting at in your paper, aren't you? Do you really think that your audience will dismiss it if you present it clearly?"

"They won't dismiss it, but I can pretty much guarantee their response won't include laughter. These are number-crunching weather geeks, Elle. And I know this may sound kind of odd to you, but weather is our baby. Whether we're academics, in business, working for the government, or on TV, we all have a pretty proprietary sensibility about the weather. Messing with it is not a charge that will be taken lightly by too many of them."

"Does that mean you're going to soft-pedal your—"

Jesus. I feel like I'm on a Sunday morning talk show. Kate shook her head. "Of course not. I want to open a discussion, but I also need to maintain my credibility." *And my job.*

Elle thought for a moment. "It's not like you'd be the first to suggest such a thing. There's a reasonably strong history of attempts at weather manipulation and control that you could use to ground your suspicions. You don't go into that at all in your paper, but it could help you in your presentation."

"Like cloud seeding for agricultural purposes, and what the Chinese intend to do to keep the rain away from the sites of the Beijing Olympics?" Kate asked with a grin. "That's not only old news, it's mild with respect to what I'm talking about. My storms show major escalations that defy explanation. If there's any sort of weather manipulation going on, it would be more like the 'mad scientist' variety." Her smile faded. "Cloud seeding has been done for decades. It's very simple, very controlled, and it produces rainfall. It doesn't cause clouds to explode into thunderheads that rise a few thousand feet in two or three minutes, and it sure as hell doesn't cause unexpected flooding in the desert in the middle of the night."

"Are you going to let Mr. Thompson see your paper?"

The urge to squirm in her seat was strong, but Kate remained still and met Elle's eyes. "I wasn't planning to. Davis Lee already approved it."

"Do you know if he's read it?"

"I presume he has. He should have by now, but it's not really his thing. He thinks my interest in these storms is kind of silly. As is submitting a paper that doesn't offer any conclusions." Kate shrugged with a casualness that she didn't quite feel and reached for the bottle of water on the cluttered windowsill. "Davis Lee's interest in weather is pretty much limited to its effects on the company's portfolio. And his social life."

"Which is busy, I'm sure."

"I don't have the slightest idea," Kate said over the rim of the bottle, raising an eyebrow.

Color rose in Elle's face. "That didn't come out right. I mean, I don't really care about—"

Kate shrugged. "Hey, relax. No harm, no foul. Even if you did care, you wouldn't be the first woman who worked here who did. He's rich, unmarried, decent looking, and charming in his own way."

"Yes, I suppose he is, but I don't care," Elle repeated emphatically.

"Got it. So why did you ask me if I'm going to send it to Carter Thompson? Why would I? And how do you know so much about the history of weather manipulation, by the way?"

Elle was quiet for a moment before meeting Kate's eyes. "I've been researching it a little bit. Mr. Thompson used to be into that sort of thing back when he was an undergraduate."

"Did he publish?"

"Sort of. He was cited in some books."

Kate absorbed this for a minute, an unpleasant itch bothering the back of her brain. "I've been doing research on this for a few months and I've never come across his name. What kind of books cited him? And what kind of issues was he writing about?"

"I wouldn't call them science books," Elle said bluntly. "Junk science, maybe. They were published in the middle to late fifties and they were fringe, even at the time. I mean, one of the authors also wrote books on how to build your own bomb shelter."

"But what did they say about weather manipulation?"

"Mostly pretty nutty stuff. That towing icebergs to the equator would stop hurricanes from forming and that dropping bombs into hurricanes would stop them in their tracks. That the winter weather that helped defeat Hitler's march through Russia was manufactured. That the great drought during the Depression was a communist experiment." She rolled her eyes. "Talk about straining the limits of credibility."

"But they quoted Carter Thompson? He was writing that kind of stuff?"

"Yes, they quoted him, but no, he wasn't supporting their ideas. His papers seemed more to flirt with the idea of manipulation than come right out and declare it was happening. He was more or less pushing the notion that it wasn't outside the realm of possibility, and that one day it would be a reality. He stopped short of saying how that would happen." Elle crossed her long legs and rested her elbow on the arm of the chair and her chin on her palm. "Maybe we shouldn't be so surprised, though. I suppose it went along with the era. You know, it seems like back then you were either into the whole Cold War mentality—Cuba, Russia, Reds hiding behind every American flag—or getting into the beatnik frame of mind. Peace, love, and flower power. And then there was the whole Buck Rogers thing, too."

Kate absorbed that for a moment, then shook her head. "It's still weird. He was a government scientist."

"Not when he wrote these papers," Elle reminded her. "I've already returned the books, but I could give you the citation list if you want to track them down."

Kate held up a hand in surrender. "No thanks. My research quota for this year is done. What are you working on that you have to find all this stuff?"

"A biography," Elle replied. "It's for private publication around his sixty-fifth birthday, which is in a month or so."

"One of the richest men in the world turns sixty-five and all he gets is a book about himself?" With a grin, Kate lifted the water bottle to her lips again. "I suppose it's better than getting him a lap dance. Good Queen Iris wouldn't like that at all. Whose idea was it?"

"Davis Lee's, I guess."

"He's keeping you pretty busy?"

Stifling a yawn, Elle gave her a wan, rueful smile. "I think that's what he had in mind when he brought me up here. I don't know many people, so I'm available all the time." She pulled herself to her feet reluctantly. "Speaking of which, I should probably get back to the mines."

Kate set the water bottle back on the windowsill and let her chair return to the upright and businesslike position. "Don't let him take up all your time. New York is a great city. Make sure you enjoy it."

"I like it here," Elle conceded, her hand on the doorknob. "But it's so big. It's hard to know where to go and what to do. Sometimes there are too many choices, and other times

I don't feel like going places alone. That's getting old," she replied, looking away as her voice dropped to a murmur. It was an affecting gesture, which made Kate wonder if it was genuine or if she was angling for an invitation.

"How long have you been here?"

"About a month."

"Have you been to any outdoor concerts? Practically every park in the city has something going on during the weekends."

Elle met her eyes and shook her head. "Not yet."

"Well, if you're interested, a few friends and I are heading out for some drinks and then over to Battery Park tonight. There's some local jazz-reggae fusion festival." She lifted her shoulders with a laugh. "Not my idea, but I'm going along with it. Why don't you join us? It will be casual and even if the music is lousy, the people-watching should be interesting. I keep having this image of metrosexuals sporting tie-dyed silk shirts and blond baby dreadlocks getting a totally civilized high by taking hits of designer pot with sterling silver, engraved roach clips."

Elle laughed but behind it looked genuinely surprised. "Kate, I wasn't—"

"I know."

Elle paused for a second, then smiled the first genuine smile Kate had seen cross her face. "Really? That's awfully nice of you. You're sure it would be okay with your friends?"

"Of course. I'll e-mail you about where and when we're going to meet up. It will probably be around eight thirty or so. See ya later."

Friday, July 13, 3:45 P.M., the Pentagon, Washington, D.C.

The first thing Jake noticed when he walked into the conference room was that of the dozen or so people in the room, he was one of only three who weren't in uniform. Tom Taylor and Candy were the other two. Even as the meeting got started, Jake was still reeling a little from the high-speed briefing he'd received from Candy on the drive over from Langley. Stealth aircraft and weather manipulation equipment. Terrorists and wartime terminology.

It wasn't quite what he'd expected to be dealing with when he'd decided to go for a doctorate in climatology.

Tom turned, fixing those mostly dead eyes on Jake's. "What's with this storm?"

"At the moment, it's stalled east-northeast of Puerto Rico after traveling at a fairly slow but steady clip for the last forty-eight hours."

"After that sudden build-up, why is it stalled?"

Jake shrugged. "It happens sometimes. No one really knows why. In 1998, Mitch stalled for thirty-nine hours off the coast of Honduras."

"And then died."

"After blasting the hell out of Honduras, eastern Mexico, and a whole bunch of Caribbean islands, it died a very slow and highly destructive death," Jake corrected.

"So is this one going to die soon?"

"There's no way to tell for sure. Its barometric pressure is still dropping, and its wind speeds are staying steady. It's still a Category 2, so it's not a big concern right now, especially if it stays at sea." He shrugged. "It could start moving at any time, or it could dissipate."

Tom looked bored. "Jake, are we looking at fifty-fifty odds?"

"I doubt it. My gut is telling me that it's not going to disappear any time soon. The sea surface temperature down there is just too hospitable."

"Anything we can do to change that?" Tom asked.

All around the table, heads shook silently.

He frowned. "Well, let's start thinking about that. I have a bad feeling that this storm is not going away. Not until we find out who's behind it." Abruptly he stopped talking and pulled his Blackberry from the clip hanging from his belt, looked at the screen, then stood up. "I have to cut this short. My apologies."

And he left.

**Friday, July 13, 4:30 P.M., the White House,
Washington, D.C.**

Tom Taylor followed the intern down bustling corridors and
through a labyrinth of offices to one of the few closed doors.
She tapped lightly, smiling at the man who opened it.

"Mr. Taylor is here, Mr. Benson."

"Thanks." Win Benson, the president's son and one of
his unofficial advisors, pulled the door open farther and
gestured, unsmiling, for Tom to enter the office.

It was as large and comfortably decorated as your basic
executive suite. Nice furniture, deep carpets, original art.
And two additional grim-faced people whose faces were
familiar from Sunday morning television: the White House
press secretary and a national security advisor.

With tight, bland smiles, they introduced themselves
and shook Tom's hand. The press secretary got right to the
point.

"Mr. Taylor, the owners and crew of a small pleasure
boat that capsized in the eastern Caribbean were on TV a
little while ago reporting that after they were rescued by a
Navy ship, they were debriefed by Navy officials about
the sudden build-up of Hurricane Simone. Their stories
are clearly incredible, and therefore the media can't get
enough of them. They're lined up to be on with Matthews,
Hannity, and Larry King, and that's just tonight. They're
making it sound like there's a mad scientist at large, and
implying government-backed experimentation. Reporters
are crawling all over this. May I ask what's going on?"

Just what he needed. Publicity. "Ma'am, we believe that
the hurricane may have been artificially enhanced through
technological means."

"You think someone's manipulating the weather?" she
asked, more than a little incredulity in her voice.

"Yes, ma'am."

"Who? And how? Does the president know about this?"
She turned to the national security advisor. "Was this in
the PDB?"

"Excuse me, ma'am," Tom interrupted. "This is an emerging issue and I believe it has not reached the point at which it would be included in the Presidential Daily Briefing. There are still too many questions we're trying to answer, including the ones you just asked."

"Do you have any more information on who you think is behind this?"

He met the security advisor's eyes. "No, sir."

"Who's 'we,' Mr. Taylor?" The president's son moved into the center of the room as he asked the question.

Tom turned to face him. "I'm running a task force at the request of the DNI. It's inter-agency, and there's broad involvement. CIA, FBI, Homeland Security, all branches of the military. A few others. Some civilians."

"And you don't know anything yet?"

He turned back to the press secretary and kept his irritation off his face. "We know plenty, ma'am, but we don't know everything. Yet. We're still coming up with a big picture."

"Well, it's sharing time, Mr. Taylor. Tell us what you know," she said in a low, sarcastic voice completely at odds with the cultured diplomacy she was renowned for. "Little pictures will do just fine."

Her pretty, telegenic face was hard. He'd seen more warmth on the faces of interrogators at Gitmo.

"We know that a person or persons have the ability to successfully manipulate weather systems. We know they have recently begun working within the borders of the United States and that they're well organized, well funded, and extremely elusive. We know that there are no reputable researchers taking part in such activities. We're considering it a terrorist threat and have people working twenty-four-seven to find out who it is and what their next move will be. And we're pretty damned sure that they have built Simone into the storm she is by deploying their technology."

"Anything else?"

Isn't that enough? "Not at the moment."

"We want to be kept informed, Mr. Taylor."

Realizing he was being dismissed, he nodded at Steel Balls Barbie and her buddies and turned toward the door.

"Do you consider the U.S. to be under a threat from Simone? Weather-wise, I mean?"

He turned back to face the president's son. "I think it's a good possibility, Mr. Benson, but at the moment we can only say for sure that we're at the same level of risk as we are whenever there's a hurricane in the Caribbean. If you're heading to Florida in the next week, I'd cancel the beachfront room."

"Thank you."

He nodded at the group and left the room.

CHAPTER 19

Friday, July 13, 6:57 P.M., Upper East Side, New York City

Elle stepped out of the car on the 4-5-6 line and let out a breath that registered somewhere between exasperation and relief. The trip uptown was always aggravating and even the prospect of a relaxing night out couldn't change that. The Lexington Avenue line was the city's most heavily traveled route and had the worst performance, something the hundreds of people packed into the cars during rush hour were well aware of. By waiting until six thirty she was usually able to avoid the worst of it. If she left the office at five, she'd have to deal with the crush of Wall Street administrative staffers heading home, and if she left at six, it would be the mid-level managers who had to make it back to Connecticut and New Jersey in time to kiss their kids good night. So she left at six thirty, after most of the Financial District had cleared out and she only faced a crush of bodies for a short time as she moved through Midtown.

She stepped out of the subway car at 68th and Lexington. After she climbed thirty-three grimy stairs, the steamy, smelly, subtropical microclimate of the subway tunnels gave way to the blast furnace of the streets and she began counting her steps until she could turn onto Park. From that point it was only three and a half blocks—about 425 steps on average—to her building, nestled on East 73rd between Park and Lex, where she could finally escape the noise and the odors of the street. Initially a game to keep her mind off what she had agreed to by coming up here, counting her footsteps had become a neurotic ritual. It kept her moving toward her favorite moment, when she closed her apartment door behind her and the public portion of her working day was finally over.

If she'd had to live in any other part of the city, she'd never have taken the job. Not that she'd wanted to take it at all, but this job truly had been the proverbial offer she couldn't refuse. For one thing, she'd been told she couldn't refuse it and hadn't been able to come up with any credible counterargument. And rather than walk away from the future she was carving for herself as a political strategist, she'd agreed to get her hands dirty. So here she was, working for a hick, dressing like a troll, and gaining so-called valuable experience that could backfire at any moment.

Just looking at the carved, graying limestone façade of her building helped some of the day's irritation fade, and, as always, she glanced up to the roof of the building where evidence of the penthouse tenant's terrace garden teased her imagination. She'd heard that the garden was pretty amazing. It wrapped all the way around the building, so that the apartment appeared to be set in the middle of a yard. She knew there was no way she'd ever get to see it, so she made do with her daily ogle. The only indications visible from the street were full-sized trees rising from enormous terra-cotta tubs and flowering greenery that trailed over the parapet and swayed in the fifteenth-story breezes. It was as close to nature as she got most weekdays.

"Good evening, Ms. Baker." The doorman was never curious, never chatty, just pleasant. "Going to be a gorgeous night."

"Hello, Shel. I think you're right," she replied with a tired smile. His timing was so impeccable she didn't even have to slow down, she just sailed through the open door into the cool, soothing haven of the Corinthian pillars and crown molding of pre-war New York. Her thin-soled loafers slapped softly across the bronze-colored marble as she headed for the elevator.

"Good evening, Ms. Baker."

"Good evening, John," she replied absently, not bothering to make eye contact. The concierge had eyes like a snake, or maybe a pornographer. She was convinced his second job was pimping.

She rode the elevator to the eighth floor in peace but didn't fully shake off the day until the apartment door clicked shut behind her and she dropped her canvas book bag on the floor, where it would remain, an untouched blight in the pristine, aged elegance of the richly furnished apartment, until seven thirty Monday morning.

It was the end of another hellish week. They all were hellish, whether Davis Lee was in the office or not. Putting up with his brand of pseudo-polite condescension took a lot out of a girl. At least she was paid enough to make her smiles and simpering worthwhile. God willing, she'd be able to execute her exit strategy soon.

She crossed the foyer and living room heading for her bedroom and a cool shower, to be followed by a cold martini and some culture. As she walked, she began peeling off her nondescript and therefore despised "uniform"— Gap linen pants and a plain blouse—with as little care as the garments required.

Crossing the threshold to her bedroom, she stopped short in the doorway, her heart bursting into a panicky sprint as she saw a figure rise from the wing chair in the corner. Recognizing his face didn't do much to slow her pulse.

He wants me back.

It was a ridiculous thought and the rational part of her brain knew it. So did her heart. She swallowed hard and took a shaky breath.

"Win. I . . . I didn't know you were— Did we have a meeting scheduled? Nobody . . . ," she stammered, then stopped. He wasn't a man to whom you ever showed weakness unless you wanted it used against you. She'd learned that the hard way, recently enough that the memory still stung.

"Hello, Elle. No, no appointment. This was a spur-of-the-moment decision. Seeing you in Iowa last week made me realize that I haven't come up to see how you're doing since you moved up here." He smiled.

It was a beautiful smile, a practiced, lazy smile that belonged at the beach or, appropriately, in the bedroom. But she didn't want it in hers. Not right now. Maybe not ever again. Maybe. But what she wanted had never really mattered to him.

He'd always intimidated her, from the time she'd met him at her parents' home during his father's first presidential campaign. Home for a visit between semesters, Elle had been underwhelmed by Win's arrogance and hadn't been discreet about it. Rather than putting him off, her attitude had intrigued him. He'd turned on the charm, keeping in touch with her and arranging for her to get the internship she wanted. A year after that he'd gotten her a better one, and by then her defenses were gone. She was local, loyal, and too much in love to complain about anything.

As the president's son, Win had a high public profile and was on the A-list of every socialite and celebrity. When he could, he told her, he spent every available minute with her, but always out of sight of the press and any other interested parties. Their relationship had been quiet and private and, she realized later, completely one-sided. She'd lived for him, deliberately staying as far from the spotlight as a person could; in return, he'd slept with her whenever it was convenient or there was no one more exciting available. It still surprised her that it had taken so long for her to realize that he was such an ass and that she—the smart, sensible, levelheaded girl—had been such a fool. That her stupid declarations of love had made it easier, not harder, for him to use her.

And despite the lesson, here she was, still being used, still not sure how to stop it.

Feeling a tense muscle flex in her cheek, she stared at his beautiful, tanned face and reminded herself that the truth about Win was that he cared only for himself and his political future. Even his father came second to that.

He pushed his hands into his trouser pockets casually, his eyes never leaving hers. "No one knows I'm here. Officially, I'm still in Washington. I just thought I should check on you, see how you're doing." The caring note was false and the familiarity in his voice didn't soothe her. It wasn't meant to. "Is the apartment okay?"

She nodded, still too unsettled to trust herself to speak.

"Glad to hear it. I guess I'll let you get dressed and then we'll talk."

His eyes drifted over her and, belatedly, she remembered that she was holding her pink blouse and the belt to her slacks in her hands. She felt heat rise to her face. "Of course. I'll be right out."

"Take your time, Elle. I'm delighted to see you again."

She stepped aside as he moved past her, and she knew the brush of his knuckles against her linen-clad thigh had very little to do with the narrowness of the doorway.

"Thank you, Win. It's lovely to see you, too," she murmured with automatic politeness as the door shut gently behind him.

Gritting her teeth at the intrusion or the intruder or maybe both, she stepped out of the rest of her clothes and made a beeline for the shower. Five minutes later, freshened up, fully clothed in a sleek, polished-cotton Ann Taylor sheath and slim-heeled Prada sandals, wearing her own identity instead of that of the office drone she played for fifty-something hours a week, Elle entered the living room with her back straight and her chin up. She nodded a cool, blasé greeting at the pair of Secret Service agents on the far side of the room. Where they'd been when she'd been doing her inadvertent striptease was something she preferred not to consider.

Coming to a stop a few feet away from Win, she cleared her throat, causing the president's son to turn from the window and smile at her again. The agents disappeared from view.

As she lifted a cigarette from the highly polished sterling silver box on the coffee table, the diamond tennis bracelet she'd bought for herself after he dumped her slid along her forearm to rest loosely around her wrist. It wasn't Tiffany, but it was real, and the setting sun flashed off the stones like the lightning from an Independence Day sparkler. She knew he'd see it and wonder where she got it. Pathetic, she knew, but that was the reason she'd nearly emptied her checking account to buy it and that was the reason she had just put it on.

Lighting the cigarette from the matching lighter, she inhaled deeply, then aimed the thin stream of smoke at the ceiling as she decided what, if anything, she was going to tell him.

"I thought you gave that up."

"I did," she replied coolly, then sat down on one of the silk-covered settees. She noticed him noticing her legs, long and bare and evenly tanned, so she crossed them, sending the abbreviated hem of her dress higher on her thigh. She let the sexy sandal dangle from the joints of her red-tipped toes.

As she watched him drag his eyes away from her feet, she let the hint of a smile appear on her lips.

"What do you have for me?"

A silver stake to drive through the space where your heart should be. She took another slow drag, then leaned forward to tap the ash into a heavy crystal ashtray that bore some sort of crest. "I'm still gathering information. I've sent a report—"

He pulled one hand from the trouser pocket of his suit

and dismissed her words with a brusque wave. "Old news. I want your impressions, Elle. That's why you're there. I want to know their vulnerabilities. Where they are, what they are, *who* they are." He announced his displeasure with a refined, unamused snort. "I didn't expect to have to go over this with you again."

His words, the tone behind them, sliced into her and she kept her eyes fixed on his. Pale blue and cold, they were as forbidding as a glacier.

If only he knew how much a little civility would gain him.

As it was, the look in his eyes made her decide against imparting the possibly interesting information she'd learned about Carter Thompson this week.

She inhaled again, slowly, elegantly, and breathed out. "I know what you want, Win, and you know that I'll find it. But I haven't found anything significant yet." She lifted one shoulder and let it drop, unconcerned.

"Significant?" he repeated slowly. "Would we define that word the same way?"

She counted one heartbeat. "I mean I haven't found anything exploitable."

He looked down, biting the inside of his lip as if he might be stifling a smile. Knowing him, though, he probably just liked pain. "You've been inside for how long, Elle?"

"Four weeks."

"If, in that time, you haven't found anything of political significance, that means either Carter runs a clean operation or you aren't working hard enough. Knowing what I already know of Carter, I think it's the latter." He paused, and when he continued, his voice had dropped to a near whisper that made chills run up her back. "We don't have time to put someone else in place, Elle. Davis Lee likes you. Apparently he trusts you. That means you've effected change. You've transformed him from a fortification into a liability. *He's* the vulnerability you're looking for, Elle. You need to exploit that to the very best of your ability."

He paused again, longer this time, and Elle didn't say a

word, didn't take her eyes off him. She knew he wasn't done speaking, and she wasn't interested in offering him any unsolicited insight. Leaning forward slightly, she tapped another length of ash from her cigarette.

"I asked you to do this because you have the skills necessary for this sort of operation. I believe in you, Elle. Don't make me start doubting you," he said slowly, then lifted his shoulders in a shrug. "That would mean I must doubt myself. It's something I've never liked doing."

Pushing aside all the comments she could make in response to that admission, she stubbed out her cigarette and stood up in one movement, her anger lending grace to the gesture. "At your insistence, I maneuvered my way into this organization, Win. I played the role of the drab little mouse; I caught Davis Lee's attention and won his confidence, as you say. I'm doing the job you asked me to do, which is pretty miserable and, frankly, far beneath my abilities. But here I am, searching for dirt on an honorable man so that you and your father can keep him off the ballot next year. For the record, I find it offensive, Win. I find everything about this job offensive, but I'm doing it anyway, to help your father and to move forward in my career. To prove my commitment to the cause. And, by my accounting anyway, I've been successful so far. I'm finding things. I just haven't found enough to create any meaningful 'big picture.' But I will. And I'll do it my way." She took a step closer to him, not letting her eye contact waver. "I was your girlfriend, Win. That doesn't make me your whore."

His laugh was for real this time, and the broad mockery in it ripped open the wound that hadn't healed despite six months without him. She was sick of his hold on her.

"Brilliant speech, Elle. And delivered with all the profundity a twentysomething can summon. But you're wrong. We're all whores. It's just a matter of what we're selling, to whom, and for how much. You want to be a strategist, right? Well, you can't do that without getting those lily-white—and, if I remember correctly, quite talented—hands of yours a little grubby."

They both knew the Secret Service agents were within earshot and that the unsubtle reference to their relationship was meant to humiliate her, but she refused to let it show. "You're asking me to sleep with him."

His eyes held genuine amusement as he gave her another easy shrug. "I'm not asking you to do a thing. I'm telling you to do what I'm paying you to do, which is gather information. I don't really want to know about your methods, whether they involve hacking his networks, pilfering his trash, or banging him on the floor of the Stock Exchange at the closing bell." He paused. "I'm just awaiting results, Elle. I expect a reasonable return on my not inconsiderable investment." He glanced around the spacious room pointedly. "This place isn't exactly low-rent."

Elle said nothing and he smiled.

"Replacing you would cause a setback for us, certainly, but it wouldn't be irrecoverable. The experience you've gained, however, would be lost, wouldn't it? To you, I mean. Granted, it might help when you go home and try to get your neighbor elected to the local school board, but as far as working in Washington any time soon—well, Washington is a small world with a very long reach. Word travels, unfortunately." His voice had gone soft again, the gentle syllables at odds with his intent.

And there it was in all its startling simplicity. This was a one-way project with no margin for error. If she didn't perform to Win's satisfaction, she'd be outed. She'd be another expendable Washington female exposed for blindly following orders and therefore subject to ridicule and slaughter in the public arena, following in the tarnished footsteps of Fawn Hall and Linda Tripp.

Except that Elle knew what she was doing was completely unethical in the first place. He'd left her without any moral high ground on which to anchor a potential defense.

What a fool I am.

She forced herself to nod once in response to his words and resisted the temptation to argue or defend herself.

Both would be pointless. Because it came from Win, she had no illusions that the threat was idle.

He nodded back, his smile satisfied. "I'm glad we understand each other. You know who to call if you need anything."

"Yes, I do. Thank you," she replied tightly. *Maureen Dowd, your father's biggest fan.*

His smile widened then and she felt a familiar and futile downward shift in her mood as he seemed to shrug off the conversation. It only took a few steps for him to close the gap between them. She fought off a shudder and took a step back.

"Now that we've dispensed with business, it really is good to see you again, Ellie May," he said, using the pet name he'd given her while they were dating. She despised it.

He pulled her close, ignoring her stiff resistance.

"Win, don't."

"Oh, come on, Elle. Grow up. Business is business, but this—" He tilted her face to his with a cool finger crooked under her chin, then eased his knuckle along her jawbone. "This isn't business, is it?"

His other hand slid into her hair and shook free the clip holding it in a conservative coil. His eyes had taken on a familiar warmth that was impossible to misunderstand.

Old desire and more recent loathing warred within her, but she knew neither would have any role in the outcome. The man with his hands on her had a saying he was fond of, and that was "Win wins." Elle knew from experience that the statement was more than just a play on words. It was a self-fulfilling prophecy. Win rarely lost, and then it was usually temporary.

"I have about an hour to kill before I have to leave," he murmured, his mouth brushing her ear as a hand slid down the front of her and snaked around her waist. "Just long enough for a drink. Or something."

**Friday, July 13, 7:20 P.M., Financial District,
New York City**

Like so many days so far this summer, it had been beautifully clear. The New York City sky had displayed its best keep-the-tourists-happy blue and the only clouds in evidence had begun life as contrails. Slow upper-atmosphere winds had diffused them slowly throughout the day, turning the heavens into a canvas of high, castellanus cirrus clouds, what some ancient, poetic skywatcher had christened "mare's tails." They lay before the setting sun, ready to be painted with colors at the higher end of the spectrum. It would be a gorgeous night. The carriages in Central Park would have waiting lines half a block long, and from Harlem to TriBeCa the streets would be teeming with life as the city gave up the heat of the day and let the night air cool it down.

Kate turned away from her window, thirty floors above Wall Street and the massive hole in the ground near it, and looked again at the documents open on her computer screen. She had at least a few more hours of reading and number crunching to do, but that would have to wait until tomorrow. She had friends to meet and music to hear.

Set so near the water, Battery Park would be balmy and breezy, and she was going to enjoy the night. If the music wasn't any good, at least the conversation would be. And she'd even be doing a good deed by introducing Elle to some new people. Feeling pretty good about herself, Kate started putting away her files and closing down her computer.

Ever since that quick conversation with Davis Lee at the party in Iowa, where he'd given her permission to present her paper, she'd been making notes and crunching data for her talk whenever she could spare the time. The three storm events that had triggered the paper would seem ordinary to a layman, and maybe even at first glance to most meteorologists. After all, a hailstorm in Montana, a flood in Minnesota, and a straight-line windstorm in Oklahoma were hardly unusual given the time of year and the geographical locations. That's probably why no one but she seemed bothered by them, she thought with annoyance. But they'd cost her traders some calls, and that was never a trivial thing. Coriolis didn't have the reputation it did because it made bad calls; its reputation was based on performance. High, reliable, consistent performance that rested on *her* group's ability to give the traders the right advice within the right time frame.

Early dry runs of her presentation had come up five minutes short of the allotted time. She always talked too fast when she was nervous, and speaking in front of groups always made her nervous. And if she was five minutes short of material while talking to her bathroom mirror, that might translate to fifteen minutes in front of a crowd. That's why she'd decided to include data about the Caribbean storm that had nearly knocked Richard off the roof and, thank God for coincidences, even tragic ones, that freak storm that had just happened in Death Valley. And now she could add Simone's escalation. She just hoped what she said would start to chew away at somebody else's brain. Someone with some answers.

"Darlin', you need a man."

Kate smiled at the sound of Davis Lee's deep Southern voice and swiveled to face him. As bosses go, she couldn't wish for a better one. He was easygoing, paid her lots of money to do what she loved to do, and stayed out of her way. "I don't need a man; I need a wife. Men just cause trouble. I need June Cleaver."

He laughed, stepped into her office, and settled himself in the same chair Elle had sat in earlier in the day. It was the only one that wasn't stacked high with manila folders, bound reports, and printouts from the plotter. "What's keeping you here so late, Miz Kate?"

"Notes on the mystery storms."

He shook his head slowly. "I hope delivering this paper will mean that you let it go, Kate. I can pretty much guarantee there will be other ones down the road you'll find just as strange," he replied, stretching his long legs out in front of him.

The comment brought a quick frown to her face, but she gave herself a shake and looked him up and down. "Where were you? Client meetings?"

He nodded, his expression either bored or tired, and let out a slow breath. Everything he had on, from his suit to his shoes, was conservative and probably custom-made. He exuded confidence and good taste and was every inch a high-level Wall Streeter.

She pointed to the leather gym bag blocking her doorway. "You came here straight from Kennedy on a Friday night and you think *I* need a social life?"

"I came from Westchester. Smaller airport, shorter lines. And yes, I think you need a social life. I'm going out later. I'll bet you're not."

Folding her arms across her chest, she leaned back in her chair. "As a matter of fact, I am."

"Glad to hear it, because all work and no play makes Kate—"

"I'm not dull; I'm determined, Davis Lee. There is something very odd about those three storms *beyond the fact that I failed to predict them*," she said, raising a hand to silence his argument before he could launch it. "But that fact alone is a big deal because, first of all, I don't like to make mistakes. Secondly, if I can figure out why I missed them, I'll be able to be more accurate the next time those conditions arise. Thirdly, I like to maintain my street cred around here. And fourth, the company lost out on some sweet money because of my inability to predict them."

"The company comes fourth in line? I thought you were a company gal."

"Davis Lee?"

He sighed and rubbed his eyes, then gave another silent laugh. "You must've been hell on wheels growing up."

"You have no idea. So, I believe this is customary about now." She reached into her bottom desk drawer and pulled out a three-quarters-full bottle of Macallan single malt and watched Davis Lee's eyebrows rise.

"Well, damn. Just when I thought you couldn't surprise me anymore."

"This okay with you?"

"I'm generally a bourbon man, honey, but I'll make an exception. I'm not sure which question to ask first, why you've got it there or what happened to the first few fingers of it?"

She laughed. "Why don't you go over to the kitchen and get a few coffee mugs and some ice cubes and I'll tell you."

He obliged her, then reseated himself.

"It was a Christmas present," she said, pouring two healthy drinks into the logoed mugs. "And the giver drank it. I'm not much of a drinker."

"Now that's a damned shame." He accepted the offered mug with a nod. "How am I supposed to take advantage of you then?"

"Like any other guy would. Dazzle me with expensive gifts and get me drunk on luxury," she said drily. "Now, do you want to hear more about the mystery storms? Or was there something else you wanted to talk about?"

"A combination of the two."

"Don't be cryptic."

He took a sip from the mug, then set it on the stack of papers next to his chair. "Since you're hell-bent on some sort of confessional track, I won't lie to you, Kate. Not everyone missed those storms."

The man whose eyes met hers was the real Davis Lee, the financial wizard and smooth politician with the pedigree of a Georgia aristocrat and the survival instincts of a subway rat. That was the Davis Lee she trusted.

Ordinarily.

Right now something in his tone made her wary, and like a cold breeze on a warm day, it was unexpected and unwelcome.

"What do you mean, not everyone?" she asked.

"There were one or two deals called against your advice. Successful deals."

That chill, wary breeze brushed past her again. She shivered this time. "Whose deals?"

His glance flicked over her. "Mine."

The word might as well have been an angry hand across her face. She snapped bolt upright in her chair. "*You* ordered deals against my advice? *You?*"

"Don't look so stunned. I was raised on a farm. I know a few things about weather."

"Excuse my candor, Davis Lee, but you know jack shit about weather," she protested, not caring that his expression changed from tired to annoyed at her blunt pronouncement. "What made you go against my advice?"

"Kate—"

"Don't patronize me, Davis Lee. This is not good news. I want answers."

"The only answers that matter are the results."

They stared at each other for a long moment. His unsubtle warning didn't change her thinking. She knew—*knew*—there was something very wrong about those storms, but looking for that something wasn't reason enough to threaten her. Or shouldn't be.

She thought of Richard's warning and, fighting a shiver, broke eye contact and looked out the window at the darkening sky.

Kate looked like she'd just finished a sprint, as if there was too much adrenaline and not enough oxygen in her blood. That was fine. He'd let her poach in her own hot water for as long as she needed to.

Davis Lee leaned back in the chair in Kate's cluttered office and took another sip of the scotch. How anybody could stand the stuff was beyond him. It smelled worse than a mange bath and tasted like kerosene. A nice, smooth bourbon, like the eighteen-year-old Elijah Craig he had waiting for him in his own office, was what he would have preferred, but it went against a Southerner's nature to turn down a hospitable invitation. Besides, he had business to discuss, and this sort of business was always better conducted with a drink in hand and no one else around.

"What were the results?" she asked eventually, turning to face him.

"We didn't make a lot on the calls. The other side made some money."

The "other side" was Coriolis Engineering Corporation, the older sister to the boutique investment firm Kate worked for, Coriolis Management. CEC specialized in cleaning up and rebuilding disaster-stricken areas, so her reports made it to the CEC planners' desks, too.

Her surprise was fading. She sank back into her chair and picked up a pen to fiddle with. "You told them what you were doing?"

"No, they spun on a dime after the fact."

She went quiet again for nearly a minute. "So all the staff meteorologists missed these storms and you—"

There was a line between stubborn and stupid, and Kate was closer to crossing it than he ever thought she'd get. He shook his head and lifted the mug of scotch to his mouth. "Kate, don't split hairs. It's not helping anything, including your career," he replied over the rim, and watched her sit up straight again.

Okay, that one sunk in.

"My *career*? Davis Lee—"

"Carter's the one who caught your mistakes, Kate," he lied without preamble, and watched her recoil as if he'd poked her with a live wire. Her brown eyes widened with surprise and she started gearing up for another fight instantly.

"What do you mean he 'caught' them?" she demanded.

That firecracker personality would have sat better on a redhead than a dirty blonde, he thought lazily. He set the mug on her mess of a desk, folded his hands behind his head as if he were settling in for a chat, and kept his eyes, half lidded, trained on hers.

"He reviews everything. Tracks some things. Always has." He shrugged. "He tracked those storms and differed with your opinion."

As he'd anticipated, she stayed quiet. No doubt she was busy calculating the odds of keeping her job.

"It's damned convenient that we have the construction side of the business to offset the investment side sometimes," he continued. "But when these sorts of things happen, especially clustered like these were, it glows like a big red 'kick-me' sign in his eyes." He let out a heavy sigh. "You know I don't like having to 'manage' you, Kate, and that's why I let you be. But I have to warn you, darlin'. You're on his radar screen now, and that's not a good place to be."

"But you don't want me to try to find the problem?"

She was incredulous and he wished she weren't. That she was too damned stubborn by half was only part of her problem. Not knowing when to keep her mouth shut, that was the other.

"That's right. I don't," he said.

"Why not?"

For Christ's sake, woman, stand down. "It's a matter of perspective, Kate. One perspective is that there's an environmental variable out there that went undetected for each storm." He paused for a beat. "Another is that the one constant across the three storms was the forecaster." He took another sip of the mange bath and tried to look sympathetic.

She tossed her long hair over her shoulder and maintained eye contact, but the hand gripping the pen was white-knuckled.

It was a good start.

"Cut to the chase, Davis Lee. Am I a short-timer?" she demanded after a moment.

"Not yet. It hasn't happened often enough. But the next time might make it often enough."

"What do I do?"

"Pay attention to what matters, Kate, and that's the future. Move on. The word is 'focus.' "

She let out a harsh breath and reached for the mug, then lifted it to her lips. "If I focus any more both of my eyes will merge into one," she muttered.

Mission accomplished.

Davis Lee stood up, then bent to pick up his duffle with one hand and his scotch with the other. "Duck and cover, Kate. I have no idea what the hell it is you do, so I can't tell you how to do it better. Buy some new software. Get some new hardware. Hire another college kid. Just stay crouched in the tall grass and try to make sure it doesn't happen again. It would be a damned shame to lose you."

He walked out of her office, crossed the quiet and mostly empty trading floor it flanked, and headed for the kitchen, where he dumped the remains of the scotch in the sink and rinsed out the mug. Once back in his own office at the far end of the floor, he shut the door and poured himself a real drink in the short, heavy, chilled Baccarat tumblers he favored. Settling into his chair, he let God's gift to Southerners slide down his throat and swiveled to watch the darkening city come to life.

Why the hell was Kate getting her panties in a bunch? The whole conversation had been bullshit, designed to rattle her branches. Carter didn't give a rat's ass about missing those storms, but she'd set herself up for it by going on about them. Who the hell knew if it would work. The woman was a street fighter. A bird dog that wouldn't come in from the field despite a lack of prey.

She hated to lose, hated to fail. She might be unpredictable, but her results were pretty damned consistent, which made the firms' margins consistently high. That's why he needed her focused on her job and not trailing her fingers in water best left alone. He couldn't afford to lose her, but he wasn't about to let her know that. There was no point in letting her get cocky.

Davis Lee swirled his drink, idly listening to the two

artificial ice cubes bump dully against the crystal. Real ice would have sounded better, but he preferred the taste of liquid gold unsullied.

Sooner or later Kate would figure out that Carter Thompson didn't care about the odd failure as long as he profited somewhere along the line. And it was rare that he didn't.

The story was that Carter was a poor farm boy from Iowa who put himself through school working construction sites until he'd started getting enough scholarships and grants to support himself. But after ten years in a dead-end mid-level job as a NOAA bureaucrat, he'd left low-paying government work to return to profitable pursuits by starting up a small construction company. Odd choice for a University of Chicago–trained meteorologist, but it had to have been the only thing open to him. What reasonable person would hire him? He was an arrogant bastard behind that grass-chewing, toe-in-the-sand façade. Nevertheless, all that hard work made him the down-home billionaire he was today.

Carter Thompson was Everyman and he'd achieved the American Dream.

That's the story the PR department spewed on a regular basis anyway. It had to be horseshit, even though Davis Lee hadn't been able to find any holes in the story so far.

Whether or not the story was true, he couldn't deny it had an element of genius about it. Carter's understanding of the weather had enabled him to transform his pissant little construction company into an emerging player on the international scene in only ten years by specializing in emergency mobilization for disaster zones.

Halliburton with a heart was what they called it in the liberal press, which didn't bother Carter at all. The reality was that Carter Thompson had gotten filthy rich by profiting from other people's troubles, yet there was no public outcry about it. Nobody picketed his sites; no whining victims' organizations protested when the government granted his company hundreds of millions of dollars in no-bid contracts. Nope, the nation revered him because he wasn't some behind-the-scenes, sweet-smelling, Armani-wearing executive no one ever saw. Just like Bill Gates, Carter had given the nation a face to go along with the company—a face that looked like the friendly old guy down the street who helped you fix your flat tire, went to church on Sunday, drank Budweiser out of a can, and played Santa every year at the local children's hospital.

America had embraced Carter as some kind of folk hero because he favored flannel shirts over French cuffs and gave the impression that he was still humbled and somewhat surprised by his success. And as far as Davis Lee was concerned, anyone who could take the American public's predisposition to a mob mentality, neutralize it, then twist it into an illogical but adoring lovefest had the kind of business sense he couldn't help but respect.

The man had also become a private-sector force on the public-policy horizon: He infuriated Republicans by giving them lots of money and then challenging all their policy decisions, and he pissed off Democrats by arguing their side without providing any funding for the privilege. Regardless, politicians fawned over him because the electorate loved him. In Washington, that was the only currency that mattered.

Contacting Carter under the auspices of a graduate school research project, Davis Lee had gradually worked his way into the man's good graces. By the end of the project, Davis Lee had been offered the position of Carter's chief strategist and, at his urging, Carter had quietly launched his investment firm.

The general perception from the outside was that Davis Lee was window dressing, maybe the son Carter never had, a golden boy who could provide small-town Carter with the social and political connections and polished image that Carter himself could never achieve. It wasn't particularly flattering, but few people other than Carter and Davis Lee understood the reality: Carter was a man with secrets. And Davis Lee knew most of them and how to protect them.

There were the obvious ones, like the calm, slow voice that hid a hatred for the president as deep and unforgiving as that godforsaken Iowa mud they'd had to slog through last week, and the careful and deceptively simple language Carter used to cloak an intellectual vanity swollen beyond all reason. But there were other secrets, deeper, darker secrets, and the only way to learn them was to continue to learn the man.

Davis Lee had discovered that Carter Thompson was insanely ambitious. Highly disciplined and with the mechanical patience of a trained scientist, Carter had held those ambitions tightly in check until his companies turned seriously profitable, until they hit the Fortune 500, and then the 400. But it wasn't money that Carter was after. The man barely knew what to do with it. He gave a lot of it away.

No, money didn't drive Carter. Carter wanted power.

Specifically, he wanted the presidency.

The latter had only become apparent to Davis Lee after Winslow Benson had taken office nearly three years ago. Life had changed then. Carter had become a man with a mission. His philanthropy had become ridiculous while his companies' profits surged. Both occurrences enhanced his public profile and now he wanted to call more of the shots. All the shots.

Davis Lee had every intention of doing what he had to do to get Carter into the White House and himself into the West Wing. Chief of staff, maybe. Sounded good.

He put his feet up on the windowsill and lifted his drink to Lady Liberty. *Sounded real good.*

CHAPTER **21**

Win checked the time as he slid the heavy Rolex around his wrist and fastened it. Three hours before he needed to be back in D.C. and thirty minutes before he had to be across town to put in an appearance at some supermodel's birthday party. He glanced over at Elle, who was still in bed, the sheets modestly tucked under her arms but outlining every long, lean inch of her.

"Sorry I can't take you to dinner. I'm late as it is," he murmured as he slipped a cuff link into place.

"When are you coming back?"

Her voice held no emotion. She was good at that, playing everything cool. Even though she'd been anything but cool ten minutes ago. She'd been biting and clawing, acting a little crazy, as if it was the last time and she knew it. Not that it necessarily was. He tried never to walk away from a good thing, especially if it was free.

He swallowed a satisfied grin before it made an appearance. It didn't take much to get underneath that ice princess exterior of hers and turn her into something hot and dirty. At least, it didn't for him, and he really didn't give a damn how long it took other guys. If there were any. She was insanely loyal, and it had probably never occurred to her that loyalty was an option, like everything else in life.

"I couldn't say. This trip was spontaneous." He didn't bother looking at her as he smoothed his shirttails flat and gathered his pants around himself. "I'm heading to Paris at the end of next week for those trade talks. I'll be gone about ten days. Too bad you can't get away for a long weekend over there. I know I'll be in the mood for some R and R at the end of it all."

"I didn't say I couldn't."

He glanced at her again and flashed her a smile. "You have a big job to do right here, Elle, and I can't afford to have you gone for four days."

She shifted from her side to her back and leaned against the pillows, sliding that silky hair away from her face. "I might be done by then."

"By when?"

"A few weeks from now."

"You won't be."

Her face tightened, but her voice remained even. "How do you know?"

"Because you'll be done when I say you're done, that's how," he said without skipping a beat.

"What's the real point of what I'm doing, Win?"

Other women would have gone pouty by now, but not Elle. She really would be a great asset once she got over that trusting streak. It was the only unsophisticated thing about her. And it was so unprofessional.

"You don't know?"

She let out a breath that revealed some of her exaspera-tion. "Look, I know there has to be more to it than just find-ing whatever dirt is out there on Carter Thompson. He's a Midwestern businessman and a tree and cloud hugger in his spare time, and the public loves him. I understand that you want to neutralize a potential threat, but what is it you want me to find? There are no women to unearth, no bad business deals, no dishonorable actions, no criminal activ-ity. The guy has never smoked a cigarette, looked at porn, or drunk anything stronger than coffee." She shrugged, dis-playing annoyance that was probably much greater than the gesture indicated. "Knowing what you want to know would help me synthesize things and fashion them into a big picture. Right now I'm just collecting facts and impres-sions, Win. Give me enough information so that I can arrange what I've got in some semblance of, I don't know, coherency." She tossed the sheet away from her and swung her legs over the side of the bed in a smooth motion that he found elegant and erotic, and he knew he could be persuaded to forgo the birthday party.

Still sitting on the bed, Elle bent from the waist to pick up her dress from the floor and slipped it on, then smoothed her hair together, flipped it around a few times, and clamped some sort of a clip around it.

She walked toward him, not a hint of playfulness or desire on her face, just taut irritation. Barely out of arm's reach, she stopped and leaned one sleek shoulder against the closed bedroom door. "So? Are you going to tell me what's the real fascination with Carter Thompson? He's a big contributor even though he's an outspoken critic of your father. Why is he worthy of so much of my time and your money?"

Ignoring her questions, Win just said, "I want to fuck you again. Right now."

She lifted an eyebrow and her mouth tightened, turning slightly down at the edges. "What a charming sentiment. Thank you, Win. Unfortunately, I have plans for this evening and have to be somewhere in half an hour. Are you going to answer my question?"

He took a step toward her, then reached out and slid a finger down her bare arm. "No, I'm not. Figure it out on your own. You're a smart girl. Come on, Elle. Once more."

"No."

"Where are you going?"

She glanced away and waited one or two breaths before answering. "The Union League Club."

His hand stilled. "For only being here a month, you sure are moving in the right circles."

She said nothing and a distinct sense of unease settled into the back of his mind.

"Who are you meeting?"

She remained silent for another moment, returning her eyes to his and holding his gaze with one that was as cool as the air blowing down on them from the ceiling vents.

"Davis Lee, actually. We're going to have a drink. Perhaps you're right, Win. Maybe I can find out on my own what your fascination is."

After a split second of holding his breath in surprise, Win's reaction was to laugh. *She's threatening me.*

Stepping back from her, he finished buckling his belt, slipped on his Ferragamo loafers, and reached for his jacket. "I have no doubt you'll be able to do just that, Elle, in your own thorough, and thoroughly enjoyable, way." He cupped one of her breasts in his hand and brought his face close to hers. "Just keep one thing in mind, darling. Remember who's paying your salary."

"It's always on my mind, Win. You both are."

Little bitch. He was so God-damned hard— He brought his mouth onto hers, pressing her back to the door, grinding his hips into hers as his free hand snaked up her dress to grab her tight, naked ass.

She didn't participate and she didn't push him away, but her eyes were spitting cold fire at him when he lifted his head. He didn't give a damn. "I like your games, Elle," he said, catching his breath. "They're very sexy, and so are you. And I still want to fuck you."

He took a step back and reached for the door handle next to her hip. She moved away.

"The feeling's entirely mutual, Win," she said softly, giving him a cold smile.

CHAPTER **22**

The storm had remained in place for nearly thirty hours, spinning at a constant speed and gaining breadth. The marine wildlife that could move away from all the turbulence below the storm did so, leaving the coral and the less mobile creatures to be battered by the relentless action of the

*waves and the debris that got caught in the vortex and then
flung out or forced down to crushing depths.*

*The sea around the storm rose in response and pushed out
from the core in surging concentricities. Thrust forward by
the heavy winds, some of the waves would travel great distances and diminish on their way to somewhere or nowhere.
Others retained their full power as they reached nearby island shores and pounded beach and reef, which relented
without a fight and allowed themselves to be reshaped or
simply destroyed. Palm trees swayed and bent, some giving
way with sounds as loud as thunder, others holding fast, releasing their fronds and fruits as missiles. Islanders huddled
in suddenly puny man-made structures, waiting for respite
as they listened to the violent changes taking place around
them and praying the wind and the water would spare their
lives and their livings. Others, seeking danger or feigning
courage, faced the storm unarmed, challenging its superiority, questioning its strength, as they waded through surging
streets to tempt their fate. One by one they would learn the
lesson of a lifetime.*

*An electrical power line, freed by the wind and excited
by the water, arched and coiled in mid-air, snapping to the
ground and up again with the erratic, violent chicanes of
a freshly beheaded snake. Mesmerized by the sight and the
sparks, one of the rain-soaked men watched the wire's
fevered dance as he clung to the metal pole of a flailing
street sign. Attempting to remain stationary in the face of
the terrifying wind, he reacted too slowly when the hiss-
ing, fire-spewing black serpent reached for him.*

*Searing pain and paralysis seized him as the unleashed
force of Vulcan threw him into the air and then smashed
him to the ground. Retching, writhing, screaming as his
soft tissues cooked slowly, he finally tore free of its angry,
convulsive grip and lay twitching in the street, barely
breathing. The wire, a thin black whip against the furious
sky, lashed forward again, hurling his limp body like a
child's toy toward the grasping fingers of the encroaching
sea.*

Nearby, speechless with disbelief and terror, the man's friends watched the surging waves push his body along the roadway until it was thrust again and again with increasing urgency onto the sharply splintered carcass of a fallen tree. Spurred by belated courage and sheer foolhardiness, one man broke from the dazed pack and ran to his friend, intent on saving if not his life, at least his body from the anonymity of a watery grave.

The wind screaming in his ears and the rain pelting him like gravel shot from beneath an angrily spinning wheel focused his attention as it had never been focused before until he reached the smoking, lifeless corpse. Grasping the collar of his friend's favorite now-charred and sodden shirt, he meant to drag the body toward a safer haven. He no sooner turned than he stopped abruptly to watch in fascinated horror as the severed heads of his other two friends bounced down the street as if part of a macabre wind-driven game of boules. Their decapitated bodies were still standing, propped against the ravaged building by the bloody, twisted length of galvanized steel roofing that had sheltered them all just seconds before.

No longer able to comprehend the Hell surrounding him, the man fell to his knees and wept for himself, for his friends, for the world that was ending before his eyes. There was nothing else he could think to do.

Far offshore, the water beneath the storm had become exhausted by the churn and relinquished the last of its heat. As the cooler water rose from the depths, the vortex, hungering for more heat and finding none, began to shift minutely, the stability of its core wobbling as if to begin its death throes. The slight action moved it incrementally forward to warmer, shallower waters, and thus encouraged, Simone began to grow again.

CHAPTER 23

Sunday, July 15, 9:00 A.M., Campbelltown, Iowa

As he always did, Carter sat at the very end of the first pew of their small church, holding his wife's hand, his head bent, his eyes closed, as the pastor led the congregation in prayer. It was his long-established habit to block out the words and let the familiar, reverent cadence of the pastor's voice serve as a backdrop to his private thoughts.

The fact that Simone had stalled hadn't pleased him. He'd been watching the storm carefully, keeping his impatience under tight wraps. He knew taking additional action too soon would have been too risky. It had worked against him nine years ago with Mitch, and the results had been suboptimal. As it turned out, this time his patience had paid off and Simone had started to move on her own yesterday afternoon. And of all the directions in which she could have gone, she had begun moving in the right direction. No corrections were necessary. He couldn't help but consider it a vindication of his plans.

As if she were flexing her muscles while she debated where to go, Simone had gotten bigger. Her eye remained tight and cohesive, but her outer wind bands stretched for nearly one hundred miles and her storm surge was already being called impressive. There had even been reports of minor wind and water damage and a few deaths on some of the small islands that lay scattered around the eastern Caribbean.

Now that she had decided on a course—the right course—the Dominican Republic and Cuba would be spared a direct hit, but the Bahamas would likely suffer as the storm moved toward warmer continental waters. Once she was past the Bahamas, though, Carter knew he would have to take control again to make sure she remained on track. The success of that dangerous and delicate operation loomed largest in his mind, primarily because Raoul was getting sloppy.

Casualties were an unfortunate ancillary outcome of many of their operations, but the demise of those campers in that desert canyon last week had turned out to be more than unfortunate. That event had turned out to be pivotal, followed as it was by those damned boaters who'd seen Raoul make his pass over the storm.

If that weren't bad enough, bloggers had started making noise about some drunken pilot in Port-au-Prince who'd been telling barroom stories about using airborne lasers to create storms. No one had seen him for forty-eight hours, though, and no one knew his name, but the timing was too coincidental to his team's presence in the region. Raoul knew better than to leave trails that could lead back to the foundation, but if that pilot had, in fact, been a disgruntled past or present member of the crew, things could get messy. Some cheap Euro-trash whore had already tried to capitalize on the story, saying that the pilot had been American and that they'd been engaged.

The decision to retain only one crew had been strategic, but in retrospect, Carter was debating whether it had been prudent. Fewer people who knew what was going on meant fewer potential vulnerabilities. It also meant there was no backup when things went wrong, as they had been lately. It also meant there was no alternative to Raoul, and his ability to affect the outcome of the operations. Whether the issue was flight conditions or personnel changes, Carter had never had reason to second-guess the laconic Brit. Until now.

Carter heard the shuffle of the congregation rising to its feet for the closing hymn and followed suit. The fellowship that followed the service was always a special time for Iris, and after that, they'd go home and have a quiet afternoon. Just Iris and him.

And Simone.

Sunday, July 15, 3:15 P.M., Santa Rita, Yucatán Peninsula, Mexico

Raoul glanced up as a shadow fell between him and the sun. He shifted the warming, dripping bottle of beer to his left hand and lifted his right to his forehead to protect against the glare. His gaze traveled up the lean, no-nonsense body of his navigator, Carrie—no last name—who stood beside him with a grim look on her face.

"It's about bloody time you made it to the beach. Have a beer," he murmured, then lowered his hand and looked out at the choppy sea again.

"It's not a social call," she replied, and dropped into the beach chair next to him.

He looked at her again, from eye level this time. "What does that mean?"

"It means I want to know what's going on." She held out a slim, folded news sheet and tapped her finger against a headline in the lower left corner.

He took the paper and squinted at the dark print dancing on the page in the brilliant light.

U.S. Flier's Dog Tags Recovered from Belly of Shark.

Fuck. He rested the paper on his thigh and took another pull from his beer, looking straight ahead. "Poor son of a bitch."

"You aren't interested in reading the rest of the article?" she asked, her voice neutral.

"What's left to read about? A midnight snorkling trip gone awry? 'Please don't feed the wildlife' signs ignored?" He shrugged.

"The Americans sent a team to investigate some claims being made in Haiti that he was murdered."

"By a shark?" He eyed the newly empty bottle in his hand and flagged down the half-dressed boy dragging a battered cooler across the sand.

"By an Englishman."

Raoul completed his transaction and waited until the boy was out of earshot and the first chilled sip had flowed down his pipes before he replied. "He was a fool and a drunk. God only knows what he got up to. He didn't show up when we were scheduled to leave, so he got left behind. I'm not a fucking nursemaid."

"No one's looking for a nursemaid. They're looking for a short Brit with an old helicopter and a lot of cash."

He turned to face her. "Do you need a lift home, or shall I just leave you here?"

Her look was stony as she rose to her feet. "My next flight is my last. I want to be paid in advance."

With the briefest of nods, he turned back to the beach and the sky.

CHAPTER **24**

Monday, July 16, 7:00 A.M., McLean, Virginia
"Tell me again why you think this stuff is interesting?"

Not quite suppressing his exasperation, Jake Baxter looked at Paul Turk, his running partner. They'd joined the CIA at the same time, gone through part of their training together, and still went running three times a week before work. Paul wasn't a meteorologist or even a scientist, but he was a smart guy. As an analyst in the Crime and Narcotics Center, he knew all about watching trends develop, so why this conversation was giving him such trouble could only be attributed to one of two things as far as Jake was concerned. Paul was playing stupid for the hell of it or, more likely, his mind was on the blonde he'd gone out with last night.

Jake kept his grin to himself and increased his speed slightly just in case the reason for his buddy's dementia wasn't the blonde. "It's interesting because these climate patterns are like clockwork. They're almost like tides or ocean currents or—" He shrugged. "They're just consistent. For decades they've been predictable, and then for no reason there's an anomaly."

"Yeah, but you're talking about weather," Paul replied, breathing harder as he tried to match Jake's longer stride. "You might as well be talking about the stock market. It's a chaotic system to begin with. 'Prediction' is just a nice word for educated guesswork, right?"

It was Paul's usual argument, designed to annoy.

As if analyzing the movements of South American drug lords is an exact science. "It's chaotic but not entirely random, which makes it predictable. Certain conditions that include specific sets of variables will produce specific results." Jake glanced at him. "We're about one-third of the way through the North Atlantic hurricane season, okay? We know it's going to be a real active one, but it hasn't kicked into high gear yet and probably won't for another month. El Niño has been only moderately strong and, until recently, we had a stationary high-pressure ridge—"

"Hey, I'm not stupid, okay? I know El Niño happens in the Pacific," Paul snapped.

Jake increased his stride again. "Yes, it is a Pacific phenomenon," he replied with patronizing patience. "But a strong El Niño creates wind shear in the upper atmosphere, which affects Atlantic weather. And if there's not a lot of wind shear over the Atlantic, the storms that blow off the western coast of Africa every few days all summer long have nothing to prevent them from turning into something big. There's also been some really strange weather in western Africa lately, which, for reasons I'm not going to bother explaining, isn't going to help us any."

"Would you quit speeding up?" Paul gasped.

Grinning in response to his friend's glare, Jake pulled up the front of his favorite, grungy Marine Corps T-shirt and wiped the sweat from his face without breaking stride. "Suck it up, pal. You're starting to look middle-aged."

"That's because I *am* middle-aged. I'm thirty-nine and

don't expect to surpass the average life expectancy, which is seventy-eight. But, God damn it, if you don't slow down, I might not live past today's first cup of coffee."

With a laugh, Jake shortened his stride. "Happy now?"

"Bastard. I still don't get where you think this research of yours is going," Paul said on an exhale. "After Katrina hit, all you gurus were saying we were in a new cycle of strong storms for the next twenty years or something. But last year was a bust and so far this year is, too."

"It's all relative. Compared to recent history, this hurricane season will probably be pretty average, which means busy by fifty-year standards. Don't forget that we're not even halfway through the season and on the verge of the busiest part of it and we've already had nineteen named storms. Granted, only six have even hit hurricane speeds and most of them disintegrated before they got anywhere near land. Simone could be the turning point."

"If it ever moves. It's just parked there and it may die there."

Everyone's an expert. Jake swallowed his exasperation. "It's already moving. But there are four and a half months left of the hurricane season and since it's been so busy already, even if it hasn't been destructive, I think we'll have at least nine or ten more named storms and that five or six of them will reach hurricane speeds. Two of them will hit the U.S. as Category 1 or 2 storms. Three of them will escalate beyond that. Maybe one will become a Category 4."

"You're full of shit," Paul wheezed. "You can't predict that."

"I just did."

"What's Simone right now?"

"A Category 2."

"What's that one going to do?"

Depends on who's driving. He shrugged. "Depends on what she does. If she decides to take a ride on the Gulf Stream, we could be in trouble."

"We? As in those poor suckers down on the Gulf Coast, or us? Isn't the East Coast due for the big one?" Paul asked as sarcastically as he could between pants. "That's been all over the news since Katrina."

"The East Coast is due for a big one. Overdue, in fact. But I'm taking about probability, not possibility." Jake stopped running as they reached the last workout area on the circuit and began his pull-ups without further comment. He watched with satisfaction as Paul, older by a few years, shorter by a few inches, and heavier by more than a few pounds, stood bent over with his hands on his thighs, catching his breath. When finished, Jake stepped aside to let Paul have his chance, but as he expected, Paul waved dismissively at the equipment and they started back on the track that wound through the wooded grounds of the CIA's headquarters in McLean, Virginia.

Easily resuming their argument and their pace, Jake glanced at his buddy. "Fifty bucks says I'm not full of shit. We'll talk again on November thirtieth when the season ends. But the patterns I was talking about, the ones I'm seeing rupture, aren't as big as something like the hurricane season. They're smaller regional patterns. Like the Santa Ana winds, or the Southeast Asian monsoons that for no statistically valid reason just malfunction."

"They're not machines."

"They might as well be; that's how predictable and consistent some of them are. But, okay, what about this one?" Jake argued as they emerged from the woods and began the last stretch of track that led to the buildings. "A few months ago in an otherwise easy spring, there was a rainstorm in a fairly barren part of Minnesota. Hardly anything there but cropland. It was a low storm, localized and moving fairly slow. The upper air was smooth. There was nothing to indicate it would be anything other than a basic spring rainstorm. Then, for no reason that any equipment could predict ahead of time or explain afterward, the storm cell became superheated and shot up to forty thousand feet. Hundreds of acres of crops were destroyed with hail and flooding. Three tornadoes spun out of it and destroyed buildings. Six people working in the fields were injured. And then it hit a stable air mass and just dissipated. It lasted maybe twenty minutes. It was incredible."

"It wasn't incredible. It was Nature, Jake. Look, even people can spontaneously combust, okay? It doesn't happen often, but it's happened. Obviously there was some condition that you missed that sparked the storm."

Jake glanced at him. "Don't be a moron. People don't spontaneously combust. That's an urban legend. And I checked and rechecked all the land and atmospheric conditions recorded before, during, and after that storm. There is no logical explanation for what happened." He shook his head and looked straight ahead. "There was a catastrophic rainstorm at the edge of Death Valley a few days ago. You had to have heard about it. It caused a flash flood. The ground is so hard packed in that region that it was as if the rain was falling on concrete. A group of college kids who were camping nearby died." He shook his head, anger churning in him as he thought about it. "I'm still collecting data on that one. The bottom line is that I've come across enough scattered events like these lately that I think the topic bears looking into."

"Wait a minute. There's no *logical* explanation? What the hell does that mean? Are you trying to link it to global warming or butterfly migrations? Rogue Nikola Tesla fanatics? The wrath of God? Look at what's happening to those guys on the boat who said there was a plane that flew into Simone right before it got big. They're getting hammered in the papers. They look like wing nuts. You might want to figure out what you want your answer to be before you start walking that plank, buddy," Paul wheezed as they slowed to a walk outside the doors leading to the gym and locker room.

Jake shot him a dirty look but didn't reply. He couldn't. Paul was right. Jake didn't know what answer he wanted. But he knew which one he was hoping to avoid.

CHAPTER 25

Monday, July 16, 11:40 A.M., Midtown, New York City

Richard had finally gotten around to starting to read Kate's paper, and he wasn't far into it when he realized there was no need to finish it. What she had hoped would be construed as nothing more than a hint was way more than a hint. It was the next best thing to an assertion. Or an accusation.

He laid aside the small sheaf of papers and stared unseeing at the multi-hued blur of weather maps glowing on the computer screen in front of him, the weight of the knowledge pressing against his chest, an awful roaring in his head.

The sudden, inexplicable escalations, the frenzied turbulence of the air—the storms were pinpoint strikes, exactly what he and Carter had talked about during long hours spent waiting for computers to generate the models they hypothesized.

Carter had said more than once that if he was given the opportunity to leave a legacy in this world, that's what it would be: custom-made weather, but not to be used as a weapon. He'd turn a sword into a plowshare, he'd said. He'd help save the world and reverse the brutalities humans had wreaked upon her.

Richard put his head into his shaking hands and willed the burn in his gut to stop.

If the Agency wasn't behind those storms, it could only be Carter. And the Agency wouldn't use American soil as its test bed. It wouldn't sacrifice unsuspecting Americans in its pursuits, not when there were so many other places on earth, like the airspace over the oceans, that it could use freely or with relative impunity.

There was a quick rap of knuckles on his office door,

followed by the voice of his assistant producer. "You're due in makeup, Richard."

He pulled himself out of his desk chair and took a few quick breaths as he tried to focus on what he needed to do.

His last broadcast of the day began in twenty minutes. After that he'd have plenty of time to figure out what to do. And he knew he'd need it.

Monday, July 16, 1:30 P.M., McLean, Virginia

Jake Baxter stared into the middle distance, not seeing the medium blue fabric of his cubicle walls, not hearing the muted tumult of voices and tapping fingers and ignored telephones. The five flat-screen monitors on his desk formed a parabola of glowing, shifting color around him.

Thirty-six and nine.

He was up to thirty-six weather events within nine years that met the task force criterion of being anomalous for their locality, but he was no closer to seeing a critical pattern emerge from the data. That's not to say he didn't think one was there. He knew there was. He just didn't know what it looked like.

The events spanned the globe, and three of them hadn't even been on the list he'd been given. He'd stumbled across them himself, investigated them, and decided they were worthy of additional consideration. There were eight rain events, two of which were thunderstorms that had spawned several tornadoes each. There were also thirteen cyclonic windstorms of varying intensity and nine heat bursts. No obvious common denominator existed among them. The surface temperatures at the commencement of the storms had varied by almost sixty degrees, and other conditions had varied just as widely. There was no common topological or landscape feature, natural or otherwise, among them. There were no similarities in duration and no solar- or lunar-cycle correlations.

From the perspective of having been created or escalated due to human intervention, there still didn't seem to be much of a pattern among the storms other than that the frequency of occurrence had increased somewhat within the last three years. An increase in tests would be expected if a government was getting closer to reaching its goal, so that didn't count for as much as something else might, like location or temporality. But none of the escalations had occurred near major cities, critical supply centers, or commercial transportation routes, and none had happened on or near the dates of any major local or international event or anniversary.

Jake leaned back with his hands meshed behind his head and stared at the maps and charts he'd plotted. The storms had occurred in twelve countries on four continents and over three oceans. When he pulled out the few events that were truly off the charts in terms of their erratic characteristics—Hurricanes Mitch, Ivan, and Wilma—a few broad similarities emerged for the rest of them. All were relatively localized, of relatively short duration, and had caused light to moderate damage to surrounding areas, which had ranged from virtually uninhabited locales in the Third World to small American cities. The storms had happened in every month of the year, over the course of the nine years, and they'd happened at all different times of the day.

He closed his eyes and tried to see what he wasn't seeing with his eyes open.

Look into the gaps. The answers are frequently in the gaps in the data.

It was a statement he never thought he'd hear again, even in his head, yet the voice was so clear, so clipped and British and annoying as hell, that Jake's eyes popped open and his breath caught for a split second—until his consciousness convinced his imagination that Professor Rutherford Blake wasn't actually standing there, glaring at him.

Nope, the cube, the monitors, the background hum of intelligence collection at its finest—everything was as it should be.

I might as well look at the gaps.

He arranged all of the spreadsheets on his monitors so he could see them simultaneously, then let out an annoyed breath. "How am I supposed to *find* the fucking gaps?" he muttered.

Every parameter had been correlated with every other one. There *were* no gaps. He'd cross-checked everything. There were a few charts with lines that resembled one another, but the data points were unrelated, making the visual similarities nothing more than random noise.

Weather is a chaotic system, random by its very nature. That had been Professor Blake's favorite statement. He'd intoned it constantly, like a priest giving a benediction.

Jake stood up and headed for the small kitchenette near the edge of the cube farm. He needed a Coke and he needed it now. Low blood sugar was the only reason that he could possibly be revisiting classes with Professor Blake. Either that or it was sheer denial that he had the best equipment in the world at his fingertips and access to every existing archive of weather data and he was still as clueless as he'd been that first year in college. His blood needed sugar as much as his brain needed answers.

The brain absorbs chaos and sorts it. That's why people always tell you to "sleep on it."

Jake stopped short. *Which professor had said that?*

Definitely not Blake. He'd never have used a cliché to explain something. He had been one of the good ones. At least one of the few who hadn't made such an issue over the state of his term papers. And he'd written a letter of recommendation, too. Jake could picture him. Sporting a long ponytail and a shaggy beard, he'd been an aging hippie with a pipe and a Saab and a wife who didn't mind a bunch of undergrads hanging around their house trying to sound intellectual. She'd actually fed them, so, like stray dogs, they'd kept coming back.

Jake stopped in front of the machine, stuck the quarters into the slot, and, annoyed at himself for getting off track, punched the button for a Coke Classic a little harder than he had to. The reminiscences could wait for another day. Right now he needed a dose of reality as much as he needed a dose of the real thing: real caffeine, real sugar, real clues. Too bad answers didn't come in a flip-top can.

CHAPTER **26**

The waters that edged the fringe of small islands were warmer than what the storm had been feasting upon, and their seduction proved irresistible. Simone moved in a long, elegant arc toward the most easterly islands of the Bahamas chain; their inhabitants began to feel her effects well in advance of her arrival.

Dropping air pressure lent a curious euphoria to the preparations as windows were boarded up and outdoor objects secured. Land-bound wildlife took to their lairs and nests as birds fled, coasting along the strengthening wind swells. Domestic animals cowered or panicked, their instincts dulled, their caretakers attending to more important things.

The rains had begun early in the day, and the wild, duney beaches were already deeply gashed in places by runoff from the island's interior and flattened in others by the heavy surf from the sea. Sea grasses prostrated themselves before the shrieking wind, and palms swayed dizzyingly, some losing their balance and, thus, their footing. Newly freed to skid or fly, the trees careened aimlessly along the land without respect for larger, denser, or more secure features. Glass doors and stray dogs were no match for the impaling power of their momentum.

The chaos intensified in the early, eerie darkness and the storm, when she hit, brought the darkness of midnight where the sunset should have been and reintroduced the howling winds of Hell to this subtle paradise. They blew in from the sea with all the force of the curving, swirling vortex behind them, tearing, shredding, uprooting, and unstoppable. Grains of powdery beach became minute missiles violating pristine surfaces, abrading flesh, stripping color and life from everything they encountered.

Like a giant engine, the dark winds roared over the low-lying terrain, catching hold of rooflines; whether tile, slate, or tar, their secretly aerodynamic edges captured the storm's thrust and they were catapulted into the air, some falling to smash on roadways or other rooftops, others somersaulting through the darkness, stopping only when they embedded themselves in whatever object blocked their way.

In their freshly beheaded homes, people crouched under heavy furniture, in doorways, and in closets, fearing the rain pelting from above and the abrasive sludge surging under doors and through cracks in walls no longer stable. Crying for mercy and for help that would never arrive, they watched their belongings disintegrate and their existence shatter as the storm's fury stole the future, replacing hoped-for tranquility with loss and violence, mud and tears.

As if forced by a giant bellows, the winds gusted, lifting the sea. Airborne, the water smashed into obstacles, animate and inanimate. Crashing back to the earth, it surged over the land. The lucky residents were washed through doorways and remained battered but alive and afloat. Others died, entrapped where they had sought safety.

Her fury unabated, Simone maintained her forward motion and sought new waters to tease her unslaking appetite.

CHAPTER 27

Wednesday, July 18, 7:30 A.M., McLean, Virginia
Jake looked up at the sound of footsteps stopping near his cubicle. Curiosity fought surprise when he realized that his visitor was Tom Taylor.

"Got a minute?" Tom looked like hell.

"Sure," Jake said uncertainly, and stood up to follow him across the Cube Highway into a conference room.

"Do you have anything for me?" Tom asked flatly the minute Jake shut the door.

"On Simone?"

"On anything."

"No. I'm still looking for a common denominator for the other storms, but the Weather Service just classified Simone a Category 4."

"They what?" Tom stared at him. "When? It was only elevated to a 3 last night."

"About four minutes ago. It zigzagged through the lower Bahamas in twenty-four hours, making landfall five times, and then it stalled again to the west of them. It hasn't changed position in any appreciable way in three hours."

"Is that normal?"

"There really isn't any 'normal' when you're talking about weather. Hurricanes don't stall often, but it happens."

Tom let out an annoyed breath that had something profane wrapped inside. "This bitch is getting big. I need to know if our friends have had anything more to do with the latest escalation," he said, and walked out of the room.

Thursday, July 19, 5:15 P.M., Financial District, New York City
Davis Lee stared through his office window at the water and the skyline beyond it. Brooklyn was shimmering in

the heat. There was a lot of sparkle on the water and a sort of dull sheen to the hazy brown air above it. The city needed a good drenching to clear the air, and Davis Lee needed some solid answers to sharpen the focus of his brain, which had been mulling over the e-mail he'd received from Elle just an hour ago.

She was proving to be a hell of a researcher, which was both good and bad. Bad because if she could find things, so could other people. Uncovering a person's deeply held secrets wasn't much different from finding a lost civilization, or so it seemed to him. You could go for years speculating until one day you found the way in through a previously impenetrable forest. There might be a treasure trove of untouched, undiscovered information waiting there to be exploited, but the first one there always left an obvious trail. And in the case of the unsettling information Elle had already found out about Carter, that trail had to be covered up so Davis Lee could synthesize the revelations at his leisure and decide what to do about them. Everything these days had a dark side, even philanthropy, and Davis Lee had to make sure he owned the discussion and could direct the outcome. He wasn't going to let anyone swift-boat Carter. Even Carter himself.

It was widely known that Carter wasn't a man to keep his opinions to himself, and one of the things he opined about ad nauseam was the environment. True, he was on the boards of many of the major tree-, water-, and cloud-hugging organizations, but this morning Elle had discovered that Carter was a man who not only talked that talk and walked that walk in public, but he walked that walk in private, too.

Quietly, in central Africa.

About fifteen years ago, Carter had apparently established a foundation that had as its goal turning parts of the Sahara and the Sahel back into arable farmland, if not into rain forest. It was a noble goal; Davis Lee couldn't fault the man's intentions, but it seemed an odd choice. There was plenty of environmental damage he could undo closer to home.

Given the amount of money Carter had been pouring into the foundation since its inception, he'd have been able to take on a lot of local issues, which could be used as serious currency in a presidential campaign. Carter would understand that, and why he'd chosen to ignore it in favor of an unpublicized cause that was so distant, literally and figuratively, from his daily existence didn't sit well in Davis Lee's brain.

If news about the existence of the foundation came out, and it would, it would be a hard sell to convince voters that it was a good thing that a man living in rural Iowa, who had more money than he knew what to do with, cared so deeply about reclaiming a desert half a world away. The thugs on Benson's campaign staff would have a field day with it, using it to place Carter squarely on the wrong side of every issue from the fate of the UN to the ethical advancement of science.

Image wasn't quite everything, though, and the two inevitable questions Davis Lee didn't want anyone asking were the ones looming largest in his own head: Why the hell would Carter want to do something that ambitious—crazy, even—and why would he keep it so quiet?

The question that Davis Lee wasn't even sure he wanted to know the answer to was what, if anything, did the foundation's mission have to do with Carter's former obsession, weather manipulation?

He turned at the sound of a light tap on his door, followed by a quiet, "Got a minute?"

Kate stood in the doorway, looking as tired as he felt, which made him feel that much better. She ought to be tired. He'd given her a shitload of new responsibilities in the last few days to see how she held up. So far, so good, and the data she was providing was up to her usual standards. It was also paying off.

For months he'd been trying to talk Carter into expanding

the investment house to include the energy markets—to no avail. Until last week. The minute the president had announced the formation of the energy coalition, Carter had changed his mind and Davis Lee had had to swing into high gear. The extra work it would create for him and everyone else was a non-issue. Anything that allowed them to position the company better for the long term and have a better place at a bigger table was just dandy.

He rubbed a hand over his face. "I might have a minute. You gonna tell me this damned sunshine is about to stop?"

"I'm not that good a liar. But we should have some heavier weather soon."

"How soon?"

She shrugged. "Maybe tomorrow. Simone is kicking up some storms on the coast and that Gulf low looks like it's taking the express train north."

He shook his head. "Damn. You can taste the air out there."

"This is New York. People have been tasting the air here for two hundred years. Get over it."

With a laugh, he leaned back in his chair and motioned for her to come in. "How are you doing?"

"Rising to the challenge." She sat down in the chair across from his desk.

"Good. That's what I thought you'd do. When are you going to have those reports I asked for?"

"Next week."

"Can you put them on the fast track?"

"That is the fast track."

Tough girl. He smiled as he reached for the tumbler of icy San Pellegrino he'd poured a few minutes ago. "What can I do for you?"

"I'm leaving to head to D.C. in an hour for that conference."

He lifted an eyebrow, encouraging her to expand on her statement. She laughed and glanced out the window for a second, making him wonder what the hell was going on.

"Did you ever read my paper? The one about the storms."

Not this shit again. "I glanced at the abstract. You're not going to give me a pop quiz, are you?" he drawled over the rim of his glass.

"No. I just wanted to let you know that the final version contains some last-minute revisions." She hesitated for a split second, then met his eyes with something like defiance in her own. "I e-mailed Carter a copy of it, and copied you."

The news landed in his gut with a thud that he didn't bother to analyze. He set the heavy glass back onto the coaster without taking a sip and stared at her. "You what? What in the hell did you do that for?"

She shrugged. "You said he was watching me. So I—"

"Wanted to remind him of your fuckups?" Davis Lee snapped. *Our chief meteorologist dangling weather conspiracy theories in the CEO's face is the last fucking thing I need.*

She recoiled at his tone and a glint of anger came into her eyes. "He has a doctorate in meteorology, Davis Lee. He'll understand what the paper means. I think it's important for my career that he understands that I'm not dropping the ball, that I know what I'm doing, that I take my job seriously and—"

He smacked a fist onto the padded leather arm of his chair and shut her up with a look. "Oh, for pity's sake, Kate, the man doesn't need to be bothered with this shit. I've told you he only cares about results. You're not paid to be some pointy-headed academic. You're an analyst. You think he wants you to do some sort of due diligence? I've got news for you. He's going to think you're making mistakes because you're fucking around on his time. Luckily, that's only if he reads the damned thing, which for your sake I hope he doesn't."

"He might be more into it than you think," she shot back. "He's written papers on similar subjects, and he not only might be interested, he might have some answers."

He froze. "Say what?"

"He's written papers on weather manipulation." Her eyes were mutinous and her body was drawn up tight.

God damn it. Either those damned papers aren't that hard to find or Elle needs a refresher course on keeping her mouth shut.

He forced the anger inside to stand down and dismissed her statement with an exasperated look. "Where are you getting this stuff, Kate?"

"They were cited in books, Davis Lee, years ago."

Fuck. He took a deep breath. "Are you saying that you cited Carter in your paper?"

"No. I didn't."

He stood up and rubbed the back of his neck in frustration. Carter would certainly read the God-damned thing, and then there would be an inquisition. That meant that *he* was going to have to read it first. "When are you coming back?"

"Late tomorrow afternoon."

"Fine. We'll talk Monday and you can tell me what the brain trust had to say about your 'intellectualizing.' " He let out a heavy breath as the speakers on his monitor emitted a soft chime announcing the arrival of another e-mail. Glancing at the subject line, he muttered, "I have to take care of this."

Kate didn't need a second invitation. She said good-bye and scuttled out of the room.

Thursday, July 19, 5:10 P.M., Campbelltown, Iowa
This is intolerable.

Fury surged through Carter as he turned away from the computer monitor on his desk, stood up, and walked to the window overlooking the fields. They were lush and decadent in the late-afternoon sun, the evidence of a perfect summer.

At the moment, that hardly mattered. What mattered was that someone had started connecting the dots. Someone on his payroll. Someone with a connection to his past.

The author would like to thank Dr. Richard Carlisle for his assistance in the preparation of this paper.

He took a deep breath and closed his eyes in an effort to rein in the anger.

How dare Richard break the solemn oath he'd taken to safeguard the secrets of his country.

Doing so was treason. Richard had broken faith on a personal level, too, by talking to Kate Sherman, of all people. And she'd begun stirring things up.

That could not be forgiven.

Taking another deep breath, Carter forced himself to acknowledge that the scales had tipped. He no longer had the luxury of time or privacy. The time had come for him to pick up the gauntlet the president had thrown down and make his point.

He reached for one of the cell phones at the edge of his desk and punched in a number. Raoul picked up on the second ring.

"Plans have changed," Carter said, and announced a set of coordinates. "Deploy in the next twenty-four hours."

He didn't wait for a response before disconnecting. Simone was about to get a place in U.S. history, and Richard Carlisle, Kate Sherman, and Winslow Benson were about to get what they deserved.

Carter depressed the intercom button on his desk phone. "Betty, call all the girls and tell them I'd like them to come home this weekend. No arguments. Send the plane for them. And I'll need to be in New York on Saturday, late afternoon. Let Jack know, will you?" he said easily and calmly, speaking of the company's pilot.

"Right away, Mr. Thompson. Is anything the matter?"

"Not for long," he said. He didn't have to fake a smile.

CHAPTER 28

Crashing slowly through the lower islands of the Bahamas chain did nothing to diminish Simone's intensity, and as soon as the eye passed back into deeper, warming waters the storm stalled again, becoming voracious as it lingered. The tropical warmth fueled Simone's insatiable engine, tightening the vortex and creating more spin, which drove up the wind speed and drove down the barometric pressure.

Building hillocks of water pushed through the surf, which shone in the pre-dawn darkness, obsidian striated with silver. Joining with the morning's high tide and the pull of a waxing moon, the hard sea slammed onto overbuilt Floridian beaches, mauling the few hardy thrill-seeking fools in the starlit shallows. Boats built for industry and pleasure alike sailed upward and inland, coming to rest on unlikely berths from which they'd never depart intact. Rooflines opened hospitably before the wind, and unsecured windows shattered. Every surface that inhibited the movement of the sand-and-water-laden air soon bore the deep, dull scars of fruitless resistance.

The causeway leading led north through the Keys to the mainland was clogged with newly panicked skeptics, their early, blustering courage having eroded with the weather. Too late they tried to flee to safety and were instead witness to the full and indiscriminate brutality of Nature. Hundreds of white-knuckled hands gripped steering wheels as once-stalwart drivers forged on through blinding rain and lateral winds, battling for stability. Despite their efforts and prayers, their cars slid and spun across traffic channels running improbably deep with rain and seawater. Hundreds of eyes widened in horror as vehicles in front, behind, and next to them were lifted and flipped, some onto other cars, some into guardrails, and some over them, slamming into the enormous, storm-hardened concrete pilings on their descent to the fractured, seething surface of the Florida Strait.

Communities farther up the coastline were watching the growing spiral on their TV and computer screens, watching the red saw blade spin madly, knowing the worst had not yet happened, praying they would not have the opportunity to experience it, but packing their cars with their belongings nonetheless.

As winds and sea grew heavier and stronger, a capricious Simone turned ever so slightly away from the land that would diminish her. Assured now of continual care and feeding, she continued her destructive, leisurely crawl parallel to land in the deep near-shore waters, flirting with mankind as only a waiting disaster can, and destroying whatever dared to remain in her path.

CHAPTER **29**

Friday, July 20, 8:26 A.M., Washington, D.C.
Kate checked her watch. Only a minute had passed since the last time she'd done so.

Damn it.

She hadn't counted on waiting ten minutes for an elevator. It was one of the reasons she always stayed below the tenth floor of a hotel. She knew she could handle ten flights of stairs. But in a suit and high heels? She was going to be nervous enough standing in front of the room giving a talk. She didn't want to be out of breath and sweaty before she started.

She checked her watch again. Another minute had passed, which meant there were now only five minutes before her talk was supposed to start. She'd wanted to be in the room by now, smiling serenely at the poor, lost souls who had nothing better to do than listen to her at eight thirty in the morning. With any luck, they'd be half-asleep and concentrating more on their coffee than on her and wouldn't notice if her voice was shaking.

Okay. Better to be sweaty and out of breath than God knows how late.

Shifting her computer bag to her other hand, Kate turned toward the stairs. She hadn't gone three steps before a chime sounded and a set of elevator doors slid open. Wasting no time, she launched herself into the empty car and pressed the button for the lobby and the Door Close button at the same time.

Kate eased into the small meeting room and tried to keep her pace dignified as she walked up the center aisle. The moderator watched her from behind the podium, frowning over the top of bright red reading glasses. Of course, everyone else in the room had swung their heads at the sound of the door opening and they were watching her, too.

Why am I doing this?

She forced a smile as she neared the front of the room. The woman behind the microphone didn't smile back. In fact, she seemed to look more pissed off.

"Sorry I'm late. The elevator took forever," Kate whispered, setting her computer bag on the small table next to the podium.

"Are you ready?" the woman replied in a voice nothing close to a whisper. It seemed to reverberate off the flocked wallpaper, and Kate had to restrain herself from looking up to see if the faux crystals in the chandelier were swaying.

On the verge of apologizing again to the gorgon in lime green linen, Kate remembered that not only was she the speaker, but she was from Brooklyn. She stopped what she was doing for a minute and glanced at the woman meaningfully.

"Not quite," she answered at nearly the same volume.

The glare she received in return flash-froze the sweat that had started to dampen her hairline. Kate straightened up and returned to setting up her computer. A moment later she turned to the woman and raised an eyebrow above a painfully artificial smile. "So, are you going to introduce me, or do I do that myself?"

Friday, July 20, 8:36 A.M., Washington, D.C.

The thunderstorms that Simone was throwing off had finally begun to hit the area and driving had been an absolute bitch as Jake came in from Reston on the same roads as the rest of the population of Northern Virginia. A few trees were down at strategic intersections on the Maryland side of the Beltway, and that had caused ripple-effect backups all the way around in no time. After ten years in the D.C. area, he was all too familiar with the drill. Even one or two minor problems on some feeder routes and the Beltway entrance and exit ramps started backing up. Annoyed drivers were forced to break the habits of a lifetime and remove themselves from autopilot in order to actually drive and make decisions instead of shaving or putting on their mascara or hosting conference calls while maneuvering across six lanes of heavy traffic at 80 miles an hour—

He took another sip of the acrid hotel coffee and grimaced. All in all, the trip hadn't left him in a very good mood. Not to mention the fact that the speaker, who'd probably had to negotiate nothing more than a few hallways and an elevator, hadn't shown up yet.

Good thing I got here early.

He was just feeling his face settle into a deeper scowl when he saw a woman glide with speed down the narrow aisle of the room with her hair sort of flowing behind her in its own jet stream. The scowl was replaced by a choked-back laugh as he overheard her brief exchange with the moderator.

Looking more than a little pissed off, the moderator stepped to the microphone. "Good morning, ladies and gentlemen. Welcome to the presentation titled 'Extreme Anomalies in Local Weather.' The presenter is Ms. Katharine Sherman, chief meteorologist for Coriolis Management.

When you sat down, you found a brief questionnaire on your chairs. If you would please take a moment after the presentation to—"

Jake tuned out the battle-ax with the wicked-witch demeanor and professorial tone and studied the speaker. She had sandy blond hair and dark eyes, a good figure, and a nervous habit of playing with her watch. Not bad for a meteorologist, especially one who wasn't on television. He glanced down at the program. Coriolis Management. That fuddy-dud billionaire's company. He looked back at Katharine Sherman, who was smiling nervously at the polite applause that followed her introduction as she stepped up to the podium. Pushing a lock of blond hair behind her ear, she launched straight into her presentation. Her words, delivered in a voice that shook and moved a little too fast, immediately pushed all thoughts of bad traffic and worse coffee from Jake's mind.

She was talking about his storms.

Friday, July 20, 9:23 A.M., Washington, D.C.

Thank God that's over.

Kate pushed a trembling hand through her hair, a gesture she knew she'd made too many times during the course of her talk and the question-and-answer period that had followed. The faint applause faded quickly and a low hum picked up in the room as people stood and began gathering their belongings and talking with one another.

She was keeping her head down deliberately as she packed up her computer, because she had a strong feeling that the guy in the middle of the back of the room was going to come up and talk to her and she didn't want to appear too eager. He'd seemed to be paying close attention. Really close attention. She'd managed to avoid any direct eye contact, and she'd tried almost as hard not to look at him at all. It hadn't been easy, though. He was really good-looking, if sort of intense and scowly. The bottom line was that you never knew who some of these people were and, given the topic, he could be some conspiracy nut. Of course, the odds were that he was just another meteorologist, but still—

"Ms. Sherman?"

It was a nice voice. She looked up and met his eyes—they were a greeny-brown that she'd always been somewhat partial to—and waited a beat before replying. "Yes?"

He smiled. He had a nice smile. It was nicer than his scowl.

She smiled back and kept her eyes on his. This was a business conference and there was no reason for her to assess how well he filled out his faded jeans and golf shirt.

"That was a great talk."

"Thanks. I'm glad you enjoyed it." She glanced down after a second and continued to organize her notes in their manila folder. After a moment, she looked up and met his eyes again with a polite hint of a smile and waited for him to tell her why he was there.

He cleared his throat. "My name is Jake Baxter and I've been researching some similar questions about a few other storms. I was wondering if you have time to talk about them. I mean the ones you wrote about. You know, give me a little more background on them. We might be able to help each other find some answers."

She slid her laptop into her computer bag. "I'd be happy to. Did you want to talk now?"

He smiled again. "If you have time now, that would be great. Are you here for the weekend?"

Well, aren't you clever? She felt a small flush of pleasure at the implication that he might want the answer to be "yes," then straightened up and slung the bag over her shoulder. The audience for her talk had disappeared. People were drifting in for the next session and the moderator was glaring at her again. Kate smiled and gave her a waggle-finger wave before returning her attention to Jake.

"Actually, I'm only in town for this talk. I'm heading back to the city this afternoon."

"The city?"

"New York."

"Then now is fine."

The tone in his voice was more decisive than accommodating, and to make a point of her own, Kate glanced at her watch again. "I'm supposed to meet someone for coffee at ten," she lied. She could handle a half hour with him, no problem. After that, she'd wing it.

"Not a problem."

He let her precede him out of the room and made idle small talk as they walked through the crowds milling outside the suite of meeting rooms set aside for the conference.

"Is the coffee shop okay?" she asked.

"How about the lobby? Right over there. There are two chairs and a table on the other side of that pillar. I'll go get some coffee. How do you take it?"

Hmm. A nook. Out of sight, out of earshot. "Plain, thanks."

"Does that mean black?"

"That's right."

"I'll be right back. See you over there."

Kate made her way to the small alcove set off the front of the lobby. Well away from any traffic pattern, the seating area was three small steps higher than the rest of the lobby and had an unobstructed, monarch's view of the entire atrium. Sitting down, she wondered how many political deals had been hammered out in that very seat.

Jake returned a few minutes later with two coffees. "Here you go. So, how was your trip down?"

Kate took the cup he offered her and set it on the table. "Thanks. Not bad. I took the train so I didn't have to deal with the rain or the traffic. So, what are you working on that involves weird little storms?"

He paused, halfway into his seat, and laughed. "You're very direct."

She laughed and shrugged. "Just pressed for time. Typical New Yorker."

He got comfortable, then reached for his coffee. "Would you mind if I call you Katharine?"

"Actually, I would," she replied, and watched his eyebrows rise. "I'd prefer that you call me Kate."

He laughed politely. "Done. I appreciate you giving me some of your time, Kate. What I'm working on is— I'm just doing some analysis of small-scale systems to see why and how anomalies happen."

You really do just want to talk about the weather. Not sure if she was relieved or disappointed, Kate attempted to take a sip from her cup and somehow refrained from swearing as pain flared through her upper lip. She set the cup back on the table and took off the lid to let it cool. "You said you've been looking at storms other than the ones I mentioned. Are there a lot of them? I mean storms with weird commencement or escalation parameters? That's what caught my attention about these."

He nodded, managing to swallow the coffee. Kate was impressed, until she saw two ice cubes bobbing in his cup. *Wimp.*

"I found thirty-six."

She stared at him. *"Thirty-six?* In what time frame?"

"Nine years, but I searched globally."

"You went *looking* for them?" she asked, more than a little incredulous. "How? What did you start looking for? I mean, there aren't any commonalities among them except for the fact that they all lie outside the standard deviations."

He smiled at her again and she realized that her reaction was probably a little too enthusiastic. Then again, it was probably just a research question for him, but for her these storms represented job security.

"Well, how did you find yours?" he asked.

"The first three sort of landed in my lap. I was tracking them for—well, it's what I do for a living." She brushed away her own interruption with a wave of her hand. "I was tracking the first three as they were evolving, and when they went off the charts they blew my forecasts and got me into some trouble. The other three, Barbados, Death Valley, and Simone, were sort of gimmes. Last-minute add-ons in case I didn't have enough to talk about for an hour." She paused for a moment, not wanting to sound too bold. "So, who do you work for that you're allowed to do all this research into obscure atmospheric phenomena? It sounds like a great job, if you don't mind me saying so."

"Not at all. I work for the government," he said, taking another sip of his coffee. It was at least a third gone, which meant that either she was talking too much or he was seriously caffeine deprived.

Being vague is not allowed. You know who I work for, so we'll try that again, Jakester. "Which agency? What do you do?"

He gave her the briefest, pointed pause, which she chose to ignore. "Mostly forensic analysis. Some predictive analysis."

She sat back in her chair and crossed her legs with more grace than she normally would, and noticed that the movement wasn't lost on him. Then she wondered what the hell she was doing, flirting with him. "So which of the storms I discussed have you looked at?"

"Minnesota, Barbados, Death Valley, and Simone."

She nodded. "That Death Valley storm gives me the whim-whams. It literally came out of nowhere. When I first saw the radar, I would have bet money that it was a false reading." She hesitated then, wanting to continue but not wanting to give him any idea that she was inclined toward the whack-job end of the research spectrum. All that discussion with Richard had made her paranoid about it.

But, damn it, the facts are what they are and can't be ignored.

She leaned forward slightly and lowered her voice, looking straight into his eyes. "Jake, don't read anything into this, but even if I hadn't been looking so hard at the other ones, that one would have sent my woo-woo detectors into overdrive."

He stayed silent for a few seconds. "Why?"

"Because it just *happened.* For no reason. It defies most of what we know about the regional climate, about the atmosphere, about weather." She paused. "I zeroed in on it and got the tightest set of readings I could get my hands on. A tiny cloud appeared for no logical reason and exploded into a storm a little while later. There are no records of any planes being in the area; there's no record of any company doing cloud seeding. I mean, I turned into Nancy Drew, Girl Detective. I looked into everything I could think of."

He stared straight back at her, no hint of amusement in his eyes. If anything, his expression might have gotten a little cautious. "What made you think of cloud seeding?"

A shiver raced down her back and she gave a small laugh that she didn't really feel, then picked up her coffee. "Well, it happened in California. They're always doing stuff like that out west. I mean, people are growing vegetables in Arizona, in greenhouses out in the desert. Why wouldn't some doofus decide to try to make it rain on demand in the desert? It can't be more expensive than putting hundreds of acres under glass."

"It's Death Valley, Kate. It's a National Park, not an undeveloped lot."

"Yeah, I know, but the entire desert isn't a park. Someone owns the rest of it. And it's just sitting there, doing nothing. Why not put it to use?"

There was no mistaking the amusement in his look. "That's kind of a stretch, don't you think?"

She leaned back in her chair, recrossed her legs without flirting this time, and raised both eyebrows. "No, I don't," she said flatly. "I work on Wall Street, Jake. The betting that goes on there—we call it speculating or investing, but between you and me, those are just ten-dollar words for gambling—what goes on there would make you doubt your own sanity. Chronic gamblers, every one of them, but they have money, so nobody talks about it."

"Does that make you an enabler?"

She laughed and unbuttoned her suit jacket. The sun was beating through the windows behind her, making her warm. At least that was what she hoped was making her warm. "Of course I am, but it's what I get paid to do, so I'm not about to stop any time soon. But there are firms that actually deal in weather derivatives." As if on cue, his eyebrows went up. "Yes. You heard me right. Weather derivatives. Like the stock market isn't unpredictable enough. Betting on the weather must be the ultimate rush. The crack of the investment world."

He put his cup on the table and leaned forward. "Wait a minute. You have to explain that to me. What the hell is a weather derivative and what do you do with it?"

She hesitated with a smile. "Explaining it is a little weird, sort of like describing how to swim. It may not make much sense. But to put it simply, a trader places bets on the weather, like options. Do you know what an option is? Like a stock option?"

"Like the ones everyone got in the nineties from the Internet start-ups? I had a few of those."

"Didn't we all. Except these you wouldn't use as wallpaper in the bathroom. They have some value. Companies that can make or lose money based on the weather place bets on what's going to happen over the course of a season or some other period of time in a specific locality, and that could be anywhere from one city to a region of the country. Power companies started doing it about ten years ago. I think Enron was the first, not that that has much to do with anything." She shrugged. "Creative thinkers, though. I have to give them that."

"I'm sure they'll thank you from their jail cells."

"Whatever. It's about a ten-billion-dollar industry now and growing. The energy companies basically started it by betting on the number of heating-degree and cooling-degree days there would be in a city where they operated. They placed options on the outcome and then made or lost money based on what actually happened. Then insurance companies got on the bandwagon by trying to anticipate things like hurricanes and floods, and now even theme parks and ski lodge operators and beer companies get in on it, and large-scale farmers—anyone whose business can be affected by local or regional weather. So they—"

"So is this what you do? I mean, your company? You bet on storm strikes?"

She stopped and met his eyes as a small warning dinged in her head. "No. We work with commodities. More unusual ones."

"Do you mean there are more unusual things to trade than the weather?"

She swallowed a sip of coffee, which had cooled, and set the cup back on the table. "I see your point. Anyway, no, we don't deal in weather derivatives." She paused and lifted an eyebrow. "Who did you say you worked for? The SEC?"

He laughed. "I said I worked for the government, but it's not the SEC. If I did, I wouldn't need the explanation."

"Maybe," she replied dryly.

He laughed again. "Okay. *Maybe I* wouldn't need the explanation. But I still don't work there."

She let a long pause build, then folded her arms across her chest and looked straight at him. "Okay, the time for being cagey has ended, Jake. So far you've been doing most of the questioning and I've been doing most of the answering. Are you fishing?"

He relaxed into his chair and met her eyes. "No. And I'm not being cagey, either. I'm curious. I'm a meteorologist. And after fifteen years in the industry, I just found out that weather is a product."

"More like a commodity."

"See, I don't even know the terminology. But I'm still curious. Isn't one of your companies into reconstruction? You go in after storms and rebuild?"

As his question registered, she had the sensation of a spider scurrying along her spine and she sat up abruptly, shaking off the sudden commotion it caused in her brain. She wasn't imagining it. He *was* fishing and he *was* being cagey.

She cleared her throat to cover her pause. "Well, yes, Coriolis Engineering has pretty much made its name by rebuilding disaster-stricken areas, but my side, the investment side, is Coriolis Management. We're a separate company and we don't deal in weather derivatives," she repeated firmly.

"Why not? If the investment side of the company is interested enough in the weather to have a meteorologist on staff—"

"Four."

His eyes widened. "You have *four*? Is that normal?"

"It's normal for us."

"So, why wouldn't the sales force for the construction side of the company have an interest in what the weather is going to do?"

She frowned. "Well, of course they have an interest. I send my reports to them, too, but— What you're suggesting is macabre, Jake."

"What am I suggesting?"

"Are you a cop of some sort?" she demanded. "Only cops answer questions with questions."

"Lawyers do, too. And I'm neither. Like I said, I'm a meteorologist."

"A government one," she pointed out.

He started to laugh. "So back to the topic at hand. I'm not suggesting anything macabre. I'm trying to think like a businessman. Predicting a firm's business cycle is fairly standard practice, and if your business is cleaning up after stormy weather— You can't be that naïve, Kate. I mean, Home Depot executives probably file into the boardroom for some serious high fives every June 1," he replied with a shrug. " 'Yippity-doo-dah, it's hurricane season again.' Talk about having Christmas in July. And no one can blame them. It's their business to sell plywood and blue tarps and nail guns, and hurricanes and floods and tornadoes help to drive up those sales. Wouldn't they be interested in weather derivatives? And so would your company."

"Our sister company. And, well, okay, I see your point, but we're not a retail outfit." She let out an exasperated breath. "Look, I don't work too much with that side of the company. Like I said, I just send them my reports. I don't actually generate anything specifically for them, nor does anyone on my staff. Besides, from what I understand, we usually have contracts in place ahead of time. More like, if something happens, we'll be there to fix it, and in certain places, things always happen. Like the Gulf Coast and the southeastern seaboard. *That's* good business."

"True, but imagine if a company like yours had contracts in place to clean up coastal cities after storm damage and then, to maximize profits, put options on storms hitting them. It would make more money, wouldn't it?"

She put her coffee on the table. The acid wasn't sitting in her stomach as well as it normally did, and she had had about enough of this conversation. "Look, the Coriolis companies are routinely named as two of the best companies to work for, and Carter Thompson is a good guy. He runs a solid business and doesn't get into all that gouging that happens with other companies, okay? Now either you quit bashing my company and we get back to discussing those storms or I'm out of here."

He held up his hands in surrender. "Sorry. I wasn't trying to bash your company. Forget what I said. And I thought you had a coffee date in a few minutes anyway."

Damn. She blinked. "I lied," she admitted. "It was an out in case you were some kind of weirdo or pain in the ass."

His smile started in one corner of his mouth and wandered slowly to the other. "So I'm neither?"

She brushed a hair off her forehead nonchalantly. "The jury is still out on the latter."

"Fair enough. Tell me about the storms and why you started looking at them."

"Because, like I said, they got me into trouble. I called them. The traders made their deals. The deals went south. Well, some of the deals made money, but not the ones that relied on my forecasts. Anyway, I'm not paid to make mistakes, I'm paid to make accurate forecasts, and people noticed that I hadn't achieved that goal," she explained, ending with more than a little sarcasm in her voice.

"People?" he repeated.

She frowned. "Carter Thompson, the man who owns the company, apparently has me in his crosshairs. This paper evolved because I need to know what happened so it doesn't happen again."

"And?"

She shrugged. "I still don't know what happened. So now you answer some questions. Do you know what happened?"

Jake's face got that closed look on it again and then he said, "What are you doing for lunch?"

CHAPTER **30**

Friday, July 20, 10:40 A.M., Santa Rita, Yucatán Peninsula, Mexico

Raoul kept his hand wrapped around the bottle of Coke and his eyes on the bar's one television.

Carter's gone blinking mad. He lifted the heavy glass bottle to his lips, trusting neither the allegedly clean glass sitting in front of him on the shabby wooden surface nor the ice that sat within it. The man was seriously expecting him to fly inside U.S. airspace some time in the next six and a half hours and zap the storm shortly thereafter.

Escalate the storm, my ass. As if I'd be able to get anywhere bloody near it.

It would be suicide.

While operating inside national borders was always risky, he and his crew were usually working in places where no one was paying much attention. But operating in the same airspace occupied by a Category 4 hurricane that was strolling up the coast of Florida was sheer lunacy. By definition, it was a place everyone was watching. Half a dozen U.S. weather agencies had their satellites trained on the area, as did, no doubt, American military and intelligence agencies. In addition to that, and much more to the point, the Air Force and the Navy had their storm watchers and Hurricane Hunters on patrol pretty much around the clock. There would be at least half a dozen bona fide reconnaissance planes already flying inside, above, through, and around the lady Simone. If any one of those pilots looked out the window and saw a plane that wasn't visible on a radar screen, life as Raoul knew it would change rapidly and dramatically.

We're going to bloody well leave it alone until it's back over international waters.

He pushed the Coke to the side and signaled for a beer. It didn't matter because he wasn't flying anywhere today.

Friday, July 20, 6:45 P.M., DUMBO (Down Under the Manhattan Bridge Overpass), Brooklyn

Kate glanced at the clock on the front of her microwave oven. It was quarter to seven.

Damn it.

She hadn't been in her apartment for more than twenty minutes, which was barely time to breathe, much less change her clothes and her mind-set, and she was already late. Not that dinner at her parents' apartment had a critical start time, but these days anything could give her mother a reason to start nagging.

Tough.

After spending six hours on a train in the last two days, getting bitched at by Davis Lee and freaked out by Jake Baxter's great smile and weird questions, there was no way Kate was going to deny herself a few minutes of private downtime. She lay down, blessedly naked and freshly showered, on the cool wood floor in the path of her window air conditioner's air stream and breathed out.

Okay, I dropped the ball.

Not liking that serious look in his eyes, and not wanting to learn for sure that Jake had become a conspiracy nut and was working for some official-sounding think tank of crackpots, she'd refused his offer of lunch, citing her train schedule. Then she'd cabbed it over to Georgetown and shopped away the wiggy vibes he'd given her until it was time to get back to Union Station for the trip home. But the uneasiness their conversation had inspired still lingered, and she knew that she wasn't going to be able to forget about it.

Something about Jake told her he wasn't the type to indulge in crap theories. His end of the conversation, when she'd finally been able to get him to talk, revealed a hard-nosed approach to facts and a creative streak when it came to research. He'd been ROTC all during college, gone into the Marines after graduation, and come out an officer. And then got his Ph.D. in climatology.

Then again, the military and academia are hardly bastions of sound thinking. He could still be a crackpot.

Except that he'd asked intelligent questions instead of making political points or wild postulations—

She sat up and grabbed the chirping phone off the coffee table, fully expecting it to be her mother checking to see if she'd left yet. If it was, she wouldn't answer. But the number that came up began with 703.

Venting at a telemarketer bent on disturbing me might be a reasonable outlet. "Hello?"

"Kate?"

She went still, recognizing the voice. "Yes."

"It's Jake."

Why didn't I give him a fake number? "Hi," she said, her voice less than enthusiastic.

"I'm sorry to bother you. You probably just walked in the door."

"Sort of."

"I was thinking about our conversation and something you said has me kind of curious."

Not again. "Okay," she said cautiously.

"When we were talking about the Death Valley storm, you said you'd checked to see if there were any planes in the area at the time."

"There weren't."

"That's what you said. But what made you check that?"

The question made everything stop, her heart, the traffic

sounds, molecular activity, just for a second. "I don't know. I just checked."

"Were you looking for additional reports of the storm?"

Was I? "I don't really know, Jake. Probably," she replied, hearing the wariness in her voice. "I just checked it out."

He paused and it wasn't a reassuring pause. "Are you busy tomorrow? I'd really like to talk to you some more about this. I could drive up."

Drive up here to talk? She stared at the phone. "I'm diving tomorrow. And it's a five-hour drive from D.C. to New York. What's so important?"

"How about Sunday?"

She frowned. "Well, yeah, I'm free on Sunday, but we could talk on the phone, Jake. It's a five-hour drive," she repeated, not liking the muddy churn in her stomach. "I mean, don't you have better things to do?"

"No. We'll probably be under voluntary evacuation by then anyway, so I'll have to go somewhere. Give me your address. I'll be there by noon."

Friday, July 20, 7:30 P.M., Financial District, New York City

Davis Lee rounded the corner to the elevator bank, not expecting to see anyone there at seven thirty on a Friday night. Most of the office had cleared out by six. The executives left for the Hamptons at noon, and the traders left at the closing bell for the Jersey Shore. The rest of the staff slipped out one by one as soon as their immediate bosses left.

"What are you still doing here?"

Elle looked up, startled and a little guilty. "Time just got away from me."

"Bad habit to get into."

She returned his smile but didn't reply. He briefly considered checking his Blackberry for messages as a means to avoid a painful conversation, then decided against it. "Big plans for the weekend?"

"Not really," she said, her gaze flicking back to the polished brass elevator doors. "I don't really know a whole lot of people up here yet. I went out with Kate and some of her friends last weekend, but other than that, weekends have been a little boring." She shot him a rueful smile and resumed staring expectantly at the elevator doors. "The natives would be appalled, but the truth is that there are only so many times you can Rollerblade around the Reservoir or go to MOMA or the Frick by yourself."

He smiled sympathetically for a moment, saying nothing, wondering whether his radar was absorbing the right signals. She was either helplessly naïve or laying out bait, and there was only one way to find the answer. "Well, you should at least start the weekend on an easy note. Do you want to get a drink? I'm heading to Echo," he drawled, naming the loud, bright, almost-hip bar in the building next door.

She looked up at him, unsure and grateful at the same time. "Are you sure? I mean, is it okay?"

Good Lord, girl, that's troweling it on pretty thick. "It is if you're over twenty-one and thirsty."

"But I work for you."

"Elle, don't put too much thought into this. I might be Southern, but I'm fully evolved. And I'm not looking for trouble; I'm just looking forward to a good bourbon," he said with a laugh. "You can join me or not."

She blushed then and looked away as the elevator doors slid open. "I didn't mean to imply—thanks, I'd love to have a drink."

"That makes two of us," he said, gesturing for her to enter the elevator car ahead of him.

She waited until the doors closed before looking up at him. "I've been wanting to talk to you about something, actually."

He wanted to roll his eyes. *Of course you have, darlin'.* "Fire at will."

"It can wait until we've ordered that drink," she replied softly.

She smiled then, and Davis Lee found himself looking

into a pair of blue eyes he didn't recognize; they held an expression far removed from anything he'd seen in them before, and he wondered if he'd just walked into a well-laid trap. Letting out a breath he wasn't aware he'd been holding, he realized that the night had just gotten more interesting and infinitely more dangerous. This girl was no baby.

Friday, July 20, 7:30 P.M., Gerritsen Beach, Brooklyn
"Hi. Sorry I'm late," Kate said as she opened the front door to her parents' ground-floor apartment.

Kate's mother looked up from her crossword puzzle, met her daughter's eyes briefly, then glanced at the digital clock on the VCR in the corner. "Traffic?"

"No. Work. Traffic was fine. Everyone is already on their way to the beach," Kate replied lightly. "It's going to be a spectacular weekend. It might a little cooler by tomorrow, but the rain won't start until tomorrow night."

"So they say. You're going diving in the morning, aren't you?" Teresa Sherman pushed herself out of the faded easy chair and began walking to the back of the apartment.

Okay, so Plan C is the blueprint for the night, which means the lecture won't start right away. After the last two years, Kate knew it was neither a small mercy nor a gift, just a tactic.

After all, delayed gratification is what martyrdom is all about. She winced as guilt instantly reared up and made her feel like a complete bitch. Taking a deep breath and resolving—again—to be more patient, Kate dropped her purse on the floor near the paperback-filled bookcase in the small living room and followed her mother into the kitchen.

"We shove off at five," she groaned. "From Montauk Point. I'm going to have to get up at three to get there in time."

"You should spend the night here."

In the House of Fun? Thanks anyway.

Kate bit down hard on the inside of her cheek as penance

for her inability to be reasonable for more than a nanosecond at a time. *Let's try it again.*

She kept her voice light. "Thanks, but I wouldn't want to disturb you guys that early in the morning."

From her place in front of the sink, her back to her daughter, Teresa let a small pause build before changing the subject to Kate's second least favorite. "Miriam is moving out at the end of August. She's in the upper front unit, the one we repainted last summer. I'm not going to start advertising it until next week. It's yours if you want it."

Her parents owned three small apartment buildings in their neighborhood and had been offering her vacancies since she'd moved back to the city after college. "No" wasn't the answer they were looking for, and they never quit trying to change her mind. Kate forced a smile that her mother couldn't see, then set her hands on her mother's thin shoulders and gave them an affectionate squeeze. "Thanks, Ma, but no thanks. I still like DUMBO. There's a Starbucks next door and I can bike to work when the weather is decent."

Her mother shook her head and shot a look over her shoulder. "So you move in here and buy a cappuccino machine with what you'll save on your monthly payment. The subway stop is a nice walk. You still get your exercise and your rent would be half what your mortgage is."

"I know."

"So don't move into this building. Move closer at least. You could buy a two-bedroom loft out here for what you paid for that shoe box."

Would you drop it? "What can I say? I like shoes." Kate dropped a kiss on her mother's hair-sprayed head and moved to the fridge. A glass of wine was quickly becoming a necessity.

"Don't be a smart-ass."

"Hey, I learned from the best," Kate replied, turning toward the hallway as she heard her father's slow, slippered shuffle-and-squeak coming from her parents' bedroom. A moment later, he came around the corner, pulling his wheeled oxygen tank behind him like a baby pulls a toy.

"Hi, Daddy."

"How's my girl?"

"A smart-ass, apparently." She walked over and kissed his cheek, careful to avoid the tubes. "How are you doing?"

"Still causing trouble."

"Glad to hear it. How did your doctor's appointment go?"

"She wants me, I can tell," he replied with a wink, sending a devilish grin toward his wife, who rolled her eyes and looked away.

Kate grinned. "Glad to hear nothing's changed."

"Well, she changed my meds. I'm going to start something experimental next week."

Kate felt her eyebrows shoot up. "You're kidding." She looked from her father to her mother, who was looking over her shoulder again, wearing an expression that signaled an impending storm of extreme intensity and infinite duration.

Great.

"Don't look at me for any information. I don't claim to understand a thing he's thinking anymore," her mother huffed. "The stuff he's on has been working fine."

"God damn it, Terri, this new stuff might keep me out of a wheelchair for another few months," Kate's father snapped, his words ending with an involuntary wheeze.

Her mother turned around sharply, fire burning behind the tears in her eyes.

"Let's talk about this a little later, okay?" Kate said hurriedly, before her mother could launch a counterattack. "Daddy, let's go into the living room for a minute. Mom, do you need any help? I'll be right back." She gently steered her father out of the kitchen and got him situated in the one chair he could still get out of unassisted. "What's going on?"

"Your mother wants to make all the decisions even though it's my lungs we're talking about," he snapped.

"Did you talk to her about it?"

"Talk to her? What do you think I am, a miracle worker? She doesn't want to talk. She wants to give orders."

"Dad, she's concerned—"

"I know she is, but she's not the one wearing tubes and pulling around this tank, and she's not the one with the nightmares. Nearly six God-damned years later and what do I have to show for it? They got my granddaughter and my son-in-law, sent one of my daughters over the edge, and stole my health. And now your mother wants me to stop fighting for whatever's left." Frank Sherman stared out the window, the clenched jaw and stubborn, angry tilt of his head telling Kate everything she needed to know about who was going to prevail.

Kate swallowed hard and let out a breath softly, keeping her exasperation in check. "She doesn't want you to stop, Dad. She wants you to fight. And win."

"She wants to move."

"I don't blame her. The doctor said that dry air might be better—"

"What the hell are they going to know about this crap in Arizona that they don't know here? They'd know less, that's what they'd know." He pounded the padded arm of the chair with a hand that was still large but soft now, and white, from several years that had had no manual labor in them. "Here's where it happened. Here's where they know what there is to know. Twenty-five years with the city, doing an honest day's work every day, and this is what your mother wants now, to move to God-damned Arizona. Not in my God-damned lifetime." His words, though not his anger, subsided to a grumble, and with a pat on his shoulder Kate left the room.

"Why didn't you tell me?" she asked her mother quietly after closing the swinging door between the kitchen and small dining room.

"You were here two minutes. Besides, what's to tell? He's turning into a guinea pig next week." She shrugged and wiped away a tear with the corner of the dish towel in her hands.

"Is this because he doesn't want to move?"

"I don't know what it's because of other than all the junk put into his lungs by those . . . those animals. As if they haven't done enough to this country. How much more is my family supposed to pay?"

Kate took a deep breath and reined in her own emotions. "Mom, it happened. Dad helped—"

"He didn't have to," she snapped. "He was retired. He could have stayed home. He could have just given blood. Or money. He—"

"Mom," Kate said sharply, as much to stop the tirade as to release some of her own anger.

The fires had been out for nearly six years, but the rage still burned. After twenty-five years hauling New Yorkers' trash off their curbs and out to transfer stations, Frank Sherman hadn't been able to sit on the sidelines and watch as outsiders came in and hauled away the Financial District on the backs of dump trucks. First he'd volunteered and later he'd taken a job working at ground zero. Eighteen months later, his lungs had begun to give out.

Kate took another calming breath. "Mom, he had to like everyone had to. He had to do something. It's who he is. He wasn't going to sit by and do nothing then any more than he's going to move to Arizona now. It's his city. He didn't have a choice."

"He didn't ask me, Kate. This clinical trial—he didn't discuss it with me. He just decided to do it. And it might keep him out of a wheelchair, but it might not do a damned thing except raise his hopes."

"Why is that so bad?" she demanded. "What else does he have to look forward to?"

Her mother's posture assumed the rigidity of a field marshal's and her eyes narrowed. "Don't get snotty with me, Kate. And have some respect. That's your father you're talking about."

Kate let out a harsh breath. "I know. I'm sorry. But why not try this new drug? What's the problem?"

"The problem is that they don't really know what this drug will do, if anything. And for the privilege, he gets to deal with going to one of the clinics over at NYU for injections three times a week, and then wait around for two hours after them."

Kate stared at her mother, incredulous. "That's it? The commute? That's what has you so upset?"

Teresa stared back at her. "That's enough."

"What? You don't want to drive him and wait around?"

Her mother hesitated for a long time, too long; then her eyes finally dropped and she turned back to the cucumber she was slicing for the salad. "I'll have to quit my job."

Kate frowned. *This is getting surreal.* "What job?"

Her mother shrugged. "I took a job."

"Where? Doing what?"

"Teaching at the adult literacy center."

"Since when? You said you'd never go back to teaching."

"Since we needed the money. Working with adults is different."

What the hell? Kate slid into one of the maple chairs at the small kitchen table. "You need the money?" she repeated. "What about—?"

"Your father's insurance isn't going to cover everything, and neither will our pensions or Social Security. And he refuses to discuss selling any of the buildings until there's a real need."

"If you have to go back to work, there's a real need, Mom."

"Not in your father's opinion," she snapped.

"So—," Kate stopped, not sure what she was supposed to say.

"He won't sell because he says I need something to live on." Her mother's whisper was raw, as if it had been scraped out of her throat. "The drugs are free in the trial. But what if he ends up in the control group and doesn't get anything at all? Then he's doing nothing but dying."

Damn it. Kate clenched her teeth, pushing back against the pain constricting her throat. "Mom, he's already beating the odds. He's not only still here; he's still walking and talking while some younger guys died a while ago. He's a hero in the local support group and he's constantly online researching things." Kate stood up and put her arms around her mother's unyielding shoulders. "You know he wouldn't do anything to jeopardize—" She swallowed hard. "Things."

Her mother said nothing, just looked straight ahead, through the window to the small raised flower bed that ran along the fence at the back of the property. She handed Kate the cut-glass salad bowl. "Put this out on the table, will you? The dressings are in the fridge."

CHAPTER 31

Friday, July 20, 9:00 P.M., Old Greenwich, Connecticut
Through the open window above his kitchen sink, Richard watched the last of the day's sunlight flash on the Sound's darkening surface. The night sounds were at full volume all around him. The rain from Hurricane Simone, which was inching up the coast of Florida, destroying a lot of beachfront in its wake, would be here by tomorrow afternoon, but tonight the weather was still perfect.

He'd been a weather hound since he was a child, reading everything he could on the subject, making graphs and charts and forecasts from the time he could handle a pencil and a ruler. Turning his passion into his life's work, he'd studied meteorology in college. His interest had quickly become more scholarly, focusing on the physics and small-scale interactions that drove larger weather systems. He knew weather and how it worked, and he'd spent ten years trying to subvert that, with significant success.

It wasn't something he was proud of.

He put the last dish in the rack and dried his hands,

nudging Finn with the edge of his flip-flop, bringing the massive hound to its feet. "Feel like a swim, buddy?"

The dog pushed past him to get to the screen door, waiting impatiently to be let into the yard. Moving like a ghost through the shadows, he headed toward the small dock with a long, loping trot. Richard followed at a slower pace.

Kate's paper would certainly attract some attention among the conference attendees. While her sample was small, the three storms she discussed were clustered within a three-month time frame, which would intrigue the forecasters who'd missed them. The addition of the other three she intended to talk about would provide another layer of interest. And while her presentation of the data was rational and academic in tone, she offered no explanations, which would delight the bottom-feeders who thrived on conspiracies.

Sitting down on the wooden bench bolted to the end of the dock, Richard threw a tennis ball into the water, smiling at the limber grace of Finn's white body as the dog stretched in a long, elegant arch above the dark water. The minute he hit the water with a thunderous, ungainly splash, he began scrambling toward the bobbing fluorescence.

Kate's storms had a signature, or lack of one, that strongly resembled what he and his team had painstakingly devised at the CIA. That signature had been of almost as much interest to the Agency as their results. It was essentially stealth technology, although that term hadn't been coined at the time.

The equipment had operated from within the belly of a retrofitted C-130 Hercules, a standard military transport that would garner no undue attention from the ground or high-flying aerial reconnaissance operations. One or even a series of seconds-long pulses from the laser would appear to be nothing more than flashes of lightning to observers on the ground who, Carter had pointed out with a laugh, would quickly have other things to worry about. Observation from space hadn't been of significant concern, either, because in those days satellite reconnaissance had been an infant technology whose use was pretty much limited to the Soviet and U.S. military forces. All of which meant that their ability to escalate storms was part of the American arsenal of rapid-deployment, first-strike weapons suitable for use in covert and guerilla operations.

But Carter had persuaded the Agency that mere escalation wasn't enough; you couldn't escalate what wasn't there, and certain parts of the world didn't have the reliability of American weather, where highs from the West collided regularly with lows coming up from the Gulf. The winner of the game, he told them, would be the one who could develop an equally rapid, equally undetectable method of *creating* storms that could then be manipulated. Carter had said they could do it, and they'd done it.

"He couldn't have continued it," Richard said, the sound of his voice breaking the stillness of the night and surprising himself.

It was a ridiculous thought. Preposterous.

He picked up the cold, soggy ball Finn had dropped in his lap. Eyes trained on the ball, the dog moved in a backward prance to show his readiness. Richard drew back his arm and threw the ball back into the Sound. Finn followed seconds later, hitting the water before the ball did.

Watching as Finn swam to the rocky shore and clambered onto it, ball in his mouth, Richard decided it was time to get some answers. He walked toward his house, meeting the dripping dog on the pier.

"Come on, boy. Fun's over. Time to get you dried off."

A violent shake that flung water in all directions was the dog's only reply before he raced toward the house.

Two hours later, Richard walked away from his cluttered desk, leaving the computer screen lit and a number of printed-out news articles stacked in a loose pile next to the monitor. Pulling the three-quarters-full bottle of Irish whiskey from its place in the small cabinet above the sink, he poured himself a healthy shot and took it to the porch. The first sip flowed like fire down his throat, scorching the edges of his anger.

Every storm Kate had written about had caused some sort of destruction in the surrounding areas. One town had been pretty much flattened. In all cases, subsequent local news stories had announced that Coriolis Engineering had been awarded contracts to clean up at least part of the damage and restore infrastructure.

The son of a bitch was playing God.

The second sip went down softer and cleared away some of the fog in his head. The evidence was circumstantial and far-fetched. But knowing Carter as he did, Richard couldn't stand by and do nothing. Maybe it was time to see about a reunion.

Friday, July 20, 11:30 P.M., Greenwich Village, New York City

This may not be so bad after all. Fucking over Win is going to be a breeze and leave me much more satisfied than actually fucking him ever did.

Elle watched Davis Lee's smiling mouth moving as he told another story. She was feeling confident about her ability to do this and was even feeling a little warm toward him. Being in his company was easier than she'd anticipated, and he was considerably more entertaining than she'd imagined. Though the Southern gentleman thing had never held much appeal for her, it had thankfully disappeared over the course of the evening along with most of the man's arrogance, leaving a much more genuine and therefore interesting Davis Lee in its wake. Elle had even loosened up a little herself as the evening had progressed.

They'd moved beyond small talk by the time she'd finished her first martini and beyond shop talk by the time she'd finished her second. The cab ride across town had been punctuated by a lot of laughter. They'd gotten out at Washington Square and walked for a few blocks before stopping at a small bistro where Davis Lee knew the owner. Mild flirting had occurred over dinner, and then they'd laughed about how much trouble they'd get in if they took it any further. And that's where the conversation had turned back to more general topics.

It was with some surprise when, over a dessert she barely tasted, Elle realized that the thought of sleeping with Davis Lee no longer turned her off. In fact, it might be appealing if it weren't for Win wanting it to happen. Making Win happy was not what tonight was about. To the contrary, tonight was about making herself happy by making Win look like a fool.

Setting the china coffee cup back on its saucer, she slid the tip of her tongue across her upper lip and, a heartbeat later, met Davis Lee's eyes. He was so ripe for the plucking.

"Will you level with me, Davis Lee?" Her voice had dropped into the bedroom register, which didn't seem to startle him.

His amused gaze swept her face before settling on her mouth. "Maybe."

Good boy. A smug coziness surged inside her like a warm ocean wave and she smiled. "Am I really researching a biography?"

"What else could it be?"

She lifted one shoulder and let it drop. The movement seemed more abrupt than she'd wanted it to be. Her attention shifted as she saw the waiter walk away with their empty wine bottle. *How much of that did I have?*

"Elle?"

She brought her eyes back to Davis Lee's craggy face. "It could be a fishing expedition."

"For what?"

"A past with some smudges that need to be erased."

He shook his head and finished the last of his coffee. "That would be a ridiculous waste of your time, wouldn't it? To send you fishing in such a small barrel? Carter knows his own past, as does anyone who's ever cared to look. Why would I—?"

Davis Lee, I'm no fool. "Let me rephrase that. Maybe it's reconnaissance," she said lightly. "A thorough dusting and cleaning in advance of, oh, maybe announcing a candidacy."

He grinned at her, a second too late. "I think you spent too much time in Washington."

"Two years in Washington can provide a girl with a very well-rounded education." She paused. "I liked living there and I liked working there, especially in the White House. It keeps your brain limber. There's always another angle to things despite what you might think."

He digested that in silence for a few moments, then smiled. "What does that mean?"

"It means that even after you think you have an issue or a person all figured out, there are still angles you haven't considered," she said smugly, and lifted her coffee cup to her lips, setting it back on the saucer when she discovered it was empty.

He didn't seem to notice. "New York isn't like that?"

"New York is different." She rested her elbows on the table and her chin on a palm. "For instance, on this project, I think I'm finding things that Carter Thompson never wanted found.

"Am I right?" she asked when Davis Lee didn't reply.

"About what?"

"That Carter doesn't want certain things made public, like that foundation of his. Or that early hobby. Or maybe it's just that *you* don't want them to be public."

He leaned against the back of his chair, idly spinning a cell phone that lay on the table. She wasn't sure if it was his or hers. He said, "His foundation is a non-profit corporation, which means that between all the state and federal documentation it has to file, there's a hell of a paper trail. If he wanted it to be private, he wouldn't have had to go to the trouble of incorporating. He could have just funded other groups anonymously."

"He couldn't have directed the research then."

"He might not be directing any research now. Besides, if you give enough money to an organization, any organization, it'll behave," he drawled. "You don't think a university would have welcomed his money and any agenda he might have?"

"What about the articles? Do you think he wants them made public?"

"They're cited in library books, Elle. That's hardly private. In fact, I think the term is 'publicly available.' " His smile looked forced and his voice was less indulgent.

She sat up straight and picked up her empty coffee cup again. "In name only. They've been out of print for so long—"

"Are we done?" His voice held a laziness that was almost believable.

"No." She dropped her voice to nearly a whisper and reached out her hand, placing her fingertips on the table-cloth a fraction of an inch from his. "Look, Davis Lee, let's cut to the chase. I know I'm doing this research for *you*. And given who Carter Thompson is and how he makes his money, this isn't the sort of information you want to be made public. But I want to know why you want it in the first place."

"Elle, you've got a vivid imagination."

"I've got a lot more than that. I've got brains, Davis Lee, and really good analytical skills. And I think you have ambitions beyond Wall Street and that's why you hired me."

"Well, the first few things you said are on the money, but I hired you to be a research assistant, darlin'. That's it."

Right. She let her mouth curve into a patient smile. "Would you like to know how I think the news of Carter's private research foundation and his early fascination with the junk-science fringes of weather research would play on the campaign trail?" she asked, looking straight into Davis Lee's eyes. They were looking straight back at her, unimpressed.

"I can't say as I do."

"It would define him, Davis Lee, and he'd never get elected. All the good he's done in the world and in business would be buried and the Benson campaign wouldn't even have to get involved."

"The Benson campaign?" Davis Lee repeated with a laugh. "I know you said a candidacy, but you think Carter Thompson wants to be president? Elle, you're—"

"Anything else would be too small-scale, Davis Lee, and you know it. He's an entrepreneur approaching sixty-five and he's the fourth-wealthiest man in America. What else would satisfy him?" she asked. "But all the power and fame he's accumulated would count for nothing if he's made to look like a believer in things that sound more like science fiction than science. It would be like Edmund Muskie's tears or Michael Dukakis's tank ride. It would follow him forever and he'd never be able to deflect or soften it."

Davis Lee dropped the affectation of amused boredom and sat back again. His hand stayed where it was, within reach of hers, draped over the cell phone. "Why do you say that? Isn't saving the environment still a noble cause or have I been asleep at the wheel?"

She smiled wider, feeling him give slightly in the face of her argument. "That depends on the motivation. Being green didn't do much for Al Gore's real-world political reputation when he was running for office. It was exploited to pretty good effect by the opposition and made into a liability, or at least a vulnerability."

"Carter's cause is apparently trees, which you can see, not air, which you can't. In most places," he added with a slight twitch of his mouth. "He's borderline fanatic about the environment. It's almost a religion with him."

"Yet he thrives on its destruction. It's how he makes his money, right? Cleaning up after Mother Nature's temper tantrums."

"That's one way of looking at it," Davis Lee said with a small nod of acknowledgment.

"And another way of looking at it is that the synergy of his companies reflects an acute business strategy."

"Yes." He took in a slow, patient breath. "This is hardly groundbreaking conversation."

"There's another way of looking at that synergy, Davis Lee. Carter makes a profit on both sides of a disaster by putting options on the outcome and cleaning up the mess."

"The press has been there and done that, Elle. In fact, they trot it out after just about every storm."

"Now factor in the foundation and the articles and Carter's early interests." She watched his eyebrows twitch downward and felt within herself an answering surge of triumph. "It puts a very creepy spin on the entire issue, doesn't it? Or at least it would in the hands of the Benson campaign. As soon as knowledge of it becomes public—"

"Will it?"

"If I found it, they can find it. And when they do, there will be lots of discussion, which means lots of questions," she continued.

"All of which can be answered."

"No, they can't, Davis Lee," she said quietly, feeling smug again. "They can't be answered in such a way that you own the discussion. The other side won't let you. There's no way to spin this that won't make Carter look like Dr. Strangelove. Think about it. Achieving reforestation of desert areas means years of conducting studies and experimentation. Presumably he's doing that already. But why is the research being done in private? Why not fund existing organizations? Like you said, universities would be happy to carry out his wishes, but he's never collaborated with them. Why? And that question leads to more questions focusing on what kind of experimentation is under way."

"You're quite the little conspiracy hound, aren't you?"

She leaned forward again so their faces were barely a foot apart. "No, I'm not, but I know what conspiracy nuts can do, and if they hear about this, they'll start conjecturing, and who could blame them? After all, what kind of experimentation would reforestation involve? Planting trees? Okay, fine. But trees need water and arable soil. With enough hard work and resources you can create soil in the desert, but no one can produce water—unless you're conducting an entirely different kind of research and experimentation. Which leads us to those early articles he wrote on weather voodoo." She smiled. "And that's when the electorate comes up with the label the other side wants them to use: mad scientist."

"Oh, come on, Elle. Carter's no—"

"Maybe not," she said in a voice that was almost a hiss, "but Carter Thompson is well-known as a man who doesn't engage in pointless endeavors. Wasting time and money is not part of his business model. So if his model is that he profits from all sides of a disaster and channels those profits into secretive research, is it such a stretch to persuade the great unwashed that he might be creating the disasters in the first place?"

Davis Lee set his napkin on the table. "I hate to say it, honey, but I think maybe you've had too much—"

She gripped his hand, silencing him. "Davis Lee, I'm not drunk and I'm not crazy. I'm trained to look at the details and, from them, find the big picture."

"Well, I think you *are* a little drunk, darlin', and you're taking a lot of mighty big leaps in the process of creating that big picture of yours. Bigger leaps than you might take under other circumstances." He slid his hand out from under hers and signaled for the check.

"Am I? The news is full of bad-weather scenarios. Bigger storms are hitting us and the scientists say it's a trend that will continue for the next twenty years. Everyone has heard that. The devastation is increasing proportionately, which means Carter is making more money. And now he wants to run for president." She paused. "Even if the Benson campaign doesn't get there first, I think the real leap of logic is to think that people will see all of this and *not* come up with a conspiracy theory."

She watched him squeeze his eyes shut and pinch the bridge of his nose as he took a deep breath. "It's too far-fetched, Elle. No one would believe it."

What is his problem? "I can guarantee that lots of people—make that voters—will believe it when the president's team gets done spinning it," she snapped, sitting back in her chair and looking away in annoyance.

"I think it's time to change the subject some. Let's talk about you. Tell me, Elle, at what point in your short career did you become a political analyst?" he said as he scribbled his name on the slip of paper the waiter had just placed before him.

The muttered question, though half-serious, was a threshold, and the realization rose in Elle like a spring tide.

Her answer could change everything.

She met his eyes. "I grew up around politics, Davis Lee."

"I know." He stood up and helped her to her feet. "Your daddy was a local big shot."

"Yes, he was and is, but I doubt he'd appreciate that description. What else do you know about me?" she asked as she stepped ahead of him into the steamy quasi-darkness of Greenwich Village.

"Not everything."

"What do you want to know?" she asked after the briefest pause.

"You don't mind taking a little walk, do you? I think you could use some air." Slipping a hand around her elbow, he propelled her forward without waiting for an answer. The traffic was heavy, making talking a challenge until they turned onto a quieter, residential street.

"I wouldn't mind knowing how you landed in the White House," he said, glancing down at her. That lazy smile was back on his face.

"Like most people, I got there through a combination of hard work and family connections."

"Whose family?"

She smiled, feeling the headiness roar through her. *This is it.* Coming to a stop in the middle of the sidewalk, she turned to face him.

"The Benson family, Davis Lee," she said softly. "I've known them all my life. My mother went to boarding school and college with Genevieve Benson, and our families vacationed together every year when I was growing up." She paused. "In fact, I dated Win until about six months ago."

He went very still, his eyes registering the unpleasant surprise and quickly growing cold.

"That's how I landed here, too, Davis Lee," she continued. "Win wanted me to find out what you're up to. He knew I'd catch your eye and he played you, Davis Lee. I was bait. You snapped."

He turned and began to retrace their steps, leaving her to hurry a few steps to catch up with him. Even after she did, he was silent for half a block.

"Davis Lee, I'm not the enemy anymore."

"That's mighty good to know, Elle."

"Davis Lee, stop," she said, tugging on his arm. "I didn't have to tell you any of that. If I still wanted to work for Win, I wouldn't have said anything."

"When did you decide that? What was the real plan, Elle? Did he tell you to come on to me, too? To sleep with me?"

She stumbled as though she'd been slapped, and he finally stopped walking and turned to face her, his anger and disgust evident. "Well, did he?"

"Yes," she whispered, watching his face. "But I told him I wasn't going to."

"Imagine that. You've got morals."

"Stop it. I didn't have to tell you anything," she repeated.

"Then why did you?"

"Because I thought you'd like to know."

"So now I know," he said flatly. "What do you want?"

She shook her head and heard a nervous laugh escape from her mouth. "Nothing. I mean, not money, if that's what you're asking. I want to work with you." *Against Win.* She smiled and slid her hand into his. "For the future President Carter Thompson."

He disengaged her hand. "Why should I believe you?" he asked coldly.

She laughed. "What's your option?"

"Throwing you back."

Her smile faltered as his words penetrated her brain, making her heart stop, then start beating too quickly.

My God.

She could barely take in a breath. "What do you mean?"

"What do you think I mean, Elle?" he asked, his contempt raw and undisguised.

"You'd tell Win?" Her question, a little too loud and a little too horrified, earned her a few wary glances from passersby as he steadied her, both hands on her elbows. His eyes were icy.

"Damned straight."

She knew her eyes were wide with fear. She could feel her kneecaps start to quiver. "You're serious." Adrenaline swamped her bloodstream and she clenched her hands around his forearms. "That would be a bad move, Davis Lee. He's ruthless. He doesn't like to lose. He does what he needs to do to win. I was just—"

"I don't care what you *were*. Traitors don't have a place on my staff."

"I'm not— I'm betraying *him,* Davis Lee, not—" Hot tears burned tracks on her cheeks.

"Don't matter a damn," he snapped, his drawl heavy. "You're a liar and a traitor. The first is unfortunate; the second is intolerable. You go on back to Win and give him my regards."

Panic flooded her brain. "I can't," she whispered, staring at him as the reality of what she'd done engulfed her, drowning her. "I can't go back to him. He'll—he'd—Davis Lee, he's the president's son. I don't know what he'd do to me."

"Then I guess it's time you found out." Keeping one hand on her elbow, he walked her the last few yards to the corner, where he hailed a cab. Turning to look at her as it slid to a stop, he gave her a cold smile and flipped open the cell phone in his hand. Finding the address book, he scrolled through it, pressed a button, and finally put it to his ear. "Hey there, Win, it's Davis Lee. . . . I hope you don't mind that I'm using Elle's phone to call you. We've been out for dinner and what all, and I just thought I'd let you know that you can take your whore back. I'm all done with her." He flipped the phone shut and handed it to her.

Rigid with fear and disbelief, she backed away from the phone as if it were poison. "You're bluffing," she said in a strangled whisper.

"I don't bluff about this sort of thing. Check the number I just called." He shoved the phone into her purse, then placed her ungently in the dark pungence of the cab's back-seat. "I'll have someone clean out your desk, Elle, and mes-senger your stuff to you. And I sure hope you consider mitigating the damage to your career by keeping all those thoughts of yours to yourself. Politics is a big, ugly thing with a long memory. And it chews up little fools like you."

He shut the door, straightened, and began walking away from her. Ignoring the cabbie's repeated request for an ad-dress, she stared at his back and started to shake.

I might as well be dead.

Saturday, July 21, 12:15 A.M., Georgetown, Washington, D.C.

Win rolled over, still out of breath, and picked up his cell phone, pressing the button on the side to silence its chime.

"That's the difference between European men and Amer-icans, you know." The sultry, Italian-inflected voice was right next to his ear. "No European man would interrupt making love to answer the phone. But you Americans, you are always afraid of missing the call, of missing the action."

"We've already finished making love, in case you hadn't noticed. And, for the record, I'm not answering the phone; I'm screening my calls—something I wouldn't be doing if I weren't the son of the current head of state," he mur-mured, squinting at the intensity of the bright blue screen. "We have a Category 4 hurricane doing some serious dam-age to some very loyal constituencies, and if my father wants to talk about it, I have to listen. *Capice?*"

"I'm Italian; I have to say no to that. Making love comes first."

He felt the tip of a wet tongue flick his earlobe and moved his head away. Had she waited a few minutes, her warm breath might have started a chain reaction, but at the moment, all he could do was slip his arm around her and pull her naked body closer to his as the screen finally came into focus. *Elle.*

He let out an annoyed breath and put the phone face-down on the nightstand. Rolling over onto his companion, who rewarded him with a low, sexy laugh, he continued his advanced tutorial in foreign relations, any thoughts of Elle already dismissed.

CHAPTER **32**

Saturday, July 21, 6:00 A.M., Montauk Point, Long Island

The sun was barely up as Kate jogged the length of the dock. The chilly, wet air hugged her bare legs and invigorated her senses. The beaches to the west were showing signs of life. A few early walkers were out, some powering up the beach with elbows pumping, others meandering in the head-down position favored by shell seekers. The lines of private docks along the shore were where the real action was. Greetings floated on the morning air as fishing tackle and dive equipment were hefted onto the decks of huge cruisers, tiny inflatables, and every size boat in between.

It's too perfect a day for size to matter, Kate thought with a grin. *Everyone just wants out on the water.*

The first engine came to life with a guttural roar next to where Kate was walking, sending the sweet, familiar smell of marine fuel into the air to mingle with the scents of salt water and drying seaweed that dominated. Puffy cumulus clouds hung like cotton balls glued to pale blue construction paper, as gray-white slashes of seagulls wheeled and dove above mild swells.

It would be a perfect day to dive. The group she was heading out with was a loose collection of college friends and assorted add-ins. Sometimes the group was bigger than others, but the core of it had been together for nearly ten years, getting together for a dive twice a month in the summer and a little less often in the off-season, when their meetings were heavier on conversation and commiseration about not having moved to the tropics.

Today, by mutual agreement, they were heading to their favorite wreck, the USS *San Diego*, the only American warship lost in World War I. Depending on which account you preferred to believe, eighty-nine years ago almost to the day, the *San Diego* was struck by a German torpedo or a German mine off the coast of Long Island and sank in twenty-eight minutes. She now rested upside down in 110 feet of water off Fire Island.

The last few weeks had seen little precipitation, which meant the water would be as clear as the Atlantic could be, and exploring the wreck would be as easy as going to Disneyland, although given that the *San Diego*'s anniversary had fallen two days earlier the crowds might be just as plentiful.

Kate tossed her dive bag onto the deck of the *Loch Ness* and followed it, landing lightly. "Anybody home?"

"Be up in a sec." Brad Scofield's voice was muffled as he called up from belowdeck.

Her Starbucks skim latte still hot in her travel mug, Kate walked to the bow and leaned against the railing. The breeze was light, out of the west, and within the next few hours the air would heat up to a seasonable high in the upper eighties. Perfect.

The thud of another duffle hitting the deck drew her attention to the back of the boat.

"Hey, Katie."

"Hey, Doug. Hi, Angela. Are you going diving for

two?" Kate called as she watched Doug Hansen, a college friend and meteorologist at NOAA, help his pregnant police-officer wife onto the deck.

"Not quite," Angela responded with a laugh. "My diving days are over for this year. I get to be the boat tender. How have you been?"

"Fine. Busy."

Angela moved gingerly across the deck to one of the benches in the stern and sat down. "I hated getting put on desk duty, but now I know why it's a requirement. Forget all the hormonal nonsense. My balance is completely shot. I trip over nothing these days. And I'm not even at the waddling stage yet."

"Well, just stay there and don't move around."

"The good news is that if I fell overboard, I think I'd bob like a buoy. No need for a life vest. Just give me a flare gun."

"What, so you can take out half the marina? I'll get you a seat belt instead," her husband said. He pulled a big, girly sun hat out of their duffle and clapped it on her head as he walked past her.

Angela flashed Kate a grin. "So what's keeping you so busy? There haven't been any storms."

"Well, that's actually part of it. We're all trying to figure out what was up with the jet stream, but now we've got Simone to worry about."

Brad, who had just emerged from belowdeck, greeted them, then glanced at Kate. "Did you see what it did to the Bahamas? Looks like freaking Baghdad with water damage. And it just keeps starting, stopping, and then getting bigger. What's up with that? Is this the big one that we've been hearing about ever since Katrina? The one that's going to take out the East Coast?"

"Brad, if I knew the answer to questions like those, I'd be diving off a bigger boat."

"Come on, I thought that's what you get paid to do: predict the weather. Your boss must want to know what this storm is going to do. After all, if it hits us, he's got to get his bulldozers out of the Gulf Coast and up here in time to clean up the mess."

Kate rolled her eyes and looked back at Angela. "What did you ask me?"

"I asked you what was keeping you so busy. We missed you last time."

She took another sip of her rapidly cooling latte. "Just work. They changed the corporate structure and now I'm not only managing three other meteorologists, but I have to produce all these forecast reports covering ridiculous time frames. Either Davis Lee thinks I have a crystal ball in my office or he wants to get rid of me." The words came out of Kate's mouth on a laugh, but hearing them surprised even her.

Doug and Angela were staring at her, surprise registering on their faces.

"Trouble in paradise?"

She forced a laugh. "No. Of course not. It was a joke. I'm as safe and secure as one can be on Wall Street."

"Which isn't saying much," Brad added lightly, glancing at his watch. "Figures that Tony is the last to show. Why the hell does he make such a big thing about checking his watch against the atomic clock four times a day if he can't manage to get anywhere on time?"

"He's a theoretical physicist, that's why. Give him a break," Doug replied. "He's been that way for as long as we've known him."

"I'm tired of giving him a break. He lives in Stony Brook, for Christ's sake, and he's late every time. You live in Manhattan and you're usually early," Brad snapped.

"So, does Simone have you as worked up as it does Doug?" Angela asked, smoothly changing the subject as Kate sat down next to her.

"As of when I went to bed last night it had stalled again, off the coast of Florida this time. Around Melbourne. I haven't heard anything about it since then, though. I was listening to CDs on the drive out." She looked at Doug. "What's up?"

"It started moving again."

"How fast?"

"It's still holding at a Category 4, but it's moving up the coast at three miles an hour. Strangest damned thing I've ever seen. The leading edge is like a rototiller, chewing up everything for five miles inland." He shook his head. "All of coastal Georgia is under mandatory evacuation. The Carolinas are still under voluntary evac, but that will probably change pretty soon. If this thing picks up some speed, it's going to be ugly."

"Well, we're overdue. Last year was a nice break," Kate said lightly, in direct contradiction to the distinct clench in her stomach his words had inspired.

Brad shook his head. "You guys gotta get your stories straight. This has been the best summer I can remember. That thing's not going anywhere. It will fizzle out."

"It's *huge*," Kate pointed out. "If it fizzles, it will take days."

"The Atlantic storm season is typically slow early on and picks up around late July. Which is now," Doug added. "And I agree with Kate. Even if it starts to destabilize soon, we'll feel something. Maybe just heavy winds and rain, but it will still pack a wallop."

"Hey, guys, am I late?" Tony Figueroa shouted from the shore as he jogged onto the dock.

Rolling his eyes, Brad said nothing as he walked to the cockpit and fired up the first engine. Both engines were humming with power held in check by the time Tony finally stowed his gear and threw off the lines. The big, V-hulled cruiser pulled away slowly, following the channel markers and gradually increasing speed as they headed away from the marina.

An hour and a half later the boat was drifting lazily at anchor, well away from the two charter boats that had beaten them to the wreck by a few minutes.

"It's like bathwater. I'm so jealous," Angela said, trailing her hands in the water.

"Get over it. That crazy woo-woo childbirth consultant

your sister insisted we meet may have talked about underwater births, but the North Atlantic is *not* what she meant," Doug said as he pulled up the thermometer he'd tossed overboard as they'd come to a stop. He glanced at Kate. "Eighty-one."

She looked at him in shocked silence for a moment. "No way. It can't be. It's only the middle of July."

"Lighten up, Kate, it's the upside to global warming," Brad cracked as he hauled the air tanks up from belowdecks. "I kinda like the idea of palm trees going native on Long Island. Going subtropical would add about three months a year to my business cycle, not to mention more beer and bikini time all around."

"How do you like the idea of that beautiful beachfront house of yours becoming an artificial reef?" Kate muttered as she took the instrument from Doug's outstretched hand and checked it herself, then looked up at him again.

"A reef? Katie, Katie, Katie, we'll never get there," Brad replied in a tone that held cocky amusement. "You just watch. Vermont will never have a coastline. The Finns won't let naked snow rolling disappear without a fight and the Norwegians aren't about to turn their cross-country skis into water skis any time soon. Mark my words. Either governments will go up to the North Pole with some serious snow-making equipment and bitch-slap Mother Nature into shape in the next few years or that guy who wrapped some island in pink Saran Wrap a few years ago will volunteer to go up there and wrap Santa Land in white. Presto change-o. No more problem."

"Instant albedo." Kate smacked her palm against her forehead. "My God, Brad, that's brilliant. Of course! We'll just shrink-wrap the poles. Then all the thousands of scientists who've been researching global warming for the last thirty years can turn their attention to something really important." She turned to Doug, who was laughing. "Imagine that, Doug. A guy who plants flowers for a living just solved the crisis of the millennium. How come *you* never thought of doing that?"

"Because I'm obviously not sucking enough nitrogen. You should watch that mix, Brad."

"Yeah, yeah. And thanks for turning me from a land-scape architect into a day laborer, Kate." Brad brushed off the good-natured teasing with a laugh. "Just watch. The Saran Man will get an NEA grant to do it, too. Then we'll be cursing him for putting us into a new ice age. So, any-body ready for some diving?"

"I'm definitely making it into the boiler room this time," Kate replied, opening her duffle and pulling out her gear. "I feel the need to scavenge some contraband as a souvenir."

"Not with Captain Courageous in the neighborhood." Brad jerked his head toward the larger of the two charter boats anchored a few dozen yards away. "He acts like he owns the damn thing."

Despite the unusually high water temperature, Kate was glad she'd opted to wear a thermal suit as she backrolled off the boat a few minutes later. The North Atlantic would never truly be *warm*. *Not cold* was about the best a diver could hope for below the surface, and that's what it was to-day. She bobbed at the surface for a few minutes to fix her mask, adjust her mouthpiece and regulator, and make sure her underwater iPod was set to keep a steady flow of Enya coming at her. Then she sank beneath the water, trading the harsh sparkle of the surface for the hypnotic green translucence of everything below it.

She took it slow and easy as she followed the anchor chain down. Ordinarily, Kate would now be in her "zone," the New Age music working in tandem with the filmy light and sense of weightlessness to clear her head of everything but the present. But she couldn't shake a dis-tant, uncomfortable sense of foreboding. She knew it had nothing to do with the dive and everything to do with the weather and her research on those storms—and Jake's. She'd been trying to ignore it all, but the more she tried to work around it the more space it took up in her brain:

There was something very strange going on with the weather, and that wasn't just her opinion. The chatter on the blogs, from the ones populated by weather professionals to those populated by more diverse weather geeks, had been getting steadily more concerned.

For most of the spring, American weather had been too good to be true, which made weather people nervous. Real weather—not that she'd figured out precisely what made these storms seem not real to her—was a system built on churn, and destruction was its natural and not uncommon outcome. When the sun shone too much, things burned up and died. When it rained too much, things drowned. Too much wind, too many clouds— everything had a natural and, from a human perspective, negative result. But lately, the weather hadn't been causing anyone trouble. Until Simone had kicked up unexpectedly and begun knocking the hell out of the eastern Caribbean.

For two months, a succession of high-pressure fronts had formed over the Plains and rolled across the Midwest toward the East Coast, disrupted only briefly by occasional Gulf lows that brought steady, gentle rains. Meanwhile parts of the West that had suffered from droughts for the past few years were getting plenty of Pacific rainfall. Not enough to cause damage but enough to replenish water tables and nourish crops. Even the hurricanes had stayed away from the U.S. coastline, inexplicably taking unusual turns toward equatorial waters and breaking up as they lost their spin, or stalling in the Caribbean and doing very little harm before dissipating.

To Kate, it had started to get downright eerie, but as far as the general population of the U.S. was concerned, the summer had been pretty close to perfect. To the nation's meteorologists and environmentalists, though, that only meant the coastal waters would continue to warm, leading to a busy and deadly second half of the hurricane season, which was exactly what was happening now.

With a start, Kate realized she was over the huge gun barrels that stuck up out of the sand and followed the rest of the team into the gaping black hole that had ended the *San Diego*'s career.

CHAPTER **33**

From her location fifteen miles off the prosperous and populated South Georgia coast, Simone was making her presence known. Screaming winds lashed the barrier islands, changing their shape, ripping out the carefully planted sea oats, flattening the nurtured dunes, demolishing the enormous seaside "cottages." Tabby walls crumbled back to their humble origins, reduced to no more than piles of shattered oyster shells and sharp concrete. Driverless cars skidded down the flooded roadways. Furious waters shoved under doorways and buckled terraces, leaving them heaped with the twisted debris of uprooted gardens and human vanity.

The only objects moving under their own power were vans sporting the brightly painted logos of news organizations. They patrolled the devastation, seeking not survivors but to feed the salacious appetites of residents of other, drier places. One stopped in front of a once-beautiful mansion, its storm shutters torn off and dangling sickeningly from the lightning rods ringing the fractured roofline.

Gingerly, a young woman climbed out of the van, her bright yellow anorak sleeked against her body, her shoulders braced and head bowed before the wind. A few steps away from the van, she stopped and turned around, leaning against the warm-colored brick of a pillar that had once borne the gates to the house.

At her signal, the van door slid open again and a similarly dressed figure clambered out, the heavy, shrouded camera on his shoulder diminishing his already-impaired stability. The small satellite dish on the roof of the van began turning slowly, its antenna cone seeking a signal. The cameraman leaned against the vehicle and pointed the lens at the reporter, and at his gesture the woman brought the microphone to her face, pushed back her hood, and began speaking, straining to be heard over the wind.

The wind bit into her face, driving water into her eyes and grit and sand into her ears, nostrils, mouth, and skin. A lightning bolt made thunderous contact with the antenna, tossing the van onto its side—and onto the cameraman. The camera skidded to the woman's feet, water running red behind it. Her screams went unheard in the dark morning and she ran to the van, which was now beginning to slide away with the force of the wind, leaving pulpy human smears on the puddled asphalt. The satellite dish snapped off and flew up and into the trees, coming to a precarious rest in a thicket of twisted branches.

The passenger door, now facing the sky, opened, and a dazed, bareheaded young woman crawled out, looking around. An awkward, ungainly jump brought her into harsh contact with the street. The first woman helped her to her feet, and hand in hand they began running toward the relative shelter of the destroyed house. A few steps later, the bareheaded, T-shirted girl, the producer, broke away and ran back toward the wall. Stooping to pick up the battered camera, she made sure the red light was still glowing and scuttled back across the road to her colleague.

As she approached, a heavy gust caught the edge of the reporter's anorak and lifted it, filling it with wind and making it billow like a sail. Helpless to fight it or deflate it, the reporter stumbled as the gale forced her into motion. In the next moment, the woman was aloft, her terrified screams lost in the wind, her panicked face caught on tape.

The van's satellite mast, bent at a useless angle, stopped her before her body rose too far from the ground. Impaled, she went instantly silent. Her limp, lifeless arms *and legs flailed at the mercy of the wind, twisting her body. Shaken, retching, the producer turned away, turned off the camera, and crossed the sodden yard to the house now open to the storm. Finding an interior staircase, she took shelter beneath it and sat and shook and prayed.*

CHAPTER **34**

Saturday, July 21, 2:00 P.M., McLean, Virginia

Jake stood up and stretched. He'd spent most of the day hunched over the microfiche reader in a small, secure carrel in the Agency's otherwise spacious library, and the experience hadn't done anything for his back or his eyes. Visine had become his closest friend. But he was making progress. Right around noon, he'd finally eased out of the 1960s.

That decade had been the heyday for both overt and covert weather research as far as he'd been able to tell. Of course, the sixties had been the heyday for the CIA in general. Everything had been less complicated then. Decisions were made and operations executed without, apparently, a whole lot of discussion or review, and certainly with no navel-gazing. Cuba and the Eastern Bloc had been the Agency's enemies, and Central and South America had been its playground. The White House had been its defender, and the Senate had been its willing benefactor. The media had been unsuspecting allies. In short, the world had been the Agency's oyster.

Then came the 1970s. Budget cuts. Internal leaks and external exposures. *Washington Post* reporter Jack Anderson and President Richard Nixon. Daniel Ellsberg and the Pentagon Papers. Senator Claiborne Pell and the Senate hearings that eventually quashed Operation POPEYE. Jimmy Carter.

That decade had been a hell of a comedown.

After the unfortunately public acknowledgment and disbandment of POPEYE, funding for many—too many—other covert weather research operations had been cut as well. Most of them had been orderly, methodical scientific operations with clearly identified objectives like steering the jet stream or using a variety of electromagnetic frequencies to do a vast, weird assortment of things. But the workings of one group of weather specialists in particular had caught Jake's eye.

Running a highly classified project with a big budget and little to no oversight—much like the task force he was currently on—this group's experimentation and research were significantly more advanced than anything he'd ever come across. Their goal hadn't been benign and their work hadn't been just theoretical. They had been successful—until their funding was cut off with a single blow from the Senate.

The notes and descriptions of what they'd been working on could be extrapolated into a blueprint for what was going on right now. The creativity and detail were unsettling, and given the speed and abilities of the computers they'd had to work with, their calculations and predictions, not to mention their successes, were nothing short of amazing. He'd felt a similar awe when it had finally sunk in that Einstein had honed his theories using a slide rule and a pencil. It was practically unfathomable.

The identities of the team members had been redacted from the microfiche, but the odds were good that some of those guys were still around. Somehow he was going to have to track them, even though gaining access to their names and concocting a cover story so he wouldn't reveal to them what he was really working on would take longer than devising a work-around.

Saturday, July 21, 7:50 P.M., Old Greenwich, Connecticut

The cab ride from the small airport in White Plains to the apartment he kept in New York City was both uncomfortable and uneventful. Carter had done what he could to keep the small talk to a minimum, but he'd had the misfortune to encounter one of the most talkative, law-abiding, and unfortunately well-informed cabbies in the tri-state area. The cabbie had recognized him immediately and, in an apparent attempt to bond with him or maybe just get a good tip, subjected Carter to a right-lane ride the entire way into the city, with a complimentary non-stop narrative on everything from crop circles to the war in Iraq. By the time Carter arrived at his small Midtown flat, the normally claustrophobic space seemed like a haven. He didn't spend much time there, having made plans to meet Richard Carlisle at his home in Old Greenwich at eight, which was where he was headed right now.

Carter pulled off I-95 at Exit 5 and drove first through moderately seedy areas and then increasingly nicer parts of town until he finally reached the quaint, old-fashioned village within a village. Elegant, authentic Victorians stood cheek-by-jowl with modern McMansions and older, larger estates as he wound through narrow lanes with Waspy names until finally reaching Ford Lane, the small private road that ended at Richard's secluded and unassuming gravel driveway.

Compared to the houses Carter had passed as he'd made his way down the street, Richard's house looked like the neighborhood eyesore. It wasn't in disrepair, but it could use some attention. No doubt the only thing saving it from the neighbors' wrath was that you couldn't see it from the street or neighboring houses. A thick border of tall trees and unmanicured shrubs blocked the view on all sides and cast long shadows across the grass.

Carter brought the car to a halt and was about to open his door when an enormous lean white dog bounded out of the house and covered the fifty or so feet from house to car in what seemed to be three strides. The dog didn't seem menacing, but there was no way Carter was getting out of his car with it standing right there. It practically had to bend down to look into the window of Carter's BMW sedan.

A moment later a casually clad Richard emerged from the house and called to the dog, which immediately loped back to the house. Alone, Richard proceeded to the car while Carter got out and began crossing the drive to meet him.

"Sorry about that. He gets excited when we have company," Richard called with a grin. "He's gentle as a lamb, but his size scares people."

Richard had aged well, showing none of the padding or slouching that most men their age, Carter included, usually sported. He was tanned and fit, with the unnaturally white smile and deep, resonant voice required of TV personalities.

"I've got a few with the same habit," Carter replied, returning the smile as they met at the edge of the raggedy lawn and shook hands. "It's been a long time, Richard. It's good to see you. You're looking well."

"It has been a long time," Richard agreed. "I'm keeping busy. Come on inside."

The inside of the beachfront bungalow—it really wasn't much more than that—was as unkempt as the outside, with books, papers, videocassettes, and clutter covering every available surface. Carter wasn't surprised. No one on the team had been more meticulous than Richard when it came to analyzing data and designing models, but his desk had always been a mess of paperwork, overflowing ashtrays, and half-filled coffee cups.

"We can get some drinks and head down to the water. I built a small patio there in the shade a few years ago. What's your preference?"

"Any sort of pop would be fine. Thanks."

Richard pulled two cans of Coke from the refrigerator, filled two glasses with ice, and handed one to Carter. "I was surprised to hear from you. I've been thinking of you lately."

I'll bet you have. "Really? I catch your forecasts on television every now and then," Carter replied as he walked ahead of Richard out the old-fashioned screen door.

Richard smiled his thanks. "One of my former students works for you here in the city. Kate Sherman. Do you know the name? She's—"

Okay, so you want to get this over with as much as I do. "Yes, I know Kate. Not very well, but I'm familiar with her work. She's very good. An excellent forecaster."

"Yes, she is," Richard said as they crossed the lawn. "So what brings you out here after all these years?"

"Your name came up recently and I started thinking about how long it's been since we've spoken."

They reached the small flagstone patio that perched on a patch of land a few feet above the waterline. The tide was going out and there was a narrow, rocky strip of beach beneath the pilings of a short wooden pier. A small outboard-motor boat bobbed against the end of it. The sun was still bright but nearing the cloud-filled horizon and casting long shadows across Long Island Sound.

They sat in chairs facing the water, separated by a weathered teak table.

"It has been a long time," Richard said with a too-casual note in his voice. "Maybe ten years. How did you say my name came up?"

"I didn't." Carter smiled thinly. "That student of yours, Kate, wrote a paper that she presented at a conference yesterday, and she sent me a copy." He took a sip of his soft drink. "She thanked you in a footnote."

Richard swung his head to look at Carter, clearly startled by the news. "She did?"

"Yes, she did. Given the content of the paper . . ." He paused. "Maybe I'm getting ahead of myself. Have you read it?"

"I didn't finish it."

"Ah. Well, it was interesting." Carter shrugged. "She makes a lot of suppositions. It's not the sort of paper that would have withstood scientific scrutiny when you and I were publishing, but I can see how it would attract some attention." He paused again. "Did you read far enough to get to the part where she starts hinting about an unnatural cause for the escalation of the storms she tracked?"

Richard nodded.

"I'm surprised you let your name be linked to it," Carter said mildly. "That footnote made me wonder just what your input was."

"I didn't have any 'input,' " Richard replied, his voice marginally cooler than it had been moments before. "We discussed the storms a few times. When she told me she was writing a paper, I counseled her to leave well enough alone because all her questions would do would be to raise other, uglier questions and put her on the periphery of good science."

"She didn't pay attention."

"She's a grown woman and a professional. She didn't have to listen to me. She doesn't work for me."

"That's right. She works for me." Carter pulled his gaze away from the sparkling Long Island Sound and met his former colleague's eyes. "And I, too, think her questions were better left unasked. So I'd like to know exactly what you discussed with her."

Richard said nothing for several minutes, a muscle in his cheek working, all vestiges of his casual demeanor gone. "If you're asking me what I think you're asking me, I'd prefer that you left my property."

"Without the benefit of an answer?"

"You don't deserve an answer," Richard responded coldly, his voice dropping to a volume that Carter had to strain to hear. "I've never said a word about my past to anyone, and certainly not to Kate. Her questions are valid ones, as much as it scares me to admit that." He paused. "Let me tell you what I think of those storms, Carter. They're too damned similar to what I saw a long time ago. And I think they have your fingerprints all over them."

Carter raised an eyebrow, then gave a short laugh to cover his pleasure at the acknowledgment. "*My* fingerprints? When I read Kate's paper, I'll admit that I saw the similarities to some of our early research, too. She has a sharp eye for detailed analysis. But why would you think of me rather than our old friends? Or perhaps our foreign friends? I'm a little flattered."

"Nobody else carried on that research," Richard said flatly. "If the Company had wanted it to continue, we would have been the ones to work on it. And our foreign friends never had the technology and never knew we had it, either. The evidence points to you, Carter. You left the Company with a bad taste in your mouth."

"You're talking about millions of dollars, Richard, if not billions."

"Another component that you, and you alone, have. And costs are much lower when you're operating outside the system, aren't they? There's no oversight or regulations to worry about."

"I wouldn't know."

"What is it that detective novels are always asking for? Means, motive, and opportunity? I'm not sure what your motive would be, but I'm sure you've got one. And the means and opportunity are already there."

"Detective novels? You disappoint me. You always struck me as a more literary type."

Richard shook his head, wearing a grim smile. "Give it up. They were small-scale storms, too much like our early test runs for my comfort. What are you waiting for? Or are you already planning something more dramatic?"

"You know that what you're suggesting is fantastic. In fact, it sounds like you've crossed over. Next you'll be hosting *Star Trek* conventions."

Richard got to his feet, clearly losing patience with the conversation but still in control of himself. "I know what to look for, Carter," he said flatly. "I saw your signature. I slowed down the pictures and went in deep, nearly to the pixel. I saw the infrared bursts."

Carter went still. "Lightning strikes."

"No. Wrong wavelength, shorter duration, dead straight.

They were low-altitude infrared bursts, Carter. The only time I've ever seen anything like them was thirty-odd years ago, when they came from the business end of our laser. And the results killed people back then and they killed people last week and last month and the month before that. The only difference between then and now is that back then we called ourselves scientists. As of right now, you're a sociopath and a mass murderer. Please leave."

His heartbeat accelerated and jumped as the offensive words sunk in and Carter got to his feet slowly, fighting dizziness and measuring his breath. He knew the sweat at his hairline had nothing to do with the warmth of the summer night. "You're wrong, Richard." He had to force the words from his chest.

"I'm not wrong. You're sick." Richard turned and began to walk away, then stopped and met Carter's eyes again. "What I can't figure out is what the hell you think you're doing. Playing God? What's the next thing on your agenda, Carter, now that you can make storms? Are you out to save the world like you used to say you were? Or are you going to try to control it, like you try to control most things you touch? You're a sick, twisted, egomaniacal bastard, Carter. You can't do this. I don't know what your end goal is, but you can't do this."

His breathing and his equilibrium restored to normality, Carter's anger flared. "But I can," he said softly, and watched Richard's expression change from contempt to disbelief. "And I'm not a murderer, not any more than you are. Or have you forgotten what we did in our final test? Super Typhoon Bess was the most destructive storm in the Pacific that year, Richard, and she was our baby. One-hundred-sixty-mile-an-hour winds at the peak, one-hundred-thirty when she made landfall in Taiwan, and she still packed some punch when she crossed the strait and hit the mainland. Thirty-two dead, thousands displaced. And she was only one of our creations. There were others. A lot of rice was ruined that year, wasn't it, Richard?"

The sun had dropped below the horizon. The long pause

between the two men was filled with the sounds of an evening at the shore, cicadas, bullfrogs, the occasional low hum of a distant motorboat, the muted laughter of a nearby cocktail party.

"How did you do it?" Richard asked, staring past Carter to the Sound.

"Just as you described. Without oversight and with my own money." Carter smiled, empowered by the look in Richard's eyes, an expression bordering on fear. The loathing that accompanied it didn't bother him. "Offshore. Poor countries will take funding where they can get it, as will their researchers and their bureaucrats."

He could see his former colleague's throat move as he swallowed hard.

"You built the laser?" His voice was low and almost hoarse.

Carter nodded once, imperiously. "It's not like the other. It's more powerful and compact. You'd be impressed."

"What do you plan to do with it?"

"Good things, Richard. Necessary things. I'm going to undo some of the damage we've done to the earth and free the people Western technology has enslaved. I'm going to start in east-central Africa, in what once was the cradle of life." He rocked from his heels to his toes and back again, almost gloating. "I'm going to restore Eden. But first I have to provide some context so that people will understand."

Richard frowned. "What are you talking about?"

"I've found that people learn better and faster when you teach using an example. Surely you've discovered the same thing during your years in the classroom," Carter jeered, his voice finally revealing his contempt for everything Richard had come to symbolize over the course of the conversation.

"Carter, what are you going to do?" Richard demanded, his voice rising slightly.

"No, Richard. You mean, what am I already doing."

They stood in the fading light, staring at each other.

Carter's smile widened as he watched Richard synthesize their conversation and come to the correct conclusion.

"Simone," he said at last, his voice sounding somewhat strangled.

"Yes, Richard, Simone." He paused and released a breath that was almost a sigh. "She was a small cluster of dirty clouds when I first saw her on the satellite footage, and she spoke to me, helped me understand what I needed to do." He shrugged. "She was destined to do nothing until I discovered her. And now, she'll transform the world's understanding of how and why mankind and Nature must work together. She'll never be forgotten. And neither will I."

"You have to be stopped." Richard turned on his heel and began walking toward the house with too much purpose in his stride to please Carter.

He's going to make a call.

It didn't matter to whom. Without stopping to plan what he would do next, Carter ran after Richard and launched his full body weight at the taller, more fit man, bringing him to the ground with a heavy grunt.

The breath knocked out of him, Richard couldn't react immediately and Carter took full advantage of those few seconds. Grabbing his former friend's head, he jerked it back and slammed it forward, then did it again, and again, the wet, sickening thuds barely registering in his brain. After a few moments, reality cleared away the cloud of fury in Carter's brain and he realized that there was no resistance left in the man beneath him. There was no life left in him.

Carter rolled off Richard's body and lay on his back, breathing hard as he stared at the darkening sky and the thin slashes of clouds adorning it. The painful pounding of his heart thundered in his ears, blocking out the night sounds. He closed his eyes and tried to ease his breathing.

It hadn't been a matter of choice. He'd had to do it.

No one knew he was here, unless Richard had mentioned it to someone. Carter had told no one. Not his assistant, not even Iris, knew he'd made plans to meet with

Richard. The only thing that could link them was the phone call he'd made yesterday evening.

Given the hour and nature of their meeting, there was no risk of anyone discovering his body tonight. Tomorrow was Sunday; Richard wasn't due on the air until Monday morning. This spot could not be seen from the road. If no one came to visit, Carter would be able to put nearly thirty-six hours between now and the discovery of the body. That was plenty of time to get out of here, out of New York, and back to Iowa. He'd keep his appointment with Davis Lee in the morning and fly home as planned. By then, the world would have more pressing things to think about. Raoul would already be airborne and approaching the strike zone. Simone would be a Category 5 in less than an hour.

Satisfied with his decision, his breath slowing, Carter opened his eyes and sat up gingerly. His body ached from the unaccustomed activity. He brushed the dirt and blood from his hands, careful to smear it in the grass rather than on his clothes, and glanced at the dead body next to him. He'd never seen one up close. There was a stillness about it that was eerie and couldn't be mistaken for mere lack of consciousness.

Rising laboriously to his knees and then his feet, Carter brushed the grass and bits of leaves off his clothes and retrieved both his Coke can and his glass from the patio table. With a stride as purposeful as Richard's had been, he walked to his car, got in, and drove away.

Saturday, July 21, 8:00 P.M., McLean, Virginia

It hadn't taken Jake long to get the names of the weather researchers. All he'd done to sidestep the protocols was phone Tom Taylor. He still wasn't sure who the hell Taylor actually was, but the original, unredacted microfiche had been delivered to his carrel within the hour, along with the news that, several hours earlier, the mayor had called for voluntary evacuations. Jake shrugged it off and went back to his research without a second thought.

The composition of the research group had surprised

him. Most of the names were familiar, but two had leaped off the page, sending his brain into overdrive. Richard Carlisle, "The Nation's Weatherman," and Carter Thompson, Mr. Green Jeans with billions of greenbacks.

Both were nationally known and respected, but neither had ever been linked to weather research—publicly. Yet both were linked to Kate Sherman, and Kate was stirring up some serious interest among conspiracy theorists while venturing a little too close to something called national security.

It could be coincidence.

Then again, maybe it wasn't.

Shaking off the cold feeling that had settled into the pit of his stomach, Jake had returned to his cubicle several floors up and begun going over his data in light of this last bit of information. Two hours later, he found himself staring at one of his monitors, wondering if his brain was overtired and he was seeing things that weren't there or if he'd stumbled onto something that he'd overlooked. At this stage, he was willing to consider almost anything.

The storms he'd been analyzing had taken place across several months and across a widely dispersed area roughly bounded by the equator, the north of France, the west coast of the U.S., and the eastern edge of Africa. If they were man-made storms, this wild disparity could only have been a deliberate attempt to disguise them. When the list was aligned by date, it reflected normal, random weather. But when he realigned the list according to the storms' locations irrespective of their dates of occurrence, he noticed a pattern emerge. The timing clumped, and when translated to universal time, the clumping became even more apparent: Regardless of the month, year, or geographical location, each of the storms had commenced within the same two-hour time frame.

From a meteorological perspective, it was a pretty damned weak correlation. Storms could spring up at any time based on local conditions, and while it might look like a pattern, it was completely random. But from an intelligence perspective, it looked like evidence that could help triangulate the location of the perpetrator. The timing corresponded to early evening in the Middle East, early afternoon in Africa, late morning in Britain. Pre-dawn in the continental U.S.

He'd been told to assume the operations were based within the U.S. borders.

He reached for his coffee cup, realized it had been hours since he'd filled it, and dropped his hand.

Could be our pals are early risers.

Could be they prefer light traffic on their communication channels.

Or want to stay under the cover of Nature while they're operating within our borders.

If it hadn't been for Wayne's genius at unearthing barely noticeable discrepancies, most of these storms would have gone unnoticed by anyone other than a local weather expert, and no one without a reason to do so would have grouped them like he had. And, as a group, they were impressive in their similarities, which, if reviewed through the lens of being a coordinated effort, were chilling.

Jake ran through the list of locations again, even though he had it committed to memory at this point. None of the locales were urban, and most were rural or uninhabited, making them perfect test beds. The storms that had taken place within the U.S. had begun before dawn, making their initiation invisible to the local inhabitants. Natural early-morning convection cycles had further helped to mask each storm's abrupt escalation.

Other than the recent Death Valley storm, the U.S.-based storms had caused no deaths and only moderate damage to infrastructure. That made them non-events in the minds of the media. And if the media don't pay attention, neither does the rest of the world.

Damn it. Whoever these terrorists were, they were no ivory tower academicians. They were playing to win.

He went back to the satellite footage of the most recent U.S. storm, Death Valley. Running the radar and infrared feeds simultaneously on a split screen with near-surface measurements tracking on another monitor, he viewed the images slowly, almost frame-by-frame. He watched the cloud cover and the rain bands from the radar readings, comparing them with wind speed and direction, relative humidity, then core temperature and lightning strikes. He didn't know what he was looking for, but just like Justice Potter Stewart had said about porn, Jake had a feeling he'd know what he was looking for when he saw it.

An hour later, eyes burning from the glare of the screens, he saw it, zooming in and replaying it four times to be sure he wasn't imagining it.

He wasn't. Adrenaline poured into his bloodstream and his brain switched to red alert. There, in the seconds before escalation, a blip appeared that was different from the rest of the lightning strikes. Under the highest resolution, the thin streak showed a higher heat than any strikes recorded during the storm, lasted for a full second less than the average strike, and appeared to blast the very center of the convection cell. And the heat's vector was dead straight.

Lightning was never perfectly straight.

Leaving the image frozen on the screen, Jake swiveled to another monitor and typed in a rapid command to pull up lightning strike data collected on the ground. Scrolling through the hundreds of lines of data, he slowed as he reached the significant time and scanned the numbers closely, enlarging them on the screen to ensure he'd read them accurately.

Nothing.

He sat back in his chair for a moment, breathing as if he'd just sprinted up a flight of stairs.

Only one piece of machinery could produce that sort of heat pulse with that sort of trajectory.

The sons of bitches were using some sort of laser.

He put his hands back on his keyboard and began reviewing the available data for each of the storms. An hour and a half later, he'd corroborated his findings on all of the domestic storms and as many as he could of the foreign storms. The signatures were close enough to the experiments in the seventies to possibly be the next generation.

Mr. Taylor, we have an answer.

CHAPTER 35

Simone continued her deadly, destructive, northerly path, hugging the U.S. coastline and smashing homes, businesses, and lives without leave or apology. Shaking off her reticence, Simone turned suddenly when she reached the Southern jewel-box city of Charleston, South Carolina, and let her winds venture farther inland. The eye of the storm, that tranquil core, stopped short of making landfall, preferring to send its signature call sign, a towering storm surge, ahead of it. The city, well used to feeling the awesome effects of an angry sea and fortified against it, stood tall. Her residents, the few who had remained, cowered before the twin furies of wind and water.

The small constellation of luxury-oriented barrier islands took the brunt of the storm's new strength, their balconied, glass-fronted homes shattering on impact. Expensive debris was flung with abandon along stretches of rapidly eroding beaches and hurtled inland to litter the roadways and gardens now flooded with the wrath of a writhing, moonless sea. Trees that had withstood more than a century of storms snapped, their tops rushing through the air like tumbleweeds, their torsos crashing to the ground, buckling houses, pancaking cars, pulling down wires. Water rushed into homes immune for decades, trapping their terrified inhabitants, who fled up elegant twisting staircases better suited for graceful descents. Wrought ironwork lost its allure as bars and grates were wrenched free of their brick moorings and flung like missiles through walls and storm shutters, embedding themselves in whatever didn't splinter on impact.

The leading winds curled into the inland suburbs, wrapping them in a deadly embrace. Row upon row of newer homes were ripped from their foundations, exploded, and shattered like so many dollhouses smashed by an undisciplined child, their contents scattered obscenely for miles. The surging muddy water rose past bureaucrats' worst-case predictions, forcing its stench and violence into the schools where thousands huddled, clinging to misguided assurances of security. Roofs were peeled back like foil wrap, letting in the torrents and airborne debris. Panicked parents clutched terrified children, and elders were abandoned to their fates as water swamped them from below and pummeled them from above. The filthy surge blocked their escape as it pushed against doors that needed to be pulled, turned wide hallways into flash-flooding rivers, and transformed broad, banistered staircases into raging, sucking cataracts.

Churning in the overly warm continental shallows, Simone picked up speed and slammed into North Carolina's Outer Banks with a fury beyond the scope of words before swerving back to the sea and resuming her parallel track. Coastal dwellers farther north in Norfolk and Richmond, making slow progress into the highlands, felt the merest shred of hope that they might be spared the full wrath of the storm.

In the nation's capital, the recommendation to evacuate had been rephrased as an order, and the roads north and west were waterlogged and filled with anxious residents and terrified visitors. Rain pounded the drenched city, flooding even the quaint, exclusive high ground, turning hilltop streets into cascading torrents of filthy water. Waves slapped at the upper steps of the Jefferson Memorial, having already obliterated the elegant Ellipse. The Washington Monument stood proud, a pale, slender, unlit obelisk atop a small hillock of green that continued to shrink in the face of the unprecedented deluge.

Boats rode high in the marinas dotting the shores of the Potomac. Tilted at precarious angles as their mooring lines pulled them down in a parody of security, they rocked into pilings, making contact several feet above the docks' protective bumpers. National Airport had closed, its primary runways submerged with the brackish water and vast quantity of debris coughed up by the Potomac's tidal churn.

New York City, no stranger to devastation or threats and no weakling when faced with defending itself, recommended to its citizens that they consider seeking shelter away from the shorelines in the face of Simone's expansive reach. And New Yorkers, life hardened and incapable of abandoning their city, ignored the warning.

And then Simone, furious, fickle Simone, swept into the open ocean and that warm, nurturing river within it, the Gulf Stream. Twelve hours later, replenished and confident, the once sluggish storm had become a raging monarch and meteorologists reluctantly acknowledged she was now a Category 5.

CHAPTER **36**

Sunday, July 22, 5:20 A.M., Midtown, New York City

Carter sat in his Midtown apartment, staring through the large window at the choppy rows of skyscrapers and the neon signs that never stopped glowing. The early-morning sky was dark gray and overcast, with clouds layered thickly across its expanse. The first true rains from Simone were on their way and mandatory evacuation of the city was being discussed with increasing intensity on the news, the talking heads breathless with an almost orgasmic need to be the first to announce the impending order.

He hadn't slept for much of the night, too busy researching how his storms were being discussed on weather blogs and conspiracy sites, whether anything about Kate's paper could point back to him. So far, nothing had. In fact, everything pointed to government experimentation.

The unnaturally good weather the country had enjoyed earlier in the summer hadn't gone unnoticed by the conspiracy theorists, deep-ecology groups, and weather renegades, and it had only fortified the arguments and charges they had been leveling at the government for more than a decade: that HAARP, the government's huge array of antennae in remote Gerona, Alaska, was being used to alter the weather. The difference was that, now, even the real science community had gotten concerned over that prolonged and unnatural northerly flow of the jet stream. Its sudden and relatively recent return to normality had been followed closely by a dramatic rise in bad weather. It shouldn't have surprised anyone; localized storms routinely formed in the Caribbean and the Gulf, spinning up out of warm waters and over land only to crash into cool fronts that swept down from the Rockies.

But that hadn't happened this summer. Gulf waters, which had reached record high temperatures, should have been releasing that heat through typical summer storms but hadn't until recently. And now those late-forming storms were getting larger and were joining forces with the atmospheric chaos created by Simone. And the one thread that was running hot and heavy through every discussion was the cause of it all. The only explanation that recurred with much frequency was HAARP.

For centuries, the jet stream, a consistent band of relatively stable air, had sped eastward across Canada and the U.S., undulating seasonally like damp sheets on a clothesline, arching and dipping according to the recombinations of millions of constantly changing variables. The one thing that had never varied to any large degree was its overall motion. Decades of monitoring had shown that, proven that. Never before in recorded history had it dipped so dramatically and remained virtually stationary for so long, keeping weather patterns benign for an entire continent.

As the liberal talking heads and bloggers liked to point out, never before had any government had the means to make those things happen.

Not that the average person in the street or on the farm had complained until Simone arrived on the scene. Why should they, when the result for the nation had been nearly two months of perfect summer weather? Crops had surged toward early ripeness and high yields. The tourism trade had burgeoned. Employment figures rose and crime figures fell, and politicians had gotten used to basking in the glow of mostly happy constituencies.

Conservative TV pundits were dismissing global warming as a scaremonger's tactic while televangelists were trying to bolster profits by declaring it the calm before the apocalyptic storm. Meanwhile Europe shivered in one of the chilliest summers on record while Mexico withered under an unrelenting drought.

Carter didn't really care about any of that. He had bigger issues on his mind. Like the arrogance of the president, tampering with global weather to fuel his own popularity. Like how Simone was going to teach the man a lesson he'd never forget. If he survived.

Undoubtedly the president would survive. The nation's capital was already feeling the distant, undeniable fury of Simone's presence, and the president and his family had already been moved to a secure location. As had the vice president, the cabinet, and most of the Congress. The very people who should suffer the most.

Carter stared at the bleak skyline and sought to redirect his fury. He would prevail. Meteorologists were already fascinated with his mercurial creation. She had intensified much faster than Carter had anticipated, especially considering that Raoul had failed to execute the operation as ordered. However, as if in support of Carter's plan, Simone had grown to a Category 5 on her own. The added boost of the laser, whenever it happened—and it would—would intensify beyond description whatever was under way naturally. New categories might need to be created. Perhaps Category 6 or even Category 7.

The natural amplification Simone had already undergone would only serve to further camouflage his actions.

He walked away from the window, his mind years and miles away. For years he had been telling anyone who would listen that all the world needed was one bad nuclear accident and life as the world had known it would be a memory, replaced by slow, horrifying, near-ubiquitous death. Few had listened to him. Winslow Benson had, and had taken his data and bastardized it, corrupted it beyond recognition, and had returned it to the public arena in an assault on Carter's reputation that had burned with radioactive fervor. Like the subject matter, Winslow Benson's twisted argument had a long, damaging half-life and had been trotted out as a "counterpoint" during discussions ever since. It remained corrosive even now. But not for long.

Carter was going to be the triumphant one soon. In less than a week, everyone would get to see the results of what Winslow Benson stood for: Nuclear power. Environmental destruction so horrific there weren't words to describe it. Deadly pollution with a radioactive half-life longer than mankind's remaining presence on earth.

Checking his watch, Carter headed for the shower. He would complete his business with Davis Lee and Kate, then head back to Iowa, where he would stay, surrounded by his family, until the holocaust was under way. If and when Richard Carlisle's body was found, Carter would be long gone.

Sunday, July 22, 6:00 A.M., DUMBO, Brooklyn

Kate never had liked surprises, and hearing Jake Baxter's voice on the other end of her cell phone at six o'clock Sunday morning wasn't a good surprise. The fact that he was calling from his car on the street in front of her apartment was even less of one.

She buzzed him in, using the few minutes it took him to get to the fourth floor to throw on clothes and brush her teeth. Her hair would have to wait.

When she pulled open her front door, there he stood. He looked as bad as she did, only more tired.

"Hi."

She knew her expression was less than welcoming, which was fine, considering that his was less than repentant. "I don't suppose you have flowers in that backpack."

He frowned in mild confusion. "No. My laptop, a toothbrush, and clean underwear."

She stepped aside and gestured for him to enter her apartment. "I'm going to make some coffee. Would you like some or have you had enough?"

"If you have the same kind—"

"No turnpike coffee. I buy it from a little Ethiopian man on the Lower East Side. He roasts his own."

"Then I'll have some," he replied, setting his backpack on the floor and glancing around the living room. "Nice place."

"Thanks." She closed the door and crossed the small space to her closet-sized kitchen. "How was the trip up?"

"A lot longer than five hours. D.C. and the eastern shore of Maryland are under mandatory evacuation orders. Crappy drivers, heavy rain, and a generalized sense of panic make for a long ride north. I think every hotel from the Delaware Memorial Bridge to the George Washington Bridge is booked solid."

"Well, they're all going to have to get out of Dodge. Have you heard the latest?"

"No. I needed a break and listened to music for the last few hours."

"She didn't make landfall as everyone predicted. She did an about-face off the North Carolina coast and headed straight for the Gulf Stream. She's now a Category 5 and her forward speed is picking up."

Jake looked at Kate with a frown. "How do you know that? Were you up when I called?"

She finished measuring the coffee into the machine and looked at him. "No. I got up a few hours ago for a little while. My sister lives in LA and works third shift. Sometimes she forgets that normal people sleep during those hours. Anyway, I checked the Web before I went back to sleep. So what is it that couldn't wait until I'd finished sleeping?"

"Yeah, uh, sorry about that."

"So you said," she replied dryly. "So?"

"I finished reading your paper and noticed that you thanked Richard Carlisle at the end of it."

She glanced over her shoulder to see him leaning against her minuscule breakfast bar. "He was one of my professors at Cornell. We stayed in touch. He does the weather on AM/USA."

"I know who he is." He paused. "If you don't mind me asking, how close are you?"

What is it with guys? She set the small sack of coffee back in the fridge and put her hands on her hips. "Excuse me? Of course I mind. What kind of a question is that? We just met. I barely know you and you're asking me about my private life?"

He had the sense to look slightly embarrassed. "I'm sorry. I'm not asking because I'm trying to pry, Kate. He used to work for the government, doing weather research, before he started teaching. I just thought he might have given you some insight into the storms."

"I know he was at NOAA when it started, but he never talks about that." She gave a one-shoulder shrug. "His only real input on my paper was to tell me not to write it."

"Why?"

"He said it would make me the poster child for the whack-jobs of the world. Unfortunately, I think he's right. The abstract of the paper was only put up on the conference Web site a few weeks ago and I've already gotten a few dozen requests for full copies. Very few of the requestors' e-mail addresses end in '.edu,' if you know what I mean."

She finished pouring water into the reservoir, flipped on the coffeemaker, and turned to face him. "So why don't you tell me why you're really here, Jake? You could have asked me about Richard over the phone."

He met her eyes and they stared at each other for a few minutes. Then he shrugged, so she braced herself for a lie.

"You're right. I have other questions that I didn't want to ask you over the phone." He hesitated for a few seconds. "I was at work all day yesterday until I left to come up here. Can I take a shower before we talk?"

Twenty minutes later, he was clean, she was dressed, and they were taking their first steps onto the Brooklyn Bridge to watch what Lower Manhattan does between downpours when there was a mandatory evacuation on. His idea. The man was clearly a lunatic.

"How come no one is on the road?"

"It's six thirty on a Sunday morning. They just got home," she muttered.

"There's an evacuation order."

She looked at him. "It's not for everyone, just people who live on the beach, like my parents."

"Why aren't you helping them move?"

"Because they're not up yet. Then they have to go to Mass. Then they might start thinking about it." She shrugged. "This is New York. People don't get freaked out by the big things. The bagel shop not opening on time? Now that could start a riot."

"There's a Category 5 hurricane less than a thousand miles away."

She shrugged and took a sip of her coffee. It never tasted as good out of a travel mug as it did out of a real one.

"Enough chitchat. I want to know what's going on," Kate said flatly.

"I can't tell you everything—," he began.

"Why not?" she demanded.

He looked at her in surprise. "I was going to explain, okay? Let me talk."

She rolled her eyes and took another sip of coffee.

"I can't tell you everything because I don't know everything. Here's what I can tell you. I work for a government agency as a forensic meteorologist. My interest in the storms we've discussed has to do with ongoing weather research."

He can't lie worth a damn. She looked at him. "We covered this the other day, Jake. What kind of research?"

He was beginning to look pissed off, although it could just be that he was cranky after no sleep. "Would you quit interrupting me?"

"Well, cut to the chase. You started asking weird questions about those storms the minute I finished giving my paper. And now you land on my doorstep with a fistful of questions. If you were trying to get into my pants, I'm guessing you would have taken a different approach. So what gives? And no more lies. You are a really bad liar," she finished bluntly.

He choked on his coffee, and when he could finally speak his voice was still a little rough.

"I want to know what you know about Carter Thompson and Richard Carlisle."

She frowned. "Nothing."

"Bullshit."

"Hey, I'm not the one who's asking for favors here. A little less attitude would work about now," she snapped.

"You think *I'm* copping an attitude?"

"You really came up here to talk about Carter and Richard?" She shook her head. "Okay, fine. The truth is that I don't know anything more about Carter than anyone else does. He's a public figure that I've seen from a distance a few times at company events. I've never spoken to the man."

"Never?"

"No. Yes. I mean, never. I know he's heard of me because he was pissed off when I misjudged those storms. And I sent him a copy of my paper—"

"When?" Jake demanded.

"What's with you? I sent it to him the night before I left for the conference."

"Has he contacted you about it?"

"I don't know. I haven't been home long enough to check my e-mail since I got back from D.C."

"Let's go and check."

"Let's not." She folded her arms across her chest and refused to budge. "I want to know what this is all about or I'm going to call the cops."

His eyes widened. "The cops? Why the hell would you call the cops? You think I'm—"

"What I think is that I met you Friday at a conference. You spook me down there, then you're on my doorstep at six o'clock Sunday morning not sounding any more sane than the yahoos who send me e-mails from addresses like badweatherdude@conspiracy.com. You say you work for some government agency as a forensic meteorologist. Okay, maybe you do, but what do I know from that? It could be the Office of Federal Sewer Research." She shrugged. "And now you've got me standing on a high bridge over deep water presumably because you think my apartment is bugged or something. You tell me what I'm supposed to think, Jake. Better yet, just tell me what the hell is going on."

He looked partly mortified and partly angry, but mostly he just looked like he didn't know what he was supposed to say. Kate didn't help him out.

Finally, he let out a deep breath. "I've been looking very deeply at those storms you profiled, Kate, as well as at a lot of other ones. There's a signature to each of them that suggests that their escalation wasn't natural, just as you imply in your paper."

Something pinged in her brain and made her frown. "What kind of signature?"

He hesitated, which didn't reassure her. "A heat burst."

"I didn't find anything like that. What kind of a heat burst?"

"I can't tell you anything more about them. Not yet,

anyway. But I came across some old research that suggests that Carlisle might know something about storms with similar escalation patterns."

"He never said anything about that."

"Not surprising. The research he was conducting wasn't in the public domain."

Everything he said generated more questions in her head and more churn in her stomach. "What does any of this have to do with Carter Thompson?"

"They worked together on the research."

Kate frowned. "Are you sure?"

"Positive. Both of their names are on the reports."

"That's weird."

"Why?"

She took long sip from her coffee, unsure of what she should say without talking to Richard first. "I've been hanging out with Richard ever since he moved to the New York area ten years ago," she said slowly. "We see each other at least once a month, and we e-mail and talk more often than that, and he's never mentioned a thing about knowing Carter. Could there be another—"

"Kate," Jake interrupted quietly, "it's this Richard and this Carter. I've confirmed it. I need to talk to Richard. Can you arrange it?"

She nodded slowly. "What about Carter?"

"I have to talk to him, too, but I'll figure that out later."

"What about the heat bursts?"

"I can't say."

She reached up to brush away some hairs that the wind was playing with. "No problem. I can probably figure it out myself anyway," she said casually. "I mean, how many forms of heat could excite a storm cell? It had to be something natural, like maybe something metal on the ground that was radiating heat it had absorbed during the day. It wasn't a bomb, because those you can't hide. So what else could it be? If our government doesn't know what it is, then it must be someone else's machinery. Is it some Russian death beam from outer space? Oh, hell, Jake, just tell me who you work for," she demanded. "Who am I going to tell?"

"I can't tell you right now. Maybe later."

Letting out an exaggerated, exasperated breath, she rolled her eyes skyward. "This is too weird. You can't tell me now. What does that mean? You can tell me, but then you'd have to kill me? Come on, is it the CIA? FBI? DIA? Some other three-letter agency? What do you mean you can't tell me?"

He said nothing and started walking back in the direction they'd come. Kate watched his retreating back as something teased at the back of her mind.

She broke into a run and grabbed his arm as she came alongside him. "It's planes, isn't it? You were asking me why I looked for planes in the area."

"I'm not going to pursue this—"

"Could something on a plane do it? Zap a storm cell?"

"I don't know."

"Look, this really got off on the wrong foot. I'm not saying I won't help you. I will help you, Jake. But you have to level with me."

"I told you, I can't. Not right now. I need more information and more answers before I can tell you anything except hypotheses."

"In that case, Carter might have more answers than Richard," she blurted.

He stopped abruptly and she bumped into him. "Why?"

She took a step back and caught her breath. "Because he funds a research foundation for reforestation. One of the women at work mentioned it the other day. She's researching him for a special assignment."

He looked at her. "What are you talking about?"

"He funds a small research foundation that's looking for ways to reverse desertification and the deforestation of tropical rain forests. Wouldn't a large part of that rely on rainfall? He might be really up on this kind of research. I mean, all those storms had to do with unexpected, anomalous rainfall, right? If he knows who's doing what in that sort of weather research, he might know who's behind the storms. Or who could be."

Jake's eyes seemed to bore into hers. "Can I talk to this woman? The one who's researching him?"

"If she's around. I'll call her later, when normal people are awake."

They made the rest of the short trip back to her apartment in relative silence, reaching her block before the expected rain started to fall. Kate could practically hear the gears in Jake's head turning and she knew it was going to be a while before he had anything coherent to say. He was probably like most guys: When he switched his brain into high gear, his ability to multi-task ceased to function.

Once inside her apartment, Kate picked up the remote and flicked on the TV set as she walked through the living room to her bedroom.

"I'm going to take a quick shower. Feel free to watch the Sunday 'Grill the Hill' shows if they haven't all headed for high ground." She caught his attention by waving the remote, then set it down on the coffee table in full view. "I'll be out in ten minutes, and then I'll want some answers. Real ones."

CHAPTER 37

Sunday, July 22, 6:40 A.M., DUMBO, Brooklyn
Coming to New York was beginning to seem like a mistake. Kate was turning out to be somewhat of a pain in the ass with the dual bad habits of interrupting him mid-thought and asking too damned many questions. But the news about Carter's research would probably provide some leads.

Jake picked up the TV remote and, out of habit, flicked through the channels until he reached the Weather Channel. One of the network's severe-weather experts, a college friend, was on the air. Jake brought up the sound as he watched the on-screen mouse draw a circle punctuated with arrows that pointed counter-clockwise around a decent-sized patch of red that was tracking the eastern coastline of the U.S.

"—escalated rapidly overnight after it entered the Gulf Stream and has continued to travel in a northerly direction parallel to the coast. Right now Simone is centered one hundred and ten miles off Richmond, Virginia. The National Hurricane Center upgraded it from a Category 4 to a Category 5 overnight. The sustained winds have been measured at one hundred and fifty-five miles per hour, and the storm has a tight, well-developed eye wall, as you can see here on the screen. Jim?"

The camera cut to one of the anchors, who sent a grave look into the camera. "Thanks, Paul. As we continue our coverage of Hurricane Simone, we offer our condolences to the families of the twenty-two people whose deaths have been attributed to the storm, and urge residents in areas that could be affected to take necessary precautions and seek shelter. While the storm hasn't made landfall yet, low-lying areas along the coast from the Florida Keys to the Outer Banks have suffered extreme damage from the wind and the storm surge. Washington, D.C., is under mandatory evacuation and the New York City and Long Island emergency management agencies have issued mandatory evacuation orders for people living in Zones One and Two, and voluntary evacuation orders for persons living in Zone Three and other near-shore areas. Coastal residents from Connecticut to Boston should be prepared for severe winds, high tides, and storm surges that could exceed ten feet. We'll be right back with more coverage of Hurricane Simone."

Jake hit the Mute button and stared at the time-lapse image of the storm that played over the channel's storm logo before the commercials started. The escalation was impressive, but it wasn't outside the parameters of normal.

That didn't mean it *was* normal, he thought wryly, because the bastards could have scaled back their dirty tricks. He hadn't had time to start looking into it before leaving D.C. and he itched to open his computer now but knew that would only prompt more questions from Kate. He'd already endured enough of those in the last half hour. Besides, the data wouldn't go away. As soon as he got the answers to his questions and could off-load Kate he'd be on his way back to Washington, where he could download everything and take a look.

He stretched out on Kate's couch, cruised the channels for more storm coverage, then folded his hands under his head to watch the damage.

Dressed but with her hair still wet, Kate had come out of her bedroom to find the television on and Jake stretched out on her couch, sound asleep.

Why is it that guys always look so harmless when they're asleep? Even the jerks who barely know you but barge in anyway without a good reason?

Rolling her eyes and still unsure of what to make of the situation, she shook her head and walked toward the kitchen to refill her coffee mug. After a quick glance at the clock, she reached for her phone. Her father would be up already. She'd have to dump Jake somewhere and get over to her parents' place to get them to a shelter. Ridiculous as it seemed, she knew they'd never leave their apartment on their own, even though they lived only two blocks from the beach. Her father would want to face down the storm and her mother would break out her favorite Rosary and put scapulars on the both of them. None of which was likely to deflect 155-mile-an-hour sustained winds or twenty-foot storm surges.

The low voice from the television caught her attention. "And now, in a breaking story, we go to Old Greenwich, Connecticut, where meteorologist Richard Carlisle was found dead in his yard earlier this morning—"

Certain she hadn't just heard what she'd thought she had, Kate swung her head around, her eyes riveted to the TV screen.

Richard's face smiled at her from a frame to the left of the anchor's blond hair.

The words she heard couldn't possibly be real.

"—Carlisle's body was discovered at two o'clock this morning by Greenwich police, who'd been called to his property by a neighbor's complaint of a barking dog. They are treating the death as a homicide. Carlisle, who lived alone in an exclusive beachfront area of Old Greenwich, was a respected figure in the weather community and a beloved television personality. He was sixty-six. We turn now to another breaking story, this time in the Middle East, where overnight—"

The mug slipped out of her hands and shattered at her feet. She barely registered the sound or the sensation, but out of the corner of her eye she saw Jake leap from the couch where he'd been sleeping seconds before. An instant later, he was standing beside her.

"What's wrong?"

She turned her head to look at him, the motion seeming to take forever until she focused on his face. "She said he's dead," she whispered. The harsh, strangled voice didn't sound like hers. "Isn't that what she said?"

"Who's dead? I think you should sit down. Be careful. The floor is full of broken glass," Jake said quietly, taking her hand and tugging her gently toward the couch.

"He can't be dead."

"Here."

She felt Jake's hands on her shoulders, pushing down, and then her knees bent and she half-fell onto the cushions. She stared up at him, feeling unlike herself, feeling like time had become viscous. Feeling like she had when she'd watched the towers fall. It couldn't possibly be real.

"Why would they say he was dead? Turn to a different channel. I want to hear it when they say it's a mistake."

"Who did they say is dead?" he asked again, his voice gentle as he crouched in front of her, his eyes probing her own.

She stared at him. "Richard. They said Richard is dead. They're treating it as a homicide."

His eyes widened and he got to his feet. "Kate, stay there. I'll get you some water."

"I'm not thirsty, Jake. I want to change the channel," she said, her voice rising as her heart started to pump faster. "Where's the remote?"

She watched in slow motion as he picked up the remote and flashed through the channels until he came to a head-line news station, where a reporter stood in the steady rain in front of the street sign for Ford Lane, Richard's street. "Turn it up."

"—lived at the end of this private road. Neighbors called the police at one forty-five this morning to complain about Carlisle's dog barking, and that's when his body was dis-covered in his yard, approximately halfway between his house and a small dock. Neighbors recall seeing a dark sedan entering Carlisle's driveway earlier in the evening, and a neighbor reported hearing voices coming from the vicinity of Carlisle's property after that. According to po-lice, there was no sign of forced entry and it appears that burglary was not a motive. Police also said that it appears there was no sign of a struggle, indicating that Carlisle may have known his attacker. This is Brian Mitchell in Old Greenwich, Connecticut, for CNN Headline News."

The box went silent and slowly, slowly, Kate turned her head to look at a blurred Jake. Tears were hot on her cheeks and a hard, searing lump tore at her throat. "Jake—"

"I'm sorry." He knelt again on the floor next to the couch and wrapped his arms around her as she started to shake. She wasn't sure how long she sat like that, crying, alternat-ing between disbelief and profound loss.

"Kate," Jake said eventually, whispering into her damp hair, "I think you should come with me."

She pulled back and looked at him, wiping her cheeks with her palms. "Where?"

"Washington," he said after a moment.

"No." She started to pull away, but his hands closed firmly around her shoulders and he gave her a small shake.

"Kate, listen to me," he said, his voice low and grave. "There are people there who will want to talk to you about your paper and about Richard and what he might have told you."

"No. He didn't tell me anything. I need to go to—"

"Kate," he snapped, and she stared at him, feeling her eyes go wide at the intensity in his. "Kate, listen to me. You need to come to Washington with me. *Now.* So don't argue. New York is already under voluntary evacuation. Washington is under mandatory evacuation, but I will get you there literally despite hell and high water."

"But my parents—"

"Let someone else take care of them."

"There is no one else," she snapped, pushing his hands away.

"There has to be. A neighbor, someone."

"No, I—"

"Damn it, listen to me, Kate! I don't know if your paper and Richard's death and this storm are connected, but if they are you're in serious danger." He reached down and unmuted the television, filling the room with information about the latest lawn pesticide, and then brought his mouth close to her ear. "I'm not talking about the Cub Scouts. I'm talking about terrorists. I work for the Central Intelligence Agency. Someone is messing with these storms, Kate. Someone is *creating* them. We know it. We just don't know who they are. That paper of yours said more or less the same thing. Richard's death might be random violence, Kate, but if it isn't, and if it has any connection to those storms or your paper, you could be a target, too. So stop arguing with me and pack a bag."

Sunday, July 22, 7:45 A.M., DUMBO, Brooklyn

Kate closed her eyes, not wanting to see all the taillights ahead of them, crawling across the bridge they'd been walking on just over an hour ago.

Since when did New Yorkers actually pay attention to the mayor or any other bureaucrat?

"Mom, I know it's early and I know you're scared," Kate said, her nerves stretched thin and her patience nearly gone. "But this is the real thing and you've got to get out of town."

"Your father doesn't want to go."

"He doesn't have a choice," Kate said slowly and emphatically. "You have to go and you have to go now, while things are still relatively calm. Do you see the wind? You think it looks rough now, twelve hours from now it will be much worse, and in twenty-four hours there could be water up to the second floor. I'm not joking, Ma. Do you understand me?"

"Don't talk to me like I'm a child," her mother sniffed.

"Well, quit acting like one, then," Kate shot back. "I'm trying to tell you that we don't know where this storm is going to go. But if it comes at the city, which it very well could, you're the first stop on the tour. Remember those pictures of New Orleans after Katrina hit? And you couldn't believe those people had actually stuck around? Well, you'll be one of those people. You live two blocks from the beach."

"Your father—"

"Tell him he's nuts. Tell him he doesn't have the right kind of oxygen tank for breathing underwater," she snapped. "You have to get in the car and head for Aunt Molly's in Vermont. Pack food and water and blankets, because it could take you a long time to get there. Keep your cell phone charged and your gas tank topped up on the way, okay?"

"Will you come with us? Where are you? Are you coming over here?"

She grimaced and held her breath for a moment, fighting

back a sudden threat of tears. "No. I'm, uh, I'm heading out of town on business."

"On a Sunday morning? You didn't mention it the other night. Where are you going?"

"Washington." She closed her eyes and waited for the shriek, which came right on schedule.

"Washington? *D.C.?* Katharine, are you nuts? Everyone has left Washington. Even the president is gone. What are you going there for? Are you alone?"

She held the phone away from her ear and sent Jake, who had his eyes straight ahead on the road, a dirty look. "No, I'm not alone. I'm with someone from work. The trip came up suddenly. I'll be fine."

Jake glanced at her and she rolled her eyes.

"I think you should tell your boss he's crazy and come to Vermont with us."

At least she's made the decision. "I'll be fine," Kate repeated firmly. "I want you out of that house and on the road in an hour, tops. Got it? Go to one of those evacuation centers if you have to, but get away from the beach. I'll call you in an hour, and you'd better be on the road."

"I'll see what I can do about your father."

"Have Mr. O'Neal come over and pick him up and threaten to put him in the trunk if he won't go on his own," she replied forcefully. "Okay?"

"That would go over a treat." There was a long, heavy pause at the other end of the line. "Katie, did you hear about Richard?"

Her mother's voice was quiet and hesitant and Kate swallowed hard against the lump she was trying to ignore. She squeezed her eyes tight. "Yeah, I did."

"I'm so sorry, Katie."

"Thanks, Mom." She sucked in a hard breath and opened her eyes. "Listen, I'll call you in a while, okay?"

"Okay."

"I love you," she finished quietly, and there was a pause on the other end of the line.

Then, "I love you, too, Katie. You be careful."

"I will, Mom. You, too."

She ended the call and rested her head against the seat, eyes closed, and didn't even try to stop the tears.

Sunday, July 22, 8:30 A.M., Financial District, New York City

Davis Lee stopped in the opened doorway to his office and stared at the unwelcome sight of Carter Thompson's back framed by the view. His view. He clenched his teeth against the invasion and gave a small cough as he entered the room.

God-damned Carter didn't even turn around for a few seconds.

"Good mornin'. You're not usually a man for surprises, Carter. I thought our meeting was for nine," Davis Lee said easily as he set his Starbucks cup on his desk and proceeded forward to shake his boss's hand. The man looked tired. Not even just tired. Haggard. But when he smiled, an odd look appeared in his eye that Davis Lee couldn't interpret.

"Good morning. I didn't get you in here too early, did I?"

It's Sunday. "Course not," he lied with a smile as he came to a stop next to the older man. "The view is better when it isn't pissin' down rain. They're calling for an evacuation already. Can't believe it. The storm is sittin' off the Carolinas, for pity's sake."

"It's a big storm and this is a big city," Carter said absently.

They both looked out over the gray, watery city in silence for a few minutes. The lightning strikes were spectacular, and Davis Lee could feel the thunder as it boomed and cracked around them.

"So what's on your mind, Carter? Anything in particular?"

"One of our meteorologists sent me a paper she wrote. Looks like she presented it at some conference a few days ago."

Carter's hands remained in the pockets of his khakis, but Davis Lee could tell by the way he held his head that the man wasn't making casual conversation. More likely, he was boiling mad.

"That would be Kate Sherman. She's damned good at what she does."

"The paper makes her sound like she missed her calling. She should have been writing for *The X-Files*."

Damn.

"Did you know about that paper? Did you approve it?" Carter continued. He'd started jingling the change in his pocket. That was never a good sign.

"I knew she was writing it and I saw an early version, but I didn't see the finished version until you did. She sent it to both of us at the same time, after it was accepted for the conference," Davis Lee admitted. "I never thought she'd make herself sound so foolish. She's a smart—"

"She identified herself as our chief meteorologist," Carter interjected sharply, "which makes it look like the company approved the paper and her outlandish conjectures. It should never have been written. It should never have been published. It's a pity you didn't read it before this mess started. I'm surprised the press hasn't gotten hold of it yet. No doubt they will." Carter turned to face him with cold eyes. "Fire her. Immediately."

We've got enough problems on our hands. Davis Lee stared at him. "Carter, that's a bit extreme. If you're worried about the press liking her paper so well, what do you think they're going to do if she's fired for writing it?"

"Did you approve it in writing?"

Davis Lee set his feet apart as if bracing himself and folded his arms across his chest. "That's generally a rubber-stamp issue, Carter. I'm sure there's something, some e-mail—"

"Get rid of it," he said flatly. "Get someone to clean out her desk, delete her files, and get her out of the system. Then fire her, Davis Lee. Today."

The points Elle had brought up came to mind, and he

met Carter's eyes. "I just want to make sure I've got this straight, Carter. Kate Sherman has been with us for more than ten years, but we're firing her because you think she might have embarrassed the company by writing a paper that isn't going to be read by anyone but the weather weenies?" He paused. "There are other ways of handling this that won't end in a lawsuit and headlines. Hell, we could just tell her she has to move to Iowa and work at headquarters. She's a Brooklyn girl. She'd quit in a heartbeat."

Carter said nothing, just resumed looking out the window.

"Just what is it we're afraid of, exactly?" Davis Lee asked. "We're a privately held company with a solid reputation. I can't see how one crazy paper full of crap hypotheses and junk science is going to hurt us. If anything, she's just made her own life more difficult and torpedoed her next bonus package. She's no woo-woo guru, Carter, and frankly, I can't believe she made those half-assed implications. She's smart as hell and generally conscientious to a fault. I don't want to lose her. Let me deal with her. I'll make sure she gets the point."

"You'll do as I instructed you."

Anger bubbled up in Davis Lee as Carter stubbornly kept his back to him. "All right, Carter. I'll find her and fire her. But for the record, I think it's a bad idea." He glanced down at his desk then and saw a note in Elle's handwriting.

The son of a bitch is in a foul mood anyway. It's as good a time as any.

"There's another situation I think needs discussing." Davis Lee looked up again, making his voice more relaxed than it was a few seconds ago. "I've had an assistant looking into your background in advance of your declaration to run. She found some things I think we might have a hard time explaining to Bill O'Reilly."

The older man stiffened. "There's nothing in my background that should need explaining."

"That's why I had her check, just to make sure." He

paused to take a sip of coffee he neither needed nor wanted and carefully replaced the cardboard cup on his desk. "I didn't say she found anything bad, just some things that could be misinterpreted if someone felt the urge. Have a seat?"

Carter ignored the invitation, and Davis Lee remained standing.

"She came across two things that might be trouble-some. The first was a series of papers you wrote in college that were cited in some off-the-wall books on weather control." Davis Lee made sure to keep his expression neutral as he watched Carter freeze. "The other is some articles of incorporation for a foundation for—" He ruffled some papers on his desk for effect, as if he were looking for something. "Something environmental. Rain forests? And something about deserts. Based in—was it India? Are there even rain forests over there?"

He looked up to see that Carter had finally turned to face him. The sudden pallor in his boss's face both alarmed and pleased him. "Those research articles might seem sort of woo-woo to the electorate, I'm thinking, so we're going to have to count on doing some damage control. Have something prepared in case we have to explain them away. But that foundation might seem sort of . . . whimsical?"

As anticipated, Carter flushed deeply at the insult, and Davis Lee cut him off before he could reply. "Maybe that's the wrong word. I mean that it may not resonate with the electorate because it's not an issue facing Americans right now. We have a few deserts, but they're tourist attractions. And we don't have any rain forests." He shrugged. "I'm thinking there might be some questions as to why you aren't focusing your energy and funding right here at home. I mean, Buffett and Gates can plunk their money in Africa or anywhere else because they're not running for office." He paused. "On the other hand, his wife's home-grown philan-thropy didn't do much for John Kerry, did it? So maybe this will be okay."

"I've always been an environmentalist and I'm not ashamed of it. And I will fund whatever causes I deem worthy." Carter's voice was low and almost shaking with anger, and his fists were clenched at his side as he turned away. "As for the early papers, I can't stop people from citing my research. And for your information, attempts at weather manipulation have been going on for centuries. Many significant breakthroughs have occurred in the last few decades."

Well, I'll be damned. "Then that should about take care of it, I guess. Unless you've had something to do with any of those significant breakthroughs," he ended with a lazy note in his voice.

Carter turned to look at him again with fury burning in his eyes. "Yes, that should take care of it. And for the record, I have no intention of being questioned about any of it by you now or by the press or Congress later on."

He walked out of the office, leaving Davis Lee to stare incredulously at his retreating back and the small clumps of muddy grass that had fallen from the treads of his shoes.

Where do you get mud on your shoes between Westchester Airport and Midtown Manhattan? And why the hell would Congress come into the picture?

Sunday, July 22, 3:00 P.M., Camp David, Maryland

It was always nice to get into the mountains and away from the soggy heat of D.C., but when it rained, the presidential compound seemed more claustrophobic than a subway tunnel. The sound of the rain smashing through the trees and pummeling the roof and the ground was incessant, and after two days of it everyone was starting to get edgy. Sometimes, like now, it seemed to take on the cadence of a drumroll. Win, who had arrived with his parents on Saturday morning, now watched his father's senior national security advisor try very hard to maintain his neutral expression in the face of presidential anger.

"Tell me again why this never made it into the PDB?" the president demanded, referring to the Presidential Daily

Briefing, a capsulized summary of all current or imminent security or intelligence issues affecting American interests worldwide. "We have a quarter of the population on the move because of Simone and the fact that the intelligence community thinks the storm might be an act of terrorism isn't important enough to make the grade?"

"We had nothing concrete, sir. There was convincing evidence of earlier tampering with the weather but—"

"Do we have anything concrete now?"

Win noticed a shine on the advisor's forehead. "Not really."

"Why not?"

"This storm's evolution hasn't followed the same pattern as the others. Mr. President, there's a task force in place, and—"

"I want updates every hour, Tucker." The president turned his attention to the papers on his desk and Tucker Wharton slunk from the room. After the door closed, his father met Win's eyes. "Did you know about this?"

He nodded. "I was in the same meeting with Tucker."

"What do you think?"

"I think it's a great opportunity and if it weren't threatening New York, I'd say you should be getting some photo ops on the ground in Charleston."

His father stared at him for a minute, then spoke. "You're a real prick, you know that?"

Win didn't react other than to smile. *I learned from the best.*

"Where's Elle?" his father asked, walking back to his desk.

"She's still in New York. I flew up there Friday to check in with her."

"And?"

Win shrugged and leaned against the window. "She's fine. Not getting as much as I'd hoped, but I think I lit a fire under her. I'm sure she'll have something for us soon."

His father glanced over his shoulder at him with obvious loathing. "Evacuation orders were issued for the city.

Are you going to get her out of there? Your mother will kill both of us if something happens to her."

"Yes, I know. The golden godchild, the daughter she never had." He rolled his eyes. "Elle's a big girl and has never been prone to doing anything stupid. Besides, that building is on high ground on the Upper East Side and it's built like a tank. She'll be fine."

His father turned and faced him, giving him the same hard-ass look that made his cabinet squirm. Out of long habit, Win refused to look away.

"You, personally, put her up there. You, personally, will make sure she's okay. Do you understand that? I was never in favor of this. She's a sweet kid and she's in over her head because you put her there. I'm not going to let her get hurt because you wanted her out of your hair for a while so you could bang that Euro-trash trollop," the president said. "Next time I ask you about her, I expect a decent answer."

Just then an aide walked in. "Sir, I have the head of the National Hurricane Center on the phone."

Bored with the conversation and glad for the interruption, Win nodded at his father and left the room.

CHAPTER **38**

Traffic had been building all day, as had people's tempers and the level of panic across New York City. Ignoring the repeated pleas to go to the nearest staging area so they could be transported efficiently to the appropriate shelter, residents had taken to the roads themselves. The result was that every road leading from Long Island into the city or onto the mainland and every road, bridge, and tunnel from Brooklyn and Queens and Staten Island into Manhattan was at a standstill. Blaring horns competed with the roar of the gusting wind, and the incessantly drumming rain held a different rhythm than the fingers drumming angrily on dashboards and steering wheels. Freeway exits in Westchester and just over the state lines in Connecticut and New Jersey were already closed to all but local traffic. Ferries were no longer an option due to the high seas.

In the city, speed limits in the tunnels were severely reduced as the runoff began to exceed the ability of the sewers to handle it, and some of the subways had already stopped running due to standing water on the tracks. Bridges were swaying in ways their designers never envisioned, enduring torsion that wearied their seams and struts.

And still the majority of the people tried to go about their business, fighting to stay upright against the wind and ignoring the rain—the most common refrain being "at least it isn't snow."

The beaches—Long Beach, Coney Island, the Rockaways—were getting pummeled. Roofs were torn from shops and shacks, and lifeguard chairs careened across the sand. Ripped, bolts and all, from the boardwalks, benches somersaulted across sand and sidewalks, coming to a stop only when they became entangled in the metal grates that afforded only minimal protection to the plate-glass windows behind them. Boats shattered in their slips, leaving fuel slicks on the surface to tempt the lightning.

Trees crashed onto light poles and wrenched wires from their moorings, bringing darkness to places that, for more than a century, had barely known it. Sludgy, muddy water lapped into suddenly eerie, darkened living rooms, astonishing the foolhardy and terrifying the naïve. It lapped at staircases, driving the occupants upward, farther away from the unlikely chance of a late rescue, closer to the prospects of a gruesome death they were certain they didn't deserve.

Fish, driven toward the shore by the currents and made hungry by the falling pressure, delighted fishermen daring enough to brave the elements. Larger fish, the predators, followed and gorged themselves on effortless meals. A clutch of bodysurfers, young, healthy, dressed in neons and giddy from their exertions in the awesome breakers, perished together in a flailing, bloody froth of teeth, fins, and dark, sinewy speed.

The Hudson and East rivers, between which Manhattan usually nestled in insouciant comfort, swelled and pushed brackish tidal water and its effluvia farther north than it had ever been, sloshing over real estate considered more valuable for its view than its ability to drain. Wind drove the filthy, stinking water over seawalls and garden walls. The rivers' debris floated in the streets and sailed into windows.

And through it all, helicopters by the dozens fought the deadly winds above the city; those with private logos ferried the late-moving privileged away from the distressing mess surrounding them while pilots in the civic choppers alerted their comrades to impending disasters. The media birds filmed it all to satisfy the morbid curiosity of the rest of the world.

CHAPTER **39**

Sunday, July 22, 9:00 P.M., Campbelltown, Iowa
Carter barely remembered the trip home. It had taken him several hours to get from Midtown to the small airport in Westchester County, a trip that should have taken less than an hour. Once he'd gotten there, though, he'd been able to board and get airborne quickly. Private jets were good for that, for getting places fast and unhindered. He'd been so deep in thought, troubled by the recent events that were threatening the success of his project, that he'd been surprised when the tires had bumped down onto the tarmac

of the airstrip at his home. He hadn't been able to focus on anything other than the outrageous reality that for thirty years there had been no disruptions to his research, and now, with success within his grasp, he suddenly faced menace from all sides.

He took a deep breath as he stood on his back porch, overlooking the dark, sparkling pond and the airstrip behind it. He could hear the sounds of his grandchildren being put to bed for the night. His girls and their families had made the unexpected and unexplained trip without argument and would remain here until the threat of Simone and the fallout from her aftermath—literally fallout, from the destruction of the Indian Point Nuclear Power Plant—was no longer an issue. He would need them to keep things running afterward, and Iris would have been beside herself if any of them had been in danger. He let out a heavy breath.

Despite the setbacks, he was getting the situation back under control. He'd dealt with Richard Carlisle, and he'd deal with Kate Sherman as severely if he had to. The assistant Davis Lee had mentioned might have to be silenced as well.

Carter tried to force himself to relax, telling himself that in a few days' time none of it would be necessary. The country would be looking for a new leader, and he'd be ready. He was the one they needed.

Feeling the need for reassurance, he turned on his heel, opened the screen door, and stepped back into his office. Crossing the hardwood floor, dappled with tree-filtered moonlight, he grabbed the correct cell phone and punched in the only speed-dial number in its memory. Raoul picked up on the first ring.

Carter ignored his greeting. "I need you to deploy to Bermuda effective immediately."

The short silence on the other end of the call plucked at his overly taut temper. "Did you copy that?" he snapped.

"I did," came the deliberately slow reply.

"We're going to make one more—"

"No, we're not."

The surge of anger was followed immediately by the erratic double thump in his chest and Carter sat down behind his desk as the light-headedness began.

"We're going to make one more trip," he rasped, gripping the arm of his chair and closing his eyes against the sensation of falling. "Not a test. I need you up here."

"The airports are closed, Carter."

"I'll make sure one isn't. Where are you now?"

"The Yucatán Peninsula. Didn't want to be in the path of anything."

Carter loosened his grip as the dizziness began to subside. "It's well past you, which is why I need you to move. I need data. Just data. I just need you to do a flyby."

"Of a Category 5 hurricane," came the laconic reply.

"The plane can handle it."

The silence was deafening.

"I advise against it."

"You what?" Carter demanded, incredulous.

"It's in the middle of the Atlantic. There aren't any places to hide, nor are there any places to land if there's trouble. We'll be seen and there will be hell to pay."

"I don't pay you to be a coward or a consultant. I pay you to fly the plane and execute my orders. I need the data," Carter said flatly.

"It's too risky. There are all sorts of reconnaissance planes in the area, and a lot of satellite coverage. We'll be discovered."

Carter became aware of his fist slowly opening and closing where it hung at his side. "All right. Do what you can with regard to the data, but I still need to deploy you to Bermuda as soon as possible. You'll be compensated appropriately."

The pause lasted long enough to make a point. "Right. We'll be there in forty-eight hours. Weather permitting."

Carter ignored the sarcasm. "I need you there within twelve hours."

"It's not going to happen, mate. The plane needs to be

inspected. I don't know if she's ready to get through a storm that size."

"Why isn't the plane ready? You've been there for days."

"Carter, you may be the banker, but I am the commander of the fucking plane and if I say we don't fly, then we don't fly." The pilot's voice had taken on a harsh, defensive edge that made Carter's eyes narrow.

The pilot's attitude was as intolerable as it was unusual, but without a backup crew or a backup aircraft, Carter had no choice but to acquiesce, and the pilot knew it. "We'll speak again in a few hours, after you've had some time to reconsider your situation," he replied tightly, and disconnected.

Sunday, July 22, 11:50 P.M., Northern Virginia

Kate felt like she'd just driven through hell. The trip had taken more than three times longer than it should have between the insanely heavy traffic, frequent diversions to smaller roads due to accidents, downed trees, flooding, and the dark, steady downpour that kept roadways dangerous and put drivers into a semihypnotic state. It was shortly before midnight when they arrived at a fairly nondescript home somewhere west of Washington.

The drive had been tense and nearly silent, punctuated by occasional attempts at innocuous conversation, infrequent bursts of music, and pit stops at various rest areas. Despite having just made the journey north, Jake did most of the driving. Even when she was behind the wheel, Kate's mind wandered. At least her parents were safely ensconced in one of the city's evacuation centers. Assuming they hadn't started lying to her just to get her to stop calling them.

She pushed that thought out of her head. She had to trust them because there was nothing she could do for them now. Cell phone coverage had gone from erratic to non-existent as they headed south of Philly.

"Here we are. I think," Jake said, slowing down as he navigated a long, bumpy, well-puddled driveway that bisected a large swath of lawn. There were about eight cars parked near the house, all facing the street as if they had to be ready at a moment's notice. The house itself was dark, with only faint glimmers of light at the edges of the windows.

It was downright creepy, and Kate realized she'd never actually asked to see any of Jake's identification. She didn't even have his business card.

"I've never been here before. I guess it's a safe house. When I called him before we left New York, my boss told me to bring you here."

Numb with grief and worry and bone-tired, Kate felt panic set in. Being stuck in the countryside with a stranger had never been covered in her self-defense classes. Not getting into a stranger's car had, but she'd already blown that opportunity. She slid her right hand down her thigh and wrapped it around the door handle.

Trying to keep her voice from shaking, she said, "I haven't been kidnapped, have I? I mean, you are who you said you are, aren't you?"

He turned to look at her. She thought he seemed to be trying not to laugh. "No and yes. Are you okay? You look like you're freaking out."

"I expected to go to headquarters."

"Washington is under evacuation orders, remember? My town house is probably already flooded and Langley—that's the CIA building—is pretty close to the river, so even if the road is sandbagged, I'm sure it's open to emergency vehicles only. We're about thirty miles from the Beltway. There will be a bunch of people inside, all of whom know who you are and why you're with me. Okay? Nothing to worry about."

"Says you."

"Well, yeah."

He brought the car to a stop and killed the lights. Gingerly, she stepped out, straight into a puddle that covered the top of her sneaker.

Great. She reached into the backseat and grabbed her duffle.

"I'll take that," Jake offered as he came around to her side of the car.

"It's okay. I've got it."

He let her pass into the house ahead of him. The large living room, to the right of the front door, was set up with folding tables and mismatched office chairs and lots of laptops and flat-screen monitors. The dining room, on the other side of the door, was similarly arranged. A few of the dozen or so people sitting at the tables looked over briefly but offered no greeting. A moment later a woman came around a corner unwrapping a Twinkie. She greeted Jake by name.

"Kate, this is Candy Freeman, my boss. Candy, Kate Sherman."

Candy extended her free hand and Kate shook it. She couldn't help noticing that the woman's nails were perfectly manicured and painted a deep pink. It was incongruous to say the least, given the woman's rugged jeans and well-worn PENN sweatshirt.

"Hi, Kate. Thank you for making the trip." She glanced from Kate to Jake and back again. "I think we can spare a few hours for y'all to get some sleep. No offense, but you look kinda tired."

" 'Exhausted' would be a better word. Where can we drop our stuff?" Jake replied.

"Hope y'all got to be best friends on the drive down. We're under more or less battle conditions here. The bunks are upstairs. Everyone's doubling up and some of the guys are using sleeping bags. I saved you a bedroom, though, around the corner to the left at the top of the stairs. It's tiny. Twin beds. The mattresses are made of some sort of concrete and the pillows are flatter than bird shit on a fence post, but the blankets are new." She glanced at her watch. "I'll come get you at four o'clock unless I need you sooner. Tom will be getting here about then. Sweet dreams."

With a smile, she continued past them into the living room, sat down at a laptop, and took a delicate bite of the Twinkie.

Kate looked at Jake. "Is she for real?" she whispered.

Jake motioned for Kate to go up the stairs. "Totally. She was one of the first D, S-and-T geeks to take the paramilitary training after they opened it up to us. She got the highest marks in her class. Apparently the only thing she can't do is throw a grenade properly. So don't be fooled by all the girly stuff."

"Why can't she throw a grenade?"

"The instructor said she throws like a girl. Candy said pulling the pin broke a nail and she got distracted."

Not sure whether to believe him, Kate nevertheless decided to give Candy Freeman a wide berth.

Turning left at the top of the stairs, Kate led the way down the shadowy hallway, which resounded with the sound of snoring coming from behind closed doors. She reached the end of the corridor and the only open door.

There, in what had obviously been intended as a large closet, were two twin beds separated by about eight inches but made up with military precision.

"Honey, we're home," Jake said lightly from behind her.

"There's not room to turn around in here."

"It's not meant for turning around. It's meant for sleeping."

"I'll take this one." Kate plunked her duffle on the bed to the right. The mattress didn't budge. She looked over her shoulder at Jake and said drily, "Looks like I'm about to break my record of never sleeping with someone on the first date."

He grinned. "If we ever go on a date, I'll take you someplace nicer than this."

"If you ever expect me to go on a date, you'd better."

His gaze roamed over her face for a minute and became serious before he spoke. "I'm going to just give Candy the quick version. I'll be back in a few minutes. You should get some sleep. Tomorrow is going to be a long day."

"Thanks."

After an awkward pause, he left the room. As the door closed behind him, the solitude rushed over her. Kate sank onto the bed as she let her tears flow.

Monday, July 23, 12:20 A.M., a CIA safe house in rural Northern Virginia

Jake headed back downstairs and dropped into the chair across from Candy. She looked up, not surprised.

"Thanks for waiting up."

"I never can seem to sleep through national emergencies. Tell me about her."

"She's a meteorologist with Coriolis Management in Manhattan. I met her at that weather conference on Friday, when she presented a paper on a few of the same storms we've been looking at. She was friends with Richard Carlisle, the TV—"

Candy raised an eyebrow. "The guy who died?"

"He was murdered. And he worked for the Agency in the sixties doing weather research. With Carter Thompson."

Candy smiled. "That's my boy."

He glanced at the computer. "Do you mind if I check on Simone?"

"As a matter of fact, I do. You really do look like hell and you need to get some sleep, because I'm going to need all your neurons firing tomorrow. Besides, it might be the last you get for a while, so enjoy it." She smiled sweetly as she took the last bite of her Twinkie.

Resigned and not altogether unhappy, Jake headed back up to the bedroom. Kate was huddled under the blanket on her bed, her breathing quiet and regular. Moments later, he was stretched out on his own bed. He didn't remember falling asleep.

Monday, July 23, 3:45 A.M., a CIA safe house in rural Northern Virginia

Kate had a mug of coffee in one hand and was rubbing the sleep out of her eyes with the other as Jake logged onto the Web and then to the weather sites he subscribed to.

A pit formed at the bottom of his stomach as he watched the spreading streaks of red, orange, and yellow spiraling across the western Atlantic and trailing across the mid-Atlantic seaboard. With a tight eye and well-formed wind bands, Simone had achieved wind speeds that put her squarely into Category 5 and she was still moving along the predicted northerly track, although at a slightly higher than expected forward speed of 12 miles per hour. It could be worse—storms in the Gulf Stream had been known to move much faster—but it still wasn't a good sign. The warming Gulf Stream waters were potent fuel. If the water got any warmer, it could turbocharge the storm.

"Are you sure you're awake enough for this?" Jake asked.

"Yes. Go ahead. I'm all here." Kate forced a smile and looked at the screen with squinty eyes that widened as she realized what she was seeing. "Good God."

They'd been awakened five minutes ago with the news that Tom Taylor would be arriving in thirty minutes and would want a full briefing on what Jake had been able to piece together. Candy had agreed that it was time to fill Kate in on some of the background in order for her to help them fill in the gaps.

Logging onto a classified area of the NOAA site, Jake began to download the footage of the storm's buildup over the last twenty-four hours, half-hoping that further investigation wouldn't reveal the same artificial pulses that had preceded the other storms. Every other storm had been over land, short-lived, and in rural areas. If they had been tests of weather manipulation, they had been successful ones.

Which meant this was more than likely the real thing.

He looked back to the screen displaying the live satellite feed. With the exception of coastal Maine, all of the northeast coast was now under mandatory evacuation orders. Although forecasters wouldn't know for the next twenty-four to forty-eight hours if Simone was going to make landfall or begin to dissipate, the storm surge was breaking records all along the shore, sweeping multimillion-dollar homes into the sea and driving multimillion-dollar boats deep onto land.

"There's no way this thing's going to disappear, Jake," Kate whispered. "It's the biggest thing I've ever seen. And it's parked in the Gulf Stream." She looked at him, her eyes huge and a little wild. "I was diving yester—Saturday—off the south shore of Long Island and the sea surface temperature was eighty-one degrees. That's more than hospitable; that's a recipe for a frigging disaster."

"Well, the industry took a beating last year because of all the warnings issued after Katrina and Rita. The public felt ripped off when there weren't any big storms. Now they're getting one," he muttered as he watched the progression of the download and then opened the application that would let them view the days-old data at the appropriate level of detail.

Three minutes later, he could feel Kate's breath on his neck as she leaned over him. They both stared at the screen, watching as the seconds counter flashed numbers.

"What are we looking for?" she asked quietly, as if any noise would disrupt the operation.

"Wait a sec."

He slowed the pace as the counter approached the approximate time of escalation and seconds later was rewarded by a short burst of dark yellow on the monitor. His excitement faded as he realized that what he was looking at was unlikely to be caused by a laser. It wasn't hot enough.

"Damn it."

"What?"

He sat back in his chair and looked at Kate, slightly stunned. "Did you see that burst of heat?"

"The lightning? Yeah. What about it?"

"All the other storms had a similar signature, but it

wasn't lighting. When you looked real closely, it turned out to be something else."

Kate looked at him like he was crazy. "Like what?"

"It looked like an infrared burst from a laser."

She stared at him for a solid minute. "A laser?"

He nodded.

"And this one is different?"

He nodded again. "Different signature. This was lower and occurred nearly at the surface. And it happened too many seconds before the escalation."

"It was the underwater thingy."

"The what?"

"There was some underwater event. Not an earthquake or anything like that. Some vent burped or something." She shook her head. "It will come to me. Richard told me about it."

She went quiet abruptly, as if the casual mention of his name had overwhelmed her. Jake looked back at the screen to give her some privacy.

Clearing her throat, she continued. "That was the first escalation and it was minor, but go back to that and then tick forward a few more minutes. You'll see the second escalation, the big one."

He did as she suggested, moving back through the file until the storm was just a slowly organizing cluster of clouds. He watched the swirls of pixilated color move in a rapid stop-action dance across the screen. And then, just as she'd said, he saw the first small flash, followed eighteen minutes later by a second burst of heat that appeared on the screen for mere seconds.

His blood began pumping at speed as he replayed the footage, slowing it down even further. There it was. A streak of dark red commencing at an altitude of nearly fifteen hundred feet, shooting downward for less than three seconds, superheating the core of the storm and sending the ceiling of the storm cell soaring up a few thousand feet.

"Son of a bitch. We've got you," he murmured, then turned around to look at Kate, who was staring at the screen and the red streak that was stationary in the middle of it.

"That's it? That's the laser?"

"It is indeed," he said triumphantly, standing up. "Kate, I could kiss you."

She held up a hand instantly. "Don't even think about it. I never do that before breakfast, unless I've had dinner and drinks first."

He laughed, more elated than he'd been since getting assigned to the task force. "You'd better grab the shower before anyone else gets it. Tom will be here soon."

CHAPTER **40**

Monday, July 23, 4:30 A.M., a CIA safe house in rural Northern Virginia

The nubby fabric beneath her backside certainly felt real, but Kate wasn't at all sure that it actually was. Because if it was, that meant everything that she remembered happening in the last twenty-four hours was actually real, too, instead of a really, really bad hallucination. If the fabric was real, that meant she had just been invited to sit down next to Jake around a folding table in the living room of a remote farmhouse, surrounded by a few people in camo uniforms, a Twinkie-eating cheerleader who knew how to kill people, a dead-eyed guy named Tom who looked like he had killed people, and a lot of flat-screen monitors littering the table and every other available surface. It also meant that Richard was dead and that her parents were, she hoped, stewing in an evacuation center somewhere in Queens.

"Ms. Sherman, we appreciate that you made the trip down here to talk with us."

Like I had a choice. She flashed a tight smile and said

nothing. The expressionless guy gave her the creeps, and Jake, in describing him, hadn't said anything reassuring like *He's really a great guy* or *He'll warm up once he gets to know you.* Which meant he was a jerk and likely to remain one.

"How much has Jake told you about the situation?" Tom asked.

"Not much. Just that there appears to be some weather manipulation going on and that the storms I wrote about in my paper are storms that he—you, I mean, are also studying."

"Anything else?"

What the hell am I doing here? "He showed me the laser signature on Simone. Look, I choke on tests, okay?" she blurted, partly annoyed and partly just plain scared. "I don't mind answering your questions, but I haven't had much sleep and I'm still trying to absorb the fact that a good friend of mine was murdered, so I'm not operating on all cylinders. If you could just ask me what you want to know, this would go much better."

He wasn't amused, but the ruddy-faced general sitting next to him seemed to be, if the twitch at the side of his mouth was any indication.

"This is not a test, Ms. Sherman." Tom leaned back in his chair and focused his gaze directly into her eyes. "There *is* weather manipulation going on. Jake is convinced that Simone"—he jerked his head slightly toward the monitors displaying the various views of the storm—"is at least partly manufactured. We cautiously agree with him. If he's right, that could mean that the other storms, the smaller storms, were test runs and Simone is going to be a 'statement.' Unfortunately, we're still not entirely sure who is executing these operations nor are we sure what the target is." He leaned forward again, his voice shifting to a softer note. "Tell me about Carter Thompson's foundation."

"I don't know much about it. There's a woman in our office who's doing some in-house research for a biography. She mentioned that Carter funds a foundation that studies desertification and reforestation. I mentioned it to Jake only because I thought that asking Carter might be a shortcut to finding out who has rainmaking capabilities." She paused. "I imagine you'd need to be able to create rain if you want to replenish rain forests and turn back the desert," she finished weakly.

Tom stared at her for a moment. "What's this woman's name?"

Oh, she's going to love me for this. "Elle Baker. I think her real first name is Eleanor. She used to work in the White House."

The room was silent except for the tapping of a few keys on his keyboard. When he hit Enter, or more likely Send, he glanced up at her again. "What else did she tell you about the foundation?"

"Nothing. I just told you everything I know about it."

"Did she tell you anything else about Carter Thompson?"

"Like what?"

"I'm not interested in his golf handicap, Ms. Sherman."

She glared at him. "She said she found some citations to papers he wrote about weather manipulation."

"Go on."

"That's about it."

"Were they how-tos? Were they political?"

"I didn't read them and I'm not sure she did, either. I think she said that the citations indicated that he didn't think it was beyond the realm of possibility."

"What was?"

"Weather manipulation."

"How long ago were these papers written?"

"I don't know. Elle made some reference to a Cold War mindset. The fifties, maybe?"

He looked down at his computer and typed for another minute or so, then looked up at her again. "What made you look into those storms?"

"I—"

"Shit."

Kate turned to look at Jake and could see from the corner of her eye that everyone else at the table had, too. Looking more grim than she'd ever seen him, Jake pointed to the largest of the monitors, and Kate, holding her breath, did the same.

The spiral that had been compact and mostly yellow the last time she'd looked had widened, the rain bands taking up more of the screen. It had also taken a slight northerly shift.

Every new projected track included New York City.

"Holy Mother of God," she breathed as the new storm track predictions appeared on an adjacent screen. Philadelphia, Long Island, and New York City all lay within Simone's possible landfall paths. Each was a heavily populated area with lots of rivers and estuaries and shoreline to transport storm surges inland. Each was already in the grip of panic and chaos.

"Sustained winds are one hundred and sixty-two miles an hour," Jake said, looking at a different screen.

"So does that make it a Category 6 now?" one of the uniformed guys at the end of the table asked.

"There is no Category 6," Kate said weakly. "There was never a reason for one."

"Looks like there is now," the officer said. "Might as well make a Category 7 while we're at it. This bitch isn't going to die without a fight."

"Welcome to Hell, people," Tom said softly.

Monday, July 23, 6:00 A.M.,
Upper East Side, Manhattan

The sky had changed.

From her place against the headboard, Elle had been watching the sky for a long time. The artificial colors on the signs had dimmed when morning came and deepened again as night fell. That had happened at least once since she'd crawled into her bed. Maybe twice.

She blinked. Her eyes, sore, heavy, and unable to close

for very long, narrowed as her brain struggled to decide what day it was. In the end, it didn't really matter. She blinked again and looked away, her fingers working at the sheet beneath.

I have to leave.

She felt the threads pull away easily, the fabric shredding and gathering into a damp clump in her palm as the thoughts chased themselves through her head again.

I have nowhere to go.

Her hands kept working at the fabric.

Win will be here soon. He called and said so.

She closed her eyes.

Hadn't he?

Her eyes shot open again as her fingers moved farther along the sheet to pick at threads still clustered in an orderly weave.

A sharp knock at the front door stilled her hands as her heart seemed to explode in her chest.

Win.

She moved slowly, her legs not responding well to her brain's demands. She tried to stand, but her legs wouldn't support her and pain flamed from her feet to her thighs as she landed in a heap on the carpet, bracing herself with her hands. At impact, a cry ripped from her throat. Elle lay on the floor, stunned, crying, her dress twisted around her hips.

There were sounds in her living room. Male voices, but none of them Win's. They sounded concerned. She looked helplessly at the still-closed bedroom door. Hot needles shot through her feet and calves as she tried to move.

I can't get up.

Men she didn't know burst into the bedroom with guns drawn and then stopped, staring at her in dull shock.

"I can't get up." She held her hands out to strangers, seeing her raw, bloody fingertips for the first time.

"My hands," she whispered in horror, and swung her head slowly toward the bed she'd been in for—since she'd gotten home from dinner with Davis Lee.

The sheets were smeared with blood, some dried and brown, some bright red and still wet. Piles of threads lay around where she'd been sitting, a vile rat's nest built of vintage Porthault linen and fresh, overwhelming guilt.

Strong hands were beneath her arms, lifting her up. She could not tear her gaze from her hands. Most of her nails were gone, the fakes Win liked and the real ones beneath. What was left looked like the carcasses of skinned animals, like the pictures that came in the envelopes from PETA.

"Ma'am. Ms. Baker. Are you all right? Are you alone?"

"My hands."

"Ms. Baker. Ms. Baker." The hands holding her up gave her a hard shake and her head snapped back.

She didn't recognize the face in front of her.

"Are you alone?" he repeated.

She nodded and started to cry. "My hands hurt." She brought one hand to her face to wipe away the tears that felt hot on her cheeks, but the man stopped her. Sitting her on the side of the bed, he pushed her hand away from her face and wiped her cheeks with a handkerchief he'd pulled out of a pocket.

"Thank you," she said automatically. "Did Win send you?"

"Win?"

She looked up at the man, then past him to the stone-faced one behind him. "Win," she repeated. "Win Benson."

The man in front of her straightened up. "No, ma'am, he didn't. We need you to come with us, Ms. Baker. We need to talk to you."

She tried to smile at him, but his face wouldn't remain in focus. "I can't leave. Win is coming. He told me. I think he did. I have to be here. He'll be so angry if I'm not."

The one closer to her studied her for a minute, and when he spoke again his voice was gentle. "It's all right if you come with us. He won't mind. Ms. Baker, it's important that we talk to you now."

"Are you sure he's not coming? He said he would." She closed her eyes. "I think he did. Who are you?"

"We're from the government."

It was an effort to open her eyes. They were so heavy. "I know that. What do you want?"

"We need to speak with you about Carter Thompson. We need you to come to our offices."

"I don't work for him anymore. Davis Lee fired me."

"Can you stand?"

She put her hands on the bed to push herself up. Pain knifed from her fingertips through her body and she screamed. The agent grabbed her wrists and yanked her to her feet, barking something over his shoulder at the other man. A moment later, cool, wet towels were wrapped over her hands.

"Keep your hands up, Ms. Baker. We'll take you to get help." As he spoke, the agent lifted her and carried her out of the apartment.

Traffic had been horrendous. So had the rain. Cars on the road, some of them anyway, had pulled aside to let the agents through. The shrill whine of a siren had accompanied them most of the way, and lights had been flashing so much that she'd just closed her eyes against them.

They'd taken her to a hospital and, to her surprise, they hadn't had to wait even though the scene was a blur of bright light and loud noise. There was a lot of screaming and shouting going on around her, but the men with her kept their voices low and official. She'd kept her eyes closed, not wanting to look at her hands or the men she was with, not wanting to see any more of the looks people were giving her. She opened her eyes for a moment when the woman doctor had insisted. Then there had been some injections that the doctor had said would wear off, and they'd done things to her hands.

The men put her back in the car then and took her to another building. This one was sterile and bland, but it wasn't a hospital. It was an office building, clearly a government building, in an area of Manhattan she hadn't been in before. Had she been less exhausted, she might have been alarmed. As it was, though, she didn't give a damn who they were or where they were taking her.

Life had begun seeping slowly back into her brain the moment her bare feet had hit the pavement in her building's garage while the nicer of the two agents helped her into the sedan's backseat. She wasn't sure how long she'd been lying in bed, but it seemed likely to have been several days. She probably looked like a refugee from a high-school production of *Carrie*. Her dress, the same one she'd been in since Friday morning, was wrinkled and torn, streaked with dried blood and vomit. The scaly, itchy patches on her face probably had the same origin. She'd gotten sick in the taxi on the way home from dinner with Davis Lee and then again in her apartment. After that she'd gotten into bed. Win had called at some point to ask if she was okay. She thought she remembered that.

The pain in her hands had gone from white-hot needles to dull, powerful throbbing that she felt everywhere and that intensified when she let her elbows drop below her heart. Despite that, she didn't say anything as they stepped into the elevator and rose from the bowels of the building to wherever they were going.

She was walking on her own, with the nice agent's hand in the small of her back to steady her, or maybe to grab her in case she fell. Or ran.

God almighty, what have I done? She swallowed hard and made a point of keeping her eyes open and her arms up, concentrating on noticing things around her to avoid addressing the horrors—*have I committed treason?*—hurtling through her head.

By the time they got off the elevator, Elle knew something was very wrong. The atmosphere in the building was high-voltage and the activity level seemed set to Intense. No one in the corridors spoke to the agents, communicating instead with grim, tight-lipped nods. No one gave Elle more than a cursory look, although the expressions of the professionally non-curious ranged from surprise to horror.

She cleared her throat as she and her escorts stopped in front of a closed door that looked exactly like every other closed door they'd passed. "What day is it?"

The agent who was punching numbers on the door's cipher lock keypad ignored the question. The one who had been taking care of her looked down at her. "Monday. Are you okay?"

She nodded and dropped her gaze to her feet. They looked bizarre and pale against the dirty, utilitarian mottled brown carpet. "Getting there."

The other one, who'd barely said a thing since she'd laid eyes on him, opened the door and gestured for her to enter ahead of him. She stepped across the threshold of an office that was unremarkably drab. A desk, empty except for the computer sitting on it, was straight ahead. There were chairs on either side of it and a small conference table off to one side. The nice agent ushered her to the far side of the table while the other sat behind the desk and immediately began typing rapidly at the keyboard.

"How are your hands?"

"They hurt." She rested her elbows on the table. The throbbing was getting stronger. "Did that doctor give you anything I could take for the pain?"

"No."

She didn't look at the one who answered, looking instead at the one who'd been helpful. "Am I under arrest?"

He looked sideways at her. "Have you done something wrong?"

Damned cops. "Please, I need some painkillers. Those shots are wearing off."

He looked away from her and watched the guy at the desk. "I can probably find some Motrin around here somewhere."

Motrin? "Look, I know I did this to myself and I know that I might seem crazy, but I'm in a lot of pain," she said, her voice starting to shake as the strain of everything frayed her tenuous control. "Can't you get me something? There has to be someone around here with some Percodan or Vicodin or something. Isn't there an evidence room?"

The guy behind the desk looked at her as if she were crazy—*maybe I am*—and the nice one looked almost as if he wanted to smile. "I'll see what I can do."

"Could you sit up a little straighter?" the other one said as he turned the flat-screen monitor around to face her and adjusted two little protrusions attached to the side of it.

Her heart dropped with a thud. *A Webcam and a microphone.* She closed her eyes. "What's this about? Who are you?"

"We're with the FBI."

"Am I under suspicion for something? Do I need a lawyer?"

"No and no."

"Then why am I here?"

"Some people in Washington want to talk to you. Please open your eyes and look at the monitor. You don't have to look at the camera. Ms. Baker, please open your eyes."

It took a lot of effort, but she opened her eyes and stared at the Microsoft logo rotating in simulated 3-D.

"Thank you. I'll get this going and then we're going to leave the room. When you're done, or if you need anything, knock—"

"With these?" she snapped, moving her arms until they were directly in his line of vision. "Or maybe I should kick the door. Would bare feet make a sound on that thing?"

Agent Not-So-Nice-Guy looked at the other agent.

"Kick the door if you have to, or do something to make a loud noise," said Agent Nice Guy.

"Why can't one of you just stay in here with me?"

"It's classified."

"The reason I'm here?"

"The topic you'll be asked about. Ms. Baker, make whatever noise you think is appropriate when you're finished. We'll be right outside."

She tilted her head toward the monitor. "How am I supposed to get this thing going?"

"It's all set. As soon as they come online on the other side, you'll go live."

They left the room and Elle sunk down in her chair, propping her elbows on the arms and trying very hard to turn her mind away from thoughts of Win and fingers and pain.

CHAPTER 41

Monday, July 23, 8:25 A.M., a CIA safe house in rural Northern Virginia

"Just look into the camera and speak into the microphone."

They were in a small room at the back of the house, which had two computers set up back-to-back on a small table. Kate sat facing one of them. She looked away from the monitor and met Jake's eyes.

"I am *so* not comfortable with this." She slid her gaze to Tom Taylor, who sat facing the other machine and was watching her over the top of the monitor. "I don't do interrogations. I'm a meteorologist. *You* ask her what you want to know."

He still had that pissed-off look on his face, which was bothering her less the longer she was in his company.

"I will be, through you," Tom replied. "And this isn't an interrogation, it's just some questions for background."

"Bullshit," she muttered.

Jake rolled his eyes at the comment, but Tom pounced on it. "Kate, *nothing* we are doing here is bullshit. Got that?" he snapped, his face rigid and his eyes cold. "There are lives at stake. Millions of lives. Right now, we need answers from this chick and you're going to get them from her because you know her."

"I met her a few weeks ago. I've spent maybe six hours in her company. We're barely acquaintances. And for your information, she's not exactly Miss Congeniality."

"Get over it. The questions will appear along the bottom of the screen. She won't be able to see them. Okay, you're on."

The change was abrupt as the computer came out of sleep mode and Kate did a double take as she stared at the screen. The bloodied, bedraggled woman slouched in a chair barely resembled the tidy, uptight woman Kate knew.

"My God. What did they do to you?" she shouted, making Jake jump and Tom push a hand through his hair in frustration.

On the screen, Elle jerked bolt upright in the chair, then grimaced so badly it nearly brought tears to Kate's eyes. "Nothing. I'm okay. Who are—*Kate*?"

"Yes, Elle, it's Kate."

"But the FBI . . . they said people in Washington—"

"I'm in Washington. I think. How are you? What happened to you?"

Elle blinked, clearly exhausted. "I'm not exactly sure, but it's a long story. Too long. And *they* had nothing to do with it. What are you doing there? Last I remember, D.C. was being evacuated."

"It was. Is. Also too long a story."

Get on with it, flashed across the bottom of the screen.

"Are you alone?" Kate asked as she'd been instructed, and watched Elle nod. "Good. Okay, look, I know this is going to seem like a really strange request under the circumstances, but I need you to tell me again what you found out about Carter Thompson. I mean any information that might not be in the public domain already."

As dreadful and drained as she looked, Elle sent back a wary glance that was backed with more than a little steel. "I already told you about him the other day."

"Tell me again."

"Who wants to know, Kate?"

"The government."

"You mean the campaign?" Elle asked, her voice sharp with sarcasm.

Campaign? Frowning, Kate shook her head. "I don't know what you're talking about. The people who want to know are—" She stopped as Tom glared at her from above the monitors.

"Are *you* alone?" Elle demanded. "Where are you?"

"No. And I can't tell you."

"Who's with you?"

This is nuts. Kate gave her an apologetic smile. "I can't tell you that, either."

"Is it Win? Or Davis Lee?"

"Davis Lee? No. What was the first name you said?"

"Win Benson," Elle replied, frustrated.

"The president's son? No."

GET ON WITH IT. Kate glanced at the message and deliberately didn't look at Tom's face.

"Look, Elle, I know this is bizarre, but something very weird is going on and the government thinks Carter Thompson is involved. We really need your help. I've gotten dragged into this . . . this thing by accident, just like you have, so bear with me. You said something about a rain-forest research program—"

"Kate, I'm not going to—"

Furious, Tom came around the table and brought his head down next to Kate's. She scooted out of camera range.

"Ms. Baker, I'm Agent Ed Delaney of the Internal Revenue Service. We're investigating Carter Thompson for possible violations of the federal tax code. We'd really appreciate your help in corroborating some information about his foundation. But first, could you provide me with your Social Security number for positive identification purposes?"

Elle's eyes widened and she meekly supplied a number, which Tom wrote down before glancing back at the screen. "Thanks very much. Specifically, we're interested in the foundation's assets and activities. I'll let Ms. Sherman continue with her questions now, but I'll be right here in case you need any clarification. Please answer to the best of your ability, Ms. Baker."

He stood up and walked back around to his side of the table, leaving Kate biting back a smile.

"Hi, Elle, sorry about that. I wasn't sure how much I could say. So what about this foundation?"

"It's an American corporation and its business address is actually Mr. Thompson's house in Iowa, but as far as I know, it only operates overseas. In India. Its stated purpose is to fund research into practices to replenish the rain forests and to reverse desertification."

"What else?"

"It owns a facility in Hyderabad, India, and has approximately forty-five people on staff. Mostly software developers, physicists, and engineers. Lots of Ph.D.'s. I think that's its only location. I didn't see anyplace else mentioned."

Assets, finances, publications? flashed onto the bottom of Kate's screen.

"Besides the building, what are its assets?"

"I didn't look into specifics, Kate. I read the annual reports, which are pretty bland. It has computer equipment, I suppose. And a plane."

"Like a corporate jet?"

"No, a research plane. There was nothing really said about it. It was just mentioned almost in passing in the introductory text."

"What about the revenues? Has the foundation's work been cited anywhere?"

"As far as I could tell, it operates at a loss and is completely funded by Mr. Thompson. And no, I couldn't find any citations to it in scientific or academic journals or newspapers. I checked all the databases that I thought might be relevant—hard sciences, soft sciences, LexisNexis. If there was published research or even a feel-good piece out there, I'd have found it, Kate. There's nothing out there. It's almost as if the foundation doesn't exist."

Kate glanced at Tom over the monitor. He met her eyes.

Ask about other research on him. His past, appeared on the band below the image of Elle.

Kate looked back into the camera. "Just a sec, Elle." She covered the tiny microphone and looked at Tom over the monitor. "This is ridiculous, you know. She worked in the White House. She must have had security clearances. You can probably trust her. Besides, she's not stupid. If we're honest with her, she'll probably tell us what we really want to know."

Tom looked nearly apoplectic. A vein was bulging in his forehead and Kate didn't even want to hazard a guess as to the psi rating of his clenched jaw at the moment.

"Thanks for the tip, Kate," he ground out in a voice that was a cross between a growl and a curse. "And by the way, that thing you're covering with your hand is the camera, not the microphone."

"Oh. Sorry." Feeling herself shrink, Kate gently removed her hand and glanced down at the screen to see Elle trying not to laugh. Somehow the expression made her look more like her usual self.

"I like your plan, Kate," she said. "Based on my experience, your Mr. Delaney seems more like a spook than an accountant. CIA, right?"

Kate swallowed hard and glanced over the monitor again to see an absolutely livid Tom push a hand through his hair with such vehemence that she was amazed he didn't pull a clump out. Then he nodded. She looked back at the screen.

"Bingo. But now you have to make me redeem myself. Tell us about that early research of Carter's. The weather manipulation stuff. Did you actually read the papers?"

After few seconds' pause, Elle nodded. "I found as many of his early writings as I could. There are copies in the filing cabinet at the office, but there are also hard copies at my apartment. And I scanned them, so there are a few CDs as well. One is in my backpack in my apartment, and I mailed the other copies to my parents' house."

Kate glanced at Tom, who was stone-faced again, and then back at Elle. "Nothing is on the network at work?"

"No."

"Why?"

Elle smiled. "Davis Lee didn't want them to get around, but I like to be safe."

"Why didn't he want them around?"

She looked away from the camera, clearly uncomfortable with the question.

"Elle? Why didn't Davis Lee want them around?" Kate repeated at Tom's terse nod.

It took another few seconds before Elle finally looked back into the camera. "I think Davis Lee and Carter Thompson are laying groundwork for Mr. Thompson to toss his hat into the ring for a presidential nomination. I'm pretty familiar with politics and know a pre-campaign scrub when I see it. My whole project was a farce. I'm sure I was hired as pre-emptive damage control, to find things before the other side did."

For the first time, Tom Taylor's face had relaxed a little. He was staring intently at the screen.

What was in the papers? Tom wrote.

"Tell me what was in the papers."

"They were kind of similar to yours, Kate. Most of them hinted at the possibility of using technology to manipulate the weather."

"How?"

She shrugged. "They were mostly historical, identifying what had been attempted and hypothesized, and then explaining why they didn't or couldn't work."

"Did he offer any suggestions as to what might work?"

"Yes. He said the only thing that could manipulate the weather was the ability to alter temperatures. He called heat the 'fuel' and cold the 'brakes' of global weather."

Kate glanced at Jake, who suddenly looked a whole lot more serious as he met her eyes.

Get back to the foundation, Tom ordered.

"What else do you know about the foundation?"

"Nothing."

"There was no hint in his earlier works of wanting to start it?"

"No. I mean, he's well-known as a tree hugger, so it sort of makes sense, but it's not like I found his diaries or anything. But he launched it about fifteen years ago, which is the same time that his company started to make serious profits." She paused, but it seemed to Kate as if she wanted to continue.

It appeared the same way to Tom, who wrote: *Push her.*

"What else?"

"Well, this is only my opinion and it's geeky researcher stuff, okay? But that early stuff he wrote had a sort of passion to it that wasn't there in his later writings, like the papers he wrote while he was at NOAA. Those were totally dull. And it looks like he tried to get back into academia after he left NOAA—there are lots of letters to universities and applications for grants in the archives. But he didn't get offered any positions and he didn't get any money, and that's when he started Coriolis. So I just thought that maybe the foundation came about when he had enough money to pursue his interests again. You know, maybe it was his way of getting back in the game."

Tom immediately started typing, but no instructions appeared across the bottom of Kate's screen. She glanced at Jake, who was staring at Tom's monitor as if mesmerized. She looked back into the camera.

"Where are you, anyway?"

"In New York. I think I'm in FBI headquarters."

"What happened to you?"

She looked down at her lap again. "I'd rather not get into it, Kate. I won't be coming back to work. But I'll be okay," she said faintly. "Keep in touch."

A sick churn began in Kate's stomach just as *Wrap it up* appeared on the white bar on-screen.

"Elle, take care of yourself. If you need anything—"

The screen went dark and Kate glared over the top of the monitor at Tom Taylor. "I'm not even allowed to say good-bye?"

"You've got more important things to do," he replied, and tapped a few keys. The screen behind him, which had been projecting a side view of Elle, changed to an image of the Atlantic Ocean. "Simone got bigger and picked up speed in the last hour. It's two hundred fifty miles off the coast of Delaware and about six hundred miles southeast of New York City. According to the National Hurricane Center and the National Weather Service, it's on a stable north-northwest trajectory. Its pressure has continued a slow and steady drop for the last twelve hours and it's now at nine hundred and eighty-nine millibars. Tell me what that means."

"It means we're in deep shit," Jake replied.

"She's sitting on Bermuda," Kate murmured.

"Let's fast forward, Kate. It's going to hit New York, isn't it?" Tom asked.

Kate looked at him. "Unless she heads to Boston instead. In that case, it won't get much worse than it is right now in the tri-state area. We'll get the water and the wind, but not the storm. Not landfall."

"What are the odds of that happening?"

Kate looked at Jake and shrugged. "Lower than fifty-fifty?"

Jake nodded. "We have to wait and see. The next twenty-four hours—"

"Are twenty-four hours we can't afford to wait. We've confirmed the underwater seismic activity you mentioned, but if that second flash you saw was man-made, there will likely be other attempts. We've got additional satellite surveillance on the storm already to track any aircraft or sea-based vessels that get within a few hundred miles of it. I've got fighters on alert all along the coast in case we get uninvited company." Tom stood up. "We'll have people on the ground in Hyderabad in a few hours. The FBI is on its way now to bring Carter Thompson and Davis Lee Longstreet in for questioning."

"Why Davis Lee?" Kate blurted out.

"Because he might know something," Tom replied over his shoulder in a tone that couldn't be more patronizing. "I have a meeting. In the meantime, why don't you two figure out a way to stop this thing?"

CHAPTER **42**

Monday, July 23, 9:10 A.M., a CIA safe house in rural Northern Virginia

Jake set his mug down on the kitchen counter and the sound seemed to have a sort of finality to it. He looked at Kate, who was standing between the kitchen table and the refrigerator looking back at him awkwardly.

"I can't drink any more coffee. Want a Coke?"

She smiled, looking as exhausted as he felt. "I'd love one."

Jake opened the fridge. By the time he'd turned around, Kate was sitting at the small breakfast bar.

"Diet or Classic?"

"Classic."

He slid a bottle and an opener across the counter and took a long pull from his own. The cool, sweetly acrid fizz woke him up and soothed him at the same time.

"I don't know about you, but I sort of wish I could wake up and this would all be just a really bad nightmare," Kate said after swallowing a more ladylike sip.

"It's going to get worse."

"What's going to stop that monster, Jake? She's already devastated most of the East Coast. What more can happen? If Simone keeps tracking the way she is—" Kate stopped and took a breath, putting an artificially cheerful note into her voice. "Golly, all those doomsday predictions will come true."

There really was no response to that, so he just took another swallow of Coke.

She closed her eyes and took a deep breath. "Do you really think someone is behind all these storms we've been tracking?" she asked quietly.

"I have no doubt, Kate. I'm absolutely positive that every one of those heat bursts was from an airborne laser."

"That's insane. Who would do that? And why?"

He shrugged. "Looks like it might be your man, Carter. I suppose it will depend on what they find out in Hyderabad when they get there, but things seem to be dropping into place."

"But why would someone do this? Especially Carter Thompson. He's got everything anyone could want. I mean, I refuse to believe it's just so he can make money—make a mess and clean it up. That's crazy. So is it just to make some sort of a point? If Elle was right about him wanting to run for president, this is not a good campaign strategy. Millions of people could get hurt. Or killed," she mumbled, then reached up to rub her eyes. "We live in a really messed-up world, Jake. A completely fucked-up world if somebody's doing this," she said, her voice having gone from tired to shaky.

He stood on his side of the breakfast bar, not sure what he was supposed to do. Comforting her was a natural impulse, but it had the potential to get complicated, so he just said, "Yeah," and lifted his Coke to his lips.

To his surprise, she began to laugh. He stared at her until she slowed to an intermittent chuckle.

"Are you okay?"

"Sorry. That 'yeah' was just so eloquent," she said sarcastically.

"Yeah, well. I'm a scientist. We don't do emotion too well."

"No kidding."

He grinned and leaned on the counter. "So how the hell do we stop this thing?"

"You and I both know there is no way. If there were,

someone would have come up with it before now. You probably know better than I do how many people have tried over the years. That's what you were really looking at when you were looking at the storms, right?"

"No. I was looking at the storms, like I said. I just didn't tell you why I was looking at the storms. There was that little thing called national security to consider."

"So now that I'm an insider we can talk about it?"

He nearly choked on his drink. "You're not an insider. You're a fly caught on flypaper."

"I can never leave?"

"I'm sure they'll let you leave. They may degauss your brain first, though. Didn't Candy give you the pep talk? You can't ever talk about any of this."

"She was serious?" Kate asked, and he did a double take before seeing the corner of her mouth twitch. "So why didn't Tom want Elle to know who he was?"

"Three reasons. The first is that more people are scared of the IRS than they are of the CIA, and the second is that the CIA isn't authorized to operate within the U.S., and the third is that everyone in the intelligence community lies. I wouldn't take a bet that Tom Taylor is his real name, either."

"That makes me feel much better," she said dryly, and lifted the bottle of soda to her mouth, finishing it. Putting it down on the counter, she stood up. "I hate to drink and run, but I need to be alone for a while before my brain melts down. I'll be upstairs in the luxury master suite. Shout if you need me."

Jake nodded and watched her leave the room.

Monday, July 23, 8:25 A.M., Campbelltown, Iowa

"This is bloody daft."

Carter smiled at the pilot's terse comment and didn't reply as he watched the plane's progress on his computer monitor. The steady beat of a light rain on the windows of his home office was welcome after so many weeks of placid weather.

"We're flying too low and too slow and too bloody close to American airspace. They've got recon planes out here in crap visibility and we're not on their radar. If someone spots me, I'll have F-18s giving me a Sidewinder enema before I can blink. That's if we don't collide first. This is madness. I'm going to abort and get the hell out of here while it's still an option. Over."

The plane immediately began to climb in a banking curve away from the storm, although it would be a while before it was completely out of range of the sweeping counter-clockwise winds. Carter tapped the key that controlled the microphone. "Negative. You'll return to course and altitude and proceed as planned. Over."

"Wrong-o, mate. I'm signing off. Over."

Carter blinked as the communications icon went dark, then smiled wider.

"You son of a bitch," he murmured as he tapped a few keys and assumed remote control of the laser command module aboard the plane. "Let's see what you think of this."

It was clear that the pilot had had no intention of executing the operation. Raoul hadn't turned on all of the necessary equipment—an omission Carter quickly rectified by stepping through the remote sequences necessary to activate the fuel and power sources.

The plane was already picking up both speed and altitude and had changed course toward the U.S. mainland.

The communications icon lit up the instant the laser suite was online, which made Carter laugh quietly.

"You demented bastard. Shut those things down." The Brit was livid.

"It's my plane, Major Patterson, in case you've forgotten," Carter replied with a smile in his voice. "I have an operation to complete and complete it I shall, with or without your help."

"I haven't forgotten a thing. But you'll wish I had. I've contacted Philadelphia Tower and requested emergency landing permission—"

"You won't be needing it. Just calm down." Carter

closed the communication link, completed the next remote sequence, and typed in the necessary coordinates. The location wasn't ideal. The plane was too far away from the hurricane's eye to do another pulse, but now he had the opportunity to test something he hadn't tried since Ivan in 2004: targeting the ocean surface itself. Superheating the water in front of the storm wouldn't be as effective as heating its core, but the additional warmth at and just below the surface would certainly fuel the storm.

He set the pulse to last for fifteen seconds, many times longer than it was meant to last, and initiated the firing sequence. Seconds later, he watched as the small patch of sea surface changed from pale blue to green to yellow as the heat spread outward.

When the time was up, the sensors on Carter's monitor were flashing ominously. With a trace of regret, he activated the safety feature he'd had built into the plane in the event of just such a situation as this. He'd hoped never to use it, but now he had no choice.

With a heavy heart, he typed in the last password and pressed Enter to activate the small explosive devices mounted inside the wing fuel tanks. He let out a heavy breath and brought his attention back to the storm on the other monitor. The patch of ocean had calmed and was already returning to a dark green while the storm itself had begun to swerve. And grow.

"It will be all right," he said to himself as he stood up and tightened the belt of his bathrobe. "It will be all right."

Monday, July 23, 9:45 A.M., a CIA safe house in rural Northern Virginia
"Kate?"

She jumped, pushing herself to a sitting position and trying to focus on the looming figure bending over her. She heard the crack of her head hitting Jake's a split second before she felt the impact. The sensation sent her flat to her back, knocking her breathless for a second before the pain set in.

He swore as she fought back involuntary tears.

"What the hell are you doing?" she demanded. The room was still pitch-dark. The bed was still uncomfortable.

He sat down on his bed holding his head in his hands. "Tom wants us both conscious and functional and downstairs."

"What time is it?"

"You've only been asleep for a little while. Like half an hour."

She pulled herself to a sitting position against the wall as she rubbed the rising lump on her head gingerly. "Christ, you have a hard head."

"You, too. What did you do that for?"

"Me? Why were you standing so close? I was asleep. What does he want, anyway?"

"It's Simone. She just escalated again."

Kate felt her eyes shut. Her lids had never been this heavy. "Damn."

"Worse than that. About fifteen minutes ago, a plane flying near the storm made contact with the Philadelphia control tower, asking about making an emergency landing. A few minutes later, it blew up. The plane was registered to Carter Thompson's foundation."

Heavy lids and all, her eyes popped open. "What?"

"There's more. It didn't show up on radar. It had some sort of stealth capability. The Coast Guard had picked it up visually. The Navy had already scrambled some jets to escort it in, but they didn't get there in time. And before it blew, satellites picked up a high-energy laser beam directed from it into the water at the leading edge of the storm. It was the same signature as the others but it was no short burst. It lasted at least fifteen seconds. Two buoys recorded water temps of one hundred and twenty degrees at fifty feet. One surface buoy recorded one hundred and seventy before it fried."

She reached out and grabbed his arm. "Jake, are you kidding me? At the sea surface? For Christ's sake, that's nearly boiling."

"I'm not kidding." He looked at her. "Something tells me it's going to be a long day."

Monday, July 23, 12:00 P.M., East Village, New York City

The moans and screech of the wind were the only sounds Davis Lee could hear as he sat in his living room, staring out the window of his third-story flat. The sound had reached an intensity that was eerie and hypnotic. Sitting motionless in the murky darkness, he felt alternately mesmerized and alarmed at what he'd seen happening on the street below. He'd been there for hours, possibly since before dawn—except dawn hadn't occurred today. In that time he'd seen small trees ripped out of the ground, trash barrels flying through second-story windows, and an orange VW Beetle sliding sideways down the street until it smashed into the corner of a brick building. The car was nearly sliced in half, as was the driver. The passenger had climbed out in a daze and started screaming. When no one came out to help after ten minutes, she stopped screaming and stumbled down the street. Davis Lee hadn't seen her again.

That had been a few hours ago. Now, the streets were empty of people. Even the few looters he'd seen skulking around were gone. The water was running at least a foot deep in the streets, sloshing over the lower steps of those buildings that sported them. Twisted frames, denuded of their awnings, were flung wildly in all directions until they were finally wrenched loose and aloft.

His apartment was starting to get stuffy. Opening the windows wasn't an option. The power and phone service had gone out long ago. His cell phone still had some juice left in it, but there was no signal. The water was still running, but there wasn't any real food in the place.

At some point it had occurred to him that he might die. Not bravely, not nobly. Possibly quite horribly or painfully or in some way accompanied by humiliation. The thought had never crossed his mind before.

For generations, his family had considered honor an obligation and good luck a part of their heritage, but the battle Davis Lee faced wasn't one in which bullets could be dodged. This was Nature. And he was very sure that Man wasn't blameless. One man, anyway.

After Carter had left his office yesterday morning, Davis Lee had sat down and read Kate's paper and the papers Elle had found, and then he'd gotten online and done some digging of his own. Kate was probably right; the storms were odd. News reports had all noted their unusual origins and then dismissed them because of their lack of additional newsworthiness. And Coriolis Engineering had been first in line to clean up the messes. Strange, destructive weather in the Sahara had been noted by the locals as well but disregarded by the rest of the world because it was in Africa. What was one more disaster over there? Devastating out-of-season flooding was dismissed with a shrug and ascribed to global warming or desertification or some other climatological catastrophe in the making. And Coriolis Engineering had always stepped in almost before the governments could ask for help. Frequently, the Coriolis teams arrived bearing news of an extra helping of Carter's personal philanthropy.

The bastard had to be behind it all. There could be no other explanation. He was clever enough and rich enough to do it, and too vain to cover his tracks.

But trying to figure out what Carter thought he might stand to gain by trashing the East Coast when he wanted to be president was— Davis Lee stopped breathing.

President.

That was the whole point. Carter didn't just want to be president. He wanted to replace Winslow Benson. No, not simply replace him—bury him. Make his name synonymous with death and devastation.

And how better to do it than to destroy one of the most potent symbols of the nation: New York City.

The last story Davis Lee had seen on the news before the power went out last night was about the security of the Indian Point Nuclear Power Plant and how it was built to withstand 170-mile-an-hour winds, an upper limit no one had ever thought would be challenged.

Carter knew that. And had apparently decided to test it.

Davis Lee looked at his hands. By the end of this, they'd be stained with the indelible blood of thousands of lives. He'd been so adroit at finessing the company, or so he'd foolishly thought. All he'd really done in the last ten years was bring this moment to bear a little sooner than Carter might have on his own. Imagining and then building the investment side of the house had been ingenious, he'd thought. Carter, however, had realized from the start that what Davis Lee had suggested would be a cash cow; it would be Coriolis Engineering's insurance when things went wrong and its bonus structure when things went right, as they so frequently did.

I've brought this on myself.

He sat at the window for a few minutes longer, then stood up and went to the small nook in his kitchen. A few stiff fingers of his favorite Elijah Craig buoyed him as he continued into the bathroom. The array of prescription bottles on the shelf was a testament to the good life: sleeping pills for those trans-Pacific business-class flights, painkillers from ligaments torn on the tennis court and knees trashed on snowy mountains, anti-depressants for the days when he had watched Enron die and Worldcom begin to thrash.

He took them all back to the living room. Sitting on the expensive sofa a gorgeous interior designer had charmed him into buying, he began to wash them down a few at a time, as he watched the rain coutinue to fall.

Monday, July 23, 11:45 A.M., Campbelltown, Iowa
Carter had left his office early to return to the house where, as usual, he would have lunch with Iris on their deep, covered front porch. They were sitting in their favorite chairs, watching the grandchildren play a muddy game of tag on the broad front lawn. Several of their daughters stood in a cluster nearby, supervising.

A movement to the far left of the lawn caught Carter's eye, and a second later he saw his caretaker's white pickup slowly appear around the final turn in the long drive. Three black SUVs with darkened windows followed it.

An alien sense of dread floated in his gut as he set his coffee mug on the small table between his chair and Iris's. Nelson hadn't called from the gatehouse to say there were visitors even though that was the established protocol, and that was highly unusual. A retired Iowa state trooper, Nelson always followed protocol.

"Carter, what's wrong? Whose cars are those?" Iris asked, more than a little alarm in her voice.

"I think you should get the girls and the children and go inside, Iris."

"No, I won't. Carter—"

He stood up as the two lead vehicles came to a stop in front of the house. The two other vehicles peeled away from the others and went in opposite directions around the house. The children had stopped playing and were watching with open curiosity. Three of his girls called the children to them. Meggy, the lawyer, headed straight for the porch.

Nelson got out from behind the wheel of the pickup. A blond woman in a dark windbreaker climbed out of the passenger side. A badge hung on a lanyard around her neck. Four similarly clad men got out of the other vehicle and fanned out across the front of the house. One stopped Meg mid-stride.

"Mr. Thompson, I'm Special Agent Susan Lemke with the Federal Bureau of Investigation," the blond woman called out as she approached the porch. "We'd like to talk to you."

"This is a rather heavy-handed way of going about it, Agent Lemke," he said, sliding his hands into his pockets. "You could have made an appointment to meet me at my office like most other people do. This is my home. You can't have any business here."

"Please keep your hands where I can see them, sir, and move away from the stairs."

He let his hands drop to his sides and looked beyond her to his caretaker and head of security for his residence. "Nelson, what's going on?"

"They have a search warrant, Mr. Thompson. I had to let them on the property, and they wouldn't let me call you." Nelson's voice was cool and professional.

Carter turned back to the agent who was now on the porch. Another agent had joined her and stood on the bottom step against the opposite handrail. Meg was watchful. Iris was sobbing quietly, having sunk back into her chair and covered her face with her hands.

"What do you want, Susan?" he asked the agent with a smile.

She didn't react to the familiarity in his voice. Her stance on the top step was not aggressive, but she was ready to move as needed. Her eyes were as expressionless as her voice. "We have a warrant to search the premises, sir. And we'd like to question you with regard to your recent trip to New York as well as some other activities."

"Am I under arrest?"

"Carter," Iris gasped, one hand dropping to cover her heart, the other sliding to cover her mouth.

"No, sir, but if you would like to have your attorney present during our questioning, you have that right."

"That woman with the blond hair is my daughter and my attorney," he said, gesturing to Meg, who was immediately allowed to join them on the porch.

"Daddy, don't say a thing." She turned to the agent. "May I see the warrant, please?"

He could hear movement in the house and orders being given and knew they had begun ripping apart his life as well as his home. Closing his eyes, he took a deep breath against the growing pounding in his chest. Raoul, the flight crew, and the plane were gone, but the facility in India was still active and he couldn't trust anyone there to protect his work, not once the money dried up. It wasn't in Iris to lie. She would tell them everything she knew, which wasn't much but would be enough to fill in gaps.

He realized that the almost painful high he had experienced when those last tests had gone well and the small erratic episodes he felt under stress were nothing like a heart attack. That had been ecstasy, a combination of pleasure and pain. The sensation in his body now held no pleasure. The pain was shooting down his arms, the pressure crushing his chest wall, and yet he did nothing to stop it, nothing to reveal it. It was part of his pact with Nature. He'd agreed to let go when he was supposed to, and now he was supposed to. He'd fulfilled his role, met his destiny. The rest was to be written without him. The cloudiness in his head had to be Nature's way of letting him go easily. Hopefully the pain would be over soon.

He had no doubt they would find everything. It was all in his office. Beyond encrypting it, he hadn't hidden it. There was no reason to.

Their presence here was all about his success. He knew it in the depths of his failing heart. They were going to take away his dreams and demonize him for pursuing them, then secretly continue his work. This was Winslow Benson's final insult. They'd take it all. His work, his dreams, his success.

He couldn't hide a grimace as the pain increased, couldn't stop himself from gasping, from trying to grab the railing to maintain his balance. His arm wouldn't work, though. It never left his side. And he began to fall.

The agents caught him before he hit the wood, the broad planks of chestnut he'd cut himself.

"Daddy? Are you all right?" The voice was distant and followed by a scream. It was Iris's scream.

He tried to call out, to tell Iris everything would be fine, but his voice remained in his head. Locked in his head, with all of his secrets. And they began tearing at his clothes, touching him, talking about him as if he weren't there.

CHAPTER 43

**Monday, July 23, 1:35 P.M., a CIA safe house in rural
Northern Virginia**

The thunder and rain were so noisy that neither Kate nor
Jake heard the helicopter until it was practically on the
front lawn. When the sound registered, they walked together toward the dining room, which was serving as the
command center.

"Oh hell," Kate whispered on the threshold.

The same words ran through Jake's mind. The room
was filling with uniforms from every branch. They were
shaking off the rain and draping their wet jackets over the
few hangers in the coat closet.

There was very little conversation as people seated
themselves at the table or stationed themselves along the
walls. Tom went to the head of the table.

"Thank you all for arriving on such short notice," he said
in his usual flat, condescending tone. "I know you've all
been briefed about the stealth-enhanced P-3 that exploded
minutes after making contact with the Philadelphia tower.
We've confirmed that prior to the explosion it deployed a
laser burst with a one-point-o-four-five-millimeter wavelength that lasted fifteen seconds and was directed to the
ocean surface. We haven't determined yet whether this was
a misfire or a deliberate act, nor have we determined what
the target was if it was a deliberate act. We do know that the
plane was the so-called research aircraft owned by the Environmental Replenishment Foundation, which was run by
Carter Thompson as a front for weather control research.
Agents from the FBI contacted Thompson late this morning
to execute a search warrant and question him. Minutes after
they arrived, he suffered a heart attack and a massive
stroke. He's still alive and apparently cognizant, but

suffered severe motor impairment and is unable to speak. He's at the regional trauma center and the agents are monitoring him as closely as the doctors are. Davis Lee Longstreet, who ran one of Carter's companies and who may have known about the foundation's work, was found in his New York apartment a short time ago. He apparently committed suicide by taking an overdose of prescription medication."

A horrified cry escaped seconds before Kate clapped a hand over her mouth. Tom paused and looked at her. "My condolences, Ms. Sherman." He scanned the room. "That leaves us with a Category 5 hurricane less than two hundred miles from the U.S. coastline."

No one spoke as he glanced down at his notes.

"We're reasonably certain that there has been external, man-made interference with the storm on at least two occasions less than ninety-six hours apart. These also consisted of one-point-o-four-five-millimeter-wavelength laser bursts directed at the eye of the storm. Each incident preceded the storm's escalation." He sat back in his chair then and looked around the room casually. "Carter Thompson worked for the Central Intelligence Agency in the late 1960s and early 1970s as a weather researcher, as did Richard Carlisle, who was murdered approximately forty-eight hours ago. The project on which they worked dealt with creating and exacerbating cyclonic storms, and they successfully created or escalated eight typhoons in the Pacific during the summer of 1971, including two that exceeded the lower limits of a Category 5 designation.

"After that success, a congressional committee rewarded them by cutting the project's funding and Carter was out of a job. One of the members of that committee was Winslow Benson. Recent intelligence indicates that Carter Thompson had both an obsession with the president and presidential ambitions of his own. Based on that and other intelligence, we've determined with a fairly high assurance that Thompson is behind Simone's escalation, and that the probable target of the storm is the Northeast, presumably

New York City, where the president was scheduled to speak in three days' time. At the moment, all indications are that this storm will continue to grow and will continue to track to the northwest, which means New York."

He reached up and rubbed his ear thoughtfully, which made Jake's hands itch to throw a punch. The prick was playing it much too cool.

"One problem is that we don't have any intelligence on how many planes Thompson had. If there are other aircraft equipped to continue this operation, the storm could be escalated again. In addition, Carter's companies have a small constellation of observation and communication satellites in low-earth orbit. For all we know, he could have the same technology mounted on one or more of them. We won't know until we talk to the people in Hyderabad, where his sandbox was."

"What's the situation there?"

"We're trying to move under the radar. The last thing we want is the Indians getting their hands on anything before we get there." Tom moved his gaze around the room again, taking in everyone. "The DNI wants to take the offense on this, which means that we have to anticipate another escalation. I think we all know how much better it would be to avoid one. Even if this hurricane remains a Category 5, if it makes it up to New York, the impact of Katrina would look like a day at an amusement park."

"There is nothing higher than a Category 5," Kate blurted.

Tom barely glanced at her. "There is now. Which is why I'd like to hear some alternative scenarios."

The room remained silent.

"Alternatives to what?" Kate asked finally.

Tom looked at her again. "Alternatives to escalation, Ms. Sherman." Then he turned to Jake.

Great. Jake felt his mood head south.

"Dr. Baxter, what will stop a storm like Simone?"

"Nothing," Jake replied flatly. "Nothing man-made, that is. People have made attempts in the past, like spreading vegetable oil on the sea surface or seeding the storms, but nothing has ever worked. Natural phenomena that can diminish a storm would be severe wind shear or a dramatic change in temperature. For instance, if it hit a pocket of cold air or cold water, it would likely diminish, but it would have to be a very large area of water. Otherwise it might just split the storm into smaller storms."

Tom turned to one of the Navy officers. "Can we do that? Can we supercool part of the ocean?"

The guy didn't even blink. "No, sir."

Tom's eyes narrowed. "Do you mean that you know we can't, Commander, or your gut feeling is that we can't? Has there ever been any attempt made or study commissioned?"

"I don't know of any studies or attempts, and it's more than a gut feeling," the commander responded, his jaw tighter than it had been a moment earlier. "Even if such an operation were a theoretical possibility, there are logistical problems. We don't have a ship or crew to sacrifice by putting it in the path of that storm. If the operation didn't work, and maybe even if it did, it would be a suicide mission for everyone on board. Beyond that, without any studies having been done, we don't know what refrigerant would be appropriate. Once that issue was decided, we'd have to ensure there was enough of it readily available to carry out such an operation, and then we'd have to fabricate equipment to disperse it."

Tom turned back to Jake. "Would a bomb work? Could we blow apart the storm?"

Jake shook his head. "The amount of energy produced by a Category 5 hurricane is immense. It could provide enough power to keep the East Coast lit up for a long time—if we could harness it. To counteract and disrupt that sort of energy would take an enormous nuclear bomb, bigger than anything ever produced, and even that probably wouldn't work. Aside from the obvious environmental and health-related implications, that is."

The room fell silent, and after a few minutes Jake cleared

his throat. Everyone's eyes veered toward him and it was an effort for him not to back down.

"Do you have something else to add to the discussion?" Tom asked.

Here goes my career. Jake swallowed. "I have an idea that might be worth attempting."

"Let's hear it," Tom replied.

"It's an extreme long shot."

"No doubt."

Jake met his eyes. "For years, lasers have been used for warm fog dispersal for aircraft landings and takeoffs. It's fallen out of favor recently because newer heads-up displays in cockpits have made it obsolete, but it's a proven technology. Certain lasers can generate enough heat to evaporate warm fog, which is just water vapor, pretty much instantly. And water vapor is what is sucked up by the convection towers in a hurricane. If we could direct lasers into the eye walls laterally and at very low altitudes—close to sea level—we might be able to disrupt and weaken the convection cycle." No one spoke after he stopped, and no one would make eye contact with him except Kate and Tom.

"You'd need a lot of lasers," came from farther down the table.

"Or a few powerful ones," Jake replied.

Tom looked at him, frowning in confusion. "If lasers evaporate water, why did Thompson's lasers escalate the storms?"

"What he was doing was like dumping a can of gasoline on a bonfire," Jake said. "He fired the lasers at the top of the storm cell, where all the latent heat in the column of water vapor is already being released as energy. The blast of heat from his laser sped up that release of energy, creating more of an upward pull on the column of air already rising in the eye. The convection cycle expanded dramatically, making the storm taller, wider, and faster. What I'm suggesting is that we try to cut off the circulation at the bottom of the air column long enough to destabilize the storm."

Tom squinted at him. "Are you thinking of lasers mounted on aircraft that would fly through it, or lasers mounted on ships?"

"I hadn't thought that far into it, the idea just occurred to me. But that decision is outside my expertise anyway." Jake shrugged.

Tom glanced over at a skeptical officer in Air Force blue. "What do you think, Major?"

"You can't fly a jet through a hurricane. You'd need props. We don't have any of those mounted with lasers. Neither does the Navy."

"Do we have *anything* we could deploy this way? UAVs?"

The naval commander looked uncomfortable. "Well, sir, the Peregrine carries lasers, but it's still experimental—"

"It would have to be big enough and heavy enough to operate in a vortex," Jake interrupted. "What kind of engine does it have?"

The officer met his eyes briefly. "It has a rocket engine that gets it up to altitude and speed, then drops off. Props take over," he said quietly, in a voice full of condescension.

Out of the corner of his eye, he saw Kate flash a piece of paper at him.

You want to evaporate a hurricane using LASERS???
You read entirely too much science fiction. BTW,
what's a UAV?

Unmanned aerial vehicle. Drone, he wrote, and slid it back to her.

"What sort of lasers? What's its range? How big is it?" Tom demanded.

"Two hundred seventy-five pounds with a top cruising speed of six hundred miles an hour and a range of one thousand miles. It can stay in the air for three hours, but it doesn't perform as well as others in turbulence."

"What does?"

"The Predator, but that doesn't have lasers."

"Then we don't need to talk about it. What sort of laser does the Peregrine carry? Could it work in the way Dr. Baxter has described?"

"Its lasers are infrared, in the same range of wavelength as the ones used to excite the storm. What's been suggested might be within its operational capability," the commander said stiffly. "The Peregrine conducts remote reconnaissance. Search and destroy missions."

"Don't be coy, Commander," Tom snapped. "Could the lasers take out this storm?"

"The lasers are extremely powerful, sir, with a midrange beam, and are designed to destroy materiél or other assets by superheating them. It exploded armored tanks in field trials."

Jake sensed Kate's shudder.

"How quickly?"

"Under ten minutes."

Tom turned to Jake. "All you need is something to produce enough heat to evaporate vapor at the bottom of the storm, right?"

"Well, not too much, because then we'll just help build the storm."

"So sucking up hot, dry air will have the same effect as sucking up hot, wet air?" Tom asked, exasperated.

"No, a hurricane needs moisture because that's where the energy is," Kate interjected.

"So we send in a few drones to blast the shit out of the bottom of the storm, drying it up. Then what happens?" Tom demanded.

"In theory, the storm cell will disintegrate and the storm will fragment. But it could rebuild itself," she explained.

Tom shrugged. "Then we just keep at it to make sure it doesn't."

"If I could just make the point that if the beams are just directed into the atmosphere, instead of at a solid target—"

Tom cut her off. "An atmosphere that dense has to attenuate the beam significantly. And in any event, there won't be any vessels on the other side of this storm. Am I right, Commander?"

"Yes, sir."

Kate seemed to shrink in her seat. Jake looked away.

"Tell me how many Peregrines we have on the East Coast," Tom demanded.

"Thirty."

Tom raised his eyebrows. "*Thirty?* Where are they?"

"Off the coast of New Jersey aboard the *William J. Clinton.*"

Jake sat up straight at the name of the Navy's newest "next generation" nuclear-powered aircraft carrier. It was bigger than anything else afloat, and more technologically advanced.

A new voice was heard. "The *Clinton* has been deployed to sea, sir, in advance of the storm."

Tom frowned. "When did that launch?"

"It hasn't been commissioned, sir. It's been stationed there undergoing final-stage field trials and will be commissioned when those end. It's scheduled to participate in the NATO war games in September."

Tom nodded, then swung his head, skewering Jake with a look. "How close would you have to be?"

With a growing sense of dread, Jake shifted in his chair. "To what?"

"The storm," Tom replied with false patience.

Jake tried to conceal the alarm that had sped up his heartbeat and was churning its way through his stomach lining. "If the drones have a range of one thousand miles, then I suppose that's how far away—"

"No," the naval officer interrupted. "That storm is already three hundred miles wide with winds topping one hundred and sixty miles an hour. Given the conditions, the drones would have to be deployed closer to the action to make sure they reach the eye as quickly as possible. We'd need to be as close as we could get."

"How long would it take the *Clinton* to get to a position within range?" Tom asked.

The commander swallowed hard. "Top speed is thirty-five knots. Between thirty and forty-eight hours depending on where the storm tracks and how fast it moves. But, sir, it's not officially—"

"Thank you all. Commander, see if you can't get the Secretary of the Navy to carve out a few minutes to meet with the DNI later this afternoon." Tom stood up then and turned to Jake. "Go pack your stuff. Both of you." Without offering time for an argument, Tom turned to face the rest of the people around the table. "I need to make a phone call. I'll be back shortly."

Tom was already heading toward the small room in the back of the house where the webcam was set up by the time his words had sunk in. Kate sprang to her feet and followed him at a trot, trying to keep the panic she was feeling off her face. Her heart rate was much too high and her breathing much too shallow. "Wait a minute."

He stopped and looked down at her, his annoyance undisguised. "Yes?"

"Pack my stuff to go where, exactly?"

"I want you out on that carrier. You came up with this idea. You should see it through."

She could feel her eyes going wide. *On the carrier?* "First of all, this is Jake's idea, not mine," she spluttered. "I'm a meteorologist. I don't know anything about lasers. And I don't—"

"There are people aboard who know about lasers," Tom said bluntly. "You know about storms. Specifically, you know how Thompson's storms behave."

"That doesn't mean I want to be in the middle of one. *On a boat.*" She glared at him. "I'm a civilian, in case you've forgotten. You can't order me to do this."

"That 'boat' is over twelve hundred feet long, has a displacement of ninety-nine thousand tons, and is the most technologically advanced warship ever built, Ms. Sherman."

"I don't care how big it is. It will be like a cork in a bathtub in front of that storm."

"That's where you come in, Ms. Sherman. You heard me say that we don't know yet if there are other aircraft in Thompson's arsenal. If that storm escalates, the whole eastern seaboard is going to be neck-deep in serious shit. You might possibly be able to help us avoid that outcome. If I can't appeal to your professionalism, perhaps I can appeal to your patriotism. If I'm not mistaken, you watched the twin towers come down, didn't you? People you know have been affected by that attack? Family members?"

She stared into his hard, dead eyes, as breathless as if she'd been physically sucker-punched instead of just emotionally, and nodded slowly. A ball of helpless rage formed at the back of her throat, precluding speech even if she'd been able to find the words.

"Make no mistake, Kate," he continued, his voice low and flat. "What your boss has done is no less an act of terrorism than what those fuckers did six years ago. With that last laser burst, Carter Thompson let every one of America's enemies know that weather has become a strategic weapon. And he let all of them know that he chose his own country as his target. None of those points are in dispute. All we can do now is try to thwart his plans, an option we didn't have six years ago. And the bottom line is that if you don't help us now, you won't have a home or parents to go to." He paused and chewed the inside of his cheek for a minute, then looked at her again.

"You know better than I do that if this storm escalates any more before it hits the continental shelf, the destruction will be like September 11th and Hurricane Katrina combined. Long Island and an awful lot of Brooklyn and Queens are already underwater, as are much of Lower Manhattan and Staten Island. How far inland do you want the damage to go, Kate?" He paused again. "Are you aware that the Indian Point Nuclear Power Plant, which is thirty-five miles outside of Manhattan, was built to withstand maximum sustained winds of one hundred and seventy miles per hour? What happens if the winds get higher than that? Imagine one-hundred-seventy, one-hundred-eighty-mile-an-hour winds carrying highly radioactive particles. How far would they go? How many people would they kill right away? And how many would they keep killing, and for how long?"

She stared at him, fighting the tears burning behind her eyelids.

"Well, Kate? Should I send you home to sit it out with your parents? Or are you going to help me and the rest of the people in this room and on that ship stop this bastard of a storm?"

"You son of a bitch," she whispered.

"Is that a yes?"

"Yes."

"Good. Be ready in fifteen minutes."

Jake stood in the doorway of their bedroom and watched Kate throw her things into her duffle with sharp, abrupt movements that were fueled by her fury at whatever Mr. Diplomacy had said to her. The longer she was silent, the more Jake assumed there would be an explosion. Spending the last twenty-four-plus hours with her had taught him that.

"Well?" he asked as she zipped up the duffle and grabbed it by the handles.

"Well what?" she snapped through a jaw clenched so tight each word had to hurt.

"What did my favorite Martian say that made you change your mind?" He let her pass in front of him into the hallway.

"Just some old-fashioned blackmail. I'm sure you've read the same file on me he did."

"I never saw any file on you. I only mentioned your name to him on Saturday. Why would the CIA have a file on you?"

"Good question. But he seemed to know an awful lot

about me, including how low to hit me." She spared him a glance then, and he saw the tear tracks on her face.

Damn. "Anything I can do?"

She moved her head from side to side, then brought up a hand to wipe her face. "Not unless you can get me out of here and out of going on that boat."

"Ship," he corrected automatically. "Kate, carriers are huge. From what I've heard, the *Clinton* has a crew of nearly eight thousand people. Trust me, it has to be a hell of storm before you even begin to feel it rock."

"Simone *is* a hell of a storm, Jake, in case you forgot." She sniffed and began rooting in her bag. "Besides, how do you know anything about aircraft carriers?"

"When I was in the Marines, I was stationed on one briefly, doing research."

She blew her nose, then looked at him, obviously unimpressed. "How are we getting there?"

"By helicopter."

"I don't fly," she said as she started down the stairs.

He followed her. "They'll have Dramamine on board."

"I didn't say I got sick when I fly. I said I don't fly," she snapped.

"Well, we can't drive there. Why don't you fly?"

She blew her nose again before answering. "The exact time I stopped flying was shortly before nine in the morning on September 11, 2001. It had something to do with seeing planes fly into towers," she said over her shoulder as she reached the bottom of the staircase.

"Christ."

"My brother-in-law worked in the North Tower. He had taken my niece—her name was Samantha and she was six—to work with him that day because it was what she wanted for her birthday. My office faced the towers. In fact, my office faced his," she said, her voice rough and tight. "Do I need to go on, or is the picture clear enough?"

"Christ, Kate. I'm sorry. I didn't know—"

"Well, Tom Taylor knows," she snapped. "He knows

where my parents are, too. What else does he know, Jake?"

"I don't know," he said after a minute. "But he wants us out there, Kate."

"There are plenty of other people who can babysit Simone for him. Why does it have to be us? Or me, anyway? I don't work for him."

"You and I are the only two who have studied the storms."

"That doesn't mean anything, Jake. This one is different. It's over water for one thing. And it's a hundred times bigger than anything else Carter messed with."

"If it escalates again—"

"If it escalates again, we'll all be dead."

Jake paused, took a deep breath, and decided to break the law. He grabbed her by the shoulders and swung her around so they were eye to eye. "Look, Kate, you know what Tom told you about Richard and Carter. They did this thirty years ago. But there's more to it. What I'm about to tell you is highly classified. *Highly* classified, okay? I went back and checked some of the bigger or atypical hurricanes of the last fifteen years. I'm pretty damned sure that Carter had something to with Hurricane Mitch in 1998 and Ivan in 2004. Possibly Katrina and Wilma in 2005. The man is a lunatic." Her reddened eyes and tear-streaked face revealed her shock. "And I suspect Taylor thinks you know more than you do about the storms and about Carter. So he wants us out there for the storm and he wants you within reach."

"You mean he wants me in custody," she said, her voice breaking. "Why can't any of you get it into your heads that I don't know anything more than what I already told you?"

CHAPTER 44

The wind spun like it was alive. Tight and slender, it undulated above the water, enclosing and protecting the storm's core, which was brilliantly lit from above. It was a sight seen only by those few brave enough to make the trip, those few tough enough to endure hours of terrifying, bone-rattling turbulence as they penetrated again and again the hundreds of miles of dark, dirty, churning clouds and rain that comprised the outer walls, and withstood the thunderous crashes and spectacular bursts of lightning that rolled and sheeted along wings and fuselage. They alone knew that, in contrast to those ominous, protective walls, the heart of Simone was pure.

Early-afternoon sunshine spilled through the open tower, giving the light a clarity that hadn't existed outside of a storm in centuries. The eye held no pollution, no man-made trouble, only Nature at her most fearsome, her most magnificent. Sunlight sparkled off the water vapor in the rising air, lending the air a calming shimmer associated more frequently with stories of redemption than destruction.

The storm held firm to the warmth of the sea, drinking deeply, gathering strength, replenishing itself as it shifted hundreds of thousands of pounds of water and sent it toward what remained of the unprotected beaches and buttressed edifices alike. The walls of water, more solid than fluid, roared up Manhattan's riverine boundaries and exploded into shoreline neighborhoods with a terrifying roar, breaking hearts and minds and bones. Heavy, wet winds smashed into the cocky, fortified city, filling the massive pit on its southern tip.

Mesh garbage bins, emptied of weight and with their plastic liners serving as spinnakers, rolled along the streets, flipping above cars and other impediments and occasion-

ally becoming airborne, smashing into windows six and ten stories up. Voracious, sucking winds pulled cowering occupants out through shard-rimmed, gaping holes. Driverless cars slid along the congested streets, abrading the boulevards, puncturing structures, and nurturing gridlock more ambitious than city dwellers could conceive. Light poles were hurled like spears, like harpoons into the sea of air, shattering on impact and impaling whatever they encountered.

Dropping pressure defeated the best-laid plans of the world's engineers as expansive sheets of reflective, impact-resistant glass burst out of their bonds and sailed, or dropped, through the canyons of high-rises. Depending on their aerodynamics, they sliced into buildings or bounced off the steel and stone. Cartwheeling through streets and sky, the window-walls stopped only when they sheared off the heads of gargoyles or statues or terrified pedestrians fleeing damaged places that no longer offered shelter.

Oblivious to everything but the warmth and the water that gave her life, Simone spun ever faster, a creation of heartbreaking, indescribable beauty, of poetry, a whirling, ethereal goddess meant to inspire awe and respect. Her unearthly roar silenced everything else. Her touch destroyed.

And yet, as the spiritual knew, her aftermath was new life.

CHAPTER 45

Monday, July 23, 5:08 P.M., Atlantic Ocean, 200 miles southeast of New York City

Her teeth clenched so hard her jaw was aching, Kate unbuckled herself from the seat in the large, loud, mostly empty helicopter, which was now settled on the helipad of the *William J. Clinton*. The ship was moving at a steady clip away from the U.S. mainland.

"Which way did you say I should turn when I get off this thing?" she asked Jake under her breath.

"To the right. That's where the bow is. That's the pointy end."

"I know what the bow of a boat is," she hissed.

"Ship. You look that way because that's where the flag is flying. So look at it and remember why you're here," he snapped, "then follow my lead. You're going to ask for permission to come aboard."

"What's gotten into you?" she demanded. "And, by the way, I am aboard."

"Would you just do what I tell you, for Christ's sake?"

The pilot turned around with a poorly hidden grin. "It will just be another minute and then you can debark. You two honeymooners? 'Cause this ain't the *Caribbean Princess*," he drawled.

Kate let Jake handle the conversation and instead looked out the window at all the people scurrying around the helicopter and on the ship in general. The deck was huge. *Huge*. And there was nothing but dark, churning sea and pelting rain in all directions. There was no land on the horizon, which in itself was hazy and difficult to discern.

Being here under these circumstances—during a heightened state of a terror alert, heading for what had already become the most powerful hurricane ever recorded—was surreal, or maybe just too real. Too reminiscent of when the towers fell. She and everyone else in the building had been effectively quarantined for nearly twenty-four hours. They'd had no lights, no air-conditioning. No power of any kind. Just panic and grief, the sound of sirens, and roiling plumes of thick, choking, grit-filled smoke that billowed past the windows, obscuring some of the horror beyond them. She didn't want to be here. Not surrounded by people pumped up on adrenaline, excited about heading directly into harm's way to execute an operation that was foolhardy at best.

She wanted to be anywhere but here. She wanted to be home.

"Kate?"

She looked at Jake.

"We can get out."

"Great. Thanks." She accepted his hand as she crab-walked to the now-open door and stepped onto the surface of the deck. He was right. She couldn't feel the motion of the waves or the boat. Ship.

He let go of her hand and pointed, saying something she couldn't hear. She looked to the right, past what looked like a several-story-tall glass-fronted building, to the bow of the ship, where the flag was whipping in the stiff wind. From the corner of her eye, she saw Jake throw his shoulders back and salute. The sight of the flag, of the man, closed her throat and blurred her vision.

Jake turned and faced an officer about their age who stood a few feet away. Kate followed his lead, saying what he'd told her to say and shaking the proffered hand. Then she followed them both through a doorway and into the gunmetal gray labyrinth of the ship.

After being shown to her quarters, a tiny room barely big enough to turn around in, with the smallest bathroom facilities she'd ever seen, she dropped her duffle and followed the men to one of a thousand doors they'd passed. Their tour guide left them at the door, after knocking and announcing them. They walked into a tightly organized conference room complete with flat-screen monitors on every wall and swivel chairs that were bolted to the floor.

"Welcome aboard."

Kate's head snapped up at the sound of a woman's voice. It wasn't so much that it was a female voice in such a male environment. She'd already passed a number of women in the corridors. It was the tone of the voice. It held a little bit of annoyance and a little bit of curiosity. What it didn't hold was any welcoming warmth. Neither did the tall uniformed blonde's bright blue eyes. They were cold.

She turned her head slightly to meet Kate's eyes and extended her hand. "Captain Joanna Smith."

"Hello. I'm Kate Sherman."

Captain Smith turned to Jake and repeated her introduction, then motioned to the table. "Now that the pleasantries are out of the way, have a seat," she said wryly. "Everyone else will be here in a minute."

They sat down at the conference table, the captain taking the seat at the head of the table, where a sheaf of papers and an open laptop were waiting. Within a few minutes, the seats at the table were filled by a team of serious, almost grim-faced uniformed men and women. Kate's first impression, as they came into the room, was that they were much too young to be doing what they were doing. More than half wore wedding bands. Too young, and otherwise committed.

What in God's name are any of us doing here?

After the first few confusing introductions, Kate realized they were introducing themselves by their duties rather than their titles. Their names were on their breast pockets. Their ranks were on their sleeves. Their confidence was present in every move they made.

Captain Smith began the meeting without preamble, her voice calm and flat. "The crew has been briefed on our mission, which is to neutralize Hurricane Simone using whatever means are possible and necessary," she said, looking first at Kate and then at Jake before glancing around the table.

The words sounded ominous and Kate fought a shudder. Jake just blinked.

"Our meteorologists are tracking the storm and we've identified a rendezvous point, which we'll achieve at approximately twenty-three hundred hours. We'll be positioned to the north-northwest of the storm, well within the outer rain bands, and approximately one hundred nautical miles from the eye if its track remains true. That means we'll be facing one-hundred-sixty-mile-an-hour or higher winds and very heavy seas. I anticipate being at general quarters, if not battle stations, for the duration of the operation."

She looked down at her computer. "I believe you discussed using the Peregrine."

When no one answered, she looked directly at Jake. "You discussed using the Peregrine?" she repeated.

"Yes."

The captain glanced at a young woman at the end of the table. She looked like she should be in the high-school gym discussing cheerleading jumps, not sitting several decks below an aircraft carrier's flight deck discussing high-tech weaponry.

"It won't survive the winds, ma'am. I think we have to go with the Condor. It's heavier and still has the laser capability."

The captain's eyebrow rose slightly. "That's still experimental."

"We have orders to field-test it."

"This would hardly be a field test," the captain replied dryly, then turned to a man sitting to her right. "What do you think?"

"I think we have no choice but to use the Condor."

The conversation quickly filled with technical jargon Kate couldn't follow and acronyms she didn't understand. Unobtrusively, she let her gaze wander around the room. Like on an airplane, there wasn't an inch of wasted space, except that in this setting nobody had to appeal to comfort or fashion. The decorating scheme was definitely utilitarian. Blue—navy blue, she supposed—and gray predominated. The table surface was Formica and the chairs weren't heavily padded. The lights were fluorescent. The floor vibrated.

She heard the storm being mentioned by name and brought her attention back to the captain, who was speaking to an officer who had gotten up to draw a diagram on a whiteboard that had descended to cover a screen. Just then the most ungodly roar resounded in the room and Kate looked around in panic.

"What in the name of God is that?" burst out of her mouth before she could stop it, and in an instant every pair of eyes in the room was on her. Some were amused, one or two were disgusted, and Jake's were already rolling skyward.

The captain raised an elegant eyebrow and turned to the officer to her right. "Perhaps you could explain."

Youngish, sunburned, and trying to keep a straight face, the guy looked at her. "That's a Hornet taking off, Ms. Sherman," he said easily. "The Navy's newest fighter jet. Our pilots are patrolling the perimeter of the storm to make sure no more planes with storm-enhancing capabilities get anywhere near it. Takeoffs and landings are sounds you'll be hearing a lot while you're aboard. I'm sure you'll have the opportunity to watch them topside."

"Thank you," she replied sheepishly. "Please pardon the interruption."

A knock at the door was followed by a sailor walking in. "Officer on deck."

Everyone in the room immediately stood up as a short, fit Asian man beginning the slide out of middle age walked into the room. Everyone except Jake saluted, so Kate kept her hands at her sides.

"As you were," he said before the door had even closed, and everyone relaxed but didn't sit down. He walked to the head of the table. Kate noticed that the captain had vacated the seat at the end and had stepped in front of the chair to her left, which had been left empty. The newcomer gestured for her to return to her place. "Captain."

"Thank you, sir."

The man sat in the chair to the captain's left and then she and everyone else sat down. A motion caught Kate's eye and she looked down. Jake's pen was pointing to the corner of his legal pad. *Rear Admiral Takamura. Big shot* was written there in small letters. She looked away, feeling the weight on her brain increase.

"As soon as we're in position, we'll begin deploying Condors," the captain said, glancing at him.

"How many do you have aboard?"

"Ten," the weapons officer replied from the far end of the table. "We were discussing configuration when you arrived, sir."

"Carry on."

The discussion of wavelengths and burst durations, altitude wind speeds, vectors, and vortex forces spun up again. A few minutes later, Kate tuned back in when Jake moved to the whiteboard.

"What do you think, Ms. Sherman?" asked Captain Smith.

Shit. Kate met the captain's gaze. "Quite honestly, Captain, this discussion is beyond my area of expertise. I don't know anything about weapons. I know about weather."

The captain didn't blink. "Do you have any questions that haven't already been asked and answered ?"

Another pop quiz. She glanced at Jake, then back at the captain. "Well, how far do the beams go? If they're clearing the atmosphere as they move through it, do they degrade? Are they going to destroy things?"

"They do attenuate and light doesn't bend, Ms. Sherman, so the beams won't go below the horizon. As a precaution, though, the shipping channels to the south-southeast of the storm are being cleared to the thirty-second parallel," someone from the other side of the table replied.

"Thank you," Kate said quietly, and indicated to the captain that she had no other questions. She might as well have put a dunce cap on. She was far out of her depth.

CHAPTER 46

**Monday, July 23, 6:05 P.M., Upper East Side,
New York City**

Elle breathed a sigh of blessed relief. She was finally alone.

Special Agents Laurel and Hardy had insisted that she had to go to a storm shelter, but she had just as adamantly refused. God only knows what that would have been like. She would rather take her chances in her apartment, not that she believed a hurricane was really going to hit New York. But if it did, she'd be fine. The building was pre-war and built like a bank vault, and it stood on high ground on the Upper East Side.

The agents had relented only when she'd been able to track down Lisa Baynes and convince her to come stay with her. It was a good idea—both for the company and because Elle couldn't do much for herself with the bandages on her hands. The intrepid Lisa had made it to Elle's building despite conditions in the streets and was wowed into uncharacteristic silence at the sight of seven spacious rooms furnished mostly with antiques. Lisa had been a real help, despite all the questions she started asking the minute the agents left them. Thanks to her, Elle was clean and dressed in clean clothes and sitting on fresh sheets in her own bedroom, exhausted and contemplating her options.

Low-lying areas had been under evacuation advisories for the last few days, and wholesale evacuation orders had been issued yesterday morning. According to Lisa, the city was in an uproar, which was part of the reason Lisa had decided to stay. The mayor was demanding that people behave in a calm and rational manner; New Yorkers were responding, true to their character, by ignoring both the evacuation orders and the mayor. Reporters roaming the streets in search of precisely this sort of idiocy had found plenty of people whose emergency plans included seeking shelter in the subways. Which was fine, Elle thought, if you liked swimming with rats rather than sharks.

Now that she had fully regained her senses, Elle knew she had to leave this apartment, this city, this life. Every extra minute spent here was a moment wasted. Even knowing she wasn't in any danger, she didn't want to be here. Her bags had been packed since early afternoon and stood waiting by the front door for the first moment she could safely leave. Anywhere would be fine with her.

Win hadn't called; the only calls had been from her parents. The call placed by Davis Lee had definitely happened, but Win was letting her dangle. At the moment, he was certainly safe and secure somewhere with his parents. No doubt the entire family was basking in the safety and comfort of their Montana ranch or their adobe palace in New Mexico, she thought bitterly. Not that she cared.

Right now, all she cared about was maximizing the damage control to her own life. She was counting on enough chaos after the storm passed to give her some cover as she headed to Washington to clear out her apartment. Despite the flooding, she was sure subletting it wouldn't be a problem. It was half of a floor in a historic mansion perched above the city in Aurora Heights and thus very close to the Pentagon. She might even make something on the deal.

The weathercasters had run out of superlatives days ago, but glancing out the window, Elle thought again that this didn't seem like the worst storm she'd ever seen. Lisa said that until the power went out, the TV talking heads had kept saying it was going to get much worse.

The backdrop of sky was composed of dark and darker shades of gray, and the clouds looked like they were boiling in some insane stew. The wind was driving the rain nearly horizontal between buildings. The constant flashes of lightning and deafening cracks of thunder reminded her of battle scenes in *Saving Private Ryan,* and the rain did its part, too, imitating the sound of muffled machine-gun fire as it hit the windows. There was a weird sort of solitude in the midst of such violence, though, and she didn't mind it.

The harsh, unwelcome sound of the door buzzer broke into the rhythm of the rain against the windows. As Lisa's wide-eyed face appeared in the bedroom doorway, Elle realized that the doorman hadn't announced anyone. Just like last time.

Dread prickled the back of her neck. She didn't know any of the other residents, and John would never let anyone into the building if they didn't have approval. Or a badge.

"Who is it?" she asked.

"I don't know. There are three guys out there. One had his head sort of down and I couldn't see his face."

With shaking hands, Elle reached for the bedside telephone console and depressed the code for the desk with a pencil. The bandages on her fingertips made dialing awkward if not impossible.

"John?" she said when he answered. "Someone's at my door. Did you let someone up?"

"He told me it was a surprise, Ms. Baker. And I thought it would be all right. He said he was coming to take you away from the storm."

"Who? Who told you?" she demanded, panic rising in her throat like bile.

"Mr. Benson. I'm sorry for ruining the surprise, Ms. Baker, but—"

She hung up the phone as the buzzer sounded again, longer this time, as if the person pressing it was impatient or annoyed.

Or ruthlessly angry.

Her heart thundering in her chest, she glanced at Lisa, who now looked thoroughly spooked.

"Don't let them in."

"Who are they?"

"It's—he's—" She stood up. "It's Win Benson, the president's son. Tell him I'm not here. Okay? Make up anything."

"Who? Win Benson? I can't lie to him. Why—"

"I can't explain," Elle said, her voice becoming nearly a shriek. "Just tell him I'm not here!"

She practically pushed Lisa out of the bedroom and shut the door. A moment later, she heard Lisa arguing with a man. Panicked, Elle spun around, vainly seeking an escape route.

"Elle."

It was Win.

The bandages made her clumsy, but after a moment of fumbling, she opened the lock and wrenched open the window. She braced herself for the onslaught of the wind and rain before swinging a leg onto the black iron grate of the fire escape. The flat sole of her shoe slid beneath her weight, leaving her off balance, straddling the sill and hanging on to the wood of the window frame above her head. The rain felt like pebbles as it drove into the skin of her arms and the back of her head with a force that actually hurt. Her ears were popping, which made no sense since she was only on the eighth floor, and it was hard to breathe. She forced herself to take slower breaths, but it didn't help.

She had to get to the street. She could wait out the storm somewhere and start over afterward. Ignoring the pain rifling up her arms, Elle gripped the frame tighter to counteract the increasing slickness of the wood beneath her bandaged fingertips and swung her other leg over the sill. Her dress, already sodden, clung to her thighs, hampering her efforts.

A cry of frustration ripped from her as she overbalanced and landed on the grated floor of the small landing. The wind sliced at her, wrapping her hair around her neck like a garrote and slamming bits of flying debris into her. Grasping the vertical supports on the railing, she pulled herself to a sitting position.

"Are you insane? What are you doing out there?"

The hoarse shout was close, and she looked up to see Win standing just inside the window, grimacing against the wind and flanked by his Secret Service detail.

"Leave me alone," she screamed.

"Elle, you're going to kill yourself. Come back in here. Grab my hand." He reached for her, leaning halfway out the window before the agents hauled him back inside. One of the suits leaned out, telling her to inch forward and take his hand.

She looked away and down, seeking the top of the stairs but seeing instead the trash-filled alleyway behind the building. Beneath her swirled a river of upscale urban garbage, with wine bottles, milk cartons, and plastic grocery bags colliding in a filthy, tortured flow.

"Elle, give me your hand." The voice—one of the agents'—seemed closer; she turned to see the man climbing out of the window.

"I can do this," she muttered to herself, wondering when she'd started to cry. She pushed herself feet first toward the stairs. Her ass and thighs scraped along the rough iron as her dress refused to move with her.

"Elle, don't," Win shouted. "You won't make it. Come inside, for Christ's sake. What are you doing?"

There was panic in his voice, and that bolstered her courage.

"Leave me alone," she shouted back, and felt her feet ease over the top of the stairs. Pushing herself harder, she moved her hands to the next segment of railing.

I'll make it. This is easy. I just have to keep doing the same thing.

Hands grabbed her from behind, snaking under her arms and across her chest, pulling her up and back. She let go of the railing and clawed at the encircling arms with her raw fingertips, the bandages falling from her hands. Writhing, trying to get away, she felt the wet, rusty grate rip at the backs of her thighs.

"Let me go," she screamed, wrenching her body away from the agent's grip.

"Elle, stop—"

"Let me go!"

Lightning sliced through the darkness, striking something nearby. The crash, the shower of sparks that flared above the building in front of her, and the earth-shaking thunder that accompanied it disoriented her and, instinctively, she rolled toward the building. In the process, she dislodged the Secret Service agent. Realizing she was free, Elle flung herself down the stairs.

The searing impact of the edge of a step as it met her shoulder ripped a scream from her throat. Her vision clouded by tears and pain, she continued sliding down the steps, the heavy, industrial iron abrading every inch of flesh it met. She realized, as she tried to brace herself, that her left throbbing arm was limp, flopping unnaturally against her. Crashing into the enclosed landing, she felt a warm liquid trickle on her face and wiped it away, then looked up to see the agent, uninjured and intact, descending the stairs cautiously, but with a determined look on his face.

Using her good arm, Elle managed somehow to get to her feet. She leaned into the railing as she hobbled, barefoot, to the next turn in the staircase. Lightning struck again, closer, and the open staircase shook from the impact. As she turned to see how close the agent was, she saw a blur of dull orange and green, before the space above and around her exploded in a welter of mud and branches.

As Elle threw her arm up to protect her eyes from the shattering terra-cotta pot from the penthouse terrace, she lost her balance and fell heavily against the fire escape's railing. The impact of the huge potted tree had driven the body of the agent down through the grate. Mud spilled over a few large shards of pottery onto the macabre mass of clothing and body tissues that dangled for a moment before being torn away by the wind. They flew into the alley and the city beyond it. Elle vomited and turned away, dropping to her knees. The landing swayed beneath her.

She snapped her head up and focused on the brick wall

ahead of her, on the black iron bolts that were leaning away from their moorings.

"Oh God. No. I'm not going to die here." The words echoed in her head. She wasn't sure if she'd actually uttered them as she inched closer to the top of the next staircase.

Seven flights. I can do this.

She descended the stairs as steadily and smoothly as she could, ignoring her pain, keeping her breathing measured, and concentrating on keeping her footing and her grip on the railing. As her foot touched the sixth-floor landing, the entire structure wobbled and she froze, holding her breath, her gaze fixed on a bolt that had come completely out of the brick.

Hesitating won't help. Keep moving.

The wind ripped at her. She was getting colder; it was harder to control her trembling and even to move. Taking a steadying breath and gripping the hand rail tightly, she took a step forward. The agent's shoes lay ahead of her, one still attached to a foot. Muddied, bloodied, and tangled impossibly into the grate lay the pulpy remains of his legs and other things less identifiable.

Fighting the urge to vomit again, she moved on, careful to dodge what was dripping down from above and avoid stepping in what remained in front of her.

She kept her head down against the storm, glancing up infrequently to gauge her progress. The rain, driven by the icy wind and laden with the city's grit, sandblasted her already-raw skin, making each step more painful than the last, each step slower than it needed to be. Nearing the last step before the third-story landing, Elle raised her head slightly and stumbled at the sight of Win, standing alone in the alley below, almost up to his knees in water. There was actual concern on his face and he was shouting something at her that was obliterated by the thunder, the banshee screams of the wind, the metallic wallop of Dumpster lids flapping like manic sheets on a clothesline.

The trembling in her knees, compounded by the lightness in her head and the growing surreality of what she was doing, brought her to a stop. She collapsed onto the metal stairs. The groaning and shuddering of the fire escape registered somewhere at the back of her mind as she rested her good arm on her knees and began to cry. Eventually a sound that she recognized penetrated the growing numbness in her brain and she raised her head.

Win had moved farther into the alley, had come closer to her. He was standing directly beneath the fire escape in the swirling water. His suit coat, like the rest of his clothing, was plastered to his body.

"Come down." The words were faint against the howling wind.

She shook her head slowly, tears still flowing. "I can't," she whispered, knowing she couldn't go back up to the apartment, either. Wiping her tears away with the back of her hand, she felt the fire escape shudder again and looked up in time to see the remains of another potted tree falling on to the grates above her.

The sensation of falling didn't last long. Mercifully, neither did the sensation of having the weight of the fire escape land on her back.

CHAPTER **47**

Monday, July 23, 11:45 P.M., Atlantic Ocean, aboard the USS *William J. Clinton*

As the night dragged on, the faces changed occasionally as people left the room and others came in, but the tension level never lessened and the muted conversations never rose in volume. Most eyes in the room were glued to the three flat screens dominating the longest wall. Kate blinked at the satellite radar view of the storm on the screen ahead of her. It was hypnotic in its sameness and slowness, probably because white obscured everything else that would ordinarily be visible on the map. The outline of the eastern U.S. and Canada, Bermuda, and much of the Caribbean seemed superimposed on the cloud cover.

She'd always thought that the majesty of storms as they appeared on the radar screen held a twisted sort of magic. The white wisps at the far edges of the storm looked so delicate, belying the deadly force propelling them and the horrible damage they inflicted. The infrared satellite images, however, never downplayed a storm's fury.

The ragged saw blade of hot orange, with its red core and flaming yellow blades, spun counter-clockwise like an ominous Catherine wheel. Green covered much of the rest of that screen. From the Caribbean to Boston, from east of Bermuda to the Ohio Valley, the pixilated rain bands changed minutely as she watched. Kate knew it was a real-time feed, the best technology had to offer, but she still had the sense that she was watching slowed-down animation. She had the urge to speed it up and get to the natural conclusion. Except, in this case the natural conclusion was what they were trying to avoid. The natural conclusion was death for potentially hundreds of thousands of people, maybe millions, if the storm destroyed Indian Point.

She slid her focus to the middle screen, a feed from a camera mounted in the belly of an Air Force P-3 Hurricane Hunter, which was circling several thousand feet above sea level in the storm's eye. The sea's surface was bright, a thrashing, foamy blue void slashed with white. The data coming in from the dropsondes, the small sensor-filled canisters the crew dropped into the storm, was grim.

The numbers ticked over as the data from the last 'sonde was received.

"God damn it," Jake said. He didn't yell. His voice was pretty calm actually, but the silence in the room was so dense that it might as well have been a shout.

"Oh my God," Kate whispered, her throat reflexively closing as she felt fear's grip.

The barometric pressure was down to 883 millibars,

one tick above the lowest sea-level pressure ever recorded, and the sustained wind speeds in the eye wall had reached 178 miles per hour. The water temperature beneath the eye was approaching 85°F. It was far too warm for the mid-Atlantic. Far too warm even for the Gulf Stream. It was fuel for an inferno already out of control.

"Baxter. Sherman." The captain's voice was emotionless and all the more authoritative for it. They turned toward her. She stood next to one of the consoles, her face grim but impassive. "It's time to rock and roll."

She began issuing orders in that eerily calm voice, and the energy level in the room punched up as personnel further down the hierarchy began issuing orders of their own and the men and women stationed at consoles and monitors around the room began calling out information.

Kate stood transfixed as she watched the third screen. It was split into two nearly identical views. These were the views from the two UACVs, the combat-ready drones, which were armed and waiting in their firing tubes. She'd found out earlier that, although unmanned, they would be operated by "joystick jockeys" at a naval base in California.

A command was given and Kate heard a dull roar as she watched the screen flash, then blur. After that, she saw nothing but sky. Dirty, gray, churning sky. A moment later, the images on the screen changed. The right pane was the view from the drone. The left screen was the infrared view from a military satellite. Kate felt someone move up beside her. A glance to her left revealed the captain.

"It's fired with a rocket," the captain said. "The booster gets it up to just beyond its cruising altitude and speed, guides it for a while, then drops off."

"Then how—"

Kate's question was cut short as the satellite image of the rapidly moving streak on the screen began to change. She watched nearly one-third of the drone's body mass fall away in a slow arc. Her eyes widened as she saw long, narrow wings sweep out slowly from the sides. Smaller blades emerged at the rear of the vehicle. A propeller slid out from the end and, already spinning, unfolded.

"It's under its own power now."

Kate looked over at the captain, who flashed her a quick smile. "I think they call that poetry in motion. It's nearly thirty feet long, with a wingspan of nearly fifty feet, and it's carrying five hundred pounds of electronics, including the laser and its fuel and propagation equipment." She shook her head. "I have no idea how someone made it work, but I sure as hell hope they knew what they're doing," she said, then walked back to one of the consoles.

The split screen changed again, and Kate watched another launch.

She had no idea how long she stood there. The turbulence shaking the cameras made her nauseous, but the images from the drones were breathtaking as they switched from cloud-penetrating radar view, to full-color high-definition, to infrared and then started the sequence over again. From eight thousand feet, the sea was churning foam, white with slashes of darkness that disappeared almost as quickly as they appeared. Though deployed more than 250 miles away from the eye, the drones quickly penetrated rain bands well into the storm.

"Dropping altitude." The God-like voice over the speaker held no emotion as it called out the new coordinates. Then Kate heard the order to fire the laser and a brilliant streak erupted on the screen showing the infrared view. The second drone fired a minute later and both screens were lit up with the fiery, pulsing beams of light that strobed the swirling bands of rain and bisected the eye of the storm.

"Shit," Jake muttered loud enough for Kate to hear, and she tore her eyes away from the drones' images to the view from above, from the hurricane hunter, and the numbers ticking over next to it.

"What's wrong? The core isn't heating up, is it?"

"No. Nothing's happening. Not a damn thing," he replied tersely. "Everything is stable."

"Shit," she agreed, a blur of dull panic settling into her already-queasy stomach. "Can we keep firing? It's only been a few minutes. It has to work eventually."

Jake leveled his gaze at her. "No, Kate, it doesn't. We've got two thin beams of heat passing through the core of a storm that's nearly seven hundred miles wide. If this works it will be a miracle."

"But it's got to work," she said, not liking the desperate note creeping into her voice but unable to block it.

"I'll give you two more drones. After that, we'll have to abort the mission and get out of Dodge." The captain's voice cut through their discussion like a scalpel and they both turned to look at her. "We can last about another twenty minutes, but if nothing has changed, we're going to have to get out of its path." She turned to the officer to her left and gave the orders to deploy two additional UACVs. On-screen, the airborne lasers kept pulsing through the murk.

"Jake," Kate whispered, trying to control her excitement as she watched the numbers superimposed on the P-3's bird's-eye view. "Jake, the variables are changing. Look. I think it's starting."

It's about God-damned time. Jake whipped his head around, his eyes boring into the screen. Sure enough, the relative humidity had dropped by .03. He looked at the captain. "How fast can you scramble those drones?"

"They're being loaded in the tubes now," she said.

"Great." He brought his gaze back to the screens, not fully trusting what he saw.

The numbers from the P-3 were stable and would remain that way until they dropped another 'sonde, but the rougher figures from the drones' less sensitive sensors showed a drop of a full percentage point of relative humidity as they passed through the areas the beams had just swept.

As the unmanned vehicles approached Simone's eye, the tension in the room rose like a storm tide. The turbulence was jarring and the images were blurred almost beyond recognition. The beams were arcing wildly as the pilots in California fought to maintain the drones' course and altitude.

"If one of those beams hits a drone, we're screwed," Jake muttered.

About a second later, the deep drawl of the hurricane hunter pilot came over one of the speakers. "I don't suppose you'd mind turning off those high beams while you're in traffic?" he drawled.

"Cease firing before we take out the boys upstairs," the chief weapons officer said curtly. Almost instantly the drones' beams disappeared from the screens.

A terse thanks crackled from the desktop speaker.

"What's going on, Jake?" the captain demanded after a tense minute of silence as they all watched, and seemed to feel, the drones bounce like basketballs.

"The eyewall, the wind bands immediately around the eye, are coming at one hundred and seventy-eight miles an hour sustained. The eyewalls are always the strongest winds in the hurricane," Kate replied quickly. "They form the tightest circulation cell and are the most critical in keeping the storm alive. Once the drones cross them and get inside the eye, there will be an abrupt cessation of the violence. The wind speeds will probably drop by two-thirds. Then they'll have to cross into the eyewall on the other side."

"Between the air pressure and the wind speed differentials, the drones will drop like stones." Joanna's voice had gone tight and low. "Or break up after passing through."

"There will have to be some corrections," Kate admitted as the first drone burst through the wall of wind and rain into sunshine so brilliant that several people in the room gasped. Though that might have been due to the instant, uncontrolled thousand-foot drop the drone experienced before being pulled up. It blasted through the far side of the eye just as the second vehicle entered the space.

Seconds later, the second drone attempted to penetrate the far eyewall. Striking the winds at the wrong angle, it flipped and shattered, exploding more violently than a mid-sized bomb, thanks to the dangerously low pressure. Shrapnel and fuel were sucked into the eyewall and began spreading out and spiraling upward into a lethal helix. Even a small piece could slice into the metal body of an aircraft like a hot knife through butter.

Uttering his thanks for the adventure, the P-3 pilot climbed as far and as fast as he could, dropping one last 'sonde before exiting the eye.

"Well, I think I can safely say we're screwed," Joanna said as the airwing commander gave the order for the undeployed drones to stand down. Everyone in the room knew that from this point forward the only data they'd be getting would be from the satellites and whatever the deep-sea buoys transmitted. Recon by the Hurricane Hunters was over.

The weapons officer gave the command to resume the beam as the first drone moved through the stronger, forward winds of the storm. Joanna looked at Kate. "Any chance we can bring that bird home?"

"If it can be turned once it's in the outer band, and be brought back in at a different altitude, we might be able to. The debris from the drone that exploded will rise and then be flung out the top of the storm, so going in at a lower altitude shouldn't pose much risk in the immediate future. It will be more effective to have the beams working at a lower altitude, but the lower the altitude in a hurricane, the worse the turbulence." Kate shrugged. "I don't think anything can hurt at this point."

"What's another eight-million-dollar drone, right?" came the dry reply as Captain Smith turned back to her officers.

Jake turned his attention back to the satellite view and the enormous expanse of swirling white that covered the screen.

Tuesday, July 24, 12:15 A.M., a CIA safe house in rural Northern Virginia

The word from the carrier was not good. The atmosphere in the house was several degrees beyond oppressive—in more ways than one. The air-conditioning had been cut off twenty-four hours ago; the generator was being used exclusively for the computers and the comms at this point. The tension in the place was choking. Stepping into the storm for some fresh air and solitude, even though it could mean death, was preferable. And that's exactly what Tom Taylor did.

The door hadn't even shut behind him when he saw a match flare, piercing the darkness to his left.

"Shit."

The woman's voice echoed his own thoughts.

Since Kate was on board the carrier and Candy was still inside, that meant his company was the blunt, uncharming Colonel Brannigan.

"Greetings to you, too," he said dryly.

"Believe it or not, that wasn't meant for you," came the equally dry reply. "This is my last cigarette and a raindrop just landed in the middle of it."

"You shouldn't smoke anyway."

Her pause was laden with potential that she refrained from utilizing. "I was off them for eight years and went back on them after meeting you. I'm pretty confident that if I die in the next few days it won't be from these."

Another match flared, followed seconds later by the first whiff of burning tobacco and, seconds after that, by a soft sigh that was almost erotic against the dark night, the screaming wind, the driving rain.

They stood there in an uncompanionable silence for a few moments.

"How's Carter?" she asked.

"He stroked on us."

"I heard. Is he dead?"

"No. He's cognizant but not cooperating."

She let out an annoyed breath. "What does that mean?" The *you prick* was silent.

He turned to look at her. "It means that when he was asked questions to determine his mental capacity, he answered appropriately by blinking, but when FBI agents started questioning him about the foundation, the plane, and the storms, he just closed his eyes."

"Maybe he fell asleep."

"He didn't fall asleep. He's refusing to cooperate," Tom replied flatly.

Silence stretched across several minutes as they stood uncomfortably close to each other under the small overhang at the back door.

"You do realize, don't you, that you carry at least as much blame as he does for what's going on right now?"

He swung his head to meet her eyes, which were lit with undisguised loathing. It was a look he was used to receiving, so it didn't bother him. Her words did.

"Excuse me?"

"I said you share the blame for Simone. You played fast and loose with the jet stream because of the same God complex that drove Carter Thompson to bring the ocean to a boil."

He felt his jaw clench as anger ripped through him, but he didn't respond until he had himself under control. "Sometimes things have to get really bad before they can get better, Colonel. Having spent your entire military career behind a desk looking at weather maps, you wouldn't know what it's like to have even one person's life in your hands, much less the lives of millions, so I will just say this to you: Never again make the mistake of associating me with a terrorist. You have no fucking idea what I do or why I do it."

"Nor do I want to know, Mr. Taylor. I'm sure your background includes lots of sordid experiences, like interrogating—"

"You're wrong, Colonel. I've never interrogated anyone.

You know who they choose to be interrogators?" he replied, his voice once again cool and unconcerned. "The pussies who can't handle the real dirty work."

She looked suitably shocked and offended, so he went in for the kill.

"Your first name is Patricia, isn't it?"

She nodded.

"That was my wife's name."

"What is this, a foxhole confession?" she said, looking away and taking her last, deep drag on the cigarette. Her hands had developed a slight tremble in the last ten seconds.

"Maybe." He paused for a beat. "I don't really care whether you or anyone else likes me or respects me or respects what I do, but I resent being called a terrorist."

She nodded once. "You made your point."

"No, I don't think I did." He turned to face her, folding his arms across his chest. "I worked for the Agency for twenty-six years and then I retired. I set up a small business making furniture, reproductions of French period pieces." He watched her eyebrows go up. "I've always been good with my hands, Colonel. But one day, one of my tools slipped and I cut myself pretty badly. The nurse in the ER was the kindest person I'd ever met. Never asked questions, just took me as I was. I married her three months later. We had two sons."

"Let me guess. Then she left you?" Her tone was sarcastic, but her voice had gone husky.

"Yes, she did. We were on a vacation at her family's summer house on Martha's Vineyard. I left early to finish something for a client. Patricia and the boys were due home two days later, but their plane was diverted into the South Tower of the World Trade Center."

Her sharp intake of breath was followed by a stifled sob.

"A few days later, my old boss called me and asked if I would come back to help out. And here I am." He paused and watched her founder in a stew of unwanted emotions.

"I'm sorry, Mr. Taylor. I'm really very sorry for your loss," she said, stumbling over the words.

"Thank you, Colonel Brannigan." He turned back to face the storm.

It wasn't until she'd gone back inside and he heard the door close behind her that he allowed himself a grim smile.

Tuesday, July 24, 12:40 A.M., Atlantic Ocean, aboard the USS *William J. Clinton*

Kate followed Jake into the captain's office. It was nicer than any other room she'd seen on the ship, with wood paneling, furniture that looked like it might have come from Ethan Allen, and nice, *real* carpeting. It was crowded, though. The admiral and the captain were already there, as were several other officers, some of whom she'd met and some she hadn't, and a civilian who clearly wasn't having a good day.

Captain Smith turned to Jake and Kate and asked them—told them, really—to sit down.

"The drones didn't work, and that's all we were authorized to do," she said with no preamble. "I don't want to test my ship by keeping her near the storm without a good reason." She paused. "The admiral and I have been in contact with the Secretary of Defense and have received authorization to deploy a new weapon that we have aboard for field trials." She glanced over at the civilian. "Dr. Przypek, this is Jake Baxter and this is Kate Sherman, the meteorologists I told you about. Would you give them the two-dollar rundown of the weapon?"

The man stepped forward, clearly not in his element. Short, stocky, and with shaggy dark hair in need of more than a trim, he wore a faded blue golf shirt with some undecipherable corporate logo on the front of it, faded jeans, and sneakers.

"Hi. I'm Kevin." He cleared his throat and went on. "The weapon is called the Cold Core Endoatmospheric High-Energy Light Propagator, or C2EHELP. We call it 'Cold Day in Hell,'" he said with a grim, tight smile that Kate thought looked alien on his puppy-doggish face. "It fires a cold-core particle beam at an aerial target, freezing it on contact."

Kate just stared at him. Jake, after a minute, shrugged and shook his head.

"Maybe you should give me the ten-dollar explanation. Sounds too much like what we've already tried except with cold instead of heat."

The civilian laughed. The rest of the room's occupants remained silent and tense.

"It's not a laser. The beam is composed of subatomic particles called przypeks—I discovered them, that's why they're named after me. They exist only at temperatures around eighty-five kelvins, which is pretty cold. Did you see that big round thing circling the ship at the waterline? Looks like a metal inner tube?" he asked, a hopeful smile on his face.

This guy is nuts. Kate shook her head in the negative. So did Jake.

"Oh." The academic's disappointment was so evident that if they'd hadn't been in such an intense situation, Kate knew she would have laughed.

"Well, that's the accelerator that produces them." He stopped again, then shrugged. "Long story short, when the particles accrete and we have enough mass, we can launch them from a cannon and shoot them through the atmosphere at a target."

"Don't they heat up the second they hit the air?" Jake asked with a little more sharpness in his voice than was strictly necessary.

Kevin frowned a little. "Well, yeah, some of them do. The particles comprising the outer layers of the beam degrade. But since the particles are traveling at the speed of light, they reach their target before any appreciable heat can attenuate the core, which is significantly more dense than the outer layers. When the core hits the target—usually the superheated engine of a rocket or an aircraft—the particles freeze it instantly and it drops from the sky. Usually it explodes, too." He shrugged. "No sweat, no threat."

Kate cleared her throat. "So we're going to aim this beam at the hurricane?"

Kevin glanced at her. "Well, yes and no. The cannon is powerful, but it's a precision instrument. Its aperture is pretty small, only five centimeters in diameter, and the cannon has to be in a fixed position when you're firing it. So you'd have to aim it at something more specific than 'the hurricane.'"

"Like what?" Jake snorted. "There's nothing fixed in a cyclonic storm. It's volatile and in motion by definition."

"What sort of distance does it cover?" Kate asked, ignoring Jake's question.

"It's meant for short-distance fighting, to the horizon but not over it. Its range is about twenty-five kilometers." He shrugged. "The beam could go farther. It depends on environmental conditions. I mean, in space, we're talking—"

"How about at sea level?" Jake interrupted sharply. "In a hot, highly turbulent environment with lots of water vapor? Will it bounce?"

"They," he corrected. "No, the particles won't bounce, but as you're implying, the density of the atmosphere the beam is traversing will increase the rate of attenuation. We should be as close as we can get to the target."

"Which would be the eye?" the captain asked.

The physicist shrugged. "That's your call."

"The storm cell itself," Jake said. "The point of convection, at the top—"

"What about the water?" Kate asked, and all eyes turned to her.

"The water?" the captain repeated incredulously. "The stuff the ship depends on to float? You want to freeze *that*?"

Kate met her eyes. "A five-centimeter-wide beam aimed at an eye a few miles wide might not do much damage. Just a guess."

"She's got a point." All eyes swung back to the physicist. "The sensors and software the device relies on for targeting seek high-speed infrared signatures. Even though a cyclonic storm releases a lot of heat, I don't think it qualifies as an ideal target. The beam, as I said, is narrow. It's designed to hit relatively small targets, so it might not create enough of an effect to stop the convection cycle, or even destabilize it."

"Any effort at destabilization should take place as low as possible in the storm, as close to the fuel source as we can get. That's what we were trying to do with the drones, right? Stop the convective towers from building? Well, this could go one better. If nothing is coming up the pipeline, the convective towers are going to collapse." Kate turned to the scientist, who was grinning now. "Can you aim it at the water?"

"We've never tested it, but I don't see why we can't try it. The cold would diffuse, but I'm not sure in what direction."

"What do you mean?"

"Well, outward across the surface, or down into the water column. I suppose either would work, wouldn't it?"

"Look, you two," the captain interrupted. "Is this going to work? Because either we try this right now or we have to haul serious ass out of here." She looked from the scientist to Kate and then to Jake. "What do you think?"

"I think we have no other choice but to try it," he replied.

"How soon can we deploy?" the captain asked over her shoulder.

"Thirty-five minutes," the weapons officer replied. "The accelerator has been on standby since we departed Dover."

The captain turned back to them and gave them the look that had no doubt won her her command. "This had better work."

There was a definite motion to the ship now, and Kate was wishing she'd taken a pass on the opportunity to be in the glass-walled control room in "the island," the command center that stood several stories above the carrier's deck. Ordinarily it was used for monitoring flight operations, but the aviation team had relinquished their space and she, Jake, Kevin, and the captain were up there to oversee the first deployment of the Cold Day in Hell.

"Are you sure that cannon isn't just going to snap off and come flying back here to kill us?" Kate whispered to Kevin as she stood next to where he was sitting at a computer terminal.

Kevin, Jake, and the captain looked at her, their expressions ranging from amusement to exasperation.

"That baby is built for battle. Nothing's going to blow it off the deck. Besides, it has a very low profile. It only comes up a few feet. Everything has to stay supercooled."

"We don't lose too many things over the side, Kate. Maybe the odd skeptic," Captain Smith said dryly, and turned her eyes back to the many monitors ranged before them.

The storm's fury had intensified to the point at which it had surpassed what would have made it a Category 6 or even higher on the Saffir-Simpson Scale—if such categories existed. Its pressure was lower, its wind speed higher, its forward speed greater, and its eye tighter than all other storms in recorded history. And it was still heading straight toward the New York Bight.

"Okay, I think it's showtime," Kevin said, his fingers stilling over the keyboard for the first time in at least half an hour.

Jake looked at him. "You *think* it is?"

Kevin grinned. "Okay. It's showtime."

The control room, which had been working at a quiet hum, went still.

"We need the cannon on deck," the captain said, and the command was repeated by a uniformed sailor sitting at a console facing away from the deck.

"Cannon's coming up," the seaman announced a moment later.

At the far edge of the deck, Kate saw part of the floor slide away and a squat, heavy-looking box rise up in its place.

"That's the cannon?" she asked.

"The back of it," Kevin replied, pride in his voice as his fingers started flying over the keyboard again.

"Is this some kind of a joke?" the captain snapped in a

voice that froze everyone in their tracks. Kate turned to look at her, her heart thumping.

The captain's face had gone white and her eyes were spitting fire at the grim-faced sailor who had just handed her a piece of paper.

"No, ma'am."

The captain brought her gaze to Kate's face, then moved on to Jake and Kevin. "The Statue of Liberty was blown over four minutes ago." She swallowed hard, still staring at Kevin. "You make this work. *You make this work.*"

After a few seconds, the physicist turned quietly back to his console. His voice shaking audibly, he said, "The aperture is opening. Setting is three degrees above the horizon. Three, two, one. Go."

A silvery-blue translucent beam shot into infinity from twenty feet above the starboard bow, freezing everything in its path. The waves, easily one hundred feet tall, froze through their middles, sending car-sized chunks of ice crashing to the deck with the unstoppable momentum of the moving water surrounding them. Shards of solid white water tens of feet long bucked into the air, somersaulting over the deck, smashing into anything that lay in their path. Kate ducked as one came flying straight for the island and crashed into the thick Plexiglas window shielding the story below where they stood.

"God almighty, look at this," Jake shouted, and Kate and Joanna clustered next to him. The side-by-side high-definition infrared satellite images showed wide and tight views of the storm. Kate's eyes flicked from one to the other. The wide focus showed a dark blue line skewering the red-hot heart of the storm and continuing for a hundred miles out to sea before fading to green and then disappearing from the screen. The tight focus showed the eye only, bisected by blue with greens and yellow radiating from it in all directions.

After a minute of near-reverent or maybe disbelieving silence, the blue line then disappeared from the screen and all eyes turned back to Kevin.

"What?" he asked, still shaken.

"Where did it go? Why did you turn it off?" Jake demanded.

Kevin looked at him like he was crazy. "It was on longer than it's supposed to be. It's sort of point and click, right? Except that it's point and zap."

"Well, reload," Jake snorted.

Kevin frowned. "Well . . . we can't."

"We can't?" Jake repeated, practically snarling. "That one blast ain't doing enough, pal. You have to do it again."

Kevin looked faintly shocked. "Look, we're talking about subatomic particles, not bombs or bullets. You don't just go to a storeroom and get some more."

"What do you do?"

He looked bewildered by the question. "You create them in a particle accelerator. It—it takes a while."

"You said there's one on board. Come on, Kevin—"

"There is, but it's not like a toaster, Jake. It—"

"Jake, quit being an ass." Kate grabbed him by the shoulder. "Take another look at the screen. It worked."

"It did?" Kevin jumped up and nearly tripped in his haste to get to the monitor.

The blue had completely disappeared, and although the residual heat of the storm had closed in, trying to reestablish equilibrium and reenergize the cell, Simone's engine had been severely destabilized.

The silence in the room was palpable, broken only by the occasional boulders of ice hitting the deck.

"Will it hold?" The captain's question was quiet, but her voice was fraying with emotion around the edges.

Jake turned to her. "It's too early to know. But if the heat's dropping, the winds will be dropping. Can we send in some more drones to attack the smaller towers before they can re-form? The debris from the earlier one is probably long gone by now."

The captain swallowed visibly, keeping her face more or less expressionless, then nodded and gave the command to get the drones ready for deployment. Then she turned command over to the executive officer and excused herself.

Kate found her in the officers' head a few minutes later, pale, shaking, splashing water on her face and rinsing out her mouth.

"You did a hell of a job, Captain," Kate said softly.

Leaning on the sink, trying to keep the emotion off her frighteningly pale face, Joanna Smith looked at her. "Glad you think so. That's not how the Navy will see it. All they'll see is that I put eight thousand lives in mortal danger, and caused millions of dollars' worth of damage to my ship. I'll be relieved of my command before it really started."

"Not a person on this ship was harmed, Joanna. You saved millions of lives."

The captain forced a smile.

Making a split-second decision that could land her in serious trouble, Kate folded her arms across her chest and looked the captain in the eye. "Did you know the storm was man-made and the target was the Indian Point Nuclear Power Plant? Well, it was and it was. So the hell with what the Navy says. You're a hero."

Her eyes widened. "Were you supposed to tell me that?"

Kate shrugged. "I doubt it. But if you tell anyone, I'll tell your crew that I found you tossing your cookies."

That drew a genuine, if exhausted, smile from the captain. "If I tell anyone what?"

"Never saw you," Kate replied with a pretty inept salute.

When Kate returned to the bridge, much of the tension in the room had faded. Although Simone was still dangerous, the clean, clear cyclonic shape that had defined the storm on the screens had become distorted. The winds were still high enough to do some serious damage and the waves were still crashing against the bow, which sat many stories above the waterline, with undiminished ferocity, but on the screens the center of the turbulence was orange with lots of yellow rather than glowing red.

Jake and Kevin were still engaging in a controlled argument about blasting what remained of the storm.

"Guys, give it a rest," Kate said, nudging Jake's arm and indicating with her head that he should look where she was looking.

Someone had uplinked to a Department of Defense satellite that had been trained on New York City's Financial District. In silent, stunned awe the people on board the *Clinton* absorbed the devastation that lay where the center of the world's finances had pulsed so vibrantly only days ago. Skyscrapers rose out of waters that would not recede for days. It took a moment for Kate to recognize an enormous swath of surging water as the former site of the World Trade Center. And then her eyes were drawn to the top of the screen, where an arm bearing a torch rose above the churning surface of the Hudson River.

"Mother of God," Kate breathed as the images finally became too blurred from her tears. She felt the warm weight of Jake's arm come to rest on her shoulder, as he pulled her in tight.

"It's the last time, Kate," he whispered into her hair, and she couldn't tell if his voice was shaking, too. "It's the last time anyone will ever have to see that or live through it. We won."

CHAPTER **48**

Undefeated by the drones, Simone had been the perfect example of a storm of Olympian proportions poised to reassert the dominance of Nature over Man—until the bolt of icy fire pierced her heart, shattering her meticulous, organized structure. Convective towers stopped their dizzying, spinning climb in the face of the force of the atmospheric change.

Chaos erupted.

The upward spiral of warm, wet air stuttered and col-lapsed as its fuel disappeared. The inner rain bands, mas-sively tall walls of frenzied, spinning clouds, froze in place and shattered, their myriad minute droplets exponentially increasing in size, expanding in a time span that was barely measurable to become pellets of brittle ice. They fell to the roiling, now-gelid sea, which subsumed them.

Without the pulsing dual forces of life and death behind them, the winds in the outer bands began to slow, losing their fearsome coherence. The sun, no longer invisible ex-cept to the core, reasserted its supremacy and began to coax the world back to equilibrium.

EPILOGUE

May 12, 2008, 2:35 P.M., Midtown, New York City

With a start, Kate pushed herself away from the window frame and dragged her eyes away from the view.

What's left of it.

She walked back to the large table in the center of the otherwise empty conference room and picked up a short stack of files before her gaze wandered back to the windows. The late-spring sky was dirty gray, to match her mood.

She was on the twenty-second floor of an unremarkable Midtown high-rise, facing south, toward what had been the financial district. After Simone's floodwaters had receded and the sludge and immediate debris had been hauled away, wide-scale demolition had begun. The buildings that hadn't come down had been imprisoned in exoskeletons of scaffolding and, by Christmas, cranes had replaced office towers on the horizon.

My city.

There was no pride in the thought, just anger and a bleak emptiness. She closed her eyes for a moment and then firmly turned her back to the windows.

Tourists and television pundits—most of whom wouldn't know Fifth Avenue from Flatbush Avenue—had taken to saying smugly that *Midtown was the new downtown*, and every time she heard it she wanted to strangle someone. The real tragedy was that it was true. It was the middle of May, and the southern tip of Manhattan was as much of a ghost town as it had been just after the storm ten months earlier. Many residents and corporate tenants had fled; few had returned.

The rest of the country—the world—had been aghast at the extent of the damage. President Benson himself had come up as soon as the water started to recede. A much-reproduced photograph showed him standing alone on the ruins of Liberty Island, his face in his hands, his head and shoulders bowed with the raw eloquence of grief, and beyond, the Lady on her side, her face lapped by a muddy, toxic Hudson.

So many people had been devastated, so many cities and towns along the Eastern Seaboard had been decimated by the storm that New York City was pretty much on its own, left to itself to bury its dead and clean up its streets. Stunned locals had assured each other that when the funerals ended, when the mud was gone, life would come back. The neighborhoods, the businesses, the crowds; the attitude and the spark. All of it had to return; this was New York, after all. But it hadn't happened. Neither the native bluster with its quintessential cocky shrug, nor the will to rebuild, had reappeared. The city remained debilitated, its residents dazed and hollow.

Kate had been one of the lucky ones. She'd been locked out of her apartment building for weeks after the storm while the co-op board discussed whether to tear it down, but her status as a key government witness had guaranteed her a hotel room uptown, meals, and money for incidental expenses, which was good because she'd had nowhere else to go. Her parents' house was gone; Gerritsen Beach was once again the mud flat it had been a few hundred years earlier. Her parents had reconsidered Arizona.

Work was gone, too. Coriolis was in its death throes, and Wall Street itself was no longer much of an icon or a destination. Depleted by two catastrophes in six years, most of the banks and investment houses had permanently relocated. It hardly mattered to Kate at this point. While some called her a patriot, the Street considered her a pariah. When her name was mentioned at all, it was as a curse.

It wasn't as if she hadn't been kept busy since the storm. The first few months after Simone had been spent in endless interviews with government lawyers and, later, in depositions to which she was summoned by attorneys representing a panoply of interests, ranging from her former company to the White House. In her free time, she'd gone to funerals.

Finally, when most of that was over, she'd been offered a job.

A job. One. And she'd taken it.

"Hey. I've been looking for you for twenty minutes."

Kate's head snapped up at the sound of Jake's voice. "You're here already?"

"Obviously. And what do you mean 'already'? I've been here for an hour."

She grimaced. "Sorry."

He shrugged with a grin. "Working for the Agency means never having to say you're sorry. Are you ready?"

She forced a smile. "Just let me put away these folders and I'm all set."

"Are you excited?"

It wasn't necessary to meet his eyes. "No."

"Nervous?"

"No."

"Then what?"

Now she looked up. "I'm not so sure I like being used as shock therapy," she murmured as she walked past him toward the corridor that led to her cubicle in the Central Intelligence Agency's New York City field office. She'd been with the Agency for three months. It still seemed unreal.

No. Surreal.

"That guy killed a hell of a lot of people, Kate, and nearly killed you and me. Just because he's—"

"I know. I know, Jake. Carter Thompson is a maniac. But he's also an old man who suffered a massive stroke. He's gone from being a self-proclaimed master of the universe to being a vegetable. I'm allowed to have some pity for him. It's called being human," she snapped.

He slipped his hand around her upper arm and brought her to a halt. "He's a criminal, Kate. A mass murderer who can barely communicate and won't cooperate."

"He killed a good friend of mine with his bare hands, Jake. I haven't forgotten that. I never will. But why should he cooperate? What can anyone do to him? They've been grilling him for months. If he doesn't want to blink his eyes in answer to a question, he closes them and falls asleep. What's the government going to do, throw him in jail for contempt? He's already there. His body is his jail."

Jake's eyes were just as hot as she knew hers were. "He responds when he hears your name mentioned. That's why we're going out there."

"So I've been told. Am I supposed to be happy that I spike the blood pressure of a stroke victim?" she demanded, then let out a breath and let her shoulders slump. "Look, I'm tired of all this. Really, really sick of it. I just want to go back to studying the weather. Conducting forensic analysis. That's what I was hired to do, not to participate in some macabre dog-and-pony show to get Carter Thompson to reveal what's left of his mind." She was pleased rather than annoyed when Jake's Blackberry began to ring, and she left him in the conference room while she walked to her cubicle to store the files and get her things.

Ten minutes later, raincoat over her arm, computer bag slung over her shoulder, pull-along suitcase parked next to her feet, Kate leaned in the doorway of the conference room, waiting for Jake to turn around and notice her. When he ended the call and looked up at her, the look on his face was a curious combination of relief and irritation. There was the shadow of a smile behind it, though, which made her frown.

"What's up?"

"Carter's dead."

For a moment all Kate could do was blink at him. She'd absorbed so many deaths in the past few months that she couldn't feel any emotion. Her first thought was that now she wouldn't have to leave town.

"What happened?" She walked into the room, dropped

her coat over the back of a chair, and set her computer bag on the table.

"About an hour ago, his wife went in to see him. She whipped out a pair of scissors she'd concealed somehow and started cutting every tube she could reach. She only managed to slice up a few before they responded, but I guess as someone tackled her she went for a wire and—" He winced. "She got far enough through the insulation to hit some current."

Kate blinked again. "So she's dead? And he's dead?"

"Toast. Literally. An FBI agent and a nurse were injured pretty badly, too."

They were both quiet for a minute, staring past each other.

"I thought that place was guarded more heavily than the gates of Hell. How did she get in there with scissors?" Kate asked, then immediately held up her hands. "Don't answer that, even if you can. I don't care. He's dead."

A minute passed, then Jake cleared his throat. "What now?"

Kate hesitated. "Is our trip canceled?"

"Yes."

Their eyes met. "Then how about lunch?" she replied slowly.

"It'll have to be take-out."

They both froze as the too-familiar voice came from just beyond the room's open door. A moment later, the young, unsmiling face of Tom Taylor appeared. Neither she nor Jake uttered a word as Tom walked in and closed the door behind him.

Looking from one to the other, his eyes were as expressionless as ever. "What? It's been months and you're not glad to see me?"

"Got it in one." Kate tried to force a smile and failed.

Ignoring her comment, Tom set his computer bag on the table, sat down, and slid out his laptop. "Have a seat. The topic is eco-terrorism, specifically pollution. More specifically, the deliberate toxification of the oceans, genetic mutation of certain species. What I need from you two is a crash course on thermohaline convection." He glanced up at Kate. "I'll pick up the tab for lunch. I suggest we don't order sushi."

FROZEN FIRE

THE NEXT AMAZING THRILLER FROM

BILL EVANS and
MARIANNA JAMESON

Deep below the ocean's surface, a treasure trove of energy awaits those brave enough—or foolish enough—to try to tap it. Billionaire Dennis Cavendish believes he is no fool, and his scientists have been working around the clock to bring this new energy source safely online. But others are out to thwart Dennis's work, fearing the environmental consequences of the slightest mistake. Victoria Clark, Dennis Cavendish's brilliant and beautiful chief of security, races to prevent ecological disaster when saboteurs strike Cavendish's high-tech underwater habitat.

COMING JUNE 2009

978-0-7653-2008-7 • 0-7653-2008-8

www.tor-forge.com